SEND A GUNBOAT

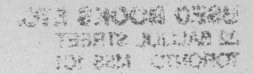

Also in Arrow by Douglas Reeman

A Prayer for the Ship
High Water
Dive in the Sun
The Hostile Shore
The Last Raider
With Blood and Iron
H.M.S. Saracen
Path of the Storm
The Deep Silence
The Pride and the Anguish
To Risks Unknown
The Greatest Enemy
Rendezvous—South Atlantic
Go in and Sink!
The Destroyers

Douglas Reeman

SEND A GUNBOAT

ARROW BOOKS

Arrow Books Ltd
3 Fitzroy Square, London W1

An imprint of the Hutchinson Publishing Group

London Melbourne Sydney Auckland
Wellington Johannesburg and agencies
throughout the world

First published by
Hutchinson & Co (Publishers) Ltd 1960
First published in paperback
under the title of *Escape from Santu* by
Panther Books 1962
Arrow edition 1973
Second impression 1974
Third impression 1976
© Douglas Reeman 1960

Made and printed in Great Britain
by The Anchor Press Ltd
Tiptree, Essex

ISBN 0 09 907060 X

To Winifred with love

Author's Acknowledgement

I wish to express my thanks to Mr. M. Ellis (Department of the Chief of Naval Information, Admiralty) for his help and co-operation in making available to me, plans and details of the 'Sandpiper' Class of River Gunboats.

It is better to light one small candle
than to curse the darkness.

CONFUCIUS

1

ANOTHER long summer was beginning, but even the dry, heavy breath which fanned the glittering water of Hong Kong's main anchorage, failed to quell the normal air of feverish activity and mounting noise, which surged back and forth in a weird ever-changing and confusing pattern.

The hard, unblinking sun fixed the white buildings around the harbour in a swimming heat-haze, making the windows glitter and twist, as if in pain. Even the mean, squalid little streets, crammed with their surging streams of colourful humanity, could not escape, although the shopfronts crouched in permanent semi-darkness. Only the uneven tops of the smart new skyscrapers, and the distant roofs of the sleepy hill-property seemed free from the stifling pressure of noise and dirt.

From the harbour these buildings made a pleasant backdrop, distance helping to mould them into a live and vital picture for the newcomer. Old mixed with new. The great temple, over-shadowed by the giant building of the Communist China Bank, and the neat white bungalows of the civil servants, lumped almost alongside the peeling tin roof of a canning factory.

The contrast was apparent too on the water. It was never quite still, as in any other harbour. It was always jammed with its countless beetle-like craft, from bobbing ungainly sampans, and the battered water-taxis, to the tall, ancient junks, which glided like great bats amongst the other craft with unerring accuracy and calm.

A P. & O. liner, her derricks clanking and jerking, lay along-side the main quay, her rails jammed with excited faces, and gay dresses, and two wharves away, the squat, eagle-crested ferry steamer sidled slowly out into the stream, about to start on yet another journey across the blue water to Macao.

Clear of the main waterway, and aloof from the bustling life of the harbour, the cruiser towered like a giant pale-grey rock, the soft wavelets shimmering and reflecting against her lofty sides. As she pulled gently at her mooring buoys, the dancing lights flickered from the brass fittings about the spotless decks, while the long taut awnings flung back the hard glare to the clear skies above.

Few figures moved about the decks, for apart from the heat, and the obvious boredom of looking at the same view, it was Sunday, and the ship's company at least showed no desire to follow the example of the busy people around them.

A marine sentry paced stolidly at the head of the accommodation ladder, his red face shadowed by the wide sweep of his tropical helmet, the gleaming rifle already hot in his grasp.

The Officer-of-the-Day, immaculate in white drill, tucked the long telescope under his arm, and licked his lips, savouring the taste of gin, and trying to remember what he had just had for lunch. Occasionally he glanced carefully at the shaded skylight in the middle of the cruiser's wide quarterdeck, as if expecting a sign to tell him of the movements of the Admiral beneath it. For this was the Flagship, and as the thought crossed his sweating mind, the officer squinted aloft to the limp flag at the masthead. The flag of Admiral Commanding the China Inshore Squadron.

He stepped back gratefully under the awning, his eyes resting momentarily on the two American destroyers which were moored side-by-side about half a mile away. Even from here he could clearly discern the wild blare of jazz which poured unceasingly from their deck loudspeakers to join the other discordant noises around them.

A police boat slid quietly between two moored junks, and prowled uneasily alongside one of the fishing yawls. The puppet-like figures waved and nodded in the age-old game of question and answer, until the launch, apparently satisfied, continued on its way.

The officer stiffened, as the Engineering Officer and the Doctor, in rumpled civilian clothes, clattered down the accommodation ladder to a waiting boat, their golf clubs rattling behind them. He envied them their freedom, but not to play golf. He whistled softly, watching the boat scud away for the shore, his mind toying dreamily with the little Malayan girl from the "Seven Seas" Club.

"Signal, sir!" The voice shattered his thoughts.

The young signalman waited respectfully while his superior collected his wits.

"Well?" The Malayan girl vanished.

"Government House, sir, just signalled to say that Mr. Gore-Lister an' his assistant are comin' over to see the Admiral."

"Is that all?" His eyes scanned the brief flimsy.

"S'all, sir."

He tugged his jacket straight, and started towards the screen-door.

"Oh, Quartermaster," he snapped. "Two Government House men will be aboard shortly. Call me when you sight the launch!"

He stepped gingerly over the high coaming, cursing these damned civil servants who thought it necessary to do their business on a Sunday.

. . . . .

Vice-Admiral Sir Ralph Meadows tossed the signal carelessly on to his desk, and walked thoughtfully to the open scuttle overlooking the harbour. His pale, china-blue eyes surveyed the colourful panorama before him with apparent disinterest, but as usual, his quick brain was summing up all the possibilities for the unexpected visit from the representatives of Her Majesty's Government.

He was a small man, built compactly and neatly. Everything about the Admiral was neat, from his thin, finely-cut features, burned to a nut-brown by his years of service overseas, to his narrow shoulders, and delicately shaped hands. Many people in the past had mistaken his fragile appearance for weakness, a mistake which had cost them a great deal, in their own comfort and security.

His eyes were perhaps the real clue to his true identity, cold and clear, yet giving the impression of his great insight and far-seeing intelligence.

At that moment, he was thinking more of his past, than of what might happen when the new crisis arose.

He had started his service as a young midshipman right here, in China, helping to patrol the great trade routes on the Yangtse, and trying to learn something about the vast, unfathomable peoples which thronged its banks. Pirates, dope smuggling, slavery, and minor wars had all made their mark on his young mind, and he had left the China Station with a true, if youthful regret. He had imagined that those experiences were to be the end of his contact with the country, but after a lifetime in other parts of the world, two world wars, and a steady climb up the uncertain ladder of promotion and appointment, he had returned, as Commander-in-Chief of the overworked Inshore Squadron.

And in a few more months, he would be leaving China, and the navy. This time for ever.

He watched the ferry steamer puffing past, the rows of faces upturned towards the British cruiser. He had changed a lot from the pink faced midshipman, but China, he shrugged inwardly, she was still about the same. Pirates and dope smugglers still abounded. The minor wars had been replaced by something bigger, but basically it was the same.

He turned slowly, and surveyed his spacious stateroom, which ran the whole breadth of the ship. The green fitted carpets, the polished brass scuttles, and immaculate white paintwork, all gave an appearance of security and well-being. A selection of bell buttons and telephones connected him with his minions and his command, and a word from him could make or break any one of them. He found it a vaguely comforting thought.

The cabin was dominated by a giant coloured chart, which was fixed right across one bulkhead, and lighted by cunningly concealed sections of strip lighting. He was very proud of this chart, which he had had specially made. It clearly showed the vastness of his command, from the Gulf of Thailand in the South, to the lonely wastes of the Eastern Sea in the North, where the Yangtse poured its yellow waters into the mass of tiny, miserable islands about its mouth.

Here and there around the chart were small, pink flags, each bearing the name of a ship, each denoting the position of one of the Admiral's scattered chain of patrols, his ever-restless and hard-pressed fleet. To his visitors from Government House the names would be meaningless, or at best, a vague appreciation of the navy's control, but to him, each flag, and each name, conjured up a clear picture of the ship, its capabilities and job, as well as a very formidable understanding of her commanding officer and complement.

He nodded, smiling slightly, the chart would look well on the wall of his study in his converted farmhouse in far-off Sussex.

The door opened carefully, and his bespectacled secretary, a tall, gangling Lieutenant, poked his head round the edge.

"Mr. Gore-Lister, sir, and er, his assistant," he announced.

The Admiral smiled thinly. "Right, let's get it over with!"

Gore-Lister, a plump, ruddy-faced man, in a neat, lightweight grey suit, was slow-speaking, and, or so the Admiral believed, equally slow-thinking, but he spent his whole life in Hong Kong, and was considered to be an authority on all matters pertaining to the Chinese "problem," as he called it.

The Admiral rarely agreed with his ideas, but for all that, they were good friends.

The other man was young and smooth-featured, with a permanently eager expression, and a new Eton tie, which might be a dangerous combination the Admiral decided, after a quick appraisal.

After the secretary had departed, Gore-Lister began to pace nervously up and down the carpet, while the Admiral sat back in his chair, his finger-tips pressed lightly together.

"Well, Paul?" he said at length. "Let's have it. What's on your mind this time?"

The other man halted reluctantly, and looked at the Admiral, who, in his white uniform with the gold encrusted shoulders, looked like a little carved figure.

"What d'you know about Santu Island?" His deep set eyes showed no expression.

The Admiral slid from his chair and moved across to the chart, and while he ran his hand swiftly across its surface, his brain was hard at work, calculating and planning. So it was Santu now. Another pin-prick from the Communists. He sighed inwardly. It was inevitable after the recent Formosa trouble, of course. Thrust and counter-thrust. His finger halted at the top of the chart, by the thirtieth parallel. "Santu Island, here it is." His voice was flat and unemotional, as if he was talking to himself. "About thirty miles West of the Chusan Archipelago. In other words, just outside Chinese territorial waters."

He turned to the others, who were watching his hand with interest, "D'you want me to go on?"

"Well, do you know the set-up there?" Gore-Lister's voice was thick.

The Admiral walked back to the desk, and perched himself on the edge, one neat shoe swinging slowly.

"Governed by some ex-general of the old régime, it's been overlooked or ignored by the Communists up to now." He raised his eyebrows questioningly. "It's almost part of that great mass of islands there, and most of them were independent less than fifty years ago. They used to be ruled by well-bred pirates, who preyed on shipping entering and leaving the Yangtse." He lifted his gaze back to the chart. "As you can see, it's about forty miles long, and fifteen wide, and not much use for anything." He turned his cold eyes on the others, "Now suppose you tell me what's going on?"

Gore-Lister sighed deeply, and lit a cigarette.

"Did you know that there are some British Nationals living there?"

"I did." He felt like adding "More fools they", but he refrained. "I believe they more or less run the tea and timber business on the island, while the old General gets on with his smuggling and piracy!"

The other man smiled bleakly, the humour not quite reaching his eyes. "That's as may be. The fact is that the Communists are believed to be going to take over the island. By force if necessary." He allowed the words to sink in.

"What d'you want me to do about it? Take my Marines up there first?" The Admiral's voice was sharp.

"No, sir, we thought you might be able to send a ship up there to feel out the facts of the matter." The young man had spoken for the first time, and the others stared at him, the Admiral with pity, and his chief with anger.

"You're here to listen, Mace," he snapped. "Sir Ralph and I are just sounding each other out! As we have done for the last three years," he added dryly.

The Admiral rubbed his chin thoughtfully. "The harbour's not much there. It's been allowed to silt up a good bit. Why can't you send one of your chaps? It'd be much cheaper!" he grinned.

"No, this is top secret stuff. If anyone got a sniff of what we're up to, there'd be hell to pay. Whereas, a visiting warship would be quite normal, surely?"

"Well, yes, we used to call there quite a lot, before the Ameri-cans began to swamp the area. It's not really necessary now, but it *could* be done."

"Good. I knew you'd help us out! What I want is this. Brief your captain to find out exactly what's happening. If it's alright, he can pull out. If it's bad, you'll have to give him carte-blanche to evacuate all the British residents at once. And I mean at once! He can contact the acting consul there, who'll be able to give him all the details."

"Why don't you ask the consul what's happening?"

Gore-Lister permitted himself a wide grin. "He's got a certain amount of money invested in the place, so he may be biased!" He leaned forward, pounding the desk with a beefy fist. "What-ever happens, this must be done quickly and quietly, we can't afford to have the Communists taking the place while our people are still there. They'd make a lot of unpleasantness and propa-ganda out of it!"

"You give me the word, and I'll take my Squadron up there in force," said the Admiral grimly. "There'll be no sea invasion then!"

"And we don't want another 'Amethyst' incident either!" Gore-Lister retorted quickly.

He leaned back tiredly. "You know the facts, Ralph. An island like this simply isn't *worth* making trouble over. With the Americans sitting in Formosa, and us in Hong Kong, we can afford to be generous. Or at least, careful."

The Admiral peered thoughtfully at his shoe, his head cocked on one side. China was like a tiger, he mused. A tiger who sleeps with one eye open. At any moment, a snatch of the claws in Formosa, or a flick of the tail in Hong Kong, and you had to be very quick on your feet.

He shook his head angrily, and concentrated on the task in hand.

"Right, leave it with me," he snapped, and pressed the bell for his secretary.

When the Lieutenant appeared, he started to issue his orders

15

to set the wheels of command in motion. "Show these gentlemen to your hideout, and they'll help you to draft out orders for a new operation. They'll include a file on local details, and I want everything you hear to be treated as secret. For your ears alone. If I hear of just one leak!" He left the threat unfinished, but his secretary's face satisfied him well enough. "I want to see the Operations Officer at once, and I shall need a Readiness Report on the *Wagtail*."

The mystified looks on the three faces as they left his stateroom, were most satisfying.

When he explained the task to his Operations Officer, Commander Pearce, his subordinate bit his lip uneasily.

"Must you send the *Wagtail*, sir? She's pretty old, and her new commanding officer has only joined the Squadron this week, he's not even seen her yet!"

"Look, Pearce, it has to be *Wagtail*, and 1924 isn't old for a ship if she's been well built! She's one of the original China River Gunboats, and very handy in shallow water, just the ship for playing hide-and-seek in and out the islands. Secondly, she's been employed lately on the refugee traffic, searching junks and so on, so she's pretty well known. It wouldn't do to send a couple of ruddy great destroyers into Santu harbour," his voice was tinged with sarcasm. "In addition to which, there's only about five feet of water in the place." He tapped his chart complacently.

The Commander still looked uncomfortable.

"The new commanding officer, sir."

"Yes, I know." The Admiral jerked open a drawer in the desk, and pulled out a manila folder. "He's come here under a bit of a cloud, hasn't he? Is that what's worrying you?"

"Well, sir, in view of his record, and the importance of this operation, I thought," he faltered unhappily.

"I know what you thought, but you don't want to damn a man before you've had a look at the rest of the picture." He skimmed briefly through the folder. "He was in command of the frigate *Sequin* in the Mediterranean up until three months ago, when it was due to be paid off for a long refit. He ended the commission by ramming the dockyard wall at Malta, and damn near sinking the ship. Court-Martial found him negligent, needless to say, but in view of his past record, they let him off with a severe reprimand, which is a nice way of condemning him to ruin in the Service! He comes out here to take command of a poor, flogged-out little gunboat, less than half the size of his frigate, which is due for the scrapheap anyway. And he must know that such a command means the finish of him. Unless," he paused, fixing the Operations Officer with a piercing stare. "Unless one particular Admiral shows a little trust in him. If he pulls this stunt off all right, it'll set his feet back on the old ladder of fame!"

He tossed the folder across the desk. "Go on, look at it. Good record. Submarine Service during the war, got the D.S.C., too. Kept his nose clean since, up till the last affair. I'd like to know *why* that happened," he muttered half to himself.

"Well, if you say so, sir."

"Yes, damn you, I do say so! Now get down to the dockyard, and tell them that *Wagtail*'s overhaul must be completed by tomorrow. She must sail in three days at the most!"

As the flurried Commander hurried away, the Admiral stood looking at the folder, bearing the name, Lieutenant-Commander Justin Rolfe, Royal Navy.

I wonder what he'd have said if he knew that this lad's father gave me such a chance when he was *my* Admiral? He chuckled, and pushed it back into the drawer.

. . . . .

Like a bright yellow beetle, the taxicab rattled and lurched its way over the cobbled road and criss-crossing railway lines which wound through the dockyard in every direction. Occasionally it would run into a patch of shade as it crossed close to the looming rusty hulks in the repair yards, or passed near to the towering grey sides of the destroyers and frigates which rested at their berths. A cloud of thick dust marked the car's slow progress, and the screech of gears clashed with the thunder of rivet guns and the clang of steel against steel.

Justin Rolfe lay back on the dusty cushions of the seat, his long legs straddled grimly across his luggage and against the driver's partition, as he fought against the painful jolting motion.

He felt a vague sense of relief to be out of the stifling streets, where the impassive faces had squashed against the cab's windows on either side, and the merciless sun had turned the interior into an inferno. Here in the dockyard at least, it gave a small impression of improvement, and through the open windows he caught the faint caress of the sea breeze.

His wide grey eyes stared fixedly at the back of the driver's head, and he tried to concentrate on the climax of the recent series of events which had started from the moment he had re-entered the Court-Martial room, and found the point of his sword turned against him, and had seemingly ended when he had arrived at Hong Kong for his new appointment. The corners of his mouth turned down slightly as he considered the matter. It would be his last appointment too, there was no doubt about that.

The throbbing had started in his head again, and involuntarily he covered his eyes with his hand, feeling the sweat moist against the palm.

He forced himself to look at the ships as they passed, putting aside all other thoughts, unconsciously gritting his teeth together with determination. Whatever else had happened in the past, and regardless of his tortured feelings, he was sure that he could mask his feelings from others, and especially from his new command.

Wagtail, he repeated the name to himself, remembering how his heart had plunged when he had looked her up in Jane's Annual. The gunboat was hardly mentioned, for apart from being apparently the oldest vessel in commission, she was due for the scrapyard at any time now. A fitting ending to a career, he had cursed.

To keep his mind free of its mounting agony, he had filled every free moment trying to find out about the quaint little ship he had to command, and as the taxi lurched to a standstill, he decided that the *Wagtail* had played no small part in keeping him sane. If only he could have a drink before he went aboard. The very thought of it made him lick his suddenly parched lips, and simultaneously, the throbbing in his head began to get worse.

He staggered out into the blinding sunlight, fumbling for his money, while the taxi driver unloaded his bags, and then stood impassively watching the naval officer who was acting so strangely.

When the cab eventually left him, Rolfe straightened up, mentally putting himself together again, in the manner which he had painfully taught himself during the last few months.

Although over six feet, his broad shoulders and slim athlete's waist gave the impression of sturdiness rather than height. He had a strong if sad face, and his generous mouth, and dark unruly hair which curled from under his white cap, added to the picture a recklessness to offset the coldness in his eyes. To the casual observer he appeared as the typical naval officer, his white drill uniform hanging perfectly on his hard-muscled body, the gold-laced shoulder straps of Lieutenant-Commander glinting in the sun. Only by watching closely would anyone notice the constant tightening of the jaw muscles, and the occasional gleam of anguish in the eyes.

Rolfe walked slowly to the edge of the dock and looked down at the little ship beneath him.

H.M. China River Gunboat *Wagtail* was typical of her class and type, of which she alone remained. Built of the best materials, at the height of Britain's overseas power, she had been shipped across from Southampton in sections, and re-erected under the watchful supervision of the naval shipwrights. Her main duty had been to protect and watch over the vast winding trade routes on the Yangtse, helping to foster the growth of the mighty chain of commerce and wealth from China to the ports of the world.

To manœuvre and navigate her one hundred and fifty feet through and across the treacherous mud banks which lurked round every curve of the wide river, she had been so designed that her hull was flat bottomed, and all her accommodation was built up above the main deck, rather in the style of the old Mississippi River steamers. Ungainly in appearance, perhaps, but she only drew a foot and a half of water, and it was said that she could sail on wet grass. Her twin screws were carefully mounted in tunnels, so that they were constantly protected from the bumps and bangs of sandbanks and wreckage alike.

All this Rolfe already knew, yet as he stared down at the high, box-like superstructure and spindly funnel, his first feeling of complete despair was eased slightly by the professional interest which was always at the back of his thoughts.

A few seamen moved about the well-worn teak decks, apparently loading stores, and an elderly Lieutenant was pacing back and forth across the seclusion of the top deck, known in these craft as the Battery Deck, because it was here that the only armament worth mentioning was mounted.

Rolfe climbed carefully down the steep rickety brow, and eventually found himself on the Main Deck, which after a frigate, or practically any other warship for that matter, seemed minute, and as he glanced round at the heavy burnished brass-work, and old-fashioned gratings, he decided that to describe it as antique, would not be unfair.

A smart seaman saluted, and then stood looking at him, somewhat at a loss. Of the Lieutenant there was no sign, yet he could not have failed to see him come aboard. A slight feeling of irritation made him snap, "Where's the Duty Officer?"

A silence had fallen over the ship, and from the corner of his eye he saw various quick movements, as members of the crew took quick glances at their new Captain.

"I'll get 'im, sir," answered the seaman readily, "I think 'e's on the Battery Deck."

I know, I saw him, Rolfe wanted to say, this point suddenly becoming important in his aching mind. But he merely nodded to the seaman, and walked to the side, gripping the guard-rail until his knuckles gleamed white in the tanned flesh.

He stared unseeingly at the scum-coated water in the bottom of the dock, wondering what had happened to himself, why he let these small matters grow to ridiculous proportions in his thoughts. Perhaps it was the heat. If only he could trust himself to take a drink. Just one. He shook his head savagely, and turned to stare at the heavy brass bell hanging by the gangway. The inscription of the ship's name had all but been polished away, but the commissioning date, 1924, was still apparent.

So we were both born in the same year. He traced the engraving with his finger, concentrating his whole will on the worn figures, which seemed to dance before his eyes.

Above his head, on the sweltering Battery Deck, Lieutenant

Albert Fallow received the Quartermaster's news with outward calm. But as the man hurried away, he felt his usual twinge of uneasiness which pestered him on every occasion that he was required to make some decision, no matter how small.

He was a big man, his heavy body running to fat, a round protruding belly rucking up the front of his jacket, which was patchy with sweat from his lonely pacing on the unsheltered deck.

His thick, red face, with loose, pendulous lips, and a swollen, purple-tinted nose, was considered fearsome by the Chinese seamen, and their British counterparts, but the deepset, brown eyes which moved constantly and restlessly in his ugly face, belied the impression of ponderous power and calm dignity, and showed only nervousness and worry.

He had been in the Service all his remembered life, being forced into a boy's training establishment by a heartless guardian, who thought that all orphans should be so punished for the inconvenience they brought to others.

He was a quiet, simple person, and soon shocked and frightened by the cruel heartlessness of life on the lower deck, his fear making him blind to the small acts of kindness which were usually hidden and blanketed by profanity and bullying.

If only as a means of escape, he had started to study for promotion, no small effort for one so slow moving, and despite the jeers of his messmates, and the open scorn of his Petty Officers, he had struggled painfully upwards. Leading Seaman brought him some measure of relief, but the small responsibility almost pushed him from his set course, and so eager was he to make a success of the position, he was mistakenly labelled a "crawler" and an "officer's pet". The real fact was, that the officers hardly knew he existed.

And then Mary had come into his lonely life. He had met her at the Southsea cigarette shop where she worked. Little, pale, trusting Mary, or so he had imagined. But behind her weakness, was a grim determination, a driving force which he was soon to appreciate. They were married, and as her letters followed him around the world, he no longer felt alone. The letters advised, guided, cajoled, and bullied, but always for the better, and as he passed his Petty Officer's examination, Mary's watchful eye hovered from the examination-room wall.

Chief Petty Officer had been their goal. He reached it and was content. But when certain reliable men were selected for Warrant rank, and later for Senior Commissioned Bosuns, Albert Fallow had found himself dragged unwillingly upwards. This was another life, and he had to start learning all over again.

It had been fine at the start, with Mary patting his uniform with its two gleaming stripes, and showing him off to the neighbours, and it had been exciting to receive letters addressed "Lieutenant", but then it ended, and he had suddenly found that the security of the messdecks which he had fought and beaten, was no longer his, and the new, devastating responsibility was twisting his insides into a hopeless funk.

He peered blindly round the deck, opening and closing his meaty hands. This should have been a proud moment. First Lieutenant of a ship, and it had certainly been better than his experiences in his first wardrooms, where the regular officers, with their snooty behaviour, and ill-disguised contempt for a lower deck man, had made him hide within a flushing silence; here at least he was practically alone, and he lavished all his old love and attention on the little *Wagtail*.

Since the gunboat had been suffering the indignities of a prolonged overhaul in the dockyard, he had become more of a caretaker than the acting Officer-in-Charge. The previous captain had been promoted, and had been flown home, and the only other officer, Lieutenant Vincent, the Boarding Officer and Interpreter, spent most of his time attending parties at Government House.

Fallow hated Vincent. To him he was the personification of all the "stuck-up, toffee-nosed" so-called officers he had ever served with, or under.

But he was prepared to put up, even with him, if he could just end the last three months of his naval service in comparative comfort, secure from the doings and goings of the real navy.

Now this had happened. Since receiving the signal about the new Captain, he had always thought of it as "this". Gone was the comfort of the pleasant, dull routine of cleaning ship, polishing brass, and sitting alone at nights in the little wardroom writing to Mary, or studying the gardening catalogues which she sent him every month, ready for their new bungalow at Southsea.

The new Captain meant that the tired old gunboat was to be

dragged out for service again, to do God knows what. A Captain who had been court-martialled too. It would mean that he would be twice as finicky and particular about everything, in order to clear his yard-arm with the Admiralty.

Fallow groaned inwardly, and dragged himself towards the ladder.

As his shadow flitted down ahead of him, Rolfe turned and waited while the big man saluted and cleared his throat.

"Lieutenant Fallow, sir," he announced huskily. "Welcome aboard."

They shook hands, and Rolfe started issuing instructions pertaining to the speeded repairs and overhaul. As he spoke, he was thinking, you poor ugly bastard, I expect you're wondering what sort of a useless article has been foisted on you for a Captain!

He heard Fallow saying something in reply, and tried to appear attentive, when his whole body was crying out to be left alone in peace.

"I've 'ad your cabin all done out, sir. You've got a good Chink boy as steward, an' I think you'll be very comfortable."

Rolfe nodded, forcing himself to answer. "I'd like you to show me round the ship first."

"Aye, aye, sir." For a moment, a brief gleam of pleasure showed in the dog-like eyes. "She's a grand old ship, sir," he added defensively.

They started off, their caps brushing against the taut awnings. Each time they passed under a gap in the white canvas, the sun smote them on the shoulders like the bars of a furnace.

The flat, broad hull was so shallow, that it only contained the engine spaces, now cool and silent, and the various store-rooms and magazine, except for one dark space right aft, with barely four and a half feet of headroom, littered with narrow bunks and scrubbed tables, and labelled "Natives Quarters."

Rolfe raised his eyebrows questioningly.

"Er, they're the Chinese crews' messes," explained Fallow, mopping his streaming face. "Bit small for us, sir, but they're mostly little chaps you see."

"They'd have to be!" observed Rolfe dryly.

He was glad to get to the Main Deck again, away from the

musty smell of those cramped quarters. The main bulk of the vessel's accommodation was built in one long, white-painted box, which ran along most of the deck, starting with the two officers' quarters, right forward under the wheelhouse, and then the wardroom, Petty Officers' Mess, sick bay, pantry and other little, cupboard-like spaces. Wide scuttles and windows opened out each side onto the side decks, and he saw that most of the cabins contained large, slow-spinning fans.

He paused, staring at a long, elaborately carved teak rack, containing a stand of gleaming pikes.

"Boardin' pikes, sir. They've always been in the ship, I suppose they were useful at one time!"

Rolfe shook his head wonderingly. This wasn't the navy any more, it was a museum, a relic of a bygone age. Somebody at the Admiralty must have smiled when he wrote out this appointment for him.

They climbed wearily up the ladder to the top deck, and Rolfe felt the heat coursing up through the soles of his shoes.

One lump of superstructure dominated the front of the deck, it included a roomy wheelhouse and W/T office, but the whole of the rear was divided up into the Captain's quarters. Port side for a sleeping cabin, and starboard for a day cabin. Rolfe refused to allow himself even a glance inside. He knew it would be fatal.

"Er, lead on," he muttered.

He followed Fallow up the last ladder to the open space above the wheelhouse. Although Fallow referred to it as the Upper Bridge, and it did in fact contain a compass and two voice pipes, it was dominated by a long muzzled six-pounder gun.

Fallow leaned on it, panting. "The main armament, sir," he gasped.

Rolfe stood for a moment, sheltering under the strip of canvas, and looking aft over his new command from this strange, lofty perch. The tall, thin funnel shimmered in a fine haze, and he stared with narrowed eyes at another small gun at the after end of the Battery Deck.

"That's an Oerlikon gun, sir. They put it there to replace the old 3.7 Howitzer that these boats used to carry for peppering the banks of the Yangtse, when things got a bit hot-like!" He watched Rolfe's face anxiously.

"Is this the only armament we've got?" He already knew the answer.

"Yes, sir. 'Cept for rifles, and a couple of Vickers guns!"

Rolfe ran his eye up to the ship's blunt bow. Ugly she was, but she was as clean as any yacht. What sort of people lived and worked aboard her? he wondered.

"What's the state of the ship's company?" he asked at length.

"We got three Chief Petty Officers," he ticked them off on his thick fingers. "That's the Chief Gunner's Mate, the Chief Engineer, and the Buffer, er, I mean the Chief Bosun's Mate, sir. Then we've got six British ratings, which includes the Signalman, W/T operator, Quartermasters, and Gunlayer. They all live in a little mess abaft the sick bay, sir, not with the Chinks."

"And how many, er, Chinks have we?"

"Twenty, sir. Mostly seamen, if you can call 'em that, and stokers. But we 'ave got three good stewards too!" he added, as if that exonerated the others.

"Thirty-two of us jammed into this." Rolfe spoke half to himself. "Well, I suppose we'll live!"

"It's not so bad under way, sir, when we get away from all this," Fallow waved his arm vaguely. "It seems cooler then," he added inconsequently.

"You're very fond of the ship, aren't you, Number One?" It seemed strange to address him as that, he'd look more at home in a C.P.O.'s uniform, he thought.

Fallow grinned nervously. "She's been good to me, sir."

Rolfe stared at him for a moment, then started for the ladder. "I think I'll go to my quarters, and freshen up." He raised his hand quickly, "No, don't bother to show me, I know the way now. By the way, what time will Lieutenant Vincent be coming aboard?"

"S'evenin', sir." Fallow's eyes were watchful again. "Would you like to come down to the wardroom for a drink now, sir?"

Rolfe tensed. "No thank you," he snapped, but at the sight of the hurt look in the other man's eyes, he added hastily, "I'll come down later. We've a lot to go over together."

He was practically down the ladder, when Fallow plucked up enough courage to ask the question which had troubled him severely since "this" had happened.

"Er, excuse me askin', sir, but you don't 'appen to know what duty we'll be doin'?" He cocked his huge head like an old dog.

"Not yet. I shall get my orders today some time."

He staggered as he hurried along the cruel deck to his quarters. As he stepped over the coaming, he looked back. Fallow was still standing out in the blazing sunlight, an expression of complete despair on his face.

For some minutes Rolfe wandered vaguely around his quarters, more relieved to be alone and in somewhere comparatively cool, than interested in his surroundings.

Both cabins were comfortably furnished and spacious, in both respects better than the frigate had been, he reflected grimly. How things had changed in the navy. In the frigate, which had been a comparatively modern vessel, the officers' and crew's accommodation had been fairly evenly distributed. In this ship, his own living space was equal to that of all the Chinese crew, and they were only at half the strength for which the ship had been designed. He marvelled at the crass short-sightedness of the early Empire-builders. We might have been a little more popular with these "Chinks" today, had they thought a little more about the even distribution of comfort.

He knew little about the Chinese, except what he had read, and the brief, hazy glimpses he had obtained passing through the town. But what he saw, he liked.

It had seemed amazing to him, that in Hong Kong, the most overcrowded place in the world, these strange, impassive people had moved heaven and earth to help their friends and relatives to escape from Communist China, even though it meant more overcrowding, and more poverty, with its aftermath of malnutrition, diphtheria, and death.

An official at the airport had told him that at the Kwong Wah Hospital in Kowloon, the maternity wards were so jammed, that one hundred and twenty-nine mothers and their babies lay in forty-three beds! His informant had been Chinese, but there had been no anger or bitterness in his voice, only a resigned but hopeful calm.

Rolfe sank down heavily in one of the big chairs, noting the steel shutters hanging alongside each of the wide windows. A weapon-slit was cut in each one. He had heard about the pirates in their apparently harmless junks, waiting for an unsuspecting prize. These simple precautions were apparently part of the answer.

He stared wearily in front of him, unable to concentrate any more, and allowing the ache to come flooding back, like an evil serpent. Face it, man! A voice nagged in his brain. This is the end. Have a drink and forget it!

He massaged his forehead with his fingers, shutting his eyes with concentration. Why did drink have to be so important? How long would this agony of mind continue?

He cautiously allowed his thoughts to go back to that last, nightmare climax of ceaseless drinking.

He had lain on his bunk, while his frigate ploughed purposefully towards Malta, the shipboard noises and routine actions only occasionally breaking through the haze of his reeling and tortured brain. He could still only vaguely remember clambering up to the bridge, as the ship made her way into the harbour approaches, and as the ragged sequence of events flashed before him, he saw again the anxious face of his First Lieutenant squinting up at him from the fo'c'sle.

Too fast, too fast, he had mumbled, as the ship bore down rapidly on the rough stone jetty, and in a last-minute effort he had tried to convey the correct orders down the misty voice-pipe. With a scream of tearing metal, the knife-like bows had torn and bumped along the wall, while the Maltese dockers had fled in confusion and panic. Somehow he had stopped the ship, and as officers bellowed orders, and a shaky crew had passed the lines ashore, he reeled faintly into his sea-cabin behind the bridge, the sour flood of vomit bringing no relief, only the final taste of failure and despair.

The next picture showed the quiet, dignified court-room. Again it was the face of his young First Lieutenant which came first to his mind. Pale and determined, he had desperately tried to defend his Captain. The grim faces of the Captains who comprised the court showed no compassion, as the Prosecuting Officer had completed his questioning.

"And did you not think that the ship was moving too fast for a safe approach, Lieutenant?"

"No, sir. The Captain always has been a marvel at ship-handling!"

One of the court permitted himself a wintry smile, and leaned forward.

"In the past? But not on this occasion?"

The witness squirmed and looked away. "It was an accident, sir!" he stammered hotly.

"We must not mistake the excellent quality of loyalty for blindness to duty, Lieutenant!" The Prosecutor's voice had been like a saw.

Rolfe shook his head wonderingly. It was really amazing that his own drunken state at the time of the collision had been kept out of the evidence by the strange loyalty of his officers.

Perhaps they had suspected it? He frowned as he tried to think of one clue, or threat, in the summing-up of the court.

No, he decided, they had certainly been curious, but had confined themselves to the facts before them, and satisfied the interests of discipline with their findings.

I'll be all right when I get to sea, he told himself, but, it seemed, without conviction. The nagging pain was still there, and he felt defenceless before its persistent onslaught.

He jumped, a loud knock on the cabin door jerking him from his painful self-examination.

Fallow poked his red face round the curtain, his loose chin sagging over the high collar of his tunic.

"S'cuse me buttin' in, sir."

He always seemed to start or end his sentences with an apology, Rolfe thought.

"But I've brought your steward, in case you'd like to give 'im some special instructions about 'ow you'd like your gear laid out?"

Rolfe nodded wearily, not really caring one way or the other, but realizing that the man was trying to make things start off well.

Fallow heaved his bulk through the door, tucking his cap beneath his arm. Rolfe was surprised to see that he had only one tongue of dark hair, slicked carefully across his otherwise bald head, as if it had fallen there by mistake, and was held down by a daily dose of water and hair oil.

Rolfe's eyes widened in surprise at the diminutive figure which stepped from behind the First Lieutenant's bulk. The white jacket and trousers, which hung loosely on his small, thin body, helped to accentuate the boy's appearance of frailty and lightness, and the round, serious face, with its almond-shaped, black eyes and wide mouth, completed a picture which was somehow appealing and rather pathetic.

"'E's not much to look at, sir, but 'e's a very good boy. Speaks English real well, too." Fallow frowned down at the small figure beside him, as if defying him to claim otherwise.

To Rolfe, accustomed to the bored and untidy indifference of past stewards, this Chinese boy was something more than just different, he seemed to hold all the elusive qualities and secrets of his race in his watchful, old-young face.

"What's your name, boy?" Rolfe asked quietly.

"Chao, sir." The voice was shrill and unformed.

"Chao? Is that all?"

Fallow hastened to explain. "The rest of it is too difficult, sir, the last Captain decided on the first bit!"

Rolfe grinned, and as if to mirror the reaction of his new master, Chao beamed widely, exposing a wide array of white teeth.

"Well, Chao, you can get my gear unpacked and stowed away. I shall probably be on to you quite a bit, until I know where everything is hidden."

"Very good, Captain-sir," he nodded vigorously, his clipped black hair jerking like an enraged hedgehog. "I sleep in pantry. You ring, I come any time." He nodded again, his button-eyes dancing.

"A very admirable arrangement," Rolfe smiled. And to Fallow, "How old is he, for Pete's sake? Under age for service, I'll bet!"

"'Ardly, sir. They takes the fit ones for this job. Age don't matter much. But Chao 'ere's about fifteen, I believe."

They watched as Chao moved the suitcases into the cabin, his bare brown feet padding noiselessly on the carpet, Rolfe with friendly interest and Fallow with his usual look of listless uneasiness.

"If you don't find 'im satisfactory——" Fallow began, and Rolfe saw the boy's thin shoulders stiffen.

"He'll be fine," finished Rolfe hastily. "Now, is everything going on all right with the ship?"

"Er, yes, sir." Fallow backed for the door. "I'll go an' get on with it, sir!" He disappeared hastily, and Rolfe heard him stumbling down the ladder to the main deck.

He shrugged helplessly. Why did the man misinterpret everything he said? Even an innocent question was taken as a hidden reprimand. He turned back to the boy, a question framed on his lips. He froze in his chair, gripping the wooden arms with fingers of steel.

Chao had the largest suitcase open on the deck, and already Rolfe's clothing was hanging in neat piles from the furniture. But his eyes were riveted on the large, silver-framed picture, which Chao had unwrapped from its thick cardboard covering, and which he now held at arm's length in a careful examination.

Rolfe's mouth was dry. Her picture. Rising up to mock him already, in his last retreat from her world.

"Put that down, blast you!" His voice cracked like a pistol shot in the confined space.

The steward spun round, his face dark with fear and misery. "Sorry, Captain-sir! I thought you'd want the lovely lady put out where you——"

"I said put it down!" His voice rose to a scream, and he jumped across the cabin, snatching the picture from the boy's frightened grasp. He stood staring at her, his breath rasping in his throat. The same white, insincere smile, the bright, mocking eyes. How could he have been so blind?

"Captain-sir?" The voice was so low that it hardly penetrated his racing thoughts. "Can I do anything?"

Rolfe lifted his eyes momentarily, and stared unseeing at the boy's stricken face.

"Yes," he said slowly. "Get me a bottle of whisky."

He stood the picture carefully on the table and sat down opposite it, not moving, or even looking up, as Chao placed the bottle and glass beside his elbow.

The door closed, and for some minutes the slowly moving fan was the only sound in the cabin.

He slopped some whisky into the glass, his eyes still on her face. Then he raised it to her, and said aloud, "To you, Mrs. Rolfe. You bloody bitch!"

The spirit burned his throat like fire, and as it flowed fiercely through him, he realized just how much he had needed it. He downed three full glasses in quick succession, and then leaned back in the chair, breathing deeply. With unsteady fingers he unbuttoned his jacket, allowing the slight movement of air from the fan to caress his heaving chest.

Perhaps it might have turned out differently if he had done as she wanted. Left the navy, and settled down in one of her father's paint factories. He laughed mirthlessly. How simple and naïve he must have seemed to her, just someone 'interesting' to show off at those endless parties in London.

He had never given up hope and never lost the nagging feeling of desire when he was near her, and he had wanted to surprise her by flying home from the Mediterranean, to tell her that when the frigate was paid off, he *would* leave the navy and try to live up to her wishes. He had surprised her well enough. He trembled, and the throbbing grew louder in his skull. If he lived for ever, he would never forget, or clean from his mind, the picture of her sitting up naked in bed, her lips parted with terror and hate. The man had been whimpering about 'not making a scene' and about all their reputations. He had still been whimpering when Rolfe had beaten him senseless on the bedroom floor. He had run blindly from the flat. He was still running.

He drank deeply, feeling the cloak of dizziness closing round him.

The man had been rather a pathetic creature really, and his short, pale legs had kicked helplessly when Rolfe had dragged him from the bed. He stared dully at the photograph, hearing her screaming after him, using words of such undreamed of baseness, that he had never been able to think of her without remembering her cruel and frightened insults.

He closed his eyes, raising the glass to his lips. He had never suspected, never even imagined such a thing possible of her. He swore loudly, but with slow, clear intonation, as if repeating a religious script. What a fool I am, he thought weakly.

He stood up suddenly, swaying against the table.

"Dear Sylvia," he mumbled. "Dear, sweet, lovely Sylvia!" He retched, and felt the sweat cold on his chest. Then, taking the picture in his free hand, he studied her face, as if for the first time. That damned smile, and those little, exciting gestures. She was always conscious of every swing and movement of her tantalizing body. And yet, and yet, he groped vainly for a sign, she must have loved him once. As he wrinkled his eyes in concentrated study, he knew he was only fooling himself, as he always had, where she was concerned. He smiled crookedly. "A thoroughly delectable tart! That's what you are, Mrs. Rolfe!" He chuckled stupidly, and as he raised his glass, he saw her face framed in the amber liquid which helped him to fight her memory.

A sudden drunken realization flooded over him, "You've caused all this!" His powerful voice rose to a frenzied shout. "You bloody bitch! You've got your divorce now. I hope you're happy," he fumbled for words, "with your newest 'interesting' person!" He reeled across the cabin, cannoning into the piled clothes and cases, which he sent flying with a wave of his arm, heedless of the whisky which slopped from the glass.

"You bloody bitch!" His head swam, and he felt he wanted to have her there in the cabin with him, so that he could tell her to her face, and then beat her to death. He knew, even in the throes of drunken fury, that he would have thrown himself at her feet, and pleaded for forgiveness.

"Forgive *me*?" He answered himself wildly. "What the hell did *I* do!"

With a savage thrust, he hurled the picture through an open scuttle, heedless of the tinkle of glass, as it dropped to the bottom of the dock.

With a moan he grabbed the bottle, and staggered through to his sleeping cabin. Once on the bed, he tilted the bottle to his mouth, some of the spirit running over his chin and neck, the rest choking him, and making him fight for breath.

He slumped back heavily, his arm, as it hung over the side of the bunk, still gripping the empty glass.

.   .   .   .   .

Lieutenant Fallow stood moodily in the corner of the wardroom, his heavy face dark with his new problems and worries.

The wardroom, which was large for such a small ship, was in a state of semi-darkness due to the overhanging walls of the dry dock, and the brass oil lamps, which were temporarily replacing the disconnected lighting, added to the stuffiness, which neither the fans, nor the first cool of evening could dispel.

Fallow's newest pile of catalogues, their bright covers ablaze with improbable chrysanthemums and dahlias, lay unheeded on one of the worn, red leather settees. He was no longer in the mood for reading them, nor could he now foresee an untroubled ending to his career.

The Captain, he glanced at the deckhead as if to locate his quarters, he was something quite new in his experience, and more than just frightening or unsettling. He was a madman. No, that wasn't the description he wanted, and his frown deepened, his overhanging lip curled in baffled perplexity.

Suppose the ratings had seen him? The very idea made him sick, and he went over the happenings carefully, to ensure he had got his facts in the right order.

He placed his hands flat on the table, studying them vaguely, as they lay like two bundles of fat sausages. The first warning had been that damned picture hurtling past him into the dock, and the Captain shouting at the top of his voice. When he had run to his cabin, he had been flaked out on his bunk, groaning and swearing like a lunatic, and the whole place stinking of booze. God, he mopped his head automatically, that's all we need now. A drunkard for a Captain, who'll probably want to leave everything to me! The very thought made him grind his teeth with frustration. He stared blankly at the framed picture of the Queen above the polished table, the light dawning slowly in his mind. So *that* was the cause of the court-martial. A woman, and then the bottle. He frowned, his eyes disappearing between the rolls of flesh. Or was it the other way about?

He belched angrily, what did it matter anyway? The Captain was off his head, there was little doubt about that.

Fallow had met plenty of drunken officers during his long career, and he had seen lots of the other kind, too. The calm and quietly efficient type, who had been respected and looked up to as the navy's best. This one was neither, or rather, he was both. Fallow permitted himself to sit down for the first time since Rolfe had come aboard. It was all too much for him to understand. He reached for his writing-pad. He'd tell Mary about it. She'd understand. Mary would know what to do.

The sound of footsteps and feminine laughter on the dockside made him sigh, and his spirits took an even lower plunge. Now Vincent had come back, and with one of his bloody, fancy lady-friends. He pushed the writing-pad away and sat back, facing the door, his hands twitching in his lap.

Lieutenant David Vincent had long ago decided that there could be little in life to enjoy without the company of a beautiful girl, or girls if possible. At twenty-four he retained the sleek, well-groomed aloofness of a head prefect in an exclusive school, and his finely chiselled features, mocking blue eyes, and fair wavy hair gave him all the physical weapons to achieve his aims. He was also ambitious, and the very reason he had elected to serve as an interpreter in this out-of-date gunboat was proof of that other hidden driving force. He had been told that it would be the first step to Flag Lieutenant to the Admiral, and once he had the Admiral's ear he had the way clear for promotion and comfort. After all, as he told himself repeatedly, in these days, when the navy was no longer run on the old lines, and when ignorant rankers found themselves in the wardroom, a really well-bred officer, with generations of captains and admirals in the family behind him, could hardly go wrong.

He raised his tennis racket negligently to return the Quarter-master's salute, and then turned to assist the dark-haired girl down on to the deck. In his open-necked shirt and impeccable shorts, his well-tanned limbs gave him the appearance of a Greek god.

"Careful, Janet," he drawled. "We don't want those little feet skidding off into the dock, eh?" He laughed shortly, watching her from beneath pale lashes. She was quite a good type, he mused, and being Gore-Lister's daughter, she was a good foot-hold at Government House.

"Isn't it *tiny*?" The girl clasped her hands, and stared round at the deserted deck. "How can you *live* here, darling?"

"I can manage for a bit," he squeezed her arm. "Now come and have a drink. I'm fearfully sorry that old Fallow is aboard, but you can ignore him!" He never referred to Fallow as the First Lieutenant unless he could not help it.

His eye fell on the gangway board. Opposite the tag labelled Captain was the word Aboard.

"Well, well, so the Old Man's arrived, eh?" He smiled with real amusement. "Another Has-Been for the old *Wagtail!*"

"Shh! He might hear you!" But the girl was laughing, too, and allowed herself to be piloted to the wardroom.

Fallow rose awkwardly and smiled.

"Miss Janet Gore-Lister, er, the First Lieutenant." Vincent's lip curled contemptuously. It was obvious that her name meant nothing to the fat fool.

The girl strolled casually round the wardroom examining the pictures and trophies with bored indifference, but pleasantly conscious of Fallow's pop-eyed glances on her long legs and tight tennis shorts.

Vincent rang savagely for the steward, and immediately Peng, the senior wardroom assistant, a tall, stooped individual with a bland and innocent expression, glided round the pantry door.

"Brandy and ginger, Janet?" Vincent looked at the girl detachedly. He was getting angry. It always spoiled his evenings out when he had to come back here. The girl nodded.

"Two Horses' Necks, Peng!" He ignored the fact that Fallow had no glass in front of him. "And answer the bell more quickly next time!" he snapped.

They sat sipping their drinks, Vincent leaning carelessly against the bulkhead, the girl in a deep arm-chair, and Fallow perched uncomfortably on the edge of the settee.

"New Captain's aboard," said Fallow at length.

"Really? What's he like? Not that I care, of course!" Vincent shot a secret smile to the girl, who blew a little kiss with her moist lips.

"Er, 'e's a bit different," began Fallow cautiously. "Not quite what I'd expected," he ended lamely. He hated the way Vincent discussed service matters in front of his painted little birds. If I was a proper Number One, I'd tell him to go to hell, he thought savagely. Both been out drinking, an' that, and then come on here to drink our stuff. He watched the girl cautiously. Mary's worth a dozen of her, he concluded, with something like triumph.

"What d'you mean, different? Has he got two heads, or something?"

The girl giggled: "Oh, David, you are funny sometimes!"

You're a bloody little twit, thought Fallow darkly. Aloud he answered, "You'll see when he comes down. He's been resting most of the day," he added inconsequently.

"Hiding, is he?" Vincent's laugh was a short, barking sound, the sign of a man lacking a sense of humour.

"No, it's not that, it's just——" he stopped and looked up, startled, as a loud thud echoed from overhead.

"Christ! What was that?" Vincent forgot the presence of the girl.

Fallow swallowed hard, and moistened his lips. "I suppose it was the Captain, er, moving something," he finished unhappily.

Vincent's eyes sharpened. "Look here," he began, watching the other man's obvious discomfort, "what's been going on? What are you trying to keep from me?" His sharp tone revealed his eagerness, as well as his lack of respect for his superior.

Fallow noticed neither, his mind was now a torment, and although he wanted to dash from the wardroom, and wash his hands of the whole affair, his heavy body felt glued to his chair. He lifted his eyes again to the deckhead, wondering desperately what he should do.

"What's come over you two men? Why are you both behaving as if you'd heard a ghost walking?" Her voice was petulant.

"Oh, shut up, Janet!" Vincent jerked his head irritably. "The First Lieutenant's got some secret or other, and I think I should be allowed to——"

"Beg pardon, sir!"

They all started again, at the interruption from the doorway. The lean brown face of the Quartermaster poked round the curtain.

"Well, what is it?" Fallow's voice was unsteady, he felt that the seaman's arrival could only bring bad news, in some way connected with the Captain.

The seaman jerked his eyes away from the girl's legs. "Telephone call from Operations, sir. Commander Pearce, the Ops Officer is on 'is way over." The man's cockney accent struck an unreal note in the little tableau.

"Coming over?" Fallow repeated dazedly. "Now? Bit late, isn't it?"

"All right, you can carry on!" snapped Vincent, who despised

Fallow all the more for showing his uncertainty in front of a rating. When the seaman had gone, he whistled absently. "You know what this means?" No one answered. "Some special orders for the poor old *Wagtail*. I thought they were in a bit of a hurry to get us out of dry dock!"

"Er, yes, I suppose so," muttered Fallow, reaching for his cap, "I must tell the Captain."

As he blundered out on to the darkening deck he heard the girl laughing.

"Blast them!" he groaned. "Blast them all!" And blinded with worry, he scrambled up the ladder to the battery deck. He staggered violently, and almost fell across the small squatting form of Chao, the steward.

"What the hell are you doin' 'ere?" He paused in his stride, his breath rasping in his lungs.

He saw the black eyes flash momentarily in the upturned face. As the boy didn't answer, Fallow steadied himself and, reaching down, pulled him to his feet. He pushed his great face forward and shook the thin shoulder demandingly. "Answer, boy! 'Ave you bin told to wait out 'ere?"

"No, Mr. Fallow, sir." The voice was a mere quaver. "Captain-sir is very ill, is very sick. But he does not call for me."

"'E's sick alright," breathed Fallow, half to himself, then gripping the boy's shoulder even tighter, as if to add force to his words, he spoke slowly and carefully. "Look, Chao, you're a good lad, and it's up to you an' me to get the Captain well again, see?" He paused, studying Chao's darkened features, and half-wondering if he had committed himself too much. "There's a big man comin' to see 'im. Now! Right now!" he added, frightening himself again by the implication his words held.

"I see, sir." The dark head nodded eagerly. "Him sick. We fix!"

"We fix all bloody right!" And Fallow advanced along the deck, the steward's white jacket flitting behind him like a shadow.

Rolfe lay on the carpet beside his bunk, his dark hair ruffled like a wig, arms and legs flung in every direction, and his breath panting against the deck.

Fallow had handled his drunken messmates a hundred times in the past, but even in this state, his Commanding Officer seemed to hold him back, undecided and nervous.

As he moved clumsily round Rolfe's body, Chao suddenly flitted past him and, bending down, started tugging Rolfe's shoulder, until with a moan, he rolled over on to his back. The white uniform was now filthy, and Chao's hands darted swiftly across it, undoing the buttons and pulling at the sleeves.

Over his shoulder he flung a quick glance to where Fallow stood uncertainly. "Please, Mr. Fallow, sir, we must get him in the shower and I cannot do it alone!"

"Yes, all right, lad," muttered Fallow humbly, and almost gratefully he reached forward to help with Rolfe's corpse-like figure.

The next few minutes were a series of anxious ones for both of them, and but for an occasional grunt from the sweating Fallow, or the hissing whispered request by the boy, the job was carried out in silence.

Rolfe was only vaguely aware of the hands which flitted across his aching limbs, and the cool air upon his naked body, but at the first icy blast from the shower, he shuddered and struggled weakly, choking under the needle-like persistance of the jets. Supporting himself by the taps, he stared down vaguely at the anxious eyes which watched him like a bird, while the busy hands pommelled his body with a wet towel. He tried to speak, but only after clearing his throat several times could he even manage a croak. His head sang unbearably, and his legs felt like two dead things.

"Thanks, Chao," he muttered at length. "This is treatment if you like."

He laughed shakily, and in the next cabin, Fallow paused to listen, trying to gauge from the sound the seriousness of the situation. Shaking his head wearily, he continued fitting the buttons and shoulder straps to a clean uniform, his thick fingers and his shattered nerves making the task doubly difficult.

Eventually Rolfe was sitting in a chair, clad in a damp towel, and grimacing horribly while Chao poured glass after glass of milk down his throat. "No time for coffee, Captain-sir!" he explained breathlessly.

Rolfe stood up carefully, and permitted himself to be dressed. As he ran a comb through his unruly hair, he used every faculty he possessed to control himself and his reeling thoughts. He concentrated instead on Fallow's news of the expected visitor.

"Very well, Number One. Go below, and receive the Commander, and I'll be down as soon as I'm ready."

Fallow ran his finger round his collar. "I 'ope you'll excuse the liberty of pullin' you about like this, sir? We, that is, I felt that it was only fair-like, when you wasn't well, an' that." His voice trailed away, and he stood awkwardly shifting his feet, his brown eyes fixed on Rolfe's face.

Rolfe grinned, and then winced as the effort made a shaft of hot iron roll over in his brain. "Thank you, Number One, I am very grateful to you." He ruffled the boy's hair, and Chao's face split into a smile, "To both of you!"

Fallow fled, charging to his next encounter like an elephant with a sore tooth.

Rolfe stared across the top of the dock wall, towards the strings of twinkling lights of Kowloon, and at the blazing arc lamps of the P. & O. liner. You fool, he thought slowly. You did it that time. Can't you ever learn? He laughed aloud, a bitter sound, now he hadn't even a picture to remember her by. As that struck another cord in his memory, he turned back to Chao, who, in his shower-soaked uniform, looked like a half-drowned monkey.

"You're a good influence around me," he smiled. "Forget about the bottling I gave you, in fact forget about everything! Understand?"

Chao nodded, and grinned happily. Everything was fine now, he decided, the Captain was sane again.

When he entered the wardroom, he gritted his teeth together in a new determination to stifle the sweeping waves of nausea which threatened to reveal his true feelings, and if Fallow's shining face was anything to go by, his jaw hanging open in astonishment, he was succeeding pretty well. He shook hands with the ruddy-faced Commander, who glanced meaningly at his watch, and then at his empty glass, and then murmured a brief greeting to Vincent. The latter's obvious scrutiny and general freshness jarred his nerves slightly, and when Vincent offered him a drink his sharp refusal brought a flush to the young man's face and a gleam into Commander Pearce's watchful eyes.

Rolfe nodded to the girl, only dimly aware of her sleek

prettiness, and the very touch of her hand brought back an edge to his troubled mind.

She smiled quickly at him, uncertain of herself for once and resentful of Rolfe's cold stare.

"I must be off now," she announced. "It's been charming meeting you all." She shook her head at Vincent. "It's all right, David, I have my car, I really must go."

"Yes." Rolfe's comment, flat and uncompromising, only added to the new air of discomfort, and as he wondered vaguely how long this nightmare would last, he saw Vincent escorting the girl out of the door while the Commander was pushing a thick sealed envelope towards him.

"Your orders, old boy," nodded Pearce softly. "You leave the dock tomorrow morning, and take on stores as arranged. I've been working like hell to get it all fixed up for you."

"Yes," said Rolfe again, and Pearce's eyebrows shot up in brief annoyance. So that's it, he thought, relieved that he had solved the problem which had been troubling him since the Admiral had started all this, it's drink which has finished him. Women, too, most likely. Then, almost cheerfully, he said, "You'll sail tomorrow at eighteen hundred." He tapped the red top secret label on the envelope, "This'll give you the whole gen. Open it when you clear the harbour limit." He stood up, thankful to be leaving this strange ship.

Rolfe saw him over the side, and then returned to confront his two officers.

"You heard that? Good. We'll sail at eighteen hundred tomorrow then." He tucked the envelope carelessly under his arm, conscious of their eyes upon it. "I'll tell you more about the operation later, when I know myself."

Fallow watched him unhappily, wondering if he should pluck up courage and ask to be relieved of his appointment before-hand, so that his relief could put up with whatever lay in store for him. Instead, he said, "Thank you, sir."

"I don't suppose I could just slip ashore tomorrow afternoon for an hour, sir?" Vincent flashed his charming smile.

"You're right. You couldn't!" answered Rolfe calmly, and with a nod, stepped out on to the deck.

The lights were still bright, and he felt somehow cleaner inside.

2

ROLFE propped his elbow on the desk, while he concentrated on reading through the typed lists of stores and fuel to be taken aboard once the ship was clear of the dock. A cold cup of coffee stood untouched at his side, and his ears were deaf to the rattle of crockery as Chao cleared away the remains of a hasty break-fast as he methodically filled his mind to the brim with details and figures. His head still ached from the previous night's drinking, and that, too, gave him a sense of urgency to get the ship mov-ing, to get clear of the harbour and the contact with the shore.

Apart from the fact that he knew he would be away for some time, he knew nothing of the operation ahead and could conjure up little enthusiasm about the venture. Anywhere would do now, and one job was much like another, or so he told himself.

He glanced at his watch and stood up stiffly, he could hold back his impatience no longer.

It was strange to find the bridge full of people. It was as if the ship itself was coming to life and enjoying it.

A tall Leading Seaman stood loosely at the wheel, his lips pursed in a silent whistle, his eyes disinterestedly watching the dockyard workers scurrying along the catwalks at the sides of the dock, casting off the lashings on the beams supporting the cradled gunboat. A steady swish of water filled the stone area with noise, as the sea poured into the opened vents and the sluggish water began to rise under the flat keel.

Vincent stood in the front of the bridge, his long hands resting on his hips, and another Quartermaster was standing by the engine-room telegraphs.

"Morning, sir." Vincent's face was expressionless. "She should be well afloat in a couple of minutes."

The seamen straightened up, suddenly conscious of their new Captain, but Rolfe only grunted and walked out of the wheel-house to the wing of the bridge.

From his lofty position he watched the busy white figures

moving about the decks in orderly confusion. Fallow's hoarse voice threatened and pleaded from a dozen directions at once and he could see his ungainly figure, even worse when viewed from above, covering the distance from the fo'c'sle to the quarterdeck in great, shambling strides, his arms swinging and pointing as he ploughed his way through a group of chattering Chinese seamen.

Rolfe looked at the latter with interest. It would be one of his first jobs to have a word with his unknown crew, as soon as he had read his orders, he decided.

The deck lurched slightly, and a little tremor ran through the ship. Still the water frothed into the dock, and when it eventually began to slacken, Rolfe watched the black, slimy doors of the basin with something like apprehension.

Out there, countless eyes would be watching him again and he knew what their owners would be thinking. He gripped the rail and stared down at the deck below him. This wasn't the navy, this was a victim partly reprieved from execution. And so am I, he thought slowly.

How would he react? What does it feel like to fall into a command like that? They would be the questions asked in the waiting ships and in the cool offices of Government House. He clenched his jaw, his eyes steely.

The gunboat rose, almost majestically on the water, as if arising from her tomb, and Rolfe caught a glimpse of the calm water in the harbour and heard the noisy clamour of the early morning traffic at the back of the port.

A wafer of sunlight split the lock gates in two, and to the chant of the labouring dockyard men the winches pulled the massive steel slabs slowly apart, and a widening path of tiny glittering wavelets opened up before the ship's bows.

A hush seemed to fall and, although from past experience he knew it to be imagination, Rolfe was again reminded of a bull waiting in its pen to enter the arena. The doors open, the bloodthirsty crowd is stilled with expectancy, and then—, he trembled slightly and shook his head angrily.

"Sir?" Vincent was framed in the wheelhouse door. "Signal from Flag to proceed when ready." The sulky eyes watched Rolfe for some sign or reaction.

42

"Very good!" Rolfe turned on his heel, and began to climb the ladder to the upper bridge. Although it was early the steel rungs were already warm in his hands.

A plump, square-faced Chief Petty Officer saluted from beside the gun, and Rolfe had the impression the man had been waiting in that position for some time. He raised his eyebrows inquiringly, and at once the man began to speak in short, tense sentences.

"I'm Chase, sir, Chief Gunner's Mate." He thrust out his chin belligerently. "Responsible for armaments and general weapons training, sir!"

Rolfe took in the well creased and pressed uniform, the small cap at exactly the right angle, and the gleaming whistle chain around his thick neck. Another one, he thought wearily. There seemed to be so many of them cut from the same rigid pattern. Even the short, ginger hair which bristled from beneath the cap, was cut exactly to regulation style. "A bit of Whale Island in China, eh?" Rolfe smiled, trying to imagine what the man beneath the wooden expression was like.

"Sir?" The slit mouth snapped open and shut like a rifle bolt.

"Alright, carry on, Chief." Rolfe had seen the voice pipes by the binnacle, and they seemed a suitable retreat.

"Bridge, wheelhouse!" He spoke sharply into the brass bellmouth.

"Wheelhouse, bridge!" The voice of the Quartermaster below him rattled tinnily back to him.

"Stand by!" He heard the jangle of bells from the bowels of the ship and a steady, pulsating rumble made the deck at his feet jump and vibrate. He leaned over the thin rail of the bridge, watching until Fallow's glistening face turned upwards.

"Single up to head and stern ropes!" he yelled. It seemed strange not to enjoy the luxury of telephones and voice pipes for passing orders to the deck, but in a way it suited both his attitude to the ship and to his new role.

"I can repeat all your orders, sir." Chase stood watching him in puzzled perplexity.

Rolfe grinned, "I think I'll get used to the ship first, thank you!"

As Rolfe turned his attention back to the movements below, the face of the Chief Gunner's Mate darkened with annoyance.

The greasy wires splashed into the water and were hastily plucked on deck by the sweating seamen, and when only two wires remained, Fallow's bellow announced that he had "singled up."

Rolfe swallowed hard, tasting the whisky in his throat. The dock entrance looked appallingly narrow. How pleased everyone would be if he repeated his last manœuvre.

"Let go forrard! Let go aft!"

The mangy-looking coolies at the stone bollards heaved the wires free and hurled them down to the waiting seamen. *Wagtail* shuddered. She was free.

"Slow ahead, together!" His voice was surprisingly calm, and he watched almost detachedly as the harsh shadows of the dock gates slid over the bows and past the bridge. He was so close to the winch platform that a small, smiling man in blue reefer and white silk trousers bowed and saluted as he moved by.

There was a twitter of pipes, and the thud of bare feet across the decks as the seamen dashed to their new stations for going alongside the loading jetty. Gingerly, but firmly, Rolfe guided the ship along the jagged stone wharf under the leaning arms of the giant cranes and gantrys. With something like a sigh he watched the lines snake ashore to the waiting hands, and the wires once more safely secured. His first trip of about fifty yards, was completed.

Now that he had handled her, he was impatient to be moving again, and after several hours of torment and irritation, while the ship took on stores, it was with real relief that he saw the jetty slide away as he moved his ship out into the harbour.

With the immovable Chase behind him, he stood silently watching the grey ships at their moorings, and listened to the shrill twitter of pipes, as marks of respect were exchanged.

The powerful bulk of the flagship loomed into view, and as Rolfe conned the gunboat between two junks which appeared to be quite motionless on the blue water, he imagined the Admiral's sharp eyes watching from somewhere on that towering superstructure.

In actual fact, the Admiral was in his stateroom, but he was certainly watching the steady approach of the *Wagtail* . . .

"Right on time," he remarked crisply. "And very nice, too!"

He saw himself as the young, innocent midshipman again, setting out in a gunboat such as this one.

Commander Pearce frowned over the Admiral's shoulder. "Doesn't look much like a warship, does she?" he commented bitterly. "Pity we couldn't send a couple of 'Darings' instead." He nodded towards the two powerful destroyers astern of the flagship.

"Hands all fallen in, too," observed the Admiral, ignoring Pearce's sourness. He watched the little ship steam abreast of the cruiser, and heard the shrill wail of the pipes, while the cruiser replied with a lordly bugle, and he raised his glasses to study the lonely figure saluting from the gunboat's bridge.

He had listened carefully to Pearce's report on his visit to the gunboat the previous night, and he had been satisfied. Somehow he knew that the job to be done in Santu was not for the ordinary, unimaginative officer, like Pearce, for instance. Rolfe's record, but for the one lapse, showed he was eminently suited for the task, and if a woman had been at the back of it, he chuckled, the sea trip would do him good anyway.

Wagtail had passed, and the Admiral craned his head round the scuttle to see her blunt bows meet the first heavy swell beyond the protecting sandbanks and walls of the harbour.

"River boat on an ocean cruise," he chuckled again. Reaching for a new pink flag from his desk, he wrote *Wagtail* on it in his firm, round hand, and with a small frown, he stuck it carefully on the wall chart.

"Well, Pearce, they're off!" he exclaimed. "Ring for my steward, and we'll drink to her success."

.   .   .   .   .

The sheltered waters of the harbour dropped slowly astern, and as the sea bottom grew farther and farther from the gunboat's keel, the colour of the sea itself changed rapidly from a deep blue to a shining, emerald green, every tiny ripple and wavelet glittering with a million sparkling gems. But the flat, comfortable calm was also gone, and in its place was the great, sullen power of the China Sea, hidden at the moment, but for the full, regular swell which trundled shorewards in a steady, ponderous rhythm.

Chief Engineroom Artificer William Louch steadied his spindly legs automatically on the gratings as the blunt bows lifted to the challenge of the ocean, and mopped his small beaky face with a piece of cotton waste. He grunted with grudging satisfaction as the two heavy engines beat out their monotonous rumble, and the fans whirred in the air-shafts, sucking great gulps of salty air down to the noisy clangour of the engine-room.

Louch was a quiet, taciturn man, who had all but lost the art of speech after a lifetime spent in similar engine-rooms, a lifetime of grunting and gesticulating to native firemen and stokers amidst the constant noise and sweat of obstinate machinery.

By now he had become immune to both, and he watched the brass dials and gauges about him with professional disinterest and allowed his thoughts to encompass the other matters and happenings which were making the ship move seawards once more.

It was certainly a rum do, he considered, what with the skipper hardly appearing anywhere on deck, other than the bridge, and the First Lieutenant scared of his own shadow. His thin mouth softened slightly at the thought of Fallow. Poor old bugger. He'd be better off in our mess than cooped up with young Vincent, he decided.

His small, bird-like eyes watched a Chinese stoker apply an oil-can to one of the many gleaming vents. The man was naked but for a ragged pair of shorts, and a fragment of cloth around his cropped head to keep the sweat from his eyes. Realizing that his chief's eyes were watching him, he bowed solemnly, and bared his teeth in a huge smile, before continuing on his tour with the oil-can. Louch grinned dourly, "Bloody savage!" he said, but the words were lost in the noise, and the short, stocky figure of the stoker, his skin gleaming under the inspection lamps, was soon lost from view. The grin faded, as the voice pipe at his elbow shrilled suddenly.

"Engine-room. Chief speaking!"

From the land of sunlight and clean decks, the world which Louch avoided and despised so much, Vincent's clear, crisp voice echoed down the pipe.

"Report to the bridge in two hours, Chief!"

Louch glared at the pipe belligerently. "Little bastard!" he muttered. No please or thank you about Mr. Vincent, just snap, snap, snap!

"Aye, aye, sir."

There was a short silence, and Louch felt a tremor of alarm that Vincent might have heard his comment.

"Captain's calling all heads of departments to a conference," the voice added, and Louch breathed again.

On the sun-slashed bridge, Rolfe leaned his weight on the warm teak rail at the side of the wheelhouse. He had just told Vincent to explain the reason for the summons to the Chief Engineer, as the terse, arrogant manner in which the Lieutenant gave all his orders, was beginning to get on his nerves.

I've been out on the flying-bridge too long, he thought, feeling the streams of sweat exploring his back, and clogging the shirt around his armpits. The harsh glare from the shimmering water made him squint painfully, but anything was better than sharing the wheelhouse with Vincent.

"Signal from Flag, sir!"

Rolfe turned at the sound of a cheerful, twanging voice at his side. Telegraphist Little, a short, snub-nosed Cockney, held out the signal patiently.

Rolfe peered at the pencilled jumble of figures, and thought of the Admiral arranging his paper flags like pawns on a chessboard.

"Alter course, oh-nine-oh, at nineteen hundred," he barked to Vincent, who had appeared briefly in the sunlight.

So we're going westwards are we, he mused, Formosa perhaps. Damn all this stupid secrecy anyway. Nobody would send a gunboat like this on anything important, so why all the fuss? And if it's pirates we're after, they'll probably know about it before we do. He glared down at the Telegraphist, who was watching him with absorbed attention.

"How long have you been aboard here?" he asked suddenly.

"A month, sir. I finishes next month, sir," he added quickly. "National Serviceman, y'see, sir."

Rolfe nodded wearily. Everyone aboard seemed to be finishing with the ship, or the navy altogether. Even the ship was finished, he thought. Dismissing the man with a nod, he walked into the comparative cool of the chart room, behind the bridge.

The charts lay in neat packs under the glass-topped table, and in half an hour, when he had read his orders, he would know which one to select. At the moment, the local chart, well-worn and criss-crossed with pencilled lines, lay on the table, the brass dividers where Vincent had last thrown them.

Another roller passed under the ship, and in the chart room loose objects clattered and banged, and a pencil rolled on to the deck. Being flat-bottomed, and with practically her whole hull above the surface, *Wagtail* was like an iceberg in reverse, and the least movement made her roll sickeningly. As the water mounted her side she would yield wearily, hanging over at an ungainly angle, and when the mass of moving water had passed under her, she would still hang for another moment, her triple rudders struggling for a grip, and then, with her ancient plates protesting, she recovered her dignity, sliding upright again to meet the next assault.

In a dead calm, too, Rolfe muttered to himself. Thank God this isn't the typhoon season. Still, typhoons were not unknown, even now. He pressed his damp face in his hands. Stop it, he told himself angrily, just concentrate, just keep——

A warning squark of the siren jerked him out of his deepening gloom, and he stepped quietly into the wheelhouse.

Half a dozen junks, their ribbed sails black against the sun, floated eerily towards the ship, their brightly painted hulls and high, carved poops adding to the air of timelessness which seemed always to be associated with China.

The gunboat's steady ten knots sent a small but impressive bow wave creaming towards them, and Vincent watched the junks carefully through his glasses, which he rested negligently against the bridge window.

"Get out of the way, damn you!" he snapped to the towering sails. "I'd like to run a few of you down!"

"Slow ahead, together!" said Rolfe calmly, and as the engines' rumble died away to a quiet throb, he, too, raised his glasses to study the junks, and their grave-faced occupants, as they glided past.

Once clear, Rolfe ordered an increase of speed again.

"They're people, not savages, Vincent!" he said coldly, his eyes still on the ships. He felt Vincent's furious gaze on his neck, and he was conscious of the Quartermaster's rigid back as he delightedly gathered a tit-bit for telling later on the messdecks.

"But sir!" The words were a protest in themselves. "We had the right of way! They completely disobeyed the rule of the road!"

"Well, we don't want a collision, do we?" Rolfe tried to keep his voice even, but as he turned to face his subordinate, he saw he had said the wrong thing.

Vincent's face was a picture of torn emotions, and he half smiled as he answered softly, "*I've* never been in a collision yet, sir!" There was a sort of triumph in his tone, like a child answering back his father for the first time and watching for results.

A nerve jumped in Rolfe's throat, and he felt as if the sides of the wheelhouse were pressing in on him.

"Meaning what?" He was amazed at the flatness in his voice.

Vincent's handsome face coloured beneath the tan, he had expected Rolfe to fly into a rage, or back down completely, but the icy coldness in the Captain's voice, and the unpitying stare from those grey eyes had unnerved him. "I just thought, sir," he stammered, "that it's part of our job to show firmness with these people."

"At the expense of the ship's safety?" Rolfe tossed the challenge to Vincent without any change of expression.

"I, I just didn't know—" began Vincent weakly.

"There are quite a few things *you* don't know, Mister! And I'll trouble you to keep your private opinions to yourself in future!"

The door of the chart room slammed behind him, but it was some time before anyone in the wheelhouse could relax.

Vincent's eyes were watering with rage, and as he stamped out on to the flying bridge, the Quartermaster began to whistle softly between his teeth. "That told 'im, Ops!" he said to his mate. And they winked at each other knowingly.

Lieutenant Fallow was quite unaware of the worsening

atmosphere on the bridge, and was more concerned with his painstaking inspection of the decks to ensure that all was secured for sea. His heart thumped painfully from his exertions, and his limbs felt heavy and sodden.

"Well, sir, looks like being a nice calm trip." Fallow's companion was Chief Petty Officer Wilfred Herridge, the Chief Bosun's Mate, and general foreman, watchdog and advisor to the ship's company and responsible to Fallow for the running and cleanliness of the ship's routine. He was a striking man of compact and sturdy build, with a long, leathery face and twinkling blue eyes, and a full mouth which was given to hardness, but for the small crinkles of humour at each corner. Born and bred of good Cornish stock, he looked every inch the professional seaman, and Fallow was, as usual, grateful for the feeling of confidence and determination which this man seemed to radiate.

Herridge was feeling even more cheerful than usual—although, like most of his countrymen he was able to conceal the more obvious appearances—as he was well on the way to achieving yet another well-deserved lift in the service, which, to him, meant everything. Just before sailing, he had been told that he was next on the list for consideration for promotion to commissioned rank, to the position of Bosun, if all went well. And he was quite sure that it would. As he thought of the prospect once more, his heart seemed to swell, and he was again overcome by the eagerness to get this trip over and collect a nice air passage home. He was not interested in leave, his one desire was to get back to Portsmouth and start the new course, with new faces about him, and a new life ahead. He watched his First Lieutenant with a small smile on his lips. He had Fallow to thank for his recommendation in the first place, and it had been almost pathetic to hear his warnings and advice about the pitfalls of wardroom life. He chuckled to himself. No fear of that for me, he thought. Nobody's going to tell me I'm not as good as he is. He flexed his powerful muscles at the thought. To Fallow, promotion had meant mental defeat; to him, it was another challenge, another interesting game, in which he was going to come out on top.

Fallow sighed deeply, watching the junks disappearing astern.

"I hope you're right, Chief," he muttered, "I shan't be sorry when we're safely back in harbour."

"That's right, sir. You'll be off home then, eh?"

Fallow smiled half to himself. "Yes. Did I show you the pictures my wife sent me of the new bungalow? I didn't, did I?"

"Er, why no, sir!" Herridge leaned forward attentively, while Fallow fumbled eagerly for his wallet. He had already seen them twice, but he wouldn't have hurt his feelings for the world.

Chase, the Chief Gunner's Mate, passed them without glance or greeting. He was still brooding over the Captain's behaviour on the upper bridge. Chase, like so many of his type, was a big man, with a small mind. Apart from that, he also disliked the ship and its outmoded atmosphere. He felt somehow that he had been drafted to her because of some old score being worked off on him by an enemy. This was partly true, for Chase was a bully, and for all his bluster, was more at home on the parade ground than he was on board ship. At Whale Island, in far-off Portsmouth, he had been in his element. In immaculate belt and gaiters, he had shouted and bellowed himself hoarse, until his red face had turned redder, earning him the nickname of 'Crabface', among others. He had also drilled potential gunnery officers, one of whom had failed, mainly because he carried his brain in his head and not in his feet. Unfortunately for Chase, that same officer had found himself appointed to drafting duties. Chase could only guess the rest.

Now, to add to his anger, the new Captain didn't seem to appreciate his smartness and steadying influence in this damned ship. Well, he'd show him all right. He kicked out at a stocky Chinese seaman who was tightening an awning.

"Pull 'arder, you yellow bastard!" he roared, "I'll 'ave you up on the bridge if I catch you slackin' again!" That's the way to treat 'em, he breathed. Thank God, Lieutenant Vincent was aboard. He at least was a proper officer, and if half he'd heard about his influence in high places was true, no doubt he'd put a word in somebody's ear for him. He arrived at his tiny cubbyhole, imposingly labelled 'Gunner's Store', and after glaring at the seaman who was carefully whitening a pile of webbing gaiters, he proceeded to read his favourite book, the *Royal Naval Handbook of Parade and Rifle Drill.*

The sky changed from pale blue to golden velvet and from somewhere astern, the beam of a beacon stabbed weakly at the gathering dusk. The gunboat ploughed on, meeting the water with her blunt bow, making it break into a frothing white moustache and letting it ripple and gurgle along her low sides until it met the fierce white flurry shot back by the racing screws. Behind her streamed a long white path, drawn as if by a ruler. A few gulls still screamed and swooped over the stern, and a group of chattering Chinese seamen lounged on the deck, throwing pieces of old food to the competing birds.

In the chart room the air was still hot and oppressive, although both the fans whirred busily above the heads of the occupants, who were jammed sweatily in the small space, watching the Captain. Rolfe pulled a chair out of the wireless room and sat down, conscious of their eyes on the wad of papers which he tossed on to the table. Fallow, his pendulous lip hanging wetly forward, perched uncomfortably on a bench, with Vincent at his side. The latter looked cool by comparison, but his eyes were dark and tense.

The three Chief Petty Officers stood bunched awkwardly together in the other corner, an ill-assorted trio. Louch, blotchy with heat from the engine-room, stood dwarfed by the others, his narrow head cocked on one side as if listening to some strange noise in the steady beat below his feet. Chase, as usual, was at attention, his square jaw clamped tight, his mean eyes devoid of understanding and compassion. Herridge on the other hand, looked calm and confident, and was watching the Captain through narrowed lids. He had heard of Rolfe's past, but, unlike the others, had known him before the court-martial. It had been while Herridge was a Leading Seaman in a destroyer of which Rolfe had been the Navigating Officer. A good and efficient officer, he mused, as he studied Rolfe's taut face. Better looking now, too. No wonder he had got engaged to that model, or whatever she was, who had visited the ship once. What an eyeful she was. What had gone wrong? he wondered. Then, as Rolfe sank into the chair, he dismissed the matter from his mind, conjecture could wait, let's get on with this job first.

Rolfe let his eyes flit around the expectant faces, and cleared his throat. "Before I start," he began quietly, "I just want to say that I'm extremely sorry I've not been given the time to get to know you a bit better. Normally, of course, I should have had a longer take-over period, during which time I should have got a fairly clear picture of the whole ship. However, we are as we are, and we have a job to do." He dropped his eyes to the papers, aware that Fallow was licking his lips, and his big hands had started to beat his knees in a steady rhythm.

"I'm afraid that I've got a bit of a shock for you," he continued, "and the work we have to do is rather more intricate than I imagined it might be." He paused, conscious that he now had their full attention. "I'll make it short as I can, we can gen up on the other details later. Our ultimate destination is Santu, on the thirtieth parallel. It's about twelve hundred miles steaming, so we should be there in five days."

Louch frowned, his mind working busily on fuel, water and a multitude of mechanical details.

"The island, as you probably realize, is independent, and governed by one of the old Nationalist generals, Ch'en-Pei. It now seems likely that the Communists are going to take over the island," he tapped the papers. "It's not yet known whether it'll be by force or by inner subversion, and in any case that's not our main concern. There is a small British community there, mostly concerned with running the island's tea and timber industries, and our job is to evacuate them in the *Wagtail*. I understand that to mean about a dozen people at the most. This ship has been chosen because she can handle the job better than anything else. The harbour's only a few feet deep, and a frigate or something of the sort would have to anchor offshore, and the whole operation would be more obvious and complicated. The great thing will be to take it quietly and calmly. I shall see what is to be done and you must make it your job to keep the thing on a routine basis. No panic, no rumours, and no show of force. Neither our people, nor the Americans want any trouble over the island, and in fact, the Americans do not yet know of our task." He paused again, watching their faces. Fallow seemed to have paled, and Vincent was smiling sardonically. "However, between now and our

E.T.A. at Santu, I want to bring this ship up to a war footing. This job will be a test to us all, and we must be ready to meet every eventuality." He studied a carefully prepared list. "So far, this is what I want. Number One. I want you to check every piece of upper deck gear, starting with the stern anchor and working right through. Chief Herridge will, of course, assist you. Pay particular attention to both of the boats. Lieutenant Vincent. You will check all the additional stores which were brought aboard, and ensure that we can deal fully with all the needs of our passengers. Chief Petty Officer Chase."

"Sah!" The heels banged together.

"Your department is most important." He watched the man rise to the offering, the piggy face flush with pleasure. "I shall want you to exercise both guns' crews from now on, until you're satisfied. All night, if necessary. Are your magazines O.K.?"

Chase mentally rubbed his hands. "Perfect, sir!" His mouth snapped importantly.

"And you, Chief," he dropped his gaze to Louch. "I won't try to tell you anything. Except to be ready for every eventuality, and then give me all the speed you can manage!"

Louch smiled dourly. That was a language he understood. "I'll do just that, sir," he murmured.

Rolfe leaned back, glad to have got it off his chest, and wondering how he had whittled down eight pages of instructions in to a few minutes talk.

"Any questions?" he asked.

Fallow swallowed hard, his face working anxiously. "Well, sir," he began, his voice unsteady, "it sounds easy enough. But will these people want to leave? I mean, sir, s'pose they don't want to be evacuated?" His eyes were clouded with fear.

"They'll leave," answered Rolfe confidently. He had, in fact, been asking himself the same question over and over again since he had opened the orders. It seemed to be the major obstacle to the whole operation. No point in adding to Fallow's misery, he concluded.

Vincent stirred his long legs. "If we run into trouble, sir," he shot a glance at Fallow meaningly, "what are our chances?"

Rolfe eyed him thoughtfully before answering. "Depends on the stage of the operation," he said at length. "Inshore, or in

Santu itself, we're on our own. We can, however, whistle up fresh forces once we're clear of the mainland." It'd be too late then, he thought.

"I see, sir." Vincent smiled slowly. "It's one hell of a responsibility for you, isn't it, sir?" he drawled.

"It is no more than I would expect from any one of you," snapped Rolfe. But inwardly he cursed Vincent for baring the thought which was uppermost in his mind. Suppose the people had planned it this way? The plan might be sound, but just suppose things started to go wrong. Rolfe knew only too well that a scapegoat might be required to placate the governments and authorities involved. Maybe this wasn't just a chance to save his career, but an opportunity to save the face of some miserable politician. He shut his mind to the nagging fear, and concentrated on Herridge who was speaking in his rich, clear voice.

"—and I was thinking it might not be advisable to allow shore leave for a bit, sir, until we know the true situation in Santu. I hope you don't mind me mentioning that, sir?"

"Not at all. I see you've not altered much since I last knew you! Still as forthright as ever!"

The others stared at Herridge with wonder, and he flushed with pleasure. So he hadn't forgotten after all, he thought.

"Right then, starting tomorrow, a full routine!" He eyed them separately, his clear eyes thoughtful. "And another thing, I fully realize that some of you are leaving either the ship or the service in the near future, but I want you to clear it from your minds completely, and concentrate on the job in hand. Completely, understand?" He stood up, and they murmured their assents.

As he left the chart room, and headed for his cabin, he said over his shoulder, "Officer-of-the-Watch, alter course as I've shown on the new chart, at twenty-two hundred!" The door closed.

Vincent, who was the O.O.W., pushed his way back to the wheelhouse, and Louch slid quietly in the direction of his engine-room. The others stared at each other. Herridge was the first to speak.

"Should be quite a party, eh, sir? Something to remember China by!" He grinned hugely, showing his strong teeth.

Chase scratched his head, pouting. "We ain't got much to fight with, if the gooks show up!"

"Never mind, Tom, you just give 'em a bit of square-bashin', that'll fix 'em!" he laughed again.

Fallow stared into nothingness, his mind jumping from one possible disaster to the next. Mary won't know about this, he groaned, she'll be expecting a letter, and if something goes wrong. He chilled, it'll be in the papers before we're back. If we get back. He twisted his hands together, locking and turning the fat fingers in time with his agony. These fools didn't understand. They didn't realize what the Captain was really like, and he was going to be the one they'd have to depend on. And this ship. He glared round like a trapped animal. What good would the poor little *Wagtail* be? The murdering swine, he thought wildly. I'll never get home now. Never. And Mary will—he lurched to his feet, "Christ!" he said aloud. The others looked at him with amazement.

"They're mad, I tell you!" He waved his arms desperately. "Mad! If we get caught by some Commie ships, we'll never make it, don't you see?" He stared at them wildly.

"We'll manage, sir," Herridge's voice was calm. "If you'll show us what to do, we'll manage!" He watched, as his words seemed to pull Fallow in to some sort of order.

"Of course, yes, of course," mumbled Fallow vaguely, and stumbled out of the room.

Chase's florid face wrinkled into a frown. "We'll be O.K., won't we, Wilf?"

Herridge clapped him across the shoulder. "Sure we will!" But as they groped their way down the ladder to their mess, he was thinking furiously. If anything blows up on this job, we'll be about as popular as a pork chop in a synagogue, he decided.

．　　　．　　　．

"Three minutes that time, sir!" Vincent screwed up his eyes against the sun's glare, as he peered up at the bridge, watching the Captain's impassive face. All morning, as the *Wagtail* pushed her way forward across the empty sea, they had been lowering the boats as far as the waterline and hoisting them again, while Rolfe timed the proceedings with his watch. Vincent had given the orders so often, that he had lost all count of time, and was conscious only of the glare and his dry and aching throat.

Rolfe's eyes, hidden by his sun-glasses, watched the little scene below him, his attention only half on what Vincent had been saying. For two days, and one morning now, they had been at sea and every available hour had been spent at exercises, as he had promised. At first it had seemed a hopeless task, and he had almost been tempted to give up the struggle. After all, he told himself repeatedly, how can you make a decrepit old gunboat, with a half-trained crew, behave like a modern frigate? Especially when most of the people in responsibility aboard were either incompetent, or disinterested. He shook his head. No. That was a stupid attitude to take. They were willing enough, but it was just that the men had been allowed to decay gently, like the ship.

He was again aware of Vincent's hot face below him. "Very good," he nodded. "Secure the boats!" And as Vincent's tense body slumped thankfully, he added sharply, "But we'll have it in two minutes tomorrow!"

He watched the boats being swung inboard. They might prove to be very useful in an emergency, and half-trained Chinese seamen would be useless without this sort of exercise. They were interesting boats. Not whalers or motor-boats in the accepted naval fashion, but two twenty-five foot sampans, one fitted with an indifferent engine, and the other with oars. With their queer twin keels and a draft of only a few inches, they would skim over any mud bank.

Vincent's voice, harsh with exertion, rang clearly across the burning teak planking of the deck.

"Avast heaving there! You! Whatsyourname! Lin Ki is it? Well put your back into it in future!" There was a pause, then, "Right, hoist away!"

Rolfe smiled slightly. All this work had, if nothing else, kept his officers too busy to get on each other's nerves.

"Tea, Captain-sir!" Chao, clad only in a large pair of spotless shorts, was watching him gravely, a tray in his hands.

Rolfe sank down on a signal locker, and drank gratefully, throwing his cap and sun-glasses in a corner. It was peaceful in the wheelhouse, and it enabled him to go over his preparations without interruption. He found that by standing most of the

57

forenoon and afternoon watches himself, he was able to keep Fallow and Vincent more usefully employed at their checking and training duties.

"Very nice, Chao," he said, putting down the cup. "You're a big help to me."

Chao smiled happily. "Will Captain-sir be requiring drinks this evening?"

Rolfe turned his face away. It was odd how easy it had been to keep off the whisky once he had got swamped by this sea of work and planning. All the same, it would be nice to have just one quiet drink with his dinner, in the seclusion of his cabin. He tortured himself for a while, and then shook his head. "Not just yet, Chao. Too much to do!"

He stared unseeingly at the boy's thin shoulders, as he padded away to his pantry, thinking of Sylvia again. She often crept back into his mind, usually at night, as he lay sweating on his bunk, unable to sleep. The more her memory tried to torment him, the more he drove himself, and the more he suffered.

Even Chase had lost pounds in weight, he thought, running hither and thither about the ship, usually followed by steel-helmeted seamen, either warding off imaginary boarders, or preparing for a landing party with all the clutter of rifles and signalling equipment rattling along behind them. Even as the thought crossed his mind, Chase's bull-like roar shattered the quiet of the battery deck. He was having another try at the Oerlikon gun apparently.

"Nah then, Ferguson, you long streak of 'addock water!" Ferguson was one of the Quartermasters, who also did duty as gunner on the Oerlikon, and he was so tall and fantastically thin, that he could never move an inch about the vessel without either banging his head or tripping over some object or other. "Jus' short bursts, that's all I want! Not poopin' off the 'ole ruddy magazine!"

There was a faint splash, as another empty crate plopped over the stern, and as it bobbed farther and farther behind on the shimmering white wake, Ferguson squinted through the ring-sight with rapidly watering eyes.

"S'long way off now, Chief!" he pleaded, watching the crate growing smaller every second.

"'Old it! Jus' think of it as a ruddy patrol boat, an' make sure of your first burst!"

Ferguson sucked his teeth. He would rather think of it as a Chief Gunner's Mate, but he sank into the leather harness of the gun, feeling the straps hot across his naked back, and gently swung the slender barrel downwards.

"Right, fire!" screamed Chase, and instantly the harsh rattle of the gun and the stench of cordite filled the air. Over and around the nodding crate plumes of spray rose lazily in a series of picturesque white feathers. Whey they had died, the gun was silent, and the crate still intact.

Chase's comments were drowned by the shrill of a voice pipe set apart from the others massed around the wheel.

Rolfe leaned over. "Wheelhouse!" he answered.

"Engine-room here, sir." Louch's voice rattled tinnily from the bowels of the ship. "Would it be possible to stop the ship for half-an-hour, sir? There's a loose gland in one of the tunnels."

Rolfe frowned at the pipe's bell-mouth. Tunnels? What the hell was he talking about? Then he remembered. These old gunboats had their screws mounted high up inside the hull in twin tunnels, so that they were actually revolving above the ship's waterline, thus enabling the ship to bump, if necessary, across a mud-flat or sandbank without damaging them. The water was seemingly sucked up these tunnels as the screws turned.

"Very good. Stop engines!"

The throbbing, their constant companion so far, died away, and the ship rolled uneasily on the green water.

Fallow paused in his work with his ear cocked. "We've stopped!" he exclaimed, and peered at Herridge as if for some explanation.

Herridge continued to check the contents of the ancient ice box against his list, and said nothing. He's really windy, he thought. It was almost as if he had some premonition of disaster. Ah well, he shrugged, perhaps I shall be like that when I'm his age!

Vincent too, raised his head wearily, as he lay sprawled out in a wardroom chair, a tall glass in his fist. Another damned delay! He downed the gin in a gulp, feeling it claw its way through the rawness at the back of his throat. He banged it on the table and signalled to the steward, Peng, unable to speak without choking.

He watched the steward broodingly, and weakly scratched the inside of his bare legs. God, it's hot, and there are still another forty-eight hours to go. He wondered what Santu would be like, and what sort of a mess the Captain would make of their mission. He sipped the second drink, and allowed his mind to drift back to Government House at Hong Kong. The white uniforms, and silk dresses, the music, and the witty conversation. His eye fell on one of Fallow's gardening catalogues, and he groaned with disgust. Thank God he'd be shot of all these dead-beats soon, for good. He picked up a copy of the Tatler, and lazily perused the photographs of the weddings and house parties, looking with interest at the bored faces which stared up at him from the glossy pages. His sense of well-being began to return, and he settled comfortably in the chair, heedless of the shirt sticking to his skin. Soon, soon now, he told himself, and he too would be mingling with reasonable people again.

Rolfe too was thinking of people, but of a different sort. He was considering the prospect of meeting Mr. John Laker, the Acting Consul in Santu. Tea planter and retired brigadier, he sounded a formidable person from the report he had re-read several times. He grimaced. How would I feel, I wonder, if some bloody government department ordered *me* off my land? His eyes sharpened, and he grabbed for his glasses. As the powerful lenses groped across the dancing water, he saw a long grey hull lift itself over the horizon, its hazy outline hardening even as he watched. The white speck at its stem gave the impression of immense speed.

Turning to the bridge messenger, he decided to test the *Wagtail*'s new state of preparedness. "Action Stations!" he barked.

The bells jangled, and the thud of feet echoed throughout the ship, as officers and seamen panted to their positions.

Vincent arrived in the wheelhouse looking fresh and cool, an unspoken question on his face.

"Destroyer! Starboard bow!" snapped Rolfe, jamming on his cap. "American, I imagine." With that, he scrambled up to the open upper bridge, where Fallow stood uneasily with the gun's crew.

Leading Seaman Clinton, the gunlayer, sat heavily on his seat, toying with his sights, his gaunt, hollow face heavy with sleep. He had just crawled into his mess for a quiet nap when the bells had started his legs moving automatically. Now, as he surveyed the approaching ship, with the Stars and Stripes flapping proudly at her gaff, he blew out his cheeks scornfully. Yanks! Always dashing about the ruddy hoggin as if they owned it! He glanced at the Captain's tall frame, the brown shoulders smooth and muscular. Ruddy officers, he thought. Always in a panic about something!

Through his glasses Rolfe saw the rows of white faces, and the brass nameplate, *Arnold P. Crane*. On the other side of her raked funnel she bore an enormous crest, and her squadron motto 'The Fastest and the Best!'

Rolfe smiled grimly, and watched as the signal lamp began to flash. Signalman Randall, an excitable young man from Birmingham, moved his lips silently as he followed the stabbing light.

"Wants to know if we're in trouble, sir?"

At that moment the destroyer moved in closer, her power slowing down, until her superstructure towered over them. A loud hailer squeaked, and then a booming voice flooded across the gunboat.

"Say, ain't you one of those old gunboats?"

Rolfe raised his battered megaphone. "Her Majesty's Gunboat *Wagtail*," he answered.

"Which Majesty is that? Queen Victoria?" The rich American voice quipped back.

Fallow glared angrily across the narrow strip of water, his fears temporarily forgotten. "Bloody cheek!" he muttered, watching Rolfe hopefully.

Rolfe was aware of Louch climbing painfully up the ladder, like a small gnome. "Ready to proceed, sir," he announced quietly.

Rolfe smiled thankfully, "Did you see the ship, Chief?"

Louch met his gaze calmly, and he wiped his neck automatically with his piece of waste. "Ship? What ship, sir?" And without a glance at the American, he turned back down the ladder.

Rolfe grinned broadly at Fallow. "There you are, Number One, that's the way to behave!"

He waved across to the destroyer. "We're alright now! Nice to have met you!"

A bell jangled, and the *Wagtail* began to move, as if eager to be clear of her present company.

Several of the American sailors were training their cameras and pointing delightedly.

"Probably think this is all the Royal Navy can afford!" observed Fallow sourly.

The ships moved apart, the greyhound of the seas and the top-heavy gunboat.

Rolfe watched admiringly as the destroyer gathered way, remembering how it had felt with forty thousand horsepower under his feet.

"Don't be taken in by their attitude, Number One. They're different in their approach to things, that's all!"

"Aye, aye, sir," answered Fallow gloomily, staring angrily after the grey shadow. "The fastest and the best! Huh!" He wiped his face clear of sweat. "They think they can do anything!"

"They couldn't get into Santu harbour for a start! And what's more, they don't know we're going to, or I don't suppose he'd have been quite so jolly!" Then briskly, Rolfe added, "Right, time for another drill! This time we'll lay out the gear for towing from aft! Carry on, Number One!"

As dusk fell, *Wagtail* crept past a sleeping Formosa, and turned on her fresh course to the north. The time for practice was over, and the game was about to start.

3

On the large scale chart of China's Eastern Sea, the island of Santu shows a remarkable likeness to a question mark, even to the extent of having a tiny formation of rocks lying entirely separate, a couple of miles off the southern 'tail-end' of the island, making a natural 'dot'. For a vessel of any size, the approaches to the island are few and treacherous, the apparently placid waters being strewn with reefs and long, uneven sand-bars, some of which are uncharted, and most of which are unknown, but to the local coast shipping. High, reddish cliffs form the eastern side, and apart from deep anchorages, there are few landing places for even the smallest craft, the only harbour being situated within the natural curl of the rough-hewn 'query' at the northern end. That too has been allowed to silt up over the years, the hosts of small fishing boats preferring to beach themselves along the flat mud banks, while larger visiting ships have had to make do with a doubtful lighterage service to and from the shore.

Rolfe stood quietly at the front of the bridge, watching for the guiding marks and stone beacons which, according to his Pilot's Guide, were the only visible aids to navigation. He was still surprised by his first sight of the island, by its lush greenness and tree-covered slopes rising above the yellow beach at the back of the harbour. The town, apparently consisting of small, single-storied white houses and huts, was strewn in a disordered and colourful jumble at the foot of a towering, red-stone cliff, the front of which had fallen down into the waters of the harbour in long flat slabs, like a handful of books tossed carelessly on a glass-topped table. The harbour wall, what there was of it, was merely an extension of this rocky formation, and looked as if it had stood for as long as the island itself. His gaze was held by the ancient, rambling walls of a fortress, which straggled along the top of the cliff, and dominated both the harbour approaches and the town; walls which were worn and pitted by weather and time, until they too seemed to be part of the rough, red stone on which they stood. From the squat, central tower, a tall flagstaff carried a long, green banner, which hung limply in the hot mid-day sun.

Apart from a few fishing boats drifting lazily nearby, the *Wagtail* had the sea to herself, and as she steamed purposefully along her set course, Rolfe felt that thousands of eyes were watching their approach, although, in fact, only a few figures could be seen on the distant harbour wall.

Fallow glanced apprehensively as a fang-toothed rock slid past the port side, and tried not to think of the others hidden below the friendly water which rippled quietly past the gunboat's hull, and concentrated instead on the shimmering face of the island. Looked friendly enough, he thought. Perhaps the job'd be over quickly after all.

"Hard a-starboard!" He heard Rolfe's terse voice, and felt the gunboat swing awkwardly off her course to avoid another grinning reef. He mopped his face anxiously, and peered down over the ship's side. It seemed frightening somehow, to be able to see the bottom of the sea from a moving vessel. They could but be in a few feet of water now, and the harbour was still half a mile distant.

He turned away from the rail, his eye falling on a group of idling seamen. "'Ere, come on then!" he growled, anxious to cover his fright. "Grab 'old of these wires an' fenders for comin' alongside the wall!" If we get there, he added to himself.

Rolfe sighed deeply as the blunt bows rounded the pointing finger of the stone breakwater. Here, at least, it was a sandy bottom, so even if they ran aground—he shook himself, suddenly angry—stop thinking of failure before you start, you're getting as bad as the others, he cursed inwardly.

As the ship manœuvred up to the jetty, the crowd of jabbering and pointing Chinese swelled, until their very numbers threatened to force some of them into the water. Many hands snatched out to collect the heaving lines as they snaked ashore, and in a very short time the mooring-wires were clamped snugly around the weather-beaten stone bollards on the top of the wall.

Another group of ragged-looking coolies, their emaciated bodies straining and grunting, swung a long, carved gangway across to the gunboat's deck, where it was secured under the watchful eye of C.P.O. Herridge, who mistrusted most other people's ability to tie even the simplest knot.

Chase, his heavy face grim with importance, stood smartly at attention at the head of the gangway, by the armed sentry, and stared fiercely at the gaping crowd, both contemptuous of them, and conscious of his own impressive appearance.

A few scruffily dressed soldiers, clad in assorted bits of uniform, but armed to the teeth with sidearms and automatic rifles, shouldered their way roughly through the crowd to stand impassively along the edge of the wall, facing the *Wagtail*.

Rolfe, straightening his tunic with slow, deliberate tugs,

watched the newcomers with interest. The soldiers of General Ch'en-Pei carried themselves with a certain confident swagger, which even their crude green uniforms could not disguise. They were definitely better fed than the townspeople, and looked more like bandits than soldiers, which they no doubt are, he thought dryly.

A hush fell over the crowd as some of the soldiers forced a passage through the packed bodies. Rolfe stepped forward to the gangway, feeling the sun on his neck like a sledgehammer, signing to Fallow to call the seamen to attention. He had seen a white panama hat floating through the lane of watching people, and he guessed that Mr. John Laker was losing no time in discovering the reason for a warship's unheralded appearance in his little domain.

John Laker was gross. To describe him in any other terms would be useless, as everything about him was big and important. His round, brown face and flinty grey eyes had the stamp of the regular army officer, but the heavy, squat body, shrouded in a well-cut white suit, was the product of extremely good living. He walked with an unexpected lightness, and as he stepped carefully across the gangway, he swept the panama from his head, revealing a mass of well-trimmed, grey hair and a smooth, unlined forehead.

Following him across the gangway came the tall, stooping figure of a Chinese officer, dressed in a smart and better designed version of the green uniform worn by the other soldiers. His long arms hung limply at his sides as he walked, and his shoulders, narrow and rounded under the flashing shoulder straps of his tunic, moved in a curious loping motion, disconnected from the rest of his long body. His features were smooth and ageless, only the deep-set almond eyes showing any interest or animation in his surroundings.

Rolfe saluted and smiled. "Welcome aboard. Mr. Laker, isn't it?"

Laker nodded vigorously. "Erm, that's right, Captain. Brigadier Laker!" There was a slight reproof in his fruity voice. He ushered his companion forward. "An' this is Major Ling," the officer bowed at the mention of his name. "He's here to welcome you on behalf of the General."

"I am also Chief of Security here in Santu!" Ling's voice was surprisingly soft and well-modulated, with hardly a trace of accent.

"Security? You mean the police?" Rolfe asked politely.

"We have no police in Santu. The army is quite sufficient!" One of his long arms waved negligently towards his men on the jetty. "As you see, Captain, they are a rough lot. But as you know, you judge a fighting dog not by its coat, but by its teeth!"

Rolfe pondered over those words, as he guided the two men into the wardroom, where he introduced his officers.

Fallow shook hands humbly, and then lapsed into silence, while Vincent flashed Laker a warm smile, and prepared himself for another conquest. The stewards had gone to great lengths to prepare for any such occasion as this, and the table glittered with a wide assortment of drinks and glasses. Even the lemons, fresh from the ice-box, still retained an appearance of newness.

Laker swilled the whisky round his glass, a tight smile on his lips. "Damn me, Captain! You navy chaps certainly know how to stock up!" He laughed harshly. "It's a real treat to see a British ship again. Thought we'd been sold up the river. Forgotten, or somethin' like that, what!"

Rolfe studied Laker's vast bulk and wondered what exactly the man had on his mind. He noticed how he laughed freely enough with his mouth, while the flinty little eyes remained sharp and cold. He realized with a start that Laker had just asked him how long the gunboat would be staying in Santu.

"About two weeks, sir. We'll be having a look round the islands generally to see that you're not being unduly bothered by pirates, and I hope you'll be able to fix me up with fresh water and so on, while the ship is here."

"Delighted, me boy!" Laker was getting into a better humour, as the whisky, which he took neat, coursed through him.

The stewards refilled the glasses rapidly on every opportunity, and the atmosphere had lost its air of tension.

"I notice you do not drink with us?" Major Ling's silky voice cut across the flow of conversation like a knife.

Rolfe squirmed inwardly and cursed himself for not thinking they would notice.

"Must be slipping!" he grinned lightly and tossed the glass

back, feeling the power of the liquid almost immediately. A prickle of sweat moved at the nape of his neck and he gripped his knee with his free hand as if to transmit a warning to himself. He watched helplessly as Peng stooped over his glass, and the sound of the whisky pouring from the bottle seemed to roar in his brain with the power of a waterfall.

Major Ling smiled softly and relaxed his long legs in front of him. "Excellent, Captain," he purred, "I always feel more at ease when my host drinks with me!"

Rolfe joined in the general laughter and was conscious of Vincent's eyes watching him curiously. Damn them, he thought angrily, must keep a sense of proportion.

He turned back to Laker. "I gather you're kept pretty busy here in Santu? I've been hearing a lot about your achievements while I've been in Hong Kong," he lied carefully.

Laker smiled happily. "So I'm not forgotten, eh? Well, that's good to know, I must say. To tell you the truth, I get a bit disheartened sometimes, the way we're ignored by the Government at home. The Major here will tell you that we've not done too badly really. I came here with me family just after the war, y'know, and had to damn well take the place apart to get things goin'. And now," he waved his glass expansively, "I've got a thriving tea business, the only one on the island, and I also export some pretty high grade camphor wood. Still a big demand for it, y'know."

Ling smiled gently, revealing small, child-like teeth. "Mr. Laker has done much for the prosperity of Santu. The General is most pleased! I hope you will enjoy your stay with us here. The General has instructed me to bid you welcome and to convey his invitation to you and your officers to his humble home."

"You mean the fortress?" asked Rolfe.

"Home," corrected Ling quietly.

Laker had been waiting impatiently for Ling to finish, and now he plunged again into his favourite theme. The achievements of John Laker.

As his thick, penetrating voice dominated the conversation, Rolfe was able to glean a great deal of useful information. Laker had retired from the army at the beginning of the war and settled in Singapore where he had various business interests. When the Japanese had struck, he had somehow managed to evacuate himself and his wife, together with a great proportion of his wealth, to India, where tea planting had taken up his full attention.

"Then, of course, our blasted Government chucked India down the drain, like they do with everything nowadays, and I heard of this place. It was a gamble, I can tell you. But as you see, it paid off." He frowned suddenly, his eyes disappearing in the folds of his cheeks. "Now we're off again!" he growled savagely. "I expect the Communists think they're on to a good thing in Santu. That's why I'm so damn glad to see you chaps here at last! Thank God our Government is goin' to make a stand at last!"

Rolfe swallowed and gripped his glass tightly. So that was it. Laker was sure of support for the British community, and when he heard the real reason for the ship's visit, it would be easy to guess his reaction.

"Will there be other ships, Captain?" Ling was watching him over the rim of a glass, his eyes dark. "Your ship is no doubt excellent but, if you do not mind my saying so, it is rather small?"

"Course there'll be others, Ling!" barked Laker, his small chin jutting fiercely. "Just wait and see, what!"

"So long as we do not have to wait too long, my dear Laker," persisted Ling softly. "The General is not happy about the many spies and agents who have been landed recently on these shores."

Rolfe pricked up his ears. "How do they get here?"

Ling shrugged. "By boat mostly, and some are already here, of course, recruited among the rabble of the town!"

"D'you ever catch any?" Vincent was leaning forward, his face flushed.

Ling turned towards him, a gentle smile on his thin mouth. "A few. You will see their heads on the prison wall!" He added, "As a reminder to others, you understand?"

"Oh, er, quite!" Vincent looked helplessly at Rolfe.

"Christ!" breathed Fallow and downed his drink in a single swallow.

Laker lurched to his feet. "Well, I must be off. Lot to do. I've enjoyed my visit immensely, I can tell you."

Rolfe kept his voice casual. "I should like to discuss certain matters with you, if I may, sir. In your other position as Acting Consul."

Laker laughed. "Oh, that! Certainly, I'll be delighted. My wife and daughter are just itching to see you, anyway. They'll bore you to death with nonsensical questions about England and so forth! You know women! You married, Captain?"

"Er, no." Rolfe saw Fallow's brown eyes dart towards him worriedly.

"Good, good! Too much trouble!" Laker laughed again.

"When shall I call on you?"

"Dammit, didn't I tell you? Must be gettin' old! You're all to come to my place tonight, if you can manage it?"

"Delighted," Rolfe murmured, trying to clear the whisky from his mind so that he could plan more easily. "We shall be there."

"Good. Six o'clock. And there'll be most of the other chaps there, all being well. They'll be tickled pink to see you, too, no doubt!"

No doubt, thought Rolfe grimly. Especially when they know what I'm here for.

"By the way," Laker added, "if any of your chaps are goin' ashore, don't let 'em wander about after dark too much. Outside the town that is. Liable to be shot at, y'know!"

"The Communist agents, you mean?" Rolfe frowned.

Ling stood up, putting on his long-peaked ski-cap. "No, Captain, my men have orders to shoot at any strangers!" He spread his hands apologetically. "The emergency, you know!"

Rolfe saw them over the side and returned to the wardroom, still frowning.

Vincent's face was working excitedly. "Dash it, sir!" he exploded, "you'll never get these people to leave here! They've done too much for the island!"

Rolfe eyed him narrowly. "They'll leave all right. Did you notice the people on the harbour?" he asked suddenly. "Half-starved, downtrodden, and for Chinese, pretty miserable. It's as our people thought," he added. "Old Laker and this General seem to have got the island sewn up between them. Where does the money go? The money Laker and his friends make? And what about the General? How do you think he has survived so long?" He shook his head thoughtfully, a deep frown between his eyes. "I'm afraid it stinks!"

"But sir!" Vincent protested, "surely that's not for us to decide, we're the navy, not the Government!"

"You're right. It's not for us to decide. It's already been decided for us. You know our orders? Well then, we shall obey them!" He glanced at Fallow, who was staring out of the open door. "Get the fresh water aboard as soon as you can, Number One. No shore leave for our Chinese seamen. It might not be advisable. In the meantime, send the Telegraphist to my quarters in ten minutes. I'm going to code up a signal for the Admiral and put him in the picture." He walked slowly to the door. "By the way, no excessive drinking this evening! I don't want any loose tongues!"

Fallow nodded dumbly, and watched the Captain hurry up the ladder to the battery deck.

"Phew, what an unholy, ruddy mess," he said slowly. "It's not right that we should be given such an impossible job!"

Vincent laughed shortly. "Not to worry unduly. Did you hear what that Chink major said about those heads? I ask you, it's like the Middle Ages!"

Fallow bit his lip. He had seen Rolfe's face when the drinks had been forced on him. Suppose something happened to him again. He remembered the Captain's inert form on the cabin floor. I'll be left to finish the job. He turned to the stewards. "Lock that damned hooch away, blast you!" He waved his hands in stabbing gestures. "I'm sick to death of the way this navy runs on bleedin' drink!"

Vincent waited until the stewards had gone, then he jumped up, his face full of questions. "Look here, Number One, what *is* all this harping on drink? Every blessed person I've met so far raves about drink! What do you know that's worrying you so much? Is it something the Captain's done? Because if it is, I've a right to know!"

His clear, sharp voice cut into Fallow's aching mind like a hot saw. He shrugged unhappily. "Don't you start, Vince, jus' drop it, will you?"

Vincent followed Fallow's broad back out of the door, his lips pursed. All this damned mystery. He brightened slightly at the prospect of the party at Laker's house. Might still be all right, he pondered. It was queer about old Fallow, though. He had never acted so strangely before, so it had to be something to do with the Captain. Drink. Was that it? And the way he had looked when Laker had asked him if he was married. As if he'd seen a ghost. He smiled thinly and pressed the bell. The steward appeared in a flash.

Vincent smiled again. "Large whisky," he drawled.

.　　.　　.　　.　　.

Once clear of the town the narrow dirt road climbed rapidly through a boulder-strewn pass, and up on to the wide plateau which covered most of the island. Here, the thick green vegetation closed protectively into the sides of the road, blotting out the sea and the shabby buildings around the harbour. Laker's cream American convertible, a Union Jack fluttering incongruously from the bonnet, rocked easily over the uneven surface, its luxury springs making short work of the pot-holes and wheel-ruts.

Vincent sat in front beside the driver, a sturdy little man called Grant, who was employed by Laker as his estate manager, while Rolfe and Fallow shared the vast expanse of the rear seat. Rolfe reflected that there was ample room for the four of them in front, but was thankful for his freedom of movement and conversation. Vincent, on the other hand, chatted happily to his companion, who handled the big car with ease and a total disregard for the occasional passer-by, who had to jump from the road to avoid the gleaming chrome bumper.

"Dashed decent of Mr. Laker to send his car for us," remarked Vincent, as a drove of chickens scattered into the bushes. "I'm really looking forward to this party!"

Grant chuckled. "Reckon you wouldn't have fancied the walk!" The blackened pipe clamped between his teeth bobbed as he spoke. "It's a bit off the beaten track, y'see, but it's worth the journey," he added proudly.

Rolfe's eyes hardened behind the protective lenses of his sun-glasses. Another one, he thought angrily. Why did these people have to choose such an outlandish place to set up their little empire? The car lurched sideways on to an even narrower road and slowed to pass through a pair of high barbed-wire gates. He caught a brief glimpse of two waving figures, and the glint of their rifles, before the car turned yet again on to a long, ruler-straight roadway which seemed to run on forever between legions of neat little trees and wide, orderly fields. There was an air of well-planned regimentation about the whole estate which made Rolfe think of Laker. As if in answer to his thoughts, Grant waved a stubby hand towards the fields. "There it is, or part of it, gentlemen. Fourteen years' hard work and a lot of capital, too!"

He pointed to the gleam of red brickwork beyond the trees. "Yon's the reservoir that the guv'nor built. No shortage of fresh water all the year round!"

"What do the inhabitants think about that?" asked Vincent.

Grant laughed in amazement. "The natives, d'you mean? Oh, it's not for them! It's for our own uses!" He chuckled as if it was a huge joke.

Vincent joined in his laughter. "I'm glad you've got the right idea out here!"

Rolfe gritted his teeth, conscious of the throbbing in his temples. Without thinking, he touched his pocket, feeling the folded signal pad containing the Admiral's acknowledgement to his message. He had decoded it himself, and his heart had quickened as he had read the news in the privacy of his cabin.

"Reliable reports indicate strong Communist forces massing on mainland due west of your position. Several large landing craft also in vicinity. Suggest you commence operation immediately. Use your own discretion."

Use your own discretion. The words had meant the death or dishonour of many naval captains in the past, whose situations had been comparatively easy when compared with his own present dilemma. It seemed fantastic that they were bowling along in this luxury automobile, when less than fifty miles away troops were probably, even at this very moment, being marched into the waiting craft for an invasion of the island. He twisted uncomfortably in his seat, and turned to face Fallow, who was showing a half-hearted attempt to listen to the conversation in front of him.

He had told neither of his officers about this new development, and he wondered if he had acted wisely. It was an unpleasant fact to face, but he knew that had his officers' roles been reversed, he would not have hesitated to take Vincent into his confidence, for he, at least, would take the news calmly. But Fallow. He watched him from behind the safety of the dark lenses, noting the twitching fingers and anxious eyes. No, he decided, Fallow would be all right when he had something to do, but now he might as well try to enjoy himself.

A long, white bungalow-type house loomed into view, and from its shaded veranda several figures watched the car's approach. Laker was the first down the steps, accompanied by several khaki-clad servants, who with military precision removed the car, the officers' caps, and then hovered respectfully in the rear.

"Like the car, eh?" Laker boomed. "This year's model. Had it shipped in from Formosa, y'know. Would have preferred a British one, of couse, but these Yankee jobs stand up to the appalling roads better."

He guided them into a wide, cool lounge which ran the whole width of the house, and Rolfe blinked to accustom his eyes to the seemingly dark interior.

With the casual grandness of royalty, Laker introduced his other guests, who crowded round the newcomers with real enthusiasm. Mrs. Laker was surprisingly small and had, Rolfe thought, once been very beautiful. Now, her thin features bore the sheen of yellow parchment, part of the price she had paid for a lifetime overseas. She welcomed Rolfe warmly, but with several nervous glances at her beaming husband, who patted her with the affection of a master to his pet dog. Rolfe sympath-ized with her inwardly and turned to the others. There was Edgar Lane and his wife, Rolfe mentally ticked them off his list. He already knew that Lane was the other of Laker's managers who handled the timber side of the estate. He was a slight, studious man with sad, watery eyes, and his wife, Melanie, looked to Rolfe like a faded chorus girl. He answered their friendly enquiries but was thankful when Laker tugged him on to the others. "Don't listen to Lane," he confided noisily. "Sticks with his damned trees so much he's forgotten how to talk to real people!" He nudged Rolfe gleefully, and a strong aroma of whisky floated around them.

"An' this is Mrs. Grant, you've already met her old man." Rolfe muttered something suitable to the cheerful, bronzed woman, and was thankful when he was introduced to the last bobbing faces. Charles and Anthea Masters were rather younger than the rest and had the appearance of nervousness. Laker announced that they were his "newest imports" to Santu, Masters being an engineer newly out from England. Anthea Masters had a shy, suburban smile which had already wilted under the glare of her new surroundings.

"Well, that's the lot, Captain! We're not exactly a Crown Colony, but we're pretty useful in our way, eh?" He laughed noisily.

Rolfe frowned, mentally checking his list. "But isn't there an English doctor here, too?"

As he asked, he felt a slight tension in the air, but Laker seemed indifferent to atmosphere of any kind.

"Oh, the Feltons? Well, they're English by birth, I suppose. But that's about as far as it goes, if you follow me, eh?"

"I'm afraid I don't." Rolfe's tone was deceptively mild and for a second a flicker of annoyance crossed the older man's face.

He rubbed his hands together irritably. "Not quite the right type, y'know. Live down in the town with the wogs!" He leaned closer, dropping his voice. "Fact is, old boy, the feller's a bloody red, no doubt about it!"

Rolfe digested this information. "How come the General hasn't asked them to leave, then?"

Grant, who had quietly approached from the side, laughed shortly. "He needs a doctor for the natives, that's the reason. Otherwise he'd have him shipped out a bit sharpish!"

Laker glared at his assistant. "Forget 'em! They don't exist! If I had my way I'd——"

"Horsewhip them?"

They turned at the sudden interruption and then Laker's face dissolved into an affectionate beam.

"Oh, Captain, I almost forgot me own daughter! Ursula, this is Commander Rolfe."

Rolfe took her hand and felt a growing uneasiness. Ursula Laker was tall for a girl, and at thirty-three had reached the fullness of her perfections. Her steady green eyes and short blonde hair, bleached almost white by the sun, clashed dazzlingly with her smooth tanned skin. If her mouth was a trifle wide, it was generous. And if her body, tantalizing beneath her light frock, was inclined to fullness, Rolfe had a feeling that it might be generous, too.

"I hope you like what you see, Captain?" Her voice was a soft drawl, with a throatiness that was vaguely exciting.

Rolfe grinned uncomfortably, and Laker, his eyes glinting watchfully, patted his arm. "Eyeful, eh? Just like her mother used to be!"

Rolfe found it hard to picture Mrs. Laker as the voluptuous creature confronting him.

A gong chimed discreetly in the background and as the servants quietly folded away some giant screens, Rolfe saw a vast, laden table glittering with food and drink.

"In yer honour!" announced Laker solemnly.

This must surely be the climax of my varied career, thought Rolfe, as with Laker at one side and Ursula on the other, he seated himself at the table. Perhaps it would be better to approach all of them on the matter of evacuation now; the idea seemed to blind him with its dreadful possibilities, Laker on his own might be too crafty an opponent. He ran his eye carefully along the happy, flushed faces. It would be worth a try.

He felt the heat rise in his body as the girl's knee pressed against his own under the table. The pain of his old memories came flooding back, and almost without noticing, he downed the tall glass of pale liquid by his plate.

"By jove!" Grant exploded admiringly. "Our very special home brew, and he takes it like water!"

Laker grunted at his side. "Damn strong stuff that, Captain! Should have warned you. Still, you navy chaps know a thing or two, what!"

The pressure on his knee increased, and he turned to the green eyes, which were regarding him with lazy interest.

"Silly old fool, isn't he?" she whispered, and the corners of her mouth twitched. She was so close to him that he could feel the hard pressure of her breast against the sleeve of his tunic. The wine flowed in his veins like fire, and for the first time in many months he felt a glimmer of his old self. He smiled back at her, immune to the babble of conversation and the stares of his officers.

It would be so very easy, he pondered, just to let everything else drop, let the others go to hell. What did anything matter any more, what did these people mean to him, anyway?

"You're pretty fed up, aren't you?" she kept her voice low, and Rolfe's eyes widened slightly.

"Does it show?"

"When you've been stuck on this place as long as I have you get to notice even the smallest bit of emotion." She wriggled her shoulders and pouted, "I'm sick to death of it!"

"Pretty lonely for you, I expect?"

"Lonely? That, my dear Captain, is the understatement of the year! I go for the odd trip each year, but what the hell! People who matter treat you like a hick when they know you live on this god-forsaken spot!" She glanced across Rolfe at her father. "Of course, you've noticed Daddy thinks it's heaven here. That's because he's the local tin god!" She eyed him dreamily. "I expect you get a bit lonely, too?"

"At the moment I feel completely alone!" admitted Rolfe grimly, although his mind was working along a different track.

"Perhaps we can do something about that?" she breathed, her lip quivering. "You'll have to let me show you round while you're here!"

Vincent watched them carefully, shading his eyes with his lashes. She's whimpering for it, he thought enviously. Wish I could hear what they're saying. Queer type, the Captain. The more you saw of him, the more surprising he became. Vincent's heart pounded as he watched the girl draw an imaginary design with her finger on Rolfe's sleeve. He shifted his eyes to his Captain's face and immediately became irritated by the blank expression in those cold, grey eyes. What sort of a man is he? Must have ice-water in his veins! One minute he looks like a young sub-lieutenant at his first party and the next his face is as hard as rock.

A servant refilled his glass and he drank deeply, feeling the sweet tang of the rice wine tingling in his throat. Wonder how Fallow feels about all this drink? The fat fool, he thought contemptuously. There was a slight disturbance as Laker heaved his huge body upright. Vincent leaned forward, showing an affected interest. Actually he was amusing himself with the mental picture of Laker and Fallow trying to pass through a door together.

"Hrrm! Ladies an' gentlemen!" Laker stared solemnly round the table. "I give you a toast. The Queen!" The glasses clinked obediently and automatically. Laker was apparently behaving as usual. He beamed at them and raised his glass again. "And another, to our guests, the officers of the gunboat *Wagtail*!"

There were several polite "Hear, hear", and Laker stared down at Rolfe, his small eyes flashing.

"We're all delighted to see these chaps, and I know you'll want me to speak for you in that respect. It makes us all proud and humble, too, to realize that we've not been forgotten in our hour of need!"

Vincent watched Rolfe's taut features for some sign of alarm or discomfort, but there was no answer to his probing glance. Rolfe sat stiffly in his chair, staring fixedly at his glass.

Vincent trembled with excitement. What a story this would make when he got back to Government House! All these pathetic characters, cut off from the outside world, but living what they believed to be normal lives, and still imagining that they were protected by the umbrella of British democracy. He shivered suddenly, gripping the sides of the chair. Rolfe had risen to his feet as Laker, flushed and breathing heavily, sat down.

Rolfe put down his glass carefully, conscious of the silence and the pounding in his veins. He spoke slowly, his clear, firm voice lending impact to his words. He thanked Laker for his kind welcome, and for a moment Vincent imagined that he was going to by-pass the main issue, but the next instant he knew that the real drama had begun.

"As you all know, the menace to this island from the Communist mainland has been growing considerably during the last few months, and the situation here, for the small British community especially, has taken on a much graver aspect. It is for that reason that I am speaking to you in this manner, as I have the unexpected opportunity of seeing you all together in this convenient and friendly setting." He paused and sipped at his glass, which had been imediately refilled. Fallow stared blankly at his plate, his fat chins working miserably as he unseeingly demolished a dish of prawns. Rolfe eyed him for a moment and continued: "Her Majesty's Government have watched your growing danger with some concern and that is the real reason for my ship's presence in Santu."

Laker nodded gravely and whispered to Grant, "Told you so, old boy!"

The muscle in Rolfe's cheek jumped noticeably and he appeared to be speaking with some effort. "It is therefore my duty to inform you all that arrangements have been made to evacuate you to Hong Kong in my ship within the next forty-eight hours!"

There was a stunned silence and Vincent hardly dared to glance at the others around him. It was like a first-night at a really good play. Rolfe had spoken his lines with terrific impact and the audience had reeled before him.

Laker was the first to recover his speech. He jumped to his feet, his mouth working frantically. "What the devil are you sayin', sir? Are you mad? Off yer head?"

Rolfe eyed him for a full four seconds without answering, his mouth pressed into a tight line.

"If you would be so good as to let me finish, Mr. Laker," he answered quietly. A few tiny beads of sweat glinted on his upper lip. Apart from that, he was outwardly the calmest person in the room.

"I was going to add," he continued, "that I have just received a signal from my Commander-in-Chief to the effect that a full military invasion is now imminent, and I'm afraid, unavoidable! So further delay, or any other solution which might once have been possible, is now out of the question. I shall make you as comfortable as I can aboard, although I'm afraid that only personal gear, and small possessions can be carried with you."

Laker was still standing at his side, his small eyes popping with rage. "You're talking rubbish! We're not leaving with you, or anyone else, d'you hear?" He glared round for support. "What the devil is happenin' here, eh? Has everyone gone completely mad?"

"Please, dear!" His wife fluttered anxiously to his side. "You mustn't excite yourself so!"

"Excite meself! I'll damn well show 'em!"

"Just a moment, suppose it's right what the Captain's just told us?" Edgar Lane interrupted uneasily. "I mean, we've seen what can happen when the Reds move in on a place!"

The young Masters couple moved closer together in alarm, their faces white.

"I can assure you I am right," said Rolfe, when the babble of voices subsided. "There is no alternative." He turned to Laker. "I would have told you about this business at once, sir, but I didn't know then what I now know to be the facts. I know how you feel and I sympathize with you deeply. "But——" he shrugged—"it is the luck of the draw."

Laker stared at him incredulously. "What are you saying? Why, it's—it's rank impertinence! I'll break you for this, if it's the last thing I do!"

Grant rubbed his chin thoughtfully. "Calm down, sir, you know as well as I do that it's none of the Captain's doing. We must face facts!" He smiled bleakly at Rolfe. "You don't pull your punches, I must say, but looking back over the last five minutes, I don't think I would have been in your place for a million pounds!"

Laker collapsed into his seat, his face suddenly very old. "God!" he whispered in a thick voice, "it's the end! The finish of everything!"

Ursula Laker hadn't stirred from her lounging position, but her face twisted into a scornful smile. "Don't be ridiculous, Daddy! We're not short of cash, and I for one will be glad to see a bit of life again!" She raised her eyes to Rolfe, the green lights dancing beneath her lashes. "Well spoken, Captain. Now tell us the rest of the good news!"

Rolfe studied her face thoughtfully without recognition and then leaned his hands on the table. "I have been instructed to tell you also that there must be no panic and no undue warning of our intentions!"

Laker roused himself from his posture of despair. "Dammit! Must we slink out of here, too?" He laughed shakily. "Just like all the others, eh? India, Africa, Palestine, Suez and all the rest! Creep out with our tails between our legs!"

"This is not British territory," Rolfe's voice was quite flat

79

and devoid of emotion. "It is practically part of the Chusan Archipelago and it has no government of its own."

Vincent thought Laker would have a fit. His cheeks wobbled and his mouth spluttered in fury. "No government? What the hell's the General doin' then?"

There was a sharp crash and everybody jumped at the sound, their incredulous eyes riveted on Rolfe's doubled fist which had slammed down suddenly on the table. He was leaning forward, the grey eyes no longer quiet and patient, but flashing with fierceness that seemed to shrivel Laker where he stood.

"Now listen to me!" he barked, "and I mean all of you! Mr. Laker has just mentioned the General. Well, I haven't met him yet, but I will tomorrow morning. He is the ruler of this island as it stands, I am not denying that! But where is the government? A couple of thousand soldiers strutting round the place like the bandits that they are, while the half-starved thousands of this miserable population exist on what they can scratch from the land or fish from the sea. If they think the Communists can offer them something better, and let's face it, they couldn't be much worse off, what choice d'you think they'll make when the troops start landing?" He glared at Laker, a lock of dark hair falling over one eye. "Is this the paradise you want the British navy to fight for? D'you honestly think this island is another Formosa? Worth another world war, perhaps?" His chest heaved under the white tunic. "Well, whatever you think, Mr. Laker, you're leaving with me. Quietly and sensibly! I would have thought that a man of your experience would realize how the Communists could make use of you and your families, as scapegoats!"

"I think you'd better stop, Captain!" Mrs. Laker's voice shook, and she held her thin arms protectively across her husband's massive shoulders.

"Stop?" Rolfe laughed wildly, but there was no mirth in the sound. "I'm sorry if I've offended you, Mrs. Laker. It's just that I've got sick and tired of hearing about the achievements here! If you want to know the Communists' strongest lever to get you out of here, just ask yourselves who have gained from these achievements. The wretched population, or you?" He dropped his arms to his sides, suddenly limp.

"Any further questions?" His face was wet under the lamp-light.

Grant nodded his square head. "What d'you want us to do first, Captain?" He spoke as a leader, and the others seemed eager to avoid looking at Laker, who had walked slowly out on to the darkening veranda.

"I shall want you to have all your necessary gear packed and ready to be moved aboard by tomorrow midday. Bring it down yourselves, altogether if possible, anyone watching will think it's stores. D'you have a lorry or something like that?"

"We've a couple of estate vans," nodded Grant, his practical face squinting with concentration.

"Good, that's fine. Don't forget, not a word!"

Ursula stretched her long legs. "What would happen if the news got around?"

Grant bit his lip. "I can answer that one, I think. There'd be quite a lot of people would like to go too, eh?"

Rolfe smiled briefly. "Right. That would very likely be the case. It would also draw the attention of our friends on the mainland, who might very well bring their invasion on a bit earlier!"

Laker shuffled past, gripping his wife's arm. "Goin' to think for a bit. Got to have time to think. All a bit of a shock!" He glared back at Rolfe with something like his old confidence. "See you damned for this!"

Vincent sighed loudly. It had been perfect, and he felt a little weak.

Rolfe's gaze swung on him suddenly. "All right, Vincent. Back to the ship. I want a state of readiness as from when you arrive. Just as I explained it to you!"

"Aye, aye, sir!" Vincent stood up sulkily, yet vaguely pleased by the audience, who watched him with mingled emotions of fear and frustration.

Fallow rose too, his belly sagging untidily, and his big hands plucking at the seams of his trousers. "Sir?" he choked, his face a mass of worry, "shall I go, too, sir?"

Rolfe grinned crookedly. "No, certainly not, Number One. We'll finish our drinks in comfort. Let the youngster do the work!"

Fallow sweated miserably and edged closer to his Captain, his ugly nose looking like part of a grotesque mask. "D'you think it'll be all right, sir? I mean 'bout us leaving'?" His throaty voice was drowned by the babble of excited conversation from the others.

"All right?" Rolfe was looking at him with a wild gleam in his eyes, "Safe as bloody houses, I should think!"

Fallow groaned inwardly. The Captain was looking odd again. Must do something. He looked appealingly at the girl, who was watching them with brazen interest.

"That was a mighty good dinner we 'ad, miss!" he blurted desperately. "Your father certainly knows how to give a party," he ended lamely.

She stretched and smoothed her dress with slow movements of her hands. "Quite so," she agreed solemnly. "And I must say the speeches afterwards were a cut above the usual!" She smiled wickedly at Rolfe, who was frowning absently at his glass. "Have another, Captain? It might help!"

Rolfe took the drink without answering, his eyes now on the murmuring groups in the far corner of the room. The party was breaking up, and with quick nods and nervous smiles, the guests began to depart.

Grant, puffing busily at his pipe, paused at the door. "Well, see you tomorrow, Captain. No doubt we'll see things a bit clearer then. I only hope you know what you're up to, for all our sakes!"

The door closed, and the three of them exchanged glances.

"You've really got 'em stirred up!" commented the girl, her voice signifying that she wanted no part of it.

"Could be," nodded Rolfe, his eyes still vague.

Fallow felt the uneasiness growing in the deserted room, and sweated accordingly. Got to do something! Must think of a way to get 'im back to the ship!

"I think I'll go down into the town!" Rolfe's voice brightened, as if he had just suggested something original. "Good a time as any to meet this doctor of yours!"

"Not mine!" she exclaimed, standing up suddenly. "Still, if you must go cantering off down there at this time of the evening, I'll drive you in Daddy's car." She marched towards the door, her long legs flashing, as if eager for the exercise. She called casually over her shoulder, "I said I'd show you round, anyway!" There was a tremble of deeper excitement in her voice.

Rolfe stared at the littered table and discarded chairs. "Pity, pity! Always mess everything up!" His gaze sharpened, "Ah, Number One, just a little left, I see." And he hurried gleefully to the oak sideboard and snatched up a bottle.

Fallow followed him dumbly. He had lost count of the Captain's consumption of drinks during the evening, but it was something quite fantastic.

Rolfe pushed the bottle towards him. "Go on," he prompted. "Fill your boots!" His eyes shone glassily, and his grave face was twisted into a smile, which was filled with bitterness.

Fallow shook his head frantically, "Please, sir, don't you think—I mean—wouldn't be better if, if you—" he stopped, beaten again.

Rolfe patted his shoulder playfully, "Don't worry, Number One, I'm all right. Jus' a little bit tired," he waved his hand, as if to clear a mist away from his face. "Quite a party, as you so right—, rightfully observed! I would say that all the natives are friendly!" With a gulp he finished the bottle, as with a screech, the car pulled up outside the veranda.

Although a cool breeze now filtered up from the sea to fan the parched earth, Ursula's bare shoulders gleamed defiantly from behind the wheel of the long, throbbing car. She shook her short curls and pushed open the door. "Come on, come on! Town tour just starting!"

Rolfe jammed his cap clumsily on his head, and slid awkwardly into the wide bench-seat beside her. As if in afterthought, he beckoned to the ponderous figure in the doorway. "Come on, Number One! Y'heard what the lady said!"

Ursula grimaced as the car sagged under the man's weight, but trembled as Rolfe was forced against her. The car whined and bounded forward along the straight estate road, the headlights cutting through the darkness like twin white swords. The estate gates were flung open hurriedly, and the girl laughed wildly, her hair rippling in the wind.

"Is it safe to be out late in the car, miss? I mean, didn't they say there's bin shootin' an' that?" Fallow tried to see her expression.

"Relax, little man!" she cried, her voice choked with laughter. "They'd rather shoot the General than interfere with this car!"

The tyres screeched in protest as the car hurtled on to the main road, loose gravel rattling up under the wings. Trees, boulders and huts flashed into the headlights, distorted into frightening shapes and were swallowed up behind them.

Fallow's body stiffened, as the luminous dial of the speedometer showed the needle quivering at eighty. She's drunk, or mad, he breathed, she'll kill us all in a second! He felt Rolfe jolting loosely with the lurching motion of the car, his face was hidden in the shadow of his cap.

Ursula pressed her foot down harder, regardless of her skirt which had blown halfway up her lap. As a wheel grated across a hump in the road, Rolfe sprawled heavily against her. Taking one hand off the wheel she groped for one of his, and breathing hard, she pressed it down against the smooth skin of her thigh. It lay there, warm and strong, but unmoving, and she twisted her head to see his face.

It was at that very second that Fallow saw the small figure standing transfixed in the swinging headlights.

"For Christ's sake!" he screamed. "Look out!" He scrabbled vainly for the handbrake in the darkness, dimly aware of the rising scrape of the brakes and the sliding, rolling motion of the car. There was a sickening jolt as the front wheels left the road, and a thousand clutching branches scratched and crackled against the metal sides. Then there was silence but for the distant barking of a dog and the patter of falling leaves across the bonnet. The headlamps still blazed, throwing their glare against the trunk of a gnarled tree in which the twisted bumper bar was embedded.

The impact and the noise of the crash, followed as it was by this shocked silence, held Rolfe completely motionless on the seat, although a surge of jumbled thoughts and emotions rocked his brain and sent a flood of shocked amazement through his tensed limbs. His mind cleared from within, although he still saw the whole incident as a picture, as if he himself was detached bodily from its implications. At his side, Ursula lay weakly on the wheel, moaning into her hands, her shoulders hunched. Fallow had left the car, and he heard him crashing through the undergrowth towards the road.

He licked his parched lips, moving his head slowly as if in a dream. "You all right, Ursula?" His voice was thick, but strangely steady.

She lifted her face and stared at him, her eyes running with tears. Her lipstick was smudged, and the wide mouth hung open almost vacantly, emitting low, strangled sobs. Then, without answering, she pushed her fingers through her hair, working her jaw and sucking in great gulps of air.

He pulled himself across to the door and stood unsteadily in the bushes, a wave of nausea sweeping over him. His head throbbed and danced, and he put up his hand as if to still the agony. Clumsily and painfully, he forced his way past the car, and stood blinking on the roadway. Fallow, his dim white shape moulded into an uneven hump, crouched on one side muttering softly.

"You hurt, Number One?" The words sounded strangely loud in the darkness.

Fallow didn't turn, but answered harshly, speaking through his teeth. "Must get 'elp, sir! She's badly knocked about!"

Rolfe strained his aching mind uncomprehendingly. "No, she's not hurt. Just shaken."

"Not 'er!" Fallow answered savagely. "This little nipper! That blasted woman drove right at 'er!"

Rolfe stared as the other man rose slowly to his feet and turned round. In his arms he was holding the small shape of a child, and as Rolfe stepped dazedly towards him, he saw with horror, that Fallow's tunic was smeared with dark stains. The child lay limply in the huge arms, her tattered clothing ripped away from the shoulders, revealing a series of cruel, ragged gashes, which gleamed angrily in the reflected headlights. For a moment he thought she must be dead, but he saw that the two bright eyes, which seemed to fill her whole face, were fixed desperately on Fallow's, the small, emaciated mouth twisted into a mask of pain.

Rolfe instinctively reached out to touch her, but Fallow drew back defensively, his heavy features grim and forbidding. "S'alright, sir, I can manage!" Then with an unusual forcefulness, "Can we get 'er to a doctor? It's 'er only chance!"

Rolfe swung back to the car, his mind forming and re-forming a series of mixed and bitter emotions. Wrenching open the driving door, he pushed the girl unceremoniously out of the way.

"What are you doing? What's happened?" Her voice suggested hysteria, but his whole concentration made him force any consideration for her from his thoughts.

The car responded shakily to his exertions, and with a rattle of loose metal, he gunned the engine and backed out on to the roadway. As the great lamps swung across the track, he got a brief glimpse of their long skid marks and the pathetic pool of blood by the roadside. Fallow stepped carefully into the back seat, muttering hoarsely, but in a low, comforting manner, which seemed to soothe the child.

As Rolfe jammed the unfamiliar gears into position and the car began to move ahead, Ursula stared from the child to Rolfe in amazement, and without warning, began to laugh in a high, strained giggle. Nobody spoke, each of the men concentrating on his own task.

"Is that what all the panic was about?" She giggled again, wiping her eyes with the back of her hand. "A damned Chink kid!" She sounded incredulous. "I thought something really terrible had happened!" A strange moan escaped her lips, "What'll Daddy say about his precious car?"

"For Christ's sake stow it, will you?" Fallow's trembling voice surprised even Rolfe, who was trying to shut out their voices and keep his strength for the effort of driving. "Don't you realize you might've killed the poor little thing?" Fallow kept his voice down, and the hissing words were all the more threatening.

"Don't you talk to me like that, you—you ugly oaf!" She wriggled in her seat, as if consumed with anger and indignation.

"Where is the doctor's place?" Rolfe spoke from between his clenched jaws, fighting the sickness which threatened to engulf him.

"If you think I'm going down there, looking like this! What's got into you?"

Rolfe followed the curve of the road as it dipped down towards the town. "Must get there quickly. If anything happens to that child—" he left his words unfinished.

"If you must make a fool of yourself! Turn right at the

first damned group of huts and follow the sea road." She tried to move closer to him, her voice suddenly pleading. "We could have left the kid at one of those houses. They're used to this sort of thing. The kids are always dying off, here!"

He eased her free with his arm, his face like a stone. "I'm not surprised," he murmured quietly.

She straightened up on the seat, pulling her skirt over her knees, and fumbling with the gaping front of her dress. Her tone was hostile, and yet ashamed. "I didn't mean it to be like this!"

"No. I don't suppose you did."

The sea spread out to greet them, and the moon shimmered coldly on the black water, the masts of beached fishing boats pointing starkly at the sky. They had by-passed the town and were twisting and turning among the little wooden buildings of the fishing village.

"You have to leave the road just up here," she directed flatly. "There is only a pathway."

Even as she spoke, he saw a long, low building, its whitewashed walls shining in the moonlight, a crude red cross painted on the corrugated iron roof.

He braked as gently as he could, and got out, hoping that Fallow might ask him to take the child, but the big man brushed past him, his face towards the house, and oblivious to the long smudges of blood on his knees and chest.

"I—I'll stop here," Ursula called after them, "I'll wait, if you like?" Again, that breathless yearning trembled in her words.

"No, don't wait." He watched Fallow's broad back, and wanted to run after him, to apologise, to help, anything. "Come in with us if you want to."

He heard the clash of gears. "I can't stand the sight of the man!" She was shouting now, "And you're drunk!" Her other words were drowned by the roar of the engine as she let in the clutch. But Rolfe was already hurrying after Fallow.

They reached the door, and even in the poor light, he could see its crude, unpainted surface, and the general air of poverty about the building.

He banged on the rough planking, conscious of Fallow's silence, and the child's sharp breathing. The door creaked open, and a diminutive man in a shapeless white smock held a lantern over his head. He studied each of them in turn, his almond eyes flickering as they rested on Fallow's burden.

"The doctor, is he in?"

The little man held the door wide, and they followed him into a wide whitewashed room lined with crude wooden benches. There was a smell of disinfectant and sweat, which made Rolfe's stomach twist uncontrollably.

He hung his lantern on a nail in the low ceiling, and reached out his arms commandingly.

"Please! The child! I take to Doctor!" He gathered the limp body with surprising ease, and pushed open a side door with his foot. A shaft of light flung his shadow weirdly across the floor, and he regarded them dispassionately. "You wait here, if you want!" The door swung behind him.

Fallow sank on to one of the benches, his face downcast. Only his hands moved ineffectually over the stains on his uniform.

Rolfe paced the room like a caged thing, his mind racing. You've done it again! You bloody, useless, self-pitying maniac! The pain in his head could hardly be endured, yet he could think with fresh clearness and bitter understanding. If only the sickness in his stomach would go. Then perhaps he could at least act like a human being. He shook his head, trying to shake off the nausea. It was more than that. It was the sickness of real despair, which held him so remorselessly.

He glanced unseeingly at his watch, having long since lost all sense of time. I can't stand this, he thought wildly. Must go and find out what's happening in there, and then get away. In his mind, the picture of his remote cabin wavered like a glimpse of heaven.

"I'm going to find out what they're doing!" Fallow jumped at the sound of his strained voice. "I'll go mad if I stop here!"

Before Fallow could utter a protest, Rolfe gripped the door handle, and softly eased his way into the other room. For a moment he blinked to accustom his eyes to the glare of a pressure paraffin lamp, which was being held over a white-sheeted table by the little servant. Rolfe held his breath, watching the bending figure of a young man who was making final adjustments to the bandaging of the child's chest and shoulders. Pieces of stained cotton-wool lay on the bare wooden floor, and the child's torn clothing had been tossed hastily on one of the scrubbed chairs. She was still quiet, her bare skin biscuit-coloured against the sheet. Rolfe looked pityingly at the hunger-swollen belly and small, stick-thin legs. Under the lamplight she looked shrunken and frail, only her eyes showed the flickering life of childhood. He watched the doctor's long hands working with swift, practised ease, and noted the dark, untidy lock of hair falling across his face, which was turned away from him. He could only make out the firm, sun-tanned cheek, and well-cut chin. About my age, he thought, as the man stood up wearily and stretched his shoulders.

The servant stared woodenly at the child, and smiled gravely. "Nice job, Doctor Felton." He pointed with his chin in Rolfe's direction, "That man's here now, Doctor."

"What the devil!" Felton swung round angrily, and Rolfe shrank back in horror, as the remaining half of the doctor's face became visible under the harsh light.

The whole of the left side had been savagely scored away from the eyebrow to the chin. It was as if a sheet of greaseproof paper had been stretched across a loose tangle of raw flesh. Above the smooth nightmare of crude surgery, the left eye squinted in horrible concentration, and the whole effect made Rolfe retch helplessly, a cold sweat breaking across his brow.

"Well, well, Chu! So the gallant Captain is honouring us with a visit!" The tone, though soft, was filled with scorn. "Have you come to see the results of your handiwork? Or did you want to have a look at me?" The dreadful eye gleamed like a chip of glass.

Rolfe pressed his palms back on the wall, digging his nails into the rough plaster. "Sorry, Doctor, I didn't realize. I mean, I just wanted to find out how she was!" It sounded empty and stupid, and the bile in his throat threatened to choke him. The face floated in a mist before him, and he knew that if he left the safety of the wall, he would fall.

"She's alright as it happens," the answer was like a slap in the face. "No doubt you enjoyed your party with the empire-builders!"

Rolfe's legs quivered, and helplessly he sat down on a carved camphor-wood chest. "Please excuse me," he choked, "I'm afraid I'm making a bit of a fool of myself!"

One half of Felton's lip curled contemptuously, the other half, a red slit, remained still and dead. "We're very sorry about that, I'm sure!"

The child made a small sound, and immediately Felton bent over her. With her eyes like dark pools, she reached up weakly, and explored the man's face with her small fingers. Rolfe felt a lump rising, and a sharp pain behind his eyes. The complete lack of fear or pain in the little creature's expression filled him with awe and a sudden humility. It was more like a wild dream than ever. All the things which were happening around him tore at his heart in a way unknown to real life.

Without leaving the table, Felton spoke over his shoulder, his calm voice trembling with anger, "Well, aren't you going? Haven't you done enough?"

"I wasn't driving. It was an accident." How ineffectual it sounded. "We got her here as fast as we could!"

"We? So there are more of you, eh? The Laker girl, I suppose! Well, this isn't her first victim by any means. Not that you care, of course!"

Rolfe dropped his head in his hands, not caring what they thought. Nothing they said could be too bad, and he felt the resistance draining from him.

He heard a door open, and he waited for Fallow's voice to add to the chaos. Instead, a new voice, a soft, gentle sound, penetrated between the protection of his clasped hands.

"I've sent someone for her father, Brian, and I—" there was a pause, and a quick intake of breath. "What's happened now? I saw the Laker's car drive off. Now who's this?"

Rolfe raised his head slowly, the figure of a girl forming mistily before him.

Dressed in a rough white overall which reached practically to the floor, the girl looked at first glance like a child. Rolfe stared incredulously at the dark cloud of rich chestnut hair, swept hurriedly back into a loose knot at the nape of her slim neck, and the perfect sun-tanned, oval face, seemingly dominated by wide, hazel eyes. Her soft, moist mouth was parted, giving her an expression of surprise and alarm. Even as he stared, she nervously lifted her small hands to her hair, the smile fading.

"It's the Captain of the gunboat." Felton spoke as if Rolfe was not in the room. "He and his friends have just brought the child here as you know. What you didn't know is, that he's actually sorry about the accident!" He turned lightly to Rolfe, and again the face glared angrily in its distorted mask. "Now get out, for God's sake! You and your kind make me sick! Keep away from me while you're here, and be damned to you!"

Rolfe staggered to the door, his eyes burning.

The girl's face was all at once hovering beneath him. "Are you alright, Captain?" Her eyes were filled with concern, which made Rolfe feel even more desperate. It was too much. First that ghastly mask, and now this soft, beautiful face, which was perfection and loveliness undreamed of.

"I'm sorry, Mrs. Felton," he muttered, groping for the door. Behind him he heard Felton laugh sarcastically. "I beg you to excuse me. I must get back—to my ship!"

With unbelieving eyes he watched her hand on his sleeve. "Are you quite sure you'll be able to manage?"

He nodded helplessly, and as the cool air fanned his face, he found himself in the roadway, with Fallow standing silently nearby.

She stood uncertainly watching him, her teeth white in the moonlight. "I'm *not* Mrs. Felton, by the way, "she said softly, "I'm his sister."

He reached out for her hand, which he seized eagerly. "Tell your brother I'm sorry," he faltered, "He thinks that I—" his voice died away.

"Don't mind him. He'll understand." She disengaged her hand, and Rolfe stood staring at the closed door.

Fallow fell in step beside him, as he walked heavily along the dark road. He was glad of Fallow's silence now, it helped him to appreciate the magnitude of his loneliness, and the realization of his recent behaviour filled him with scathing contempt.

As their feet scrunched over the uneven surface, Doctor Felton's sister was rarely absent from his thoughts.

The rasp of scrubbing brushes and the clank of a salt-water pump, mingled with the subdued chattering of the Chinese seamen, brought Rolfe slowly out of his coma-like sleep.

For some moments he lay staring at the white deck-head and the revolving fan, trying to piece together the events of the previous night. Even the sounds of the seamen washing decks, and the other friendly shipboard noises, were insufficient to drag him from his general feeling of depression, and as uneven pieces of his memory jumbled together in his aching head, he felt a real sense of frustration and loss.

"Tea, Captain-sir!" Chao's slender hands manipulated the wide cup and saucer at the side of the bunk, and his quiet, smoky eyes were watchful, as he tried to gauge his master's new mood.

Rolfe grunted, and rolled on to his side, wincing with the effort. He stared with disgust at the dirty uniform which Chao was bundling under his arm, and at the trail of disorder which had followed his own unsteady steps across the cabin a few hours earlier. Over the rim of the cup, he absently watched the boy, as he pattered about the cabin, laying out fresh white drills, and preparing the morning shower. Somewhere in the ship a pipe twittered, and Chase's coarse voice bellowed "Attenshun on the upper deck! Face aft an' salute!" He could picture the colours being hoisted to start a new day, as he had seen it done so many hundreds of times before. On the distant flagship, the Admiral would be hearing the blare of bugles, and the precise clicks as the marine guard presented arms. Gunboat or cruiser, peace or war, it made little difference to the navy's respect for tradition. He groaned, and sat on the side of the bunk, rubbing his naked stomach with the palm of his hand. The touch of the smooth flesh made him stir uneasily, and the memory of Ursula's pleading sent a stab of remorse through him.

"Blast her!" he muttered. "What a fool I made of myself there!"

"Sir?"

"Nothing, Chao. I'm getting old or something. That's all."

Chao smiled, not understanding. "Captain-sir enjoy his party?"

Rolfe stared at him balefully, looking for some small sign of insolence, but the dark eyes, and wide grin, were bare of either disrespect or disloyalty.

"It was quite a party," he answered briefly.

As he shaved, he thought about the General, or rather, he tried to concentrate on his forthcoming visit to his headquarters. But quietly and persistently, another person entered into his thoughts. He saw the rough white smock, the huge, sad eyes, and the gleaming mass of auburn hair. What had brought her to Santu? What made her stop with that distorted creature of a brother? He studied his steely eyes in the mirror, their hard stare reflecting the unanswered questions.

There was a tap at the door, and Fallow, his cap under his arm, stepped across the coaming.

He waited mutely until Rolfe had completed his toilet, his red face blank and preoccupied with inner thoughts.

"Major Ling's on the jetty, sir. Says 'e's come to drive you to the General's."

Rolfe buttoned up his fresh tunic, pondering over the announcement. "Very good, Number One. I didn't expect him, but I'm glad I shall be escorted, as it were." He stared questioningly at the other man. He's brooding about last night, he thought. "Everything all right in the ship?"

"C.P.O. Herridge has got the stern anchor laid out as you requested, sir. 'E wants to know when to start layin' it out in the 'arbour?"

Rolfe walked to the wide side-windows. The harbour gleamed and danced in the early morning sun, and only a few small craft could be seen moving on the rich, green water. "Tonight—I want the anchor carried out to the centre of the harbour. Use the pulling boat, I don't want any noise to upset the local people. The cable will lay straight from the ship, along the sandy bottom, to the anchor, so that we can pull the ship straight out to the middle of the harbour, without using the engines. Without noise or fuss, and at a second's notice."

"Yes, sir, I've explained to Herridge, an' 'e's got a party

93

detailed all round the clock, just for that duty." The pendulous lip jutted anxiously. "What might you be expectin' to 'appen, sir, if I might ask?"

"Don't know yet." He slipped his pipe and pouch into his pocket, and reached for his cap. "But if there's trouble, a mob round the ship, or something like that, we'll be safer out away from the wall!"

As he stepped on to the battery deck, he breathed in deeply, making the most of the salt air, and knowing that in an hour, the full force of the sun would be taking its toll of his senses again.

A dull-painted jeep stood on the jetty, and he could make out Ling's long shape curled comfortably in a bucket seat, the smoke from his black cheroot floating lazily over his head. He transferred his attention to the gunboat's decks, noting briefly that his orders had been carried out.

An armed sentry paced above the ship, on the jetty, and another on deck, abreast the gangway. Just inside the Quartermaster's Lobby entrance, he saw the gleam of a stand of oiled rifles, each with a bandolier of ammunition and a bayonet hanging from its snout. There seemed little prospect of trouble at the moment, but a ship tied against the wharf was always at a disadvantage.

Lieutenant Vincent was pacing the quarterdeck in a leisurely manner, and Rolfe studied his uniform carefully. He nodded, satisfied. The bulge beneath the immaculate tunic denoted the heavy Webley pistol. "Morning, Vincent!" he called, and Vincent saluted punctiliously, the puzzled look on his face again. Wondering if I'm sober, he thought bitterly.

"Alright, Number One," he said softly, "I'm off now. Manage, can you?" he added kindly, knowing Fallow's fear of responsibility.

"Send a message after you, if we receive fresh orders," Fallow droned out his instructions, like a child repeating a lesson. "Stow baggage of our passengers, when it arrives, and let no unauthorised person aboard!" He licked his lips, and dropped his gaze from Rolfe's face.

"That's right!" Rolfe tightened his jaw, and put an edge to his voice. "And if anything happens to me, don't forget that you will not only assume command, but you will also continue with, and complete, this evacuation!" He hated himself for his ruthless approach, but he knew that it was the only way.

Fallow raised his eyes, hurt and worried. "Aye, aye, sir!" he mumbled thickly.

Rolfe eyed him grimly for a few seconds, and then smiled. "Don't worry, we'll get by!" And with a salute, he stepped up the gangway, as the pipe trilled its salute to the Captain.

"Good morning, Captain!" Major Ling unwound his long legs, and smiled lazily. His clear eyes were a true indication of this man's character however, and Rolfe saw their cool intelligence and watchful alertness, also a bleak hint of ruthlessness.

The jeep lurched forward over the rough stonework of the jetty, and Rolfe adjusted his sun-glasses as a barrier against the harsh reflection of the sea. "The General is expecting me then?" Rolfe's voice was casual.

"He is, Captain." Ling chuckled quietly, and his strong hands spun the wheel easily to avoid a small donkey cart. "The General is disturbed I fear, by strong rumours," he darted a side glance at his passenger. "Rumours concerning an imminent withdrawal of British support. No doubt you have all the necessary answers for such whisperings?"

"I shall be pleased to inform the General of the facts." Rolfe spoke calmly, but his mind seethed with possible complications. Somebody must have talked too openly, or listened too carefully.

The jeep growled deeply, as it began to climb the steep and narrow road which zig-zagged up the side of the towering red cliffs like a thin yellow pencil-line. To their right, the cliffs dropped away at a sickening angle, and already the harbour was far below. The fort would be a very difficult place to storm, he thought. Up and up they climbed, even the jeep's sturdy engine protesting noisily, and then the road levelled out, and they were facing the entrance to the General's home. The high rugged wall, pitted with weapon-slits and observation holes, stretched along the whole of the summit, and the actual entrance was across a narrow causeway cut in the weatherworn rock. Two massive gates were open to receive them, and numerous slovenly soldiers eyed them watchfully from the ramparts.

Once through the gates it was strangely cool, and Rolfe stared up with interest at the ancient buildings within the guarded walls.

Of the same rough red stone, they were roofed in high green tiles, after the style of Tibet, and against the clear blue sky, he saw the intricate and fascinating carvings which adorned the curved eaves and beams which supported the roofs. Above all, the green banner fluttered limply in a sea breeze.

Past more guards, and through another courtyard into an inner set of buildings, he followed Ling's uneven stride, their feet ringing loudly on the smooth flags. At last, after a climb up a winding stone stairway, the treads of which were worn to fantastically curved shapes, they arrived at a high oak door, the wood black with age, and the wrought iron hinges gleaming dully from the light of a narrow window. Rolfe glanced through this window, as Ling rapped on the door, and caught his breath. Below, spread like a panorama, was the town, the harbour, and half the island. It was a fantastic view, stupendous in its beauty and simplicity. Like a minute toy, the *Wagtail* lay shimmering in the sunlight, the Union Jack painted on her spread awning a tiny splash of colour against the pale grey.

Ling touched his arm, his face expressionless. "Come", he said, and Rolfe stepped through the door, his footsteps now muffled by the thick profusion of animal skin rugs which covered every inch of the vast, airy room. The high stone walls were hung with rich embroidered banners and tapestries, which Rolfe guessed must be as old as they were priceless, while around the room were dark lacquered chests and gleaming tables, their rich surfaces alive with carved dragons and ornate birds. The whole room was littered with exquisite figures of carved jade, and shining bronze, and mixed incongruously amongst them, were two large portraits, one of Chiang Kai-shek and the other of Sun Yat-sen.

The far end of the room opened on to a wide stone terrace, decorated with potted palms, and the sea air mingled agreeably with the heavy, sweet smell of incense which smouldered from several giant bronze bowls.

Ling ushered him on to the terrace, a platform clinging to the side of the central tower like an eagle's nest, and giving a view even more breathtaking than his earlier one. He riveted his attention on the two men who sat comfortably on a pile of cushions by a huge chess board, their backs to the sea, and their faces frowning in unison at the ranks of carved chessmen. Each piece was over six inches high, and fashioned from jade and ivory, so that each figure was an individual masterpiece.

The General was a tiny man, and beautifully formed, like one of his chessmen. His small, round head was devoid of any hair, and although his skin was smooth and unwrinkled, it carried a kind of transparency, which gave the impression of great age. His small, dark eyes were hooded, and deep set, and his small, soft mouth was pursed like an unopened flower. His tiny, delicate hands, criss-crossed with veins, hung limply in his lap, and he was completely motionless. Rolfe watched him narrowly, sensing the aura of power and complete dominance which seemed to generate from this tiny carving of a man. Even the soft green uniform, bare of rank or decoration, added to his appearance of unreality, and made the second man, a fat, crafty-faced officer, in the uniform of a colonel, appear clumsy and vulgar.

"Lieutenant Commander Rolfe, of the British gunboat, General!" Ling drew his limp body together in a semblance of attention.

The hooded eyes flickered from the board, and Rolfe felt the cold and penetrating scrutiny from their black depths, but could read no message in the General's expression.

"Sit, Captain!" Soft and vibrant, with a strange, sing-song quality, the General's voice was nevertheless commanding, and without the weakness of age.

"You are welcome here, and I hope your mission is successful!"

Rolfe settled himself on the cushions, wishing that the brightness of the sky didn't prevent him from seeing the General's face more clearly. Ling busied himself in the background, and eventually laid a brass tray of fine crystal glasses at their feet. They sipped the wine without speaking. The General with apparent indifference and the Colonel with noisy satisfaction. Rolfe noted the savage scars on the man's fat cheek. The relic of some past fight, no doubt.

"I hope to be able to sail very shortly, General. My work is nearly finished here," Rolfe began carefully. "I understand you have heard something about my mission already?" He watched for some sign of surprise or anger, but the General folded his hands slowly in his lap.

"You should be more careful with your secrets, Captain!" His tone was a mere purr. "Your admirable Mr. Laker has already been to see me about your proposed withdrawal, or should I say, retreat?"

So it was Laker, thought Rolfe furiously, and a tremor of anger ran through him. "It was a matter for my Government to decide, General! I have my orders, and as I see it, there is no alternative!"

The General's small face crinkled slightly and a few small yellow teeth glinted in a brief smile. "Do not excite yourself, my dear Captain. It is of no importance to me!" He shrugged eloquently, "I had hoped that your government might intervene on our behalf, but it does not matter. We are quite capable of dealing with any attack from the scum across the water!"

The Colonel puffed out his cheeks, and belched loudly. "No one can take Santu from us!" he spat thickly. "We repelled the Japanese, Captain, and the efforts of many others before that." He spread his hands widely. "But, the dogs go and the pigs come! We will vanquish these animals, too!"

Rolfe sipped his glass, thinking rapidly. The General intended to fight, that was obvious, and he might be right about his powers of resistance, although the outcome could surely only be a question of time and numbers.

"I am sorry you had the story second-hand from Mr. Laker. I would have liked to explain it myself," he said evenly. "I hope that you will see my point of view?"

The General laughed, a tinkling sound. "What did you expect me to say? That I would stop you leaving? That I would sink your little ship?" He suddenly stood up, his frail body straight and proud. "Come to the wall here, Captain, I have something to show you!"

Rolfe crossed to his side, and the General pointed down to the ramparts below them. Rolfe started, for there, lined at regular intervals along the wall, were half a dozen long naval guns, their carriages mounted firmly in deep concrete beds and their muzzles pointing out across the sea.

The General was watching him closely. "There are others at the rear, and some more field pieces in the hills! So you see, we are not, how shall I put it, the lame donkeys?"

"Where did you get those guns? They look quite modern!"

"An American submarine very thoughtfully torpedoed a Japanese destroyer very close to the coast, during your last war. The rest was up to us! Well, Captain, what do you think now?"

They returned to the cushions. "I think you'll make quite a mess of any landing craft, General," answered Rolfe slowly. "And of course, from here you can command the whole island with those guns."

"Quite so! And at night, no ship would dare to try for a landing. You yourself know that the shoals and reefs would make that a particularly hazardous business!"

"I wonder why the Communists are intent on taking the island? Why not just ignore you?"

The General smiled secretly at the Colonel. "We are a nuisance here. We intercept the shipping from the Yangtse, and we are a possible springboard for a Nationalist attack on the mainland. You do not know the Communists, my dear Captain! They are like all clumsy régimes. Too many heads looking in too many directions! Colonel Kyung here will tell you how stupid they are!"

The Colonel laughed coarsely, "They are fools! We will drive them back like the dirt they are!" He lapsed into silence again, his scar gleaming whitely on his dark skin.

"What about the people here?" Rolfe approached the matter with caution. "How would they feel about a Communist attack?"

"Ah, you are thinking that they might not wish to fight? That they might wish to see me with my ancestors?" He shook with laughter. "Do not look so alarmed, Captain, I know exactly what you are thinking! They are poor creatures mostly, and unlike your happy Chinese in Hong Kong. But they have enough, and I have three thousand soldiers to back up my desires! And as you know, my Major Ling keeps a careful eye on the back-door, so to speak!"

"You speak excellent English, General." Rolfe changed the subject rapidly to give him time to think.

"Have you been to Ascot? And to Henley? Or perhaps raced at Cowes?"

Rolfe shook his head, smiling regretfully. "No, I never could get around to it."

"I have, Captain!" The little man stared past Rolfe into the far distance. "I visited your country many times, in the days of the old régime, and when the Kuomintang was all-powerful, before the scum rotted the feet of my country! Then I was great and powerful, and now, as you see, I am a mere speck of annoyance on the map of your international relations!"

Rolfe grinned uneasily. "Please, General, we must have a little charity!"

The General's eyes changed again, and were hard and black. "Charity is like war, Captain! It is not for amateurs! It must be total, to be effective!" He folded his hands suddenly, like a fan, and lowered his head towards the waiting chessmen. "Go, Captain! I wish you well!"

Rolfe stood up, surprised at the abrupt ending to the interview. "Goodbye, General. I hope we meet again!"

"I think not. To me, a man who will not fight is more dangerous than one who fights against me!"

As the doors closed behind him, he heard the General's fluted laughter, and he was almost tempted to burst back into the room, regardless of the consequences, and release some of his pent-up anger. He hardly noticed his descent from the great central tower, or Major Ling's secret smile, as he swung along beside him. When they were again settled in the jeep, Ling casually lighted another of his black cheroots, and puffed the smoke contentedly into the humid air.

"Well, Captain? How do you feel now?"

Rolfe regarded him coldly. "I'm pretty fed up with the way nobody here seems to speak in anything but riddles and stupid threats!"

Ling chuckled softly. "The General is not an easy man to impress! He has been a ruler too long!"

The jeep grated forward, and some soldiers put their backs to the high gates, letting in the brilliant glare of the outside world. As they swung open, Rolfe was reminded of the dock gates in Hong Kong, as they had opened for the little *Wagtail*, starting the ship and himself on this infuriating mission.

As they passed under the curved archway the sun smote them with cruel force, and he felt the tunic growing moist against his skin.

"Where to now, Captain? To your ship, perhaps?"

Rolfe stared out across the glittering sea, an empty plain of glass. Yet over there, beyond the lip of the hazy horizon, lay the great mass of Mother China, waiting, watching, and somehow full of menace. A shiver ran through him, and involuntarily he shuddered.

"I think I'd like to go and see Mr. Laker," he said suddenly. "That's if you don't mind the trip?"

Ling smiled secretly through his smoke. "A pleasure. I have nothing to do at the moment. Nothing to do but wait," he added slowly.

He was driving more slowly this time, steering the worn tyres round the craggy edges of the road with careful ease. Rolfe caught glimpses of his ship and a pang of something like affection touched him each time he saw the quaint hull nestled against the jetty, the spindly funnel adding to her appearance of defencelessness.

"The harbour, is it always as empty as this?" he asked.

"No, it is quite rare. The main fishing fleet is away at the moment," explained Ling, his dark eyes on the shimmering track. "They will be back any time now with the fish. A veritable harvest no doubt!" There was something not quite genuine in his tone, and Rolfe began to feel irritated again.

"I suppose it helps the General's belief that the island can be self-supporting, no matter what happens?"

"It helps," nodded the Major indifferently. "We are very cut off here, and apart from the occasional visit of a freighter, or a British warship, we hear little of the outside world. It acts both ways, of course."

"How d'you mean?"

"People hear little of us, too. We have no radio transmitters, so what we do, we keep to ourselves!"

Rolfe pulled the peak of his cap still farther over his eyes, and breathed heavily in the still, sluggish air. He cursed angrily as the jeep slewed round and stopped with a jerk, its wheels but a foot from the edge of the cliff.

"What the devil's up now?" He turned hotly on his companion, and then fell silent.

Ling's face was impassive, his eyes squinting against the

sun. He slowly removed the cheroot from his lips and blew out a thin white cloud. "Captain," he said quietly, "there are three aircraft flying out of the sun!"

He said it so calmly that Rolfe stared at him for a second, before the words and their full significance, dawned on him. Even as he stared up at the bright expanse of blue he heard the distant whine of powerful engines, and then, on the very rim of the sun, he saw three tiny silver specks, flying in a tight, arrowhead formation. From the fort behind and above him, he heard the dull booming of a big bell, followed at once by the banshee moaning of a siren, repeating the warning in the town below.

"The thin edge!" Ling's voice was a hiss and he followed the tiny shapes through expressionless eyes. He jerked the gear lever, and the jeep rocked back into the centre of the road and started to plunge crazily down the winding track at an alarming speed.

Rolfe ignored the rocking, protesting frame beneath him, and swivelled round in his seat, watching the planes with anxious eyes. Damn them, he thought desperately, yet he had known that this would come. They were nearer now and already were forming into single line, the manoeuvre being performed with such lazy grace that their whining engines clashed with their peaceful and gentle movements.

The tyres screeched, and for a moment Rolfe looked straight down the crumbled side of the cliff. "Can you take me to the ship?" he asked urgently, all thoughts of Laker banished from his mind.

"Certainly, Captain!" Ling hooted impatiently at a group of men and women, who stared open-mouthed at the intruders. They scattered from his path, the sudden movement transmitting fresh urgency to others who stood helplessly nearby, and soon, the sides of the road and the tiny hill tracks were dotted with stumbling, running figures, their mouths moving soundlessly in the roar of the jeep's engine.

Rolfe felt a sense of detached calm creeping through him, a feeling of flat resignation which he had known before when he had realized that action was imminent. He had seen such sights many times. As a young Sub-Lieutenant during the German

102

invasion of Greece, and again in the freezing misery of Korea. Always he remembered the blank, tight faces, staring skywards.

They burst into the shabby market place, zig-zagging between the deserted stalls and scattering townsfolk, and plunging recklessly past the flimsy bazaar buildings. A blind beggar in his filthy rags stood alone on a corner, his head cocked in frantic terror, and calling about him in a quavering voice. A child sat crying on some rush mats, its tiny face puckered into the misery of its generation.

As they swung on to the harbour wall, Rolfe saw the guns of the gunboat already following the diving aircraft, and heard the harsh bark of commands. Somewhere behind him the aero engines rose to a mad scream, blotting out all other sounds and forcing reason from the mind.

As the jeep braked, Rolfe flung himself across the jetty, dimly aware that Ling was already turning the vehicle round and hareing towards the town.

Chase's voice bellowed suddenly from the battery deck, "Stand by, all guns!" The machine-guns had also been mounted on either side of the bridge, and they too swung menacingly in a tight arc.

Rolfe bounded down the gangway and ran breathlessly to the upper bridge, where he found Fallow and Chase following the aircraft with their glasses.

"No firing!" Rolfe's voice was a mere choke. "Only if we are attacked!"

Fallow dropped his glasses to his heaving chest, the relief flooding to his paled face. "Aye, aye, sir!" He screwed up his eyes and pointed frantically, "There they come!"

The air was filled with the high, harsh rattle of machine-guns, and the steady thump of cannon, and as they stared, holding their breath, one aircraft dropped like a diving sea-bird and streaked across the low roofs of the town, its wings alive with spitting orange flames. As the cannon shells and bullets raked savagely along the streets and clawed across the cringing houses, they saw the woodwork and flying dust churned into an inferno of noise and fire.

Even as the plane pulled out of its dive, its engine racing

madly, the others followed in, the bright red stars gleaming clearly on their stubby wings.

Helplessly they followed the remorseless, darting attacks, and saw the growing pall of black smoke, splashed here and there by creeping tongues of flame.

A few guns answered sporadically from the high fortress, but as Rolfe had guessed, most of them could not be depressed sufficiently to grapple with the twisting aircraft, which were now flying considerably lower than the cliff itself.

Something clanged against the bridge plating and screamed away across the harbour, but Rolfe hardly flinched. He was watching the cruel destruction with anger and pity.

"Signalman!" he shouted sharply, "take this signal, and get it coded up at once!" He followed the silver shapes, his features composed into an expressionless mask. "To Admiralty, repeated Commander-in-Chief. Communist aircraft attacking Santu. Will commence evacuation immediately. Estimated sailing time twelve hundred tomorrow. Request permission to assist in anti-aircraft defence of town!" He watched the signalman scurry into the wheelhouse and tried to shut out the screaming engines. God knows what other sounds they are shielding from the town! he thought bleakly.

"Number One! Stand by to slip all wires and cable if we are attacked!"

A growing plume of smoke thickened around the funnel as Louch and his men sweated in the heat of the engine-room to raise steam.

Then at some secret signal, the aircraft turned away, their shadows flicking across the bridge itself and then bounding distortedly over the peaceful water. He could see the helmeted heads of the pilots as they set course for their distant base.

As the engines died, the spluttering crackle of burning wood-work, and the crash of falling stone, added a new horror to the scene, and as they waited, they heard the rising moan of countless tongues bonded together in their pattern of fear and agony. It was a chorus from hell.

Fallow swallowed hard, his hands rubbing the teak rail with agitation. "D'you think they'll be comin' back, sir?"

Rolfe shook his head. "No, not yet, at any rate. I think that was just a token of things to come! They'd have sent over more aircraft if they were really in earnest!" He had already dismissed the planes from his mind and was concentrating on the sudden urgency of his plans. "Number One!" he began briskly, his sharp tone hiding his gnawing anxiety. "Send for Chief Petty Officer Herridge, and I want Lieutenant Vincent as well!" He watched Fallow's slow movements and the clearly defined marks of worry on the ugly face. "Well, snap it about then! We haven't got all blasted day!"

Alone once more, he turned his gaze back to the town, the main fear in his mind taking full possession of his feelings. The hospital—would it be all right? Would she be safe? He frowned impatiently as he heard the clatter of feet on the ladder.

Herridge saluted, his strong face calm and unruffled.

"Look, Chief, I want you to take ten men ashore at once! Collect first-aid gear and stretchers and go into the town and see if you can assist the authorities. Muster your party right away and report to me before you move off."

Herridge saluted again, his face unmoved, and hurried purposefully away. His powerful voice rang along the deck as he went, already issuing orders and detailing his men.

Rolfe sighed deeply. Thank goodness someone knew how to carry out instructions without question and argument! A slight breeze wafted the pungent odour of burning across the harbour and he twitched his nostrils unwillingly, catching the tang of destruction.

Vincent panted up the ladder, his eyes smarting from the smoke.

"Go at once and see Laker! Tell him to round up the others and get them down to the ship as soon as they can manage it! I want 'em all aboard by tonight!"

"But that, that's a day earlier than you told them, sir!"

"The Communists have altered the programme slightly!" snapped Rolfe bitterly, "so get to it and I'll hold you responsible for anyone left out!"

"Yes, sir," answered Vincent, his cheeks colouring. "I shan't forget!"

He, too, hurried from the bridge and Rolfe forced himself to follow him down to the main deck, where an orderly bustle was in progress. Herridge was instructing his party quietly on the jetty and called down to Rolfe as he appeared. "All ready to move off, sir!"

He saw Fallow leaning on the guardrail, staring fixedly at the water. He looked as if he was going to be sick.

"I'm off to the hospital, Number One. Send a messenger after me if anything else happens!"

He ran across the gangway, aware that Fallow was watching him wildly, his brown eyes pleading as if to say, not again! Don't leave me alone in the ship again!

They marched briskly along the wall, Rolfe conscious of Herridge's long shadow behind him, and the tramp of booted feet on the hot stonework. As they passed the first group of dwellings Rolfe's stomach tightened and he quickened his pace.

The huddled houses beside the market place were all ablaze, and the tinder-dry wood and rush roofs flared skywards with a steady roar, great gouts of red flame and dense smoke billowing across the open roadway. A surging mass of people ran wildly from house to house, some trying to save pathetic possessions and others searching and tearing at the thin walls. Along the length of the market place several still shapes lay scattered in distorted positions, like discarded bundles of rags. The blind beggar was still in the road, but kneeling by the side of one of the flung bodies and running his thin hands dazedly across the contorted face and dead eyes which stared at the sky. As the sailors clattered by, he raised his head and croaked at them in a thin falsetto voice, his mouth wet with the saliva of fear.

"All right, old man," Herridge growled. "Keep your hair on!" And to Rolfe, "Not much we can do about him, sir?"

Rolfe shook his head briefly. "Poor bastard ! Must be nearly out of his mind!"

The aircraft had been using plenty of incendiary shells, he thought, there was so much flame and smoke everywhere. He set his jaw tightly and stepped to one side. A small child lay spreadeagled on its face, a crude wooden doll clasped firmly in one hand. The middle of the child's back gaped open in a large crimson hole, through which the shattered bones shone whitely in the sun.

Two soldiers with canvas buckets were throwing water half-heartedly into a smouldering shopfront and Rolfe saw another soldier leading some dazed and bleeding creatures from a side door.

"There you are, Chief! Get to work with that lot! But keep your party together!"

Herridge pushed his cap on the back of his head and stood feet astride in the road, taking in the chaos and destruction. "Right, you lot! Lend these soldiers a hand with the water! And you two get the bandages out!"

The white uniforms of the ratings stood out in the whirling stream of confusion and pain, like an island of sanity and order, and without question, the soldiers redoubled their efforts under the watchful eye of the tall, grim-faced Herridge.

Rolfe pressed on up the road, trying to remember his way through the labyrinth of alleys and side streets. People jostled him blindly and he had a continuous impression of gaping faces and terrified eyes, and above all, the rising wave of panic.

An old woman, her sunken face running with tears, blocked his path, her gnarled hands clutching at his arm and her toothless mouth uttering a persistent hysterical gabble of words, which he could only guess at. He gripped her thin shoulders firmly and looked down at her frantic face.

"I don't know what you're saying, Mother," he said quietly, "but I know what you mean." His calm voice had some effect, for she searched his face in wonder, her sunken eyes looking for fresh assurance. But Rolfe released her and forced his way through the press of bodies in the narrow street.

A group of men stood staring at a woman kneeling on the ground, her hands like claws in her black hair, and her slim body rocking slowly from side to side. Rolfe didn't have to hear her wailing tones, her desperate lament, to know the reason for her grief.

A twisted, fire-blackened corpse, its face gone completely, lay by her knees, the clothing still smouldering, the stench of charred cloth mingling with that of burned flesh.

It was almost a relief to break through into the coast road and to feel the sea's caress again, but as he broke into a run through the scattered fishermen's huts, his stomach contorted suddenly, and his feet faltered. The hospital, at first glance untouched, was still as he had remembered it, but across the front wall was a savage pattern of round holes.

He brushed aside two gesticulating men and ran panting up the sandy slope, for once unconscious of the sweat pouring from his body, and the heat, made more suffocating by the dense pall of smoke, which like a death-pall, lay everywhere.

He burst into the long waiting-room and almost fell headlong over a still shape by the door. As he blinked his smarting eyes he saw that every inch of the floor was filled with motionless bodies, some with their faces relaxed and dark, as if already dead, and others, whose bright, bead-like eyes followed his approach like helpless birds. As he groped his way forward, one of the bodies arched itself in the shape of a bent bow and emitted a spine-chilling scream. Those near it twisted their packed limbs as if trying to disassociate themselves from this surrender to pain. The man, for man it had once been, screamed again, the whites of his eyes shining starkly in the sunlight which streamed through the holes made by the bullets. The rough bandage across his chest burst open and a deluge of blood flooded on to the floor. The man relaxed and stared in amazement as his life gushed away. Then with a shudder he dropped back, his mouth open in an unfinished grin. A silence fell once more and Rolfe retched at the smell of fear and vomit which pressed on him from every side.

Somehow he got across the room without treading on anyone and reached the door of Dr. Felton's surgery. He hung on to the handle, not daring to think of what he might find. Beyond the door a girl cried out in pain and the next second Rolfe had the door open and was in the surgery.

Felton was struggling with a twisting body on the rough operating table, while his servant repeatedly tried to bandage the girl's foot, which to Rolfe's eyes, looked as if it was hanging by a mere thread. The sheets on the table were torn and bloody, and Felton himself was glistening with exertion and what seemed like near-exhaustion.

"Here, let me!" Rolfe stepped forward and pressed the girl's shoulders flat on the table, while Felton straightened up in surprise. His ghastly face twisted into what might have been a smile, and then he ducked round the table to his patient's foot.

Rolfe saw the girl's face darken with pain and her eyes rolled upwards until only the whites showed. "For God's sake! Haven't you got any anæsthetics?" he gasped.

Felton jerked and twisted, and Rolfe sickened as he heard something drop into an enamel bowl. "Used 'em all! Not a ruddy thing left!" He stood up and felt the girl's pulse. He nodded and dashed the sweat from his eyes. "Good! She's still with us!" Then over his shoulder he shouted hoarsely, "Judith! I've finished with this one! Come and give Chu a hand with her!"

Rolfe stood back from the table, his mouth suddenly dry, staring at the door. She was all right. She was safe. In this nightmare place, with death and suffering all round, and the terrible mangled mask of Dr. Felton, he had hardly dared to hope! The door swung back and she hurried towards him.

The untidy smock swirled round her and he felt real pain at the sight of the dark smears across it and the stains on her small hands. She had her arm under the girl's head before her glance settled on him, and even then she seemed unable to clear the mistiness from her wide eyes.

Felton coughed weakly, beating his chest with his fist. "Good girl. Not many more now!" His good eye winked. "The Captain's back, Judith! He's working for me now!"

Rolfe reached out shakily and gently eased her arm from the table. "Here, I'll do that! Just show me what to do."

She smiled suddenly and Rolfe realized that she had been very close to tears, and lifted her small chin defiantly. "I'm so glad you could come!" she said softly, and staring down at her stained gown she grimaced, her slim shoulders suddenly tired. "What a mess I must look!"

"When you've both finished!" Felton's voice was amused. "Would you mind fetching the next one in, please?"

Rolfe laid the body which had been nearest the door across the table and looked round desperately. "Have you any paper?"

Felton pointed to the littered desk. "Help yourself. Going to write to the United Nations?"

Rolfe scribbled a message on a sheet of writing-paper. "Could you have this sent to the ship? I have told my First Lieutenant to supply the bearer with a case of medical equipment. I thought it might help!" he added hastily, in case Felton's iron pride got the better of his judgement.

Felton was already examining his new patient. "Chu! Go to the gunboat with the message. Give to officer and bring back medicine!" And as the little man scuttled away he reached out awkwardly and touched Rolfe's sleeve. "Thanks!" he said shortly.

Judith had been watching them, and as Rolfe looked up at her he noticed that her huge eyes were brimming with tears. But as she ran from the room he saw also that there was a small smile on her soft mouth.

They worked on in silence until Chu returned with the heavy metal box, and then Felton examined the contents with dull satisfaction. "Not bad at all!" he breathed softly. "It'll come in very handy!"

"I'm only sorry we haven't got a doctor aboard to give you a hand."

"I can manage!" Felton's voice contained something of his old harshness, and he stooped over the gasping body on the table. "These poor devils are used to hardship!"

Judith hurried in with a tray of dressings and darted a quick glance at her brother. "Only half a dozen more," she murmured gently. "They are just minor injuries."

Rolfe watched her with a feeling of growing tenderness and a new sensation, which cleared his mind of weakness.

As she moved softly out to the waiting-room, Felton remarked distantly, "Good girl, I don't know how I'd manage without her!"

"She's beautiful!" The words came out before he could stop them, but for a moment he didn't think the other man heard him.

"Yin Fong Leung." Felton's voice was dreamy. "That's what the people round here call her."

"What does that mean?"

Felton paused in his work, his eye studying Rolfe's face with close scrutiny. "Fragrant and Beautiful Flower," he answered quietly.

Rolfe dropped his gaze, and although his hands remained steady, his heart pounded uncontrollably. He knew now that whatever happened, the visit to Santu had been more than worthwhile. It was a hope for a new future.

. . . . .

Lieutenant Fallow watched the little man scurry across the gangway clutching the first-aid box. What the hell was happening at the hospital? he wondered. Perhaps the Captain would be back soon. He shook his head vaguely and tried to bring his attention to what Leading Seaman Davidson was saying about the baggage being stowed. Two shooting brakes had just arrived on the jetty and some of the seamen were loading an assortment of boxes and wooden crates into the open hatchway leading to the forward storeroom.

It was an easy task, with no onlookers, as every single soul in the town seemed to be occupied elsewhere on other matters. He pulled at his ear impatiently as Davidson tapped at his pencilled list. "An' if that lot's personal gear, sir, I'll eat my bloomin' 'at!" he said scornfully.

"Well, I s'pect they've collected quite a lot of stuff over the years," began Fallow severely, and then his eye fell on Chase, who was ushering Charles Masters and his young wife down from the jetty. He groaned, the first blasted passengers had arrived.

Masters looked pale and was clutching his wife's arm tightly. "Oh—er—I hope we're not too early?" He gazed round him, as if seeking somewhere to hide. "We've sent our baggage along already."

Fallow forced a smile. "Captain says you're to make yerselves at 'ome. I'm afraid all the ladies will be sleeping together in the officers' cabins and the men'll 'ave to make do in the Chief Petty Officers' mess. 1 'ope that'll suit you?"

He beckoned Chase urgently with his hand. "Show these people to the wardroom, an' tell the stewards to fix 'em up!"

As they moved away he heard Anthea Masters whisper loudly, "He looked very worried, darling! Do you think everything is going as expected?"

Fallow cursed and removed his cap to mop at his perspiring head. Blast them! Why did his fear show so clearly? He peered at the town and saw that the flames had practically cleared. Only the black smoke remained to mark the attack. High on the cliff, the fort stood aloof and untouched, the banner still fluttering limply. Fallow shook his fist in sudden anger. "Damn you, too!" he mouthed. "If it wasn't fer you, we wouldn't be 'ere!"

He dropped his arm in embarrassment as he caught sight of the telegraphist, Little, gaping from the wheelhouse.

"Signal from C.-in-C., sir."

"Well, read it, boy!" Fallow brought out his gruffest tone to cover his agitation.

Little frowned at the signal. "From Commander-in-Chief. Re your one-one-three-six, stroke zero nine," he read, "concur. Your request re other duties denied."

Fallow pieced the jargon together in his aching mind. So the Admiral didn't want the *Wagtail* to get mixed up in any air battles, eh? Thank God for that. Let 'em fight their own bloody wars! he thought savagely. Always runnin' down the British, and yet they always whine fer us when they're in a bit of trouble! A feeling of remorse struck him, as some new scream of anguish rose from the direction of the town. He rubbed his hands together worriedly. If only we can get out of here without something else happening! It was like a prayer from inside his heart.

He stared along the jetty as Herridge and his small party marched wearily into view. Their white uniforms were stained and blackened and the eyes of the Chinese seamen were downcast and dull with shock. Even Herridge was tight-lipped and strained.

Fallow tried to find comfort from Herridge's return, to seek some small feeling of security. But instead, he found only the sickness of fear.

Herridge entered his mess and hung up his cap and pistol with slow, deliberate movements. He glanced round at the familiar objects, the austere arm-chairs and bookshelves, Louch's fishing rod, and a small selection of garish pin-ups over Chase's locker.

Louch eyed him steadily from his prone position on the couch. He grunted and heaved himself upright, his skinny shoulders hunched over the table. Still without speaking, he removed a clean napkin, which had served as a cover for three glasses. Three glasses of rum for the *Wagtail's* Chief Petty Officers.

Herridge slumped in a chair and picked up his glass, staring moodily at the dark contents.

"Here's looking at you, Bill!" He tossed it back, enjoying the rich power as it ran through him.

"Reckon you needed it!" Louch's beaky face creased into a wry smile. "What was it like ashore?"

"Bloody! The poor devils didn't know what hit 'em!"

"I suppose they've never had a touch of real civilized warfare before?" Louch sipped his rum pensively. "There'll be a lot more where that came from, I'm thinking!"

Herridge tensed as the door banged open, and Chase clumped noisily to the table. He grabbed his glass and smacked his lips. "Cor! Just wot I need! I've 'ad a bellyfull up there, I can tell yer!"

"It must have been hell!" nodded Louch sarcastically.

Chase perched his plump body on the table and frowned. He always frowned when he was trying to gauge the contents of his colleagues' remarks. "Poor ol' Jimmy-the-One is fair bustin' a gut up top!" he added with obvious relish. "As an orficer 'e'd make a ruddy fine plumber, I should think!"

"Well, keep those thoughts to yourself!" Herridge's blue eyes flickered menacingly. "Old Fallow's got a lot on his plate at the moment!"

Chase stared at him in surprise. "Gettin' in with the orficers already, eh? You 'aven't got your bit of gold lace yet, yer know!"

Herridge's sturdy body bounded from the chair in one quick movement and his leathery face was only inches from the other man's sweating forehead. "Say that again, Tom," he said conversationally, "and I'll ram that bloody book of rifle drill down your fat, stupid neck!"

They stayed motionless until Chase flushed even redder and sidled off the table. "'Ere, stow it, Wilf!" he muttered uneasily. "Take a joke, can't yer?"

The crow's-feet round the Cornishman's eyes wrinkled suddenly, and he winked at Louch, who had been watching the battle of wills with bird-like interest. "Fine one to criticize old Fallow, eh? The Admiral won't even let him fire his pretty guns! Reckon he must know what bloody poor shots his gunners are!"

"Now let me tell you!" Chase began to bluster, but his words were cut short by the violent clangour of the alarm bells.

All three men sprang for the door, Herridge grabbing his

pistol from its hook, and Chase already bellowing for his gunners. Louch trotted to the circular steel hatch from which issued the constant trickle of steam, and taking a last look at the blue sky and the green water, he plunged below.

Herridge ran to the bridge, overtaking and dodging the scurrying figures of the seamen. He found Fallow leaning right out on the rail, his glasses trained along the harbour wall. Hearing footsteps at his side, he spoke thickly from the side of his mouth. "There's some sort of mob comin' out of the town!" He darted a quick glance at Herridge's impassive face and then peered through his glasses again.

Herridge followed the direction Fallow had indicated and he saw that from behind the first row of buildings a straggling crowd of people was indeed hurrying for the wall. As they watched, a group of soldiers ran out of their hut and waved their rifles menacingly at the approaching mob. The mingled voices of the people merged into a sullen roar as the confined space of the harbour entrance brought them together in a tightly packed mass.

"Christ! What d'you reckon they're up to?" Fallow's voice shook.

"Us!" Herridge spat out the word. "They know we're off to Hong Kong, everybody does now! It must be this year's worst kept secret!"

The gunboat's decks were bare of running figures now and voice pipes whistled and cracked as the various parts of the ship reported their readiness for whatever lay ahead.

"Oerlikon closed up!" A/B Ferguson settled himself in his harness and swung the slender gun barrel in a practice arc.

"Six pounder closed up!" The gunlayer, Leading Seaman Clinton, spat on the deck and rubbed his horny hands.

Two seamen swung the machine-guns round on the bridge rails, the bullet-studded belts glinting evilly.

The soldiers had fallen back a bit now and the crowd was getting more daring. One or two had climbed up on the side of the wall and were trying to by-pass the sentries. A shot rang out and one of the scrambling figures pitched out of sight into the water.

The crowd halted and then, as the subdued murmur of voices

swelled to an enraged scream, they surged against the soldiers like a tide breaking over a rock, and then they were running wildly towards the end of the jetty.

Herridge tore his eyes off the terrible spectacle and turned to Fallow. There must be about two thousand of 'em there, he thought. If they get aboard here, we're done for. He watched Fallow's thick lip working wetly, it seemed he was unable to take his eyes from the glasses, although heaven knows, thought Herridge desperately, they're near enough to be seen by a blind man now!

"Sir?" He nudged Fallow's elbow gently. "Shall I carry on with the Captain's idea?"

Fallow stared at him blankly, his eyes flickering wildly. He didn't seem to hear properly, and his mouth opened and shut noiselessly.

"You know, sir," Herridge clenched his teeth as the screaming roar thundered along the jetty behind him. "Move the ship out with the cable?"

Fallow nodded slowly and swallowed hard. "Yes, yes! Do that!" It was not an order. It was a sob.

As Herridge ran to the rear of the bridge to see if his anchor party were still crouching by the stern capstan, Fallow whispered after him, "For God's sake, why doesn't he come back?"

The Captain, thought Herridge bleakly, as he cupped his hands. Well, we'll manage, old fellow! His voice rose above the din like a trumpet call. "Deck there! Slip all lines and wires! Start the capstan!"

The sentries ran like madmen along the deck, their axes flashing above their heads as they hacked and slashed at the ropes and mooring wires. From the quarterdeck a thin spiral of steam burst from the ancient capstan, as with a metallic clink, the first pawl dropped into its nitch and took the strain of the anchor cable.

The ship trembled, and with a painful jerk her stern began to swing out from the jetty. Slowly the gap widened, although the bows were still resting against the stonework.

The mob swarmed suddenly into Herridge's view as he ducked round the wheelhouse and he saw one man run wildly across the canting gangway, an iron bar raised above his head. Below his feet he heard the sharp click of a rifle bolt and he leaned out to stop the seaman from firing. At that moment, another piece of cable clattered through the stern fairleads, and the ship swung a few more feet, dropping the gangway into the water with a loud splash. An angry bellow rose from the crowd as the man in the water swam miserably back to the jetty, and then, as if of one mind, they heaved back to the only piece of the gunboat within their reach.

"Stand by in the bows there!" Herridge wished he could jump the three ladders in one go, but he knew he was needed on the bridge. Fallow hadn't even moved.

A rush of seamen ran to meet the frantic group who had managed to scramble up over the stem, and as they grappled savagely for handholds, a rain of stones and pieces of brickwork rained down on the decks. Herridge winced as a sharp stone glanced off his shoulder and watched anxiously as the tiny strip of green water around the bows suddenly widened to a ship's breadth and then, all at once, the stones were falling short and the cries of the mob grew more indistinct. He frowned as the seamen unceremoniously heaved the boarders over the side. But he knew it was useless to interfere, weakness now could do plenty of harm.

The mob was streaming back into the town, and as he stared after them he saw the glint of sunlight on several jeeps which were racing down the cliff road. There was a crackle of rifle fire, and a few screams, and seconds later, the jetty was jammed with soldiers who occasionally, and apparently without orders, dropped on to one knee and fired into the town.

"What a shower!" muttered Herridge bitterly, and glanced round at the shimmering harbour. The gunboat rode easily at her new mooring, plumb in the centre, swinging at her stern anchor. He grinned and nodded at the seamen by the capstan. "Well done!" Their oriental faces smiled back gravely, pleased with the small compliment.

He somehow knew Fallow would still be staring at nothing, and he coughed noisily as he mounted the ladder. But he needn't have worried—Chase was already there, making his report.

"No casualties or damage, sir, 'cept one pantry winder smashed!"

Fallow nodded painfully, "What about the passengers? The, er, Masters couple?"

"Fine, sir!" Chase scowled round the harbour. "Should 'ave let 'em 'ave a bit of three-oh-three!"

"Who? Masters?" Fallow seemed vague and distant.

"No, sir, I meant—" Chase began again, but Herridge interrupted sharply.

"Permission to fall out the hands from Action Stations, sir?"

"Oh er, yes. What about the Captain?" The thought which was uppermost in the man's mind burst from his loose lips.

"I'll take care of it, sir. I'll take the motor-boat and a couple of armed hands, and wait by the jetty. It'll be alright now. The soldiers seem to have the situation in hand!" He ran lightly down the ladder, as Fallow, with a terrific effort, turned to Chase.

"Double the sentries, Chief! Make sure no swimmers come nosin' around!"

As Chase stamped importantly to the main deck, Fallow let out one great big sigh, and sat down heavily on the gun mounting, unconscious of the sun beating across his fat shoulders, and aware only of the distant town, with its sullen noise and terrible menace.

.   .   .   .   .   .

John Laker pounded the veranda rail with his fist, a vein throbbing in his forehead. Silhouetted in the bright sunlight, and the green sheen of the neat trees, he seemed to dominate the view with his trembling anger.

"Damned Reds didn't fly over the estate! Did you notice that?" he shouted. "They mean to make use of all this, of all my work!"

Lieutenant Vincent watched him lazily, his back comfortably cradled in a deep cane chair. Poor chap, he thought sympathetically, but it's not going to help him any more.

Laker bounced back into the room, as if unable to torture himself with the sight of the rich estate. "I tell you, Vincent, they'll hear about this in Whitehall!" He slopped a large drink into his glass, and his face was suddenly sad, "Might as well drink it all now! Can hardly call this personal baggage!" His lip curled contemptuously. "That Captain of yours, where the hell is he?"

"I gathered he's gone to the hospital," Vincent answered slowly.

"Hospital, eh? That damned shack, you mean! I suppose he's listening to that blasted Red, Felton, or snivelling up to that little bitch of a sister!"

"Now, dear!" Mrs. Laker's voice was thin and tired. "She's a very nice girl I'm sure. She can't help what her brother is like!"

"Stuff and nonsense!" He glared at her. "Anyway, I'll give this Captain of yours a towsing when I get in the right quarter!"

"Really, sir?" Vincent listened quite affably, enjoying the peaceful house and the excellent brandy.

"Yes, dammit! Still got a few friends in the right places, y'know! My cousin is in the Colonial Office, and there are one or two fellas I know at the Admiralty who'll take care of this, this bloody upstart Captain!"

Vincent's eyes sharpened, and he saw Laker in a new, and more interesting light. "I wish I'd been able to do more for you myself, sir!" he said carefully.

"I'm sure you'd have seen things differently, m'boy!" Laker eyed him grimly. "Not enough of your kind about nowadays. Don't worry, I'll put in a word for you. I shan't forget!"

Vincent's heart sang, and he lowered his head hurriedly to hide the triumph in his eyes.

The door banged, and Ursula, fresh and cool in a pale green frock, and carrying a wide straw hat, sauntered across the room, her face flushed from the sun.

"Well, well! Another visitor!" She smiled softly at Vincent, her lashes masking her green eyes.

"I've just been visiting your manager, and so on. I expect you know about the plans for leaving the island?"

She pouted her warm lips. "Can't be too soon for me! I'm quite looking forward to the voyage."

"Huh! No fuss or panic, eh? Leave without making a scene! Is that what that idiot Rolfe said?" Laker was still smouldering. "I'll show him!"

Ursula's eyes hardened. "Leave off, Daddy! He's got a rotten job to do, and you know it!"

Laker glared and downed his drink. Then, picking up a full bottle, he stamped to the door. "I've told the boys to get the car

118

round the front for us. I imagine our gear will have been stowed on that ruddy gunboat by now! I'm going for a last look round the estate. I'll show him!" He disappeared, and Mrs Laker wandered vaguely after him. "I hope Father doesn't do anything foolish!" she murmured.

Vincent stared appraisingly at the girl, the brandy warm in his stomach. She was a picture alright. And what a perfect figure! He patted the seat beside him. "Come and join me in a drink!"

She smiled wryly. "Fair enough. Let's drink to better things!"

They drank slowly and appreciatively, enjoying the silence of the house, and hearing the shrill calls of the birds, and the distant ring of an axe against wood.

The air was warm and moist, and without warning, Ursula banged the heel of her shoe angrily on the floor. "Damn!" she exclaimed. "Your Captain is a bit queer, I must admit, but there's no doubt about it, he's got something!"

"I'm getting jealous," Vincent murmured softly, a cautious smile on his lips.

He went to the laden sideboard, and refilled the glasses. As he leaned across her to put the glass at her side, he let his gaze falter on the top of her dress, and watched the rise and fall of her heavy breasts with trembling anticipation. She stiffened as he ran his hand gently across her neck, and something like pain showed in her eyes.

The glass tinkled on the floor, and the next instant she was in his arms, panting and straining against him.

The suddenness rocked his control, but with pounding senses, he sought her wide mouth, feeling her hot tongue pressing against his. They broke, gasping, and she tried to meet his eyes, the colour mounting in her cheeks.

"I hope you don't think I always——" she stammered wildly, "It's just that it's been so long——"

Her thighs trembled uncontrollably as his groping hand began to unbutton the front of her dress, and she allowed herself to be led weakly to the screened corner of the room.

Vincent sighed deeply, as the thin garments came away in his hand, and he cupped her firm breast caressingly. She had her eyes closed, and moaned protestingly as he slipped away from her.

119

Then as he came back, muffling her cry of delicious pain with his mouth, they both allowed their longing to replace want, and desire to sweep away reason.

5

THE sun, unchallenged by even the smallest cloud, rose arrogantly in the afternoon sky, its probing beams beating and flaying the rocks and beaches with unpitying fierceness, while the trees and pigmy scrubs bent in a shimmering haze along the lip of the central plateau.

The town was strangely quiet now, and although the burned buildings still smouldered and stank of fire, only a few people remained to poke and pick at the wreckage. Small groups of soldiers idled untidily at the foot of the cliff road, and around the harbour, smoking, or playing quietly in the dust with bone dice.

Along the harbour wall there were still a number of silent groups, made up mostly of the older townsfolk, their wrinkled faces and dark eyes turned towards the Western horizon, or staring wistfully at the isolated gunboat, which glittered like a scale model in a glass showcase.

Even the cormorants, usually loud-voiced and querulous, perched moodily on their wizened legs, their long beaks tucked into their breasts, their eyes slitted with sleep. There was a general air of watchfulness and foreboding hanging heavily in the humid air.

The hospital, faded and wilting in the glare, was also quiet, the last casualty either resting uneasily on the rough beds, or sent home to his family, or already buried.

Rolfe lay back easily in the long chair, his stained uniform unbuttoned across his chest, in an attempt to trap the faint breath of air from the rickety fan, which squeaked remorselessly over his head. For all the pain and squalor which he had witnessed and had tirelessly helped to relieve, he felt unusually relaxed.

He glanced around the small, neat room with lazy contentment, aware that he should be making his way back to his ship, yet conscious that for the first time for so long, he was feeling the inner warmth of happiness.

The room, small though it was, held many of the answers to his unspoken questions, and revealed much of the lives of its owners.

Crude shelves were tightly packed with medical books and tattered magazines, mostly concerned with tropical disease and malnutrition, while around the walls were small feminine touches which brought a lump to his throat, so pathetic did they seem in this rough setting. There were several earthenware pots of bright wild flowers, and some small pictures, obviously hand painted with an almost schoolgirl simplicity, which did much to break the otherwise bleak interior of the dwelling.

Felton watched him quietly, his lips set in a tight line, as if tensed against some possible criticism or condescending remark, yet totally betrayed by the anxiety in his gleaming eye.

"I suppose you think I'm a bit of a swine to keep my sister out here, in all this?" He jerked his hand quickly.

Rolfe eyed him steadily. "I suppose you know what you're doing," he said evenly. "But, quite frankly, it must be a bit hard on her?"

Felton shrugged wearily. "Eight years," he said, half to himself, "but I've achieved so much!" Some of his drained energy flooded back. "And now, it looks as if these people might get a chance! Get a chance to live their own lives! Not just slaves of a half-mad Fascist!"

"They may not find freedom with the Communists!" Rolfe spoke carefully, watching the other man's tortured face for the return of anger. "That exhibition this morning wasn't much of a peace offering!"

Felton stood up edgily, biting his lip. "You're a servant of a military power, Justin! You must realize that today, all changes are only achieved by force. Some blood has to be shed!" He waved his hands nervously. "But in the old capitalist systems, the poor suffer for victory, and go on suffering after that victory to the advantage of the false politicians and industrialists who caused their misery! Surely after this, these wretched people will get something better!"

Rolfe's eyes widened, more at hearing Felton calling him by his Christian name, than by listening to his views.

"If this damned General had been removed before this, we should have been able to achieve so much more. There's plenty of food and natural resources on the island, but the people get none of it! The General and your precious Laker saw to that!" He kicked fiercely at the floor. "I hate everything that they stand for! And everything that all the other Lakers are doing all over the world!" His terrible face suddenly softened, as Judith's voice floated sweetly into the room. She was singing a strange French song, and the words were punctuated by the sounds of running water.

"She's making herself nice for you." He smiled crookedly. Rolfe felt himself flushing. "She sounds happy!" he stammered. Felton nodded. "She is! Are you married?" he asked sharply. "I was. It's all over, now!"

Felton studied him, and seemed vaguely satisfied. "Thought it was something like that. You had it written all over you!" He raised his hand as Rolfe opened his mouth. "Forget it! Now there's something I want to ask you, a sort of favour."

"Go ahead." Rolfe felt on safer ground.

"It's about Judith."

Rolfe felt the pain again. Judith. The very name made him feel different.

"I want you to promise me something. I want you to take her with you to Hong Kong!" He leaned forward, "Will you do that?"

"I'm taking you both!"

Felton shook his head sadly. "You obviously don't know what I've been talking about! I suppose you're so steeped in this imperialist clap-trap, that you couldn't possibly understand! I shan't be going, ever! My work is here, with these people. They trust me, and they need me. And that in itself is reason and reward enough for my staying!"

Rolfe frowned. "You know that she'll want to stay with you, don't you?"

"I do. We've been together so long now, she feels she has to look after me." He shook his head irritably, "Never mind that! This is no time for sentimentality! Will you promise me that you'll take her?"

122

"I will! By force if necessary! Although I don't think she'd like me much for that!"

"And that means a lot to you, doesn't it?" His voice was shrewd. "Well, that's a big weight off my mind! I'm not worried about my own safety. The Chinese aren't fools, and they'll realize that I'm some use to these people!" He looked searchingly at Rolfe, "Be good to her, won't you?"

Rolfe swallowed, and wondered how to answer. "I can't possibly see how you keep arriving at all these conclusions," he started lamely.

"That'll do! I'm not interested in all these irritating preliminaries!" He dropped his voice, the bantering tone replaced by one of gentle sincerity. "She's twenty-six, a woman, but for all that practically a child. She came out here when she was eighteen, straight from a ghastly finishing school, and so she has no idea really of the outside world! I trust you, Justin!" he explained simply, "God knows why! You stand for all that I hate, yet I do! And I want you to look after her, to put her on the right road."

"Have you no parents?" Rolfe's heart was pounding painfully.

"Dead! Mother quite early, and Father when his money ran out. He didn't quite approve of me, and he tried to keep Judith and me apart!" He smiled at some secret memory. "When the cash stopped, so did the finishing school! That's one thing the old man didn't bargain for!"

"I think you only like me here so that you can give me a lecture!" Rolfe laughed softly, to break the tension. "But don't worry, I'll come up for her tonight. I shall sail tomorrow forenoon, and I hope you may change your mind about staying," he finished soberly.

He jumped to his feet, as the girl stepped lightly into the room. She had combed her hair back into a gleaming, chestnut mane, which reflected every light in its silky tresses. She was wearing a plain cotton dress, which had obviously been washed and repaired many times, yet her beauty was only accentuated by her faded clothes, and her huge eyes studied his face anxiously, as if to see his reaction.

Rolfe found he was staring at her again, seeing her for the first time, as a woman.

Her small, graceful figure, its promise of curved perfection barely disguised by the newly-pressed dress, and her slim, sun-browned legs, no longer hidden by the rough smock, made his blood roar in his head, and he didn't trust himself to speak.

"I'll leave you two alone," Felton said shortly. "Just going to clean up the surgery!" He patted her arm as he passed. "Careful with him, Judith, he'll eat you alive!" They heard him laugh as he slammed the door.

Rolfe fiddled with the buttons on his tunic, unable to tear his gaze from her, yet unwilling to meet the cool candour of those wide eyes.

"He's been bullying you, hasn't he?" she asked gravely.

"Just telling me about himself, and you."

"He likes you, I can tell. He doesn't take to people like—" she stopped, a blush on her smooth cheeks.

"Don't worry. I know what you mean!" Rolfe interrupted gently. "He thinks I'm an imperialist warmonger, or something!"

"He's so keen to help these people!" Her small, well-shaped hands embraced the invisible island. "He gets very impatient sometimes!"

"Tell me," Rolfe spoke softly, his eye on the door, "how did he get that terrible injury? An accident out here?"

She smiled sadly, "No, not out here." She moved quickly to the side of the room, and tugged a battered suitcase from under the couch. She went on her knees, her hands pulling impatiently at the strap which held the case closed. A great wing of hair tumbled across her shoulder, and she bit her lip with concentration. Rolfe thought she looked at that moment, more like a child than ever before.

The case burst open, and although he tried not to appear curious, he couldn't help seeing the pathetic possessions inside. A school badge, some old English newspapers, and then with a sob, she pulled out a small leather box. Gently, and with great care, she brushed away the clinging fur of mildew which was beginning to form on the faded surface, and then she opened the lid, and held it out to his gaze.

In the box, on its bed of pale satin, lay a silver cross, and a blue and white ribbon.

"The Distinguished Flying Cross!" he murmured, and met her

124

watchful eyes, seeing the warm glow of pride and defiance. "I never dreamed!"

She touched the medal with her finger, and then closed the box, quickly stuffing it back in the case. "Nobody knows, and he'd be furious if he knew I'd shown it to you." She sat on the edge of her chair, her hand nearly touching his. "He was a very good pilot. All the girls at the school used to rave over him when he came to see me. That was before—before he was shot down in Burma." She dropped her eyes to her lap, and he wanted to crush her to him, to protect her from everything. "He was taken prisoner by the Japanese, he was terribly burned in the crash, but they didn't try to help him, they just let his face form itself into that mask!" She shuddered. "He had been a medical student until he volunteered for the air force, and that must have saved him. He more or less treated himself! Even now, I can't bear to think of it!"

Rolfe went cold, visualizing the months of agony and fear. "That explains a lot!" he murmured softly.

In the surgery he could hear Felton whistling cheerfully. "I suppose it was too late to do anything about his face when he was released from prison camp? Plastic surgery, I mean."

"Yes, too late. He threw himself into his studies instead, and he really is a very good doctor!"

"Yes I know. What made him first come out here?"

She straightened her skirt thoughtfully. "It wasn't easy for him in England, you know. They practically told him outright that he'd never hold down any position there because of the way he looked! It was terribly cruel! It made him very bitter!"

Rolfe nodded understandingly, seeing only too clearly how a man like Felton, with his forthright views, and embittered mind, would react to such handling.

Judith crossed to the window, staring out across the bay. "She's very lovely, isn't she?"

"Who?" Rolfe twisted his mind on to this new track.

"Ursula Laker," her voice was wistful. "I've often seen her driving and riding around the island. She's always so beautifully dressed and self-assured!" The slim shoulders shrugged helplessly, "She must be very happy!"

"I don't think she's very satisfied."

"Do you like her a lot?" Then she turned, shaking her head quickly, "No, I'm sorry, I shouldn't have asked! Please forgive me!"

"There's nothing to forgive, Judith. I'm afraid she only succeeded in making me very uncomfortable!" He laughed unsteadily.

He watched her walk across the room. What's happening to me? What am I doing? Have you forgotten so soon what has already happened in your life? A mental picture of Sylvia flitted across his mind, and he was surprised to find that it no longer hurt him. He watched the girl narrowly, wondering how it had all happened, and not even wanting to resist its implication.

"Brian wants me to go away from here, doesn't he?"

Rolfe started. How like her brother she was, always making sudden and unexpected statements. "Has he told you that?"

"Not in so many words. But he does, doesn't he? I can feel it."

"It's the only solution. This'll be no place for you when the trouble starts. For any of us, for that matter."

She stared at the door. "He won't be able to manage without me. I must stay with him!"

Rolfe stood up, his face set and determined. "No, Judith! I want him to go too, but even if he decides to stay in the hospital, he won't be happy with you here. It might be dangerous, and you wouldn't want him to be worried all the time, would you?"

"But where should I go?" She gazed round the room, her eyes searching, "This is my home now!"

"I'll look after you, " Rolfe answered, his throat tight. "I'll be able to get you back to England if you like?"

"I suppose the Government will pay for the fares and everything?" she sounded dazed and uneasy.

"I don't care what the Government do! I am going to look after you!"

She stared at him, showing surprise at the grim determination in his taut voice. "I think you mean it," she breathed softly.

You'll never know how much I mean it! If only I could tell you how I feel!

He grinned awkwardly, "Leave it to me. And you could always come out here again when things quieten down," he lied. "Things might be better then."

126

Her eyes were misty. "I hope so, for his sake!"

Rolfe forced himself to look at his watch, and marvelled incredulously at the speed at which the hours had passed. It would be better to leave now, he thought, before she has time to change her mind.

"I must go now. I shall either come for you tonight, or send my Lieutenant. You will be ready?" He tried not to meet her eyes.

"I shall be here." Her voice sounded far away.

"Would you like me to take some clothes and things with me now, to save time?"

She glanced down at the dress. "I've got them on!" She smiled, but her lip quivered.

Rolfe reached out and gripped her arm, his voice husky. "We'll take care of that. Don't worry!"

A jeep snarled along the sea road and halted. Major Ling called out from the distance. "Are you coming, Captain? Can I give you a lift?"

Judith's eyes flared angrily. "That awful man! When you see people like that, you realize that Brian is right!"

He gave her arm a squeeze, reluctant to go. "Goodbye, Judith! Until tonight."

"Yes." She watched him stride off, her hand touching her arm where his hand had been.

As Rolfe clambered into the jeep, she came running down the path, holding out the little leather box. "You can take this for me!" Her voice was breathless, and she avoided looking at the major.

Rolfe slipped the case into his pocket, and leaned across to her, until her hair brushed his cheek. As her eyes widened, he whispered slowly and carefully, "Yin Fong Leung."

As the jeep bounded forward, he saw the pleasure rush to her cheeks, and her teeth white in her brown face.

"A very nice girl, Captain!" Ling began to hum softly.

Rolfe smiled, his head spinning. "Yes, Major. A *very* nice girl!"

"She and the Doctor will be leaving with you?"

"All being well," answered Rolfe non-committally, "I think it would be much safer for them."

"You have no faith in the General's defence plans?" Ling spoke with heavy irony. "You feel perhaps that it will be a walkover for the invaders?"

"I didn't say that!" He glanced sideways at this strange, imperturbable man. He felt a twinge of pity for him at that moment, realizing that in a space of days, or hours, he might be dead. Ling's expressionless face showed no sign of fear, or even anger, or annoyance. His hands were relaxed on the wheel, and his long legs were curled comfortably above the metal floor. "Perhaps the Communists will change their mind," he added, without much conviction.

"You do not know them as I do, Captain! They will come, as surely as night follows day." He shrugged, as if bored with the whole matter. "But a tree must be pruned regularly to be kept alive and healthy!"

Rolfe lapsed into silence, puzzling over the last remark, and then as the jeep topped a rise in the road, he jerked upright in his seat, staring at the distant shape of the *Wagtail* at her new mooring.

Ling chuckled softly. "Do not be alarmed! I'm afraid that I unworthily forgot to mention that your ship had moved its berth. Or perhaps I didn't want to trouble you in your moment of happiness!"

Rolfe stared at him, looking for a sneer, but Ling merely chuckled again. "It was nothing, Captain, just a little disturbance in the town. Some of the rabble wanted a free ride to Hong Kong, and I think your admirable second-in-command thought otherwise!"

Good for him, breathed Rolfe softly, I'll bet poor old Fallow was upset, all the same. Aloud he said, "All quiet now?"

"At the moment. Of course, some of the most responsible citizens are away in the fishing fleet. These hot-heads are the rabble-rousers, and wasters!" His eyes narrowed to hard slits. "They will have plenty to occupy their minds soon!"

"And what about you, Major?" Rolfe asked quietly. "What are your hopes for the future?"

"The future? Maybe I shall see you in far-off Hong Kong one day!"

The wheels kicked up twin banks of white dust, as the jeep

rolled on to the market place, and slowed down by the harbour entrance. Rolfe stood at the side of the jeep, and stretched himself, feeling the heat strike upwards through the soles of his shoes.

"So long, Major! In case I don't see you again, all the best!" They shook hands, and Rolfe trudged along the wall, watching his ship, and wondering about Judith and her brother.

Some of the soldiers who sprawled in the shade stared at him indifferently, and some saluted sketchily, while others turned their faces away, gripping their rifles tightly. Probably wishing they were coming with us, he thought grimly.

Herridge's head popped up over the stonework almost at his side, jerking him from his thoughts.

"Boat's here, sir!" And he steadied the motor-boat with his foot on the stone steps, so that Rolfe could climb in.

The engine coughed, and rattled, and then with a jerk, the boat moved away from the wall, churning the water into a creamy froth. The two seamen stood smartly with their boathooks in the air, conscious of the many eyes on their precise movements, and Rolfe heard Herridge growl from the tiller. "Heads up there! Don't forget you're making history!"

"Be off to England after this, Chief? For your new job?"

"Aye, sir," the blue eyes twinkled, "I shall be sorry in a way though, to leave the old *Wagtail*."

"No ship as good as the last ship," muttered Rolfe half to himself. "The navy never changes much, does it Chief?"

The man laughed deep in his chest. "Never, sir! Who else but our navy would send a ship of this vintage on a job like this?" He dropped his eyes to Rolfe, his smile fading, "No disrespect meant to you, sir."

"None taken, Chief!" Rolfe answered lightly. He means because I'm Captain of her, he pondered. Well, the task was nearly over now, he reflected, and whatever the Admiral might say, it hadn't done him much good. Laker would see to that when he got back.

As the motor-boat curved towards the *Wagtail*'s gangway, he caught a glimpse of the distant fort, although in the heat-haze it was difficult to estimate where the cliff left off and the rugged walls began. The General was sitting at his chessmen, he grimaced, and the Admiral playing with his little flags. How strange were the men who could become powerful and unyielding.

He still couldn't get used to stepping out of a small boat straight on to a ship's main deck. Even in a frigate he'd had a long companion ladder to contend with. He saluted the quarterdeck, and acknowledged the shrill of the Quartermaster's pipe.

He allowed his body to relax, as Fallow padded forward to meet him. Get ready to deal with every eventuality, he thought. Funnily enough, it no longer seemed to bother him.

"I'm so glad you're back, sir! I had to move the ship because of the mob which came runnin' down the jetty at us!" He gulped in a fresh breath, his chin sagging over his tight collar. He looked as if he was expecting the Captain to fly into a rage, or start to bombard him with complaints.

Rolfe smiled pleasantly, and nodded approvingly. "Well done, Number One! You've done a good job! Just as well we had the old cable laid out, eh?"

Fallow peered at him nervously, and seemed on the point of smelling Rolfe's breath, at any rate, his amazement and his relief were clear to see.

"All our passengers aboard, yet?"

"Er, most of 'em sir. The Masters couple, and the Grants are fixed up, and Lieutenant Vincent's gone for the Lakers, and the other two, er, Mr. Lane an' his wife."

Rolfe frowned, and glanced at his watch. "Very good. Send the hands to tea now, and let me know if anything new occurs to your mind. Vincent ought to be here soon, I should think." Bloody young fool, he thought, probably having quite a time now that he's got the stage to himself.

Chao was waiting for him, and smiled happily as Rolfe walked into his quarters, dropping his jacket on the deck, and lazily stepping out of his trousers.

The shower felt good, and he hummed softly as he scrubbed away the dust and dirt of the town, and the fatigue of the sun.

I wonder how she'll get on with the other women passengers? he thought, rubbing the soap from his thick hair. I think I'll put her in with the Grant woman, she looked human enough.

Laker'll have to share my quarters, I suppose, blast him! The Acting British Consul could hardly be confined to the Chiefs'

Mess! He laughed delightedly at the picture, and Chao, busy as usual with a fresh uniform for his master, cocked his head with satisfaction. The Captain must have discovered something good in Santu, he decided.

Fallow sat at his usual seat at the wardroom table, watching the stewards pass round the tea and biscuits. It was worse than ever in the wardroom now, he thought darkly, with a crowd of uneasy-faced civilians eating and drinking silently all around him.

Grant and his wife consumed their tea unseeingly, Grant no doubt thinking of his wasted years, and his wife occasionally darting a worried look in his direction.

The Masters couple, and Fallow could never think of them as individuals, sat very close, and but for two or three whispered words, they added nothing but discomfort to his gloom.

Bloody Vincent'll be back soon! Still he at least would keep these people off his hands, with his yarns of Government House, and so forth! Why was he still worried? He creased his brows, trying to pin down the exact reason. In a few days he'd be safe, and getting ready to leave China for good, and all the misery and humiliation would be a thing of the past. He leaned back in his chair, momentarily forgetting his companions, and tried to picture Mary waving up at the ship as she docked. Mary, warm and understanding. She'd understand everything, and wouldn't laugh at him. He smiled drowsily, seeing the bungalow in the photograph, with its neat garden, and a view of the sea. In the evenings they'd sit together on the little lawn, and watch the lighted liners heading across to Southampton. And he'd smoke his pipe, and say, did I ever tell you about the time I was First Lieutenant of the *Wagtail*? He nodded heavily forward, the single lick of hair on his shining head dropping untidily over his ear.

Louch's head and shoulders were protruding from the engine-room hatch, while he took a breather, and a cup of strong tea, which Herridge had brought down to him.

It was cool under the awning, and a strong breath of warm air was sucked past them by the whirring engine-room fans.

Louch smacked his lips. "Nice cuppa!" he commented.

"How's the old box of tricks down there?" Herridge squatted on the hatch coaming. "Rarin' to go?"

"Too right it is! Captain's ordered me to stand by until

further notice. Just in case we decide to leave a bit earlier than we planned, I guess!"

"He's alright, the Captain! And he seems a bit more cheerful today too."

Louch grinned unsympathetically. "Not much of a job for a young two-an-a-half-striper, is it? Still, I daresay he'll get something better after this lot! He's got quite a load on his plate, an' no mistake!"

"He'll be O.K. I expect. He's a darn sight better than a lot of skippers I've known, and that's a fact!"

Louch swilled his cup, and shook it carefully over the side. "He'll do!" he said briefly.

As he eased himself back on to the ladder, he squinted across at the town. "I hope we don't forget anything when we go," he grinned, "I don't reckon we'd find it very easy to get in again, with the Commies in the place!"

Herridge picked up the cup, and nodded. "It'd be like trying to open an oyster with a bus ticket!" He laughed shortly, and wandered back to the mess, where Chase lay snoring on his bunk.

.   .   .   .   .

Vincent breathed deeply, and studied his reflection in the ornate mirror, running a comb through his fair hair. A weak, trembling sensation still clung to his loins, and he saw the gleam of wild satisfaction in his eyes. He put the comb in his breast pocket, and patted his uniform into shape.

He heard a movement behind him, and Ursula stepped round the screen, her face flushed, and eyes averted. She swayed towards him, her lips parted and moist.

"How do you feel?" he asked, the excitement still making his voice unsteady.

She rubbed the palms of her hands lazily on his shoulders, still avoiding his gaze. "It was wonderful, David! I wish it would go on for ever!" She pressed herself against him, her hair nestling his chin. "I'm glad we'll be together on the ship."

He ran his fingers along her spine, and felt a tremor run through her soft body. "You're shameless!" he laughed. "But you're also very right!" He felt as if he was riding on a wave, and he wanted her again, that very moment. He pulled her tighter,

132

thinking of Hong Kong, and the possibilities of the future. Janet wouldn't like this, he thought, but she could go to hell! Janet was a babe-in-arms compared with this creature!

He jumped violently as a loud roar shook the building, followed by a sullen rumble, which died away almost before he could recover his senses. They stared at each other, uncomprehending.

"What the hell was that?" He gently prised her arms from his neck, and walked to the window.

The sun had moved across the trees, and the low fields were pooled in purple shadows.

Behind the thick leaves, a pall of smoke was rising, and even as they watched, a red and yellow tongue of flame licked hungrily at the first rank of trees.

Ursula gasped. "There's a fire! The whole estate is alight!"

Vincent felt vaguely uneasy, and listened to the growing crackle and roar of blazing timber.

"The reservoir! It's gone!" Her voice trembled, "That must have been the explosion!" Her eyes were fearful, as she turned towards him, "What does it mean?"

Vincent reached to the table, and buckled on his heavy pistol, his face grim. "I don't know, but whatever it is, we're getting out, right now!" He forced himself to light a cigarette, and draw in the smoke calmly, for his own sake, as much as hers. "Get your mother into the car, and I'll look for your father!" He ran lightly down the steps, aware of the complete air of desertion which hung over the whole estate.

"David!" Her call pulled him up short. "Don't be long, will you?"

He grinned back at her. "Don't worry, I'm not in any state to walk much!" But when he hurried away, he felt the anxiety rising like a frog in his throat.

He hadn't covered more than a hundred yards, when he saw Laker walking slowly towards him. His big body was unsteady, and he carried an empty bottle in his hand like a club. He raised it to his mouth, and then, with a grunt of disgust, sent it hurtling into the field. "Take that!" he shouted thickly, and then he saw Vincent.

"Well, my boy! You're a bit late for the fireworks, I'm afraid!" His speech was slurred.

"What have you done, sir?" But he already knew. The fool, he thought, no chance of a quiet exit now!

"Blown up the whole blasted place! None of these yellow bastards'll ever get the chance to live off my work and sweat!" He threw back his head and laughed noisily. "What a damned shock they'll get, what?"

"I think we'd better go, sir!" Vincent said tightly. "There may be trouble!"

"Balderdash! Haven't you got any guts either?"

"Yes sir, and I want to hang on to them!" He turned back to the house, and grumbling and laughing intermittently, Laker stumbled after him.

Ursula was helping her mother into the car, and she looked at her father with disgust. "You've made a fine mess, haven't you?"

Mrs. Laker reached out weakly as Laker staggered to the car. "John, I want to know—"

"Shut up, for God's sake! The lot of you! You're worse than a pack of bloody wogs!" Laker glared defiantly. "I was just sayin' to Vincent here that—" he stopped as Edgar Lane, followed by his wife, appeared round the side of the building.

Lane's face was white with shock, and he clawed at Laker's sleeve, trying to speak. When his voice came, it was almost a scream. "My trees! What have you done to my trees?" He stared wildly at Laker's red-rimmed eyes, and he gripped his arm more tightly. "You've killed them! Oh God, my trees!" he sobbed. Melanie Lane looked from face to face, her mouth slack and pleading.

"*Your* trees? Damn your eyes, sir! They're mine, d'you hear?" Laker swayed heavily. "I always knew you were cracked, you fool! Now get out! Go to hell if you like!" He brushed the man's hand away and staggered up the steps of the house.

Vincent stepped forward. "Have you got a car, Mrs. Lane?" She nodded dumbly towards one of the estate cars.

"Well, get on down to the harbour. At once, please," he added curtly. "Can you drive?"

She nodded again, and pulled her husband's arm. "Come on, Edgar," she edged him to the car. "Try not to think about it!" She forced him into the seat, and ran round to the other door.

As the car moved away, Vincent saw Lane staring back at the growing fire. There were tears in his eyes.

Ursula slid behind the driving wheel, and they waited silently, until Laker reappeared, an oil lamp in his fist. As he stood looking back at the house, he suddenly hurled the lamp into the long room, where, half-an-hour earlier, Vincent had made love to his daughter. It exploded, as the burning oil splashed across the wooden floor in a fiery stream.

"Damn you!" shouted Laker at the house. "Burn away!" he fell in the back of the car, breathing heavily. Mrs. Laker edged away from him, making herself small in the corner.

As Ursula pressed the starter button, Vincent moved closer to her, keeping his voice low.

"Listen, Ursula! Whatever you see or hear, keep driving, got that?"

She whispered a quiet "Yes", her face pale under her tan.

"There's likely to be a bit of trouble before we get to the harbour. Everyone's bound to have seen the smoke, and heard the explosion, and maybe they won't like it much!" He set his lips in a tight line, and drew the pistol from its holster, feeling the metal warm against his leg.

The car swung on to the roadway, and gathered speed along the deserted estate, and through the wire gates. Vincent noticed that there were no guards this time.

Laker muttered and swore in a dreary monotone, and Vincent began to hate him. Blasted fool, didn't he understand the instructions about leaving quietly? Ah well, it was too late now.

"The smoke seems to have blown right down here," Ursula said jerkily, as the car dashed down the centre of the main road. Her eyes widened with fear, as Vincent answered her, his voice flat.

"That's different smoke! It's in front of us, around the next bend!"

Nobody answered him, but he saw the girl's hands tighten on the wheel, and she hunched her shoulders defensively.

Still keeping to the centre of the road, the long American car swung round the wide bend, the dust spewing from under the wings in a choking cloud.

At first Vincent could only gape at the surging mass of people who filled the road ahead, and then he choked back a gasp of horror, as he saw the blazing station wagon, crackling like a bonfire in their midst.

The roar of the fire, and the wild shrieks of the mob, deadened the sound of their car, and as they got nearer, Vincent saw the contorted face of Edgar Lane pinned against the flaming coach-work by a crude forked stick at his throat, while a forest of groping, frenzied hands clawed and battered at his twisting body.

Then the car was amongst them, and they got blurred impressions of gaping, snarling faces pressing in on them in a wall of savagery. The windscreen frosted over, as a heavy club swung across the bonnet, and Vincent heaved himself to his feet, his teeth bared, while he clung to the dashboard for support. He dimly realized that the car was stopping, and as he raised the heavy pistol, he heard Ursula cry out, as her door was jerked open, and two brawny arms seized her shoulder, ripping open her dress. She screamed again, her mouth slack with terror, as the man's broken nails clawed her bare shoulder, dragging her relentlessly from her seat.

Vincent had never fired a shot in anger in his life, but without a second's hesitation, he squeezed the trigger at point-blank range across Ursula's back, and as if in a nightmare, he saw the man's face dissolve into a scarlet blotch, and disappear beneath the car. The shot, its report magnified and distorted by the surrounding trees, made the men around the car fall back in surprise, cannoning into the press behind them.

In that instant, a sort of madness gripped Vincent, and he vaulted out of the car, kicking out savagely at the man nearest him, and firing again twice into the seething crowd of bodies. He felt no pain as a stick struck his arm, only a savage wave of exhilaration as the gun jumped in his hand, and he tasted the stench of cordite. Heedless of the screams, he ran to the burning vehicle, where Lane had fallen to his knees, his hair smouldering on a gleaming, raw scalp.

Vincent jerked him viciously to his feet, shutting out the man's cry of agony, and trying not to stare at the body of Melanie Lane, which lay a few paces from the car. She must have suffered terribly at the hands of the mob, before someone had cut her throat.

"Get back you bastards!" He didn't recognize his own voice, or realize that he had fired again, until he saw two men drop writhing at his feet. He only knew that the shining bodywork of Laker's car represented a haven, and an only chance of escape.

The car moved towards him, the driving door still hanging open, and Ursula's white face peering through a hole in the frosted windscreen.

"Get in, Lane!" He pushed the man clumsily into the car, seeing Mrs Laker on the floor, where her husband had thrust her, and watching Laker himself, a heavy tyre lever in his hand, thrashing out at the faces behind him.

"Quick, get going!" he choked, groping for the car with his foot, and then crying aloud with pain, as a hard head butted him in the back, and someone else grabbed at his ankle.

"Bastards!" he sobbed, the tears of agony blinding him, and as the car started to move from under him, he twisted sideways, feeling the foul breath in his face, and seeing the eyes filled with hate. The gun jumped in his hand, and he saw the man bare his teeth wildly, as if snapping at his last breath. The hammer clicked again on an empty cylinder, and he flung the useless weapon into the sea of heads around him. He clawed his way into the front of the car, his face brushing against Lane's limp body, and his feet still dragging along the track. Ursula leaned over, groping for his tunic, her eyes on the weaving pattern of the road ahead.

With a final gasp, Vincent plummeted into the car, and somehow hauled himself upright, temporarily blinded by the sun's reflection on the dented and scratched bonnet, and still deafened by the screams of the mob, although they were already out of earshot. As he lay against the girl, panting like a wild animal, he remembered Lane at his feet, and saw again in his mind the horribly mutilated body of his wife.

He lowered his head and retched, feeling the sour taste of vomit in his throat. Now that his blood was beginning to settle, a wave of weakness and shock swept over him.

Laker was leaning forward, mopping his face with his sleeve. "Well done, m'boy! Saved us all!"

Vincent swallowed in agony, and spoke through his clenched teeth. "For Christ's sake shut your stupid mouth!" he ground.

He reached out shakily, and covered the girl's hand on the wheel, squeezing until it hurt. "You were fine!" he croaked, and she darted a quick glance at his bruised face, her mouth quivering.

Her dress flapped in the breeze, the long scratches on her shoulder like the marks of a giant claw.

"David," she faltered, "I thought we were done for! I never guessed this sort of thing could happen!"

Vincent wearily reached for his handkerchief, and turned his aching mind to the problem of Lane's head. "It's a thing I shall never forget!" he grated, fighting back at a fresh tide of nausea.

After what seemed like an age, they drew up on the harbour wall, several people pressing round, staring at their injuries, and the damage to the car. A whisper of uneasiness rippled through the ragged figures, and Vincent thought, that but for the presence of the soldiers, they would have been attacked again where they sat.

There was a jeep parked by the guard-hut, and the fat figure of Colonel Kyung eased itself from the small seat, and waddled over to them. In addition to his tight uniform, he was wearing a pair of long, shiny jackboots, which gleamed incongruously in the dusty road.

"You make a big fire, Mr. Laker?" His small eyes glittered like stones. "I think it very foolish to damage such a fine place!"

Laker stumbled from the car, his face mottled with anger, and the sudden necessity to cover up his fright.

"My land! Do what I damn well like with it!"

Vincent watched the fat colonel, noting the cruel scars on his cheeks. Go on, he prompted inwardly, hit the silly fool in the face. I shan't help him! But the colonel merely smiled smugly.

"So long as the gallant Mr. Laker doesn't waste the time of his Government, or mine, by asking for compensation at some later date!" He shrugged calmly. "If you had not behaved so recklessly, we could have come to some arrangement of course, but now . . ." He shrugged again, enjoying the expression of incredulous dismay which flooded Laker's face. "However," he continued in a brisk tone, "I will take your car for myself. I will commandeer, is that what you call it?"

Laker stepped forward, a vein bulging in his neck. "I'll see you in hell first! I—I'll drive the thing into the sea before I let your damned body use it!"

Colonel Kyung rapped a sharp command and a handful of rifles rose menacingly. "I think it is time to say farewell," he snapped. "I am told that most of your estate is unharmed, so we are not ungrateful for your services!"

"You, you," spluttered Laker, staring round at the watching soldiers and the levelled rifles. "You'll be sorry for this!"

The colonel grinned and spat on the sand between them.

Vincent stepped forward, trying to disguise the shaking in his legs. "We will go aboard now!" he said sharply. "I think you've done and said enough, sir!"

He felt a sigh of relief in his throat as he saw the motor-boat curving towards the jetty. Suddenly he wanted to be aboard the gunboat more than anything else in the world.

He helped the seamen carry Lane into the boat where he lay moaning softly, his bloody head in Mrs. Laker's lap. Ursula sat in the tiny cabin, her forehead pressed against the seat, her hands balled into tight fists. He smiled at her, ignoring Laker completely.

"You can have a damn good bath when you get aboard and then get some sleep."

She lowered her head but reached out for the comfort of his hand.

As the boat pushed off from the jetty he saw Colonel Kyung driving the car slowly along the wall, followed admiringly by his men.

.　　　.　　　.　　　.

Rolfe laid his binoculars down on the flag locker with slow, deliberate movements, his mouth set in a tight line. He was aware that Fallow was watching him fearfully, and that but for the soft commands from Herridge—who was supervising the removal of Lane's body from the motor-boat—the ship had fallen unnaturally quiet. Not trusting himself to speak, he climbed down to the main deck, a fierce pang of anger twisting his inside into a knot.

Vincent was explaining to the stewards what he wanted done for the two limp women when he looked up and saw Rolfe approaching.

"Well?" Rolfe dropped the word coldly into the silence. "What exactly has been happening?"

Vincent swayed slightly and steadied himself by the guardrail at his back. "The fire, sir. They saw the fire and came after us!" He bit his lip and Rolfe saw the sickness in his face. "They knew we were getting out, and tried to stop us, to get their revenge!" he finished wildly.

Rolfe looked him up and down, noting the torn uniform, and bruised face. He had already guessed what had happened when the explosion of the reservoir blowing up had brought him running to the bridge. Even as he cursed himself for trusting Laker, he had watched the growing wall of smoke over the plateau.

"Why were you so long? Why didn't you keep an eye on things more carefully?"

Vincent dropped his face, writhing under the Captain's cold stare. "I did my best, sir, I couldn't stop him!"

Rolfe turned slowly to Laker who was obviously getting irritated again at being discussed so openly by the officers, in front of the women and two or three watching seamen.

"Mr. Laker," he began calmly, "is there anything you'd like to add?"

"There's a hell of a lot I've got to add! Yes, indeed!" His grey hair bristled like a wire brush. "I'm not going to be spoken to by a damned jumped-up sailor in this manner!"

The seamen hissed expectantly and even Herridge was rooted to the deck, watching their faces and waiting for the storm to break. Rolfe eyed Laker for a few moments, giving no sign of the fury in his heart.

"When I came to Santu, Mr. Laker," his tone was almost conversational, "you were reluctant to leave. You gave me certain views which as Acting Consul I was bound to listen to. Then, eventually, you realized the necessity for the evacuation and foolishly I thought you were going to be co-operative and help me with a quiet and efficient operation." The grey eyes flashed with hidden fire. "But it appears that you decided to be heroic and tried to antagonize these wretched people, as if they haven't got enough to contend with at the moment!"

Laker's chin jutted forward, his mouth champing with temper.

"I see you've been listenin' to that bloody Felton!" he was shouting now. "Damned Commie! Probably a conchie into the bargain!" he added, groping for some additional insult.

Rolfe stiffened, staring across the other man's sweating head. "Doctor Felton, as it happens, was a fighter pilot," he announced tonelessly. "Not that it has any bearing on this matter. But he did very well in the last war, now that we're on the subject, and while you were sitting on your behind making money and enjoying the high-sounding name of Brigadier, he was fighting for something he believed was worth while!"

Fallow gasped and Vincent forgot his misery as he studied Rolfe's face, which was twisted into a cruel smile.

"Furthermore, Mr. Laker, your official status here has now ceased to exist, and I am Captain of this ship!" He looked down at Laker's popping eyes, "And if I get one more bit of trouble from you, I'll put you under arrest!" He swayed back on his heels, knowing that he meant what he said, and half hoping that Laker would hit him.

"I'll see about that!" but Laker's voice was trembling. "I, at least, have done my duty!" he added weakly, the fight gone from him.

Rolfe turned his back on him and put one foot on the ladder. "You have also caused the death of an innocent woman," he said flatly, and mounted to the bridge, hearing Mrs. Laker's cry of anguish.

Another minute, and I'll have flattened him myself, he mused, letting his pent-up breath whistle through his teeth.

He busied himself with the charts, until Fallow pushed his way into the chart room.

"How is Lane getting on? Have you managed to make him comfortable?"

"'E's quiet now, sir. I've made 'im comfortable in the Sick Bay. Gave 'im a shot of morphia, too, sir."

"Good, good," Rolfe scratched his chin absently. "It's a shame we couldn't have saved his wife!"

Fallow clenched his big fists nervously. "I'm glad you told Mr. Laker what 'e'd done, sir! 'E'll 'ave to face up to the music when we get to Hong Kong!"

Rolfe regarded him stonily. That's what you think, he thought,

I'll be answerable for her death, not Laker. He forced a smile. but his eyes were still hard. "It's been quite a business, hasn't it?"

Fallow twitched, his bar-taut nerves responding to anything out of the ordinary. A deep-sounding horn, like a fog-siren, echoed across the harbour.

Rolfe grunted with irritation. "Don't take any notice of that, Number One. I was warned about it when we arrived. It's a signal from the fort to inform the town that they've sighted the fishing fleet!"

They stepped out on to the wing of the bridge, looking up at the high cliff.

"From that high tower they must be able to see a damned long way, it'll be some time before our lookouts spot anything."

Fallow glanced around the quiet harbour, his seaman's mind taking in the problem of *Wagtail*'s position.

"We'll be a bit in the way 'ere, sir, won't we?"

Rolfe's gaze wandered to the bare horizon. "Yes. Start up the capstan, and we'll shorten in on the cable!"

Eventually the *Wagtail* began to drag herself further along her cable towards her stern anchor, the slime-soaked links of the chain clattering on to the deck, and being meticulously scrubbed before they disappeared into the chain locker below.

Idly Rolfe scanned the jetty through his glasses, his lip curling as he saw the fat Chinese colonel still sitting in his new car, the bent bumper of which reached practically to the end of the stonework. He'll have a job to turn it round and drive it back to the town, he thought, as the jetty's end was its narrowest part, worn away by the breakers from the open sea beyond.

He swung his glasses on to the horizon, steadying them suddenly as he picked out a mass of tiny dots just mounting over the sun-dappled lip. He smiled secretly, thinking how he would be able to share these sights with Judith. Perhaps the future would be different, and not quite so full of uncertainty, if only she could understand what she had become for him. He shook his head, straining his ears. The sun hung like a red ball over the western sky as if poised and ready to leave the world for another night, but he didn't notice its splendour any more, he was concentrating on the far distant rumble, which crept lazily across the miles of placid sea like summer thunder.

C.P.O. Herridge, who had been quietly sharpening a knife on a stone just beneath the bridge, raised his head questioningly, his calm features immediately alert. He looked up at Rolfe, an unspoken question on his lips.

Rolfe felt a chill at the base of his spine as he met the other man's stare. "Gunfire!" he snapped briefly, and as Herridge jumped up, thrusting the knife in his belt, he reached into the wheelhouse and pressed the small red button. Even as the bell clanged madly throughout the ship, the guns on the fort began to fire.

Rolfe could see their black muzzles swinging across the ramparts before settling on the mystery target, then with a shattering roar, like a giant whiplash, each would fire independently and the heavy shells screamed overhead with the noise of an express train.

Vincent ran to his station on the bridge, his previous shock sweeping back remorselessly, and he felt something new to him, something he couldn't place, but a sensation which drained away his last reserve of calm and outward steadiness.

He nodded jerkily as Chase reported the ship closed up at action stations, not trusting himself to speak. As the guns bellowed again, he winced, biting his lip hard to prevent himself from ducking his head beneath the breast-high plating.

He glanced sideways at Rolfe who was slowly and methodically filling his pipe. The sight of his firm, grim face and the strong fingers pressing home the tobacco did a lot to steady Vincent, but he leaned heavily against the rail, not trusting the strength of his legs.

Rolfe watched him through the smoke of his pipe, sensing the change that had come over Vincent since his return on board. He could sympathize with him, remembering only too well how he had reacted to gunfire when he was first stricken by its ear-shattering roar, so many years ago it seemed now. He dropped his lighter into his pocket, shutting off that train of thought. Sympathy was useless now. "Vincent!" he barked, "are the passengers secure?"

Vincent stared dazedly, "I'm not sure sir. I—I think——"

"It was your job! Now jump about, man! I want all of them taken below to the storerooms, at once!"

Vincent staggered out on to the open wing of the bridge, flinching as another salvo crashed out, as if he expected to be shot down in his tracks.

Rolfe watched him go, thinking of the dark, airless store-rooms, which were in the actual hull of the gunboat, just above the keel. On this ship, they were about the only part beneath the waterline, and even then his passengers would have to lie down, there was insufficient room to stand!

He forgot them immediately, as his glasses followed the broad line of advancing fishing boats, scattered across the dappled sea like so many insects. They were much nearer, and from their odd manœuvring, it appeared as if some of the boats were towing several of their companions. All the dun-coloured sails hung limp and useless, yet they were making some sort of progress towards their haven. He snapped his fingers, of course, some of the boats had engines of a sort and they were helping the less fortunate ones.

Then, almost like little white feathers, he saw the fall of shot from the fort's guns, over and beyond the scurrying boats, kicking up the water in a steady bombardment. Whatever they were firing at much be pretty low in the sea, he thought.

He pounded the teak rail impatiently gripping his pipe stem until his teeth ached, cursing himself with cold, concentrated rage for not bringing Judith aboard earlier. This bombardment might delay matters, it might even—he turned sharply, as Fallow heaved himself down from the gun platform above the bridge. "Well?" He studied the fat, sweaty face, wondering how the man was reacting to this new menace.

"I put a look-out aloft, sir!" Fallow was breathless, but apart from that, he looked little different from usual. "'E can see the target quite well now!" He gulped, "Two biggish landing craft!"

Rolfe digested the information, vaguely aware that Vincent was back in his position, staring woodenly out of the window.

"Right. I'll come up with you!"

Rolfe ran lightly up the ladder, noting with satisfaction that Herridge and a few hands were removing the last of the deck awnings. From beneath his feet he heard the metallic clang of steel shutters, as the stewards moved through the ship, closing up all scuttles and ports. The quaint, antiquated gunboat, cleared for action as she now was, took on a bare but purposeful appearance.

Chase crouched amongst his gun's crew, his cap pulled over his eyes.

"What's the range, Chief? Of the target?" Rolfe's voice was sharp and impatient.

"Comin' on six thousand yards, sir! Target's zig-zagging at fairly 'igh speed, an' as far as I can judge, is avoiding the shots from the fort!"

Rolfe climbed up on to the gunlayer's seat, cursing the gunboat's ancient rangefinder. She had not been designed for this sort of thing. His binoculars, about twenty-five feet above the waterline, wavered, and then settled on the long, low shapes of the newcomers. Powerful craft they appeared, with squat bridges at the rearmost ends. Occasionally an orange flash whipped out from the long, flat decks, and seconds later he heard the sullen bark of their guns.

Appeared to be a single mounting on each craft, probably quite powerful, too, he considered, hardly enough to attack the island, but good enough to finish off the fishing fleet. The fort's rapid rate of fire, however, seemed to remove this possibility, he thought, a sigh of relief rising as the fishing fleet grew larger and larger, their uneven shapes taking on a firmer outline.

Between the wooden boats and the sinister shapes of the landing craft a wall of shell splashes crept protectively from side to side.

"Looks as if they're makin' for the 'arbour!" exclaimed Fallow, his eyes watering. "None of 'em's likely to try for the beach, I shouldn't think; it's a bit bare like."

Rolfe nodded in agreement. "We'll have to be ready to move a bit sharply! Don't want all the paintwork scratched!" he added wryly.

So the General's faith in his guns was sure-founded. Not one of the fishing boats faltered, and the enemy were being held at arm's length, with not a little danger to themselves either.

He saw Colonel Kyung was standing up in the car, waving his hands with obvious delight, probably enjoying the fact that on the end of the jetty, he was nearer the enemy than anyone. Rolfe smiled dourly, just a pirate at heart, and no doubt the General was not even alarmed!

The fishing boats were larger than the type he had seen around Hong Kong. Long, flush-decked vessels, with a deck house aft, a high sail, and very little else. Practically the whole deck of each craft was filled with a giant hold for the catch. The thud of their ancient diesels could be clearly heard now, as they struggled manfully through the outer reef, the towed craft yawing awkwardly from side to side, as they skimmed round the gleaming rocks.

Must have a good catch, he thought, they're heavy enough anyway.

"Range steady at four thousand yards!" announced Chase with professional interest. "I think they're gettin' too near the guns now!"

It certainly looked as if the two landing craft were having a hard time of it, and were no longer so keen on prolonging the action.

"It's lucky they can't get any nearer," he remarked softly. "I don't think the General's guns would depress much more!" They were firing down at a difficult angle, at what must have registered as point-blank range.

The first group of fishing boats swayed past the breakwater, and drew abreast of the jetty's end. The colonel stood stiffly in his car, as if expecting some sort of salute. Maybe he just wanted to show off Laker's car! Rolfe chuckled at the thought, poor Laker was missing the sight.

An air of relaxed tension broke over the ship, as the big ugly craft crowded across the harbour entrance. The guns still fired out to sea, but the landing craft appeared to be hiding beneath a smoke screen.

Herridge clambered to the bridge and nodded to Chase. "Clever types, eh, Tom? Attacking the fishermen with the setting sun behind them! Must have blinded the General's gunners a bit!"

Chase stared sourly at the nearest fishing boat, which moved slowly towards the jetty towing two more craft. "Not many blokes to 'andle big boats like them, is there?" he observed. "Don't know 'ow they manage wiv their nets or whatever they use!"

Rolfe stopped at the bridge ladder, his foot dangling in space, Chase's last words striking his brain like cold steel. He stared desperately at the milling boats, his mind racing. You fool, he choked, of course! Why didn't you see? Why didn't anyone see? He swung wildly on the gossiping group behind him.

"Herridge, break the cable! At once, d'you hear!" Herridge stared at him blankly, and Rolfe punched his arm savagely. "Quick, man, at the double!"

He saw Vincent's head beneath him, as he leaned tiredly on the bridge rail. "Vincent. Stand-by, both engines!"

Vincent turned as if he had been kicked, his eyes white, but automatically he ran to the wheelhouse, and they heard the clang of engine-room bells.

Herridge and two men had reached the cable now, and Rolfe saw the glint of a steel marlin spike in the man's hand. He fumed wildly, gripping his glasses with desperation.

Fallow was still staring at him, he knew, and probably wondering if the Captain had at last gone stark, raving mad! With steeled eyes he watched the first fishing boat, his heart suddenly pounding. "Number One," he spoke in a low, strained tone, "stand by all guns!"

"But, sir! What, what's 'appenin', sir?"

Rolfe didn't answer, watching the blunt stem of the fishing boat nudge the stone jetty. Two soldiers stood to receive the mooring ropes, and several other people ran along the wall towards them. The wooden hull groaned along the stone, the other boats bumping astern of her. One of the soldiers caught the rope, thrown by a ragged figure in the bows, and then it happened.

The crude canopy across the fish hold was flung back, and a short, stocky figure bounded into the dying sunlight, the last rays gleaming on the barrel of his trained sub-machine gun. His brown uniform, the bright red star on its cap, gave him the appearance of unreality, but as the gun rattled at his hip, and the two soldiers fell writhing on the jetty, unreality was finished. The next instant, a swarm of similar figures poured up from the fish hold, swamping the side of the boat in a seething horde. The other two boats had stopped, and as a bugle blared discordantly in their midst, their decks too were covered with running soldiers, and the air was suddenly filled with the bark and rattle of automatic weapons.

Rolfe watched as if turned to stone. Too late he had realized the Communists' clever ruse. He had watched their invasion fleet enter the harbour unmolested, protected by the guns of their enemies!

There was a sharp clank, followed by a splash. "All gone aft!" Herridge called faintly, his voice hardly carrying above the awful din.

He braced his legs and stood with his arms wrapped around the binnacle and voice pipes.

"Slow astern port, slow ahead starboard! Hard a-port!" His words rang hollowly in the brass pipe.

The jetty was wreathed in blue smoke now and blotted out by the running soldiers. More and more boats bumped alongside, spewing out their deadly cargo. An anonymous brown sea swept down the wall, pitted with a thousand stabbing lights as their guns swept the General's soldiers away like corn before a scythe.

Slowly the gunboat began to pivot round, the painted Union Jacks shining on her grey sides and reflecting the countless orange flashes.

"Half ahead together! Midships!" He didn't listen for the helmsman's voice repeating his orders, he watched the blunt bows of the gunboat with solid concentration, trying to close his ears to all else.

Fallow gasped loudly at his elbow. "Fer God's sake, look at 'em!"

The gunboat steadied and gathered speed, a mounting froth rising at her square stern.

Two seamen stared aghast from the quarterdeck, their eyes wide with horror.

"Get those men off the upper deck!" Fallow suddenly bellowed like a wild bull, his fear forgotten. "Keep yer 'eads down, fer Christ's sake!"

The noise was indescribable and sapped the sanity from their bodies, and the air was filled with a chorus of high-pitched whistling, and the nerve-jarring blare of the bugle.

Alone on the end of the jetty, marooned by the human sea, Colonel Kyung fell from his car and stood uncertainly on the edge above the water. An unheard shot brought him scrabbling to his knees and he screamed again as a bayonet pierced his chest.

The General seemed to have recovered from the initial shock, and a withering fire was being returned from the cliffs, cutting through the packed infantry with terrible results.

Rolfe tore his eyes away, as two fishing boats swung clumsily towards the *Wagtail*, their decks filling with soldiers, even as he watched. The bayonets glittered and without warning, a spray of bullets pattered and rang along the bridge plating below Rolfe's feet. He felt naked and defenceless on his open platform, but he gritted his teeth, the sweat cold on his back.

"Can we return fire?" Fallow dropped heavily on one knee. "Can we, sir?"

Rolfe watched the narrowing gap between the vessels. "No!" he spat. "But keep down, all of you!" He lowered his lips to the voice pipe, "Make a signal!" he shouted hoarsely, "to Admiralty! Operation commenced at . . ." He ducked involuntarily as something whined hotly past his cheek. "Give the time. And say that Communist invasion has started! Got that?" A frightened voice quivered up the pipe. "Good! I'll give you another signal when I can! Now hurry up and send that Plain Language!"

Blast the signalman! Let's hope he doesn't lose his head!

He saw the nearest boat cant over as the soldiers swarmed to one side. Their intention was obvious.

He spoke slowly and carefully, imagining Louch in the engine-room, his ear cupped to the pipe, and wondering what the hell was breaking above his head. "Chief, give me all you've got! Emergency!"

Vincent, hanging to the rail, heard the order "Full Ahead", and felt the little ship dig her stern deep into the threshing water. Everything in the bridge was vibrating and rocking as the revolutions mounted, and the spidery engine-room dials crept towards and past the red line of danger.

The first fishing boat saw the danger too late and swung hastily away from the creaming steel bows.

With a jarring crash the gunboat's stem struck the wooden hull, and for a moment the two ships hung together, the grey steel of the gunboat rising up on to the slanting deck, as if to gnaw at the feet of the toppling soldiers. Then the *Wagtail* broke past, scattering timber and decking over her own hull in a deluge of wreckage.

Rolfe watched from his jolting platform, suddenly calm and resigned, handling the gunboat like a battering ram, and swinging her round with all the speed the ancient boilers could manage, to keep the sinking boat between him and the other one, the deck of which still rippled with automatic fire.

A seaman at his side cried out sharply and fell on his back, blood already soaking through his jacket, while from below he heard the ring of steel as the bullets rattled harmlessly off the tough plating.

The smoke suddenly thinned, and as the rocks slid past unnoticed, Rolfe scrambled down to the wheelhouse, his eyes still on the distant shapes of the two waiting landing craft.

The bridge was dark and smelling of smoke and sweat as he groped through the steel shutters.

"Hoist battle ensigns!" he snapped. "If we're going to fight, I don't want any mistakes!"

The sea was dark now, the small waves pitted with shadows as the bottom edge of the sun dipped into the horizon. The *Wagtail*, her scraped bows lifting in a surge of unsuspected power, steamed out of the smoke from the harbour, her funnel streaming out an oily trail behind her.

As she tacked around the last reef, two enormous White Ensigns broke at her stumpy masts and waved defiantly over her pitching deck.

The two dark shapes ahead of her, their outlines uncertain in the red path of the sunk belched fire in unison and almost immediately Rolfe heard the abbreviated whistle and saw two columns of water rise like ghosts on either side of him. He clamped his jaw on the unlit pipe. A straddle with the first shot, he breathed. But they had fired first, that was important to everyone else but the seamen of the *Wagtail*.

Chase gulped excitedly as the gong rang at his side. "Open Fire!" he bawled, and the long six-pounder roared out in answer, the slim barrel jerking back to spew out the empty cylinder on the metal deck. The gunners sweated and chanted quietly as they went through their drill. The breech clanged shut, and as the cross wires of the gunlayer's sight hovered across the squat bridge of the nearest ship, another flash showed their tense faces in stark clarity.

The Oerlikon joined the battle with its high-pitched rattle, and a stream of tracer shells bounced and clawed their way across the shortening range.

The gunboat shuddered and a sharp, metallic bang rocked the bridge. Vincent fell to his knees, his ears ringing with the explosion. He saw Rolfe's mouth moving, but he could hear only the thud of his own heart.

He tried to rise to his feet, but the pent-up fear burst over him like flood water breaking through a dam, and he crouched on the rocking deck, his fingers crooked over the grating on which the helmsman still stood, his feet braced, and his head bent watchfully over the compass. He knew that the gunboat had been hit, but he had no past experience to tell him how bad was the damage. He only knew that if he dared to lift his frightened eyes, he would see the angry tongues of red flame licking hungrily under the wireless room door, and filling the wheelhouse with an unearthly glow. Above all else, came the repeated crash of the six-pounder over his head, and as the gun recoiled on its mounting, it sent a savage tremor straight down the framework of the bridge, as if trying to tear the whole structure from the ship. His eyes smarted painfully from the smoke and the stench of cordite and burning paintwork, and as if in a dream, he saw Herridge drive a long axe through the wireless room door, each blow widening the gap, a window into an inferno. Two Chinese seamen, staggering under the weight of a giant foam extinguisher, brushed against his arched body without a glance, their almond eyes fixed on their objective. As the foam gushed into the shattered door, the stench grew worse, and the helmsman doubled over the wheel, his face contorted with a fit of coughing.

Herridge stood back from the door, tearing off his jacket and mopping the sweat from his naked chest. He felt he could hardly breathe in the air, yet in the steel box of the shuttered wheelhouse, there was little enough for anyone, and he bit his lip, biting back the coughing, which he knew would reduce him to a useless piece of obstruction for the others. He saw Rolfe turning back to the business of handling his ship and was thankful for his trust. The Captain's eyes were slitted against the smoke, but were still calm and unemotional.

The seamen stood back, waiting for orders, and heedless of Vincent's low moan and the sudden renewed firing, Herridge pushed back the blackened door and surveyed the damage.

A shell had struck the side of the superstructure and burst against the interior bulkhead, filling the small steel room with a deluge of white-hot splinters, and setting fire to wood and paintwork in one searing flash.

Herridge slipped and skidded across the foam-slimed deck as a sudden alteration of rudder made the ship heel over, and groped his way to the pile of shattered metal boxes and tubing which represented the remains of the radio equipment. He licked his lips, which were quite dry and cracked, as his eye fell on the bundle of shredded rags and flesh, half of which was crushed beneath the toppled transmitter, and the rest splotched and smeared across the buckled plating. Poor Little, he thought, smashed down at his post without even a second's warning. He turned his eyes to the gaping hole in the side of the cabin, its blackened edges bent inwards like wet cardboard. Fresh air breathed in at him and through the gap he saw the distant flashes of gunfire. He breathed deeply, conscious of the hideous mess behind him, which had once been the spruce little Cockney telegraphist. You bastards! he choked inwardly. I hope you get something for this!

He shut off his mind like a trap and began a careful examination to ensure that there was no more likelihood of fire, or other outside damage.

He leaned on the door supports, the metal still warm under his palms. Rolfe had opened one of the shutters and was watching the dark sea through his glasses. Without turning, he said, "Much damage, Chief?"

"Radio's knocked out, sir! Little's dead!"

Rolfe lowered his glasses momentarily, his face suddenly tired. "Too bad!" Then, as if the matter was dropped, he barked, "Port twenty!" The wheel creaked round and Rolfe watched the bows begin to swing. "Come on, old girl," he whispered softly, "don't let them catch you now!"

As if in answer to his words, they heard Chase yell excitedly from the upper bridge. "A hit! A hit! Take that, you bloody sods!"

Herridge craned over the Captain's shoulder and saw the bright orange glow flickering across the still water. It was blotted out almost immediately by what he took to be the smoke of gunfire, but he heard Rolfe's grunt of satisfaction, "Smoke screen again! They're pulling away!"

A ragged cheer echoed along the darkened decks, and another as the Oerlikon sent a parting stream of shells screaming into the smoke, the tracers following the burning ship like a host of hornets.

Herridge smiled grimly. Good old lady! The Captain felt the same way about her, too, he knew that now.

The cease fire gong rang tinnily, and the ship steadied on a straight course, the telegraph in the engine-room signalling a reduction of speed.

Louch eyed the dials and sighed deeply. "Not a moment too soon!" he muttered. A Chinese stoker grinned vacantly from behind the gleaming rods, as they thrust strongly in their steam-filled beds.

"Pretty big speed?" he shouted.

Louch grinned back, in spite of his tingling nerves. "I'll pretty big you in a minute, you yellow heathen!"

He leaned back against the hot grating, feeling for his cigarettes. The *Wagtail* could still do it, he reflected. He'd have something to wipe the supercilious grins off his mates in the Fleet Canteen when he got back to the base. Them an' their bloody great frigates! He ran his tongue along the edge of the cigarette paper. Them new ships were built of plating as thin as paper. A bout of this sort of caper would have 'em in the dockyard for a year! He cursed as the voice pipe shrilled in his ear.

"Captain here! Well done, Chief! The landing craft have run for it!"

Louch snapped down the cover and pulled out his matches. So that's what we were fighting. From the din I thought we were mixin' it with the whole Chinese navy!

Rolfe watched the steel shutters being lowered and sucked in the clean salt air. It had been short and sharp, but they had come out on top. He smiled bleakly. If the two Communists had known their stuff, they could have made things much worse by keeping well apart, and dividing the *Wagtail*'s scanty armament between them. With their powerful guns and low-lying hulls, they would soon have made a dangerous impression.

During the action they had moved to the north of Santu, and as he swivelled his glasses over the ebony sea he saw the distorted flash of distant weapons glowing eerily through an invisible smoke barrier. A lump rose in his throat, and he had difficulty in preventing his eyes from misting over.

Somewhere back there, Judith and her brother would be waiting in their little hospital. I'll be back for you, Judith, he had told her. Now the sea, and a war, lay between them. He remembered the brown-clad soldiers and their fanatical advance along the jetty. They had seemed so confident and so utterly ruthless that the General and his chessmen became a mockery and a part of the past.

Why had the Communists attacked the gunboat? Why had they been so eager to entangle themselves with another power, when they were already dealing with a complicated operation of their own?

Damn them, he thought wretchedly, what did they matter, or the people he had so clumsily removed from the path of the savage invasion. Judith had been more than a mere promise of happiness for him, and not just an escape. As the island slipped away in the darkness astern, he knew that she, above all, deserved to live and had truly earned the right to be freed from her island prison.

He leaned his head on his arms, his voice muffled. "Steer Oh-nine-oh!"

"Steer Oh-nine-oh, sir!" The helmsman's face was relaxed and passive, his thin features lighted by the dim compass bulb, as he turned the worn spokes in his hands.

The *Wagtail*'s wake curved slowly and she headed into the dusk.

6

THE babble of nervous conversation died away as Vincent stepped over the coaming into the wardroom and he felt seven pairs of eyes watching him questioningly. He blinked dazedly in the sudden, harsh glare of the electric lights and faltered in his stride, as if undecided whether or not to stay, when his whole being cried out for seclusion and quiet.

The stewards were ducking and murmuring over the passengers, passing round steaming mugs of tea and glasses of what looked like rum. Vincent walked to the sideboard, determined to keep his back to their stupid faces as long as possible, if only to delay the flood of questions which he knew would come. He gulped, as he saw his hand shaking madly, trying to steer the neck of the whisky bottle towards a glass. Damn! He breathed fiercely, I must hold on! Got to keep a grip on myself! He drank deeply, keeping his aching head held back, as if to hurry the passage of the neat spirit.

"Hell, man, what's happening now?" Grant's voice behind him made him stiffen, the bottle poised in mid-air. "Are we out of danger yet?"

Laker cleared his throat. "Bloody great crash! What was it? Was the ship badly hit?"

Vincent pivoted his protesting body against the sideboard and made himself face them. "One shell hit us," his voice was thick. "There was a bit of a fire, too!"

Laker sounded querulous. "From the noise you chaps were making I imagined that we were sinkin'!" He glared round at the others. "Not like it was in my day!"

No one answered, but Ursula, her hand poised in the motion of combing her hair, turned her face sympathetically to Vincent.

He avoided her eyes, licking his lips nervously. Did she know? Did she realize that he had cracked? He stared blindly at the bulkhead beyond their heads, seeing again the blazing wireless room, with its ghastly stench of burning. And Lane's distorted face by the car, and his wife, and, and . . . he shut his eyes tightly, hearing Laker's voice continuing, gaining power and vehemence from the drink.

"When I was a young subaltern on the Marne! God, things were *really* hot there! Young fellas today don't seem to have it in 'em!"

Why doesn't someone shut him up? Vincent swallowed hard, tasting the vomit in his throat. He stiffened even more as he heard the sound of something metal being scraped over the deck above his head. God! He nearly screamed. They're gathering up all that's left of Little! The sounds went on relentlessly, and he took two steps to a vacant chair and flopped down heavily.

Ursula pretended a yawn and wandered past him. Her hand casually strayed to his neck and stayed there, firm and cool. "Pretty rough, was it, David?" Her voice was so low that Laker and the others didn't even notice.

He reached up for her fingers, gripping them fiercely. He held his cheek against them, his eyes smarting and his body beginning to shiver.

The door banged back and Fallow lumbered in. He looked slightly dazed and rather pale, but he managed to ignore the curious glances, and he wandered uncertainly around the wardroom, touching the familiar objects as if to reassure himself, He took a cup of tea from the steward, his brown eyes watching Vincent over the rim. He smacked his lips noisily and twitched his bulbous nose with appreciation.

"Drop o'good, that," he murmured, as if to himself. Then, in a sharper tone, "Captain wants you up on the bridge, Vince! You feelin' all right?"

"He's had a rough time of it," began Grant from the corner.

"Really?" Fallow's mouth drooped whimsically. "Well, that's a pity, ain't it?"

Vincent lurched to his feet, looking like death. "What's he want with me now? Can't I have a minute's rest?" His voice trailed away like that of a small rebuked child. He jammed on his cap and stumbled for the door.

Fallow breathed deeply and eyed the others keenly. "Pretty rough down in the old bilges, eh? Bet you was glad to get up an' smell the fresh air agin."

156

Laker snorted and stared at him contemptuously. "I'd have liked to see just what *was* goin' on up top, I can tell you!" There was almost an accusation in his voice.

Fallow studied him sadly, "Nobody does nothing to please you, an' that's a fact!" He kept his face straight, but he felt like skipping, or getting drunk! They were going home! They were out, and clear! The battle had left him breathless, but otherwise unmoved. He had seen too much suffering and pain in the navy to let one more little skirmish bother him. His only fear had been when he saw the troops swarming from the innocent-looking boats. Then he had felt naked fear clutching at his insides, for it was at that moment that he thought his chance of getting away had vanished for good. But, thanks to the Captain, the gunboat was thrashing her way round the north-west end of the island, and in a few hours they would be steadying on their homeward course. He felt a tremor of his old misery, as he heard Laker mutter. "Damned rankers! Never could make 'em into gentlemen and never will!"

Ursula was at his side and he frowned defensively. "I'm worried about David," she began, "I think he's sick."

No guts, you mean! he thought, but he forced a smile. "'E'll be fit enough soon, miss! Gets 'em all like that at first." He knew inwardly that Vincent would never be the same again. He stifled the chuckle—God, anything'd be an improvement on the old Vince!

She bit her lip uncomfortably. "I'm sorry about what I said to you yesterday," her voice shook. "I was a stupid clot! I've learned a lot since then!"

Fallow smiled slowly. Was it only yesterday, he marvelled? The car dashing through the night, the child, and the hospital. He gulped suddenly. "Gawd! The 'ospital! The Doctor an' 'is sister!" He stared awkwardly at the girl. "I'd forgotten about them!"

She nodded. "They'll be safe, I expect," she said vaguely. "Daddy said that Felton's one of them! A dyed-in-the-wool Communist!"

Fallow eyed her father narrowly. "Beggin' yer pardon, miss, but I don't reckon your Dad's much of a judge of character!"

Mrs. Laker sat bolt upright, her brittle face pallid under the lights. "What's that? The engines have stopped!"

Laker put his feet up on the table and eyed Fallow coolly. "I expect the Captain's having a rest!" He kept his small eyes fixed on the Lieutenant's face. "From what I've heard about him, I should say he's going to need one!" He laughed harshly.

Ursula stepped towards him, "Daddy, please! You don't know what you're saying!" She stared at him angrily.

Fallow's face was hard. "Yes, the engines 'ave stopped! Would you like to 'ear something?" And without waiting for an answer, he jerked the door open and switched off the lights.

"What the devil!" began Laker, in an annoyed but startled voice, but the others hissed him to silence.

A pale shaft of moonlight rippled across the heaving water and cast weird shadows on the deck outside the wardroom door. There was the gentle slap of water against the motionless hull, and the occasional creak of rigging and tackle.

Above it all, clear and firm, they heard Rolfe's voice reading, as if from a great distance.

"We commend unto Thy hands of mercy, most merciful Father, the soul of this our brother departed, and we commit his body to the deep. . . ."

There was a pause, followed by a slithering sound and a splash.

Rolfe's voice continued, but Fallow slammed the door and switched on the lights. He glared round at each one in turn, reading the shocked surprise in their faces.

Mrs. Grant stammered, her hands twitching at her throat, "We didn't realize anyone had been, had been——" she faltered, and her voice died away.

"Killed?" Fallow added brutally. "No, you didn't realize, any of yer. 'Cause you was all too busy feelin' sorry fer yerselves and bein' 'eroes!" He stuck out his jaw threateningly. "That poor kid the Captain's just buried 'ad more guts than all you lot lumped together, an' that's tellin' yer!" He stared down at Laker. "Well, ain't you got nothin' to say fer once? Why not tell us what you was doin' while that kid was bein' shot to bleedin' bits!" He knew he was getting out of control, but he didn't care. All the pent-up anger at these petty people, with their toffee-nosed ideas seemed to overwhelm him. Laker shrank away from him, his mouth slack. They're all scared of me, he thought suddenly, think I've gone nuts! Well, perhaps I 'ave, but it was good to let off steam!

Bells jangled and the throb of the engines continued their steady beat.

Rolfe looked grey with fatigue and there was dirt and grease on his jacket. His mouth was tight and Fallow wondered if he had heard his outburst.

Rolfe stared at his passengers coldly, with a detached, clinical interest. "All well, Number One?"

The faces turned from the Captain back to Fallow, wondering if he was going to continue with his attack.

"All well, sir." Fallow cleared his throat. "Pity about the lad, sir?"

"Yes."

He seemed to be trying to make up his mind about something, and when he spoke, Fallow had the impression that he was by-passing the main issue. There was something else which was gnawing at the Captain's mind.

"You know by now that the invasion got under way just as we were leaving. We were engaged by two Communist landing craft, although this ship is clearly marked, and we didn't fire back until they attacked us first." He shrugged wearily. "However, the niceties of neutral law and acts of war are matters for the politicians. The fact is, we gave them a bloody nose and they made off! We had one hit on the ship and we received two casualties, one of whom was killed. Unfortunately, our radio is completely written off, and we cannot send or receive signals. I informed my superiors that I had commenced the evacuation and that the island had been attacked. That was all! So as far as the Admiral is concerned we are on our way home."

"Won't they think it's queer if you don't keep in touch with them?" Ursula's green eyes watched him softly.

Rolfe shook his head shortly. "I should normally observe radio silence once the job has started, and while we were nearer the Chinese coast than our base. Secrecy is the main item here, because now that we are away from Santu, we don't want to start pouring out signals to all and sundry when, by the time we

159

get back, we may find that the situation in Santu is no different from when we left! Now, there's another matter which I wanted to put before you."

Here it comes, thought Fallow, watchfully.

"As you now fully understand," he dropped a glance on Laker's sullen face, "my job was to carry out a complete evacuation."

"And damned well you did it, too," began Grant, unexpectedly. Rolfe brushed his words aside. "I did not get the Feltons away! I failed in that respect!"

Fallow pouted worriedly, so that was what was driving him! The sharp lines round Rolfe's mouth were proof of his unsettled mind.

"Well, I don't see that should concern us!" Laker blurted, but fell silent again as the grey eyes pierced him.

"I said I would go back for them, and go back I shall!" Rolfe ended quietly.

There was a chorus of cries and wild protests. Everyone seemed to be appealing to Rolfe at once.

He raised his hand sharply. "That'll do! I think I understand your feelings! And that is why I decided to consult you!"

Grant jumped to his feet, his pipe falling unnoticed to the deck. "What exactly d'you have in mind, Captain?"

"I had hoped I might be able to contact some of the General's men, if they are still fighting, that is, and perhaps find a way to contact the Feltons and so bring them out."

Laker sprang up, his face contorted. "Are you mad, all of you? Here we are, within sight of safety, and this fellow wants to push us all back into danger! We've seen the sort of people these Communists are, yet the Captain wants to risk the ship, and our lives, just for the sake of a couple of worthless throw-outs, who are probably drinking rice wine with the Reds right now!" He glared round wildly. "Think of the women! Are we going to throw them right back into that vile mess?"

Rolfe watched him dispassionately. "Very well! Your loyalty and courage touches me deeply!" His voice was bitter.

Masters flushed hotly. "I agree with Mr. Laker, Captain," he mumbled and reached out for his wife's hand. "I, I mean, we can't afford to take the risk, can we?"

160

There was an uneasy mutter of agreement and they avoided Rolfe's cold eyes.

"I see. Thank you!" He glanced at Fallow's apprehensive face. "Come to the bridge, Number One. I have some orders for you!" He turned on his heel, leaving the wardroom strangely quiet.

They climbed to the bridge, where Vincent paced the deck in short, nervous strides.

"What're you goin' to do, sir? I mean, are you really goin' back?"

"I am. But I shall be going alone!"

"What?" Fallow stared at him, aghast. "Alone, sir?"

Rolfe leaned heavily across the chart and tapped it with the brass dividers.

"I've been having a look at the east coast of Santu. There's a little cove tucked in the cliffs just there, look!"

Fallow breathed heavily, his mind awhirl with this sudden threat of disaster. "Not enough water there, by the look of it, sir. An' all them rocks, too!"

"I know," Rolfe sounded distant. "I want to be rowed as far as the rocks in the sampan, and I'll swim the rest!"

Fallow gulped. The Captain had had it all planned before he came to the wardroom. He had known that nobody would have guts enough to back him up with his first idea. That included me, he thought miserably.

"'Ow'll you get back, sir?" he asked in a small voice.

The brass dividers moved to the bottom of the island, to the small 'dot' at the foot of the question mark. "If I'm successful I shall make my way there."

" 'Ow shall we know, sir?"

Rolfe smiled to himself. "I'll give myself twenty-four hours. If you stand off the island tomorrow night at about midnight, I'll signal to you. If I'm not there by then, if I'm delayed or something, you make straight for Hong Kong! You'll contact an American patrol about a hundred miles to the south, anyway, so you'll be quite safe."

"What'll happen to you then, sir?" Fallow lowered his eyes.

"I'll try to steal a boat, or just wait for another opportunity!"

He straightened his back. "Anyway, that's not your worry, Number One! I'll write out a set of orders for you and make the necessary entry in the log, you'll have nothing to worry about!"

"But, sir!" Fallow floundered, seeking the right words. "If you're left behind, they'll say you deserted!"

Rolfe laughed bitterly. "If I fail on this, I don't think I shall care much about that! Now carry on with your duties and call me when we're abeam of that cove. It should be in about three hours' time. I have a few things to do yet!"

Fallow watched him go, his mind suddenly blank.

.   .   .   .   .

Rolfe stood up and switched off the lamp at his desk. He eased open one of the steel shutters and allowed some of the cool air to seep into the darkened, stuffy cabin. On the desk lay the results of his hurried preparations for quitting his ship. A sealed letter for the Admiral, and additional orders for Fallow. As he groped across to his sleeping-cabin he found the time to marvel at his feeling of preoccupied calm and icy determination. The magnitude and gravity of his proposed action seemed small by comparison with his sudden eagerness to start on his journey. The doubtful prospect of success or even survival left him strangely unmoved.

He wrenched open the door of his wardrobe, his fingers brushing against the neat, swaying rank of uniforms. The stiff gold lace on the sleeves, an open record of his achievement and work, seemed unimportant and useless, and impatiently he jerked out a set of plain khaki drill shirt and trousers. He dressed quickly and pulled on a pair of rubber deck shoes, then, making sure that he carried neither papers nor any mark of rank, he made his way to the table, his hand touching the smooth, cold surface of the heavy Service revolver. He tested the weight in his hand. It was a pity the ship didn't carry anything lighter. Still, it seemed doubtful if he would have the opportunity of using it. He thrust it in his belt, wondering what action the salt water would have on the gun.

He sensed that Chao had padded in behind him.

"Captain-sir? You not really going ashore?" The voice sounded plaintive.

"I'm afraid it has to be, Chao. There's no other way!"

Chao was silent for a while, but Rolfe could sense him watching his movements in the darkness. He closed the shutter again and switched on the small reading lamp. The boy stood blinking at him, his face wrinkled with worry.

Rolfe sat on the desk, impatiently glancing at his watch. His eye fell on the small leather case by his side. He opened it slowly and stared at the medal with its faded ribbon.

"Captain-sir? You take me with you?"

He ruffled the boy's spiky hair affectionately. "No, I'm getting into enough trouble as it is!" He snapped the box shut, and laid it on the desk.

I'm coming for you. The words repeated again and again. He tried to picture her face, but he could only remember her huge eyes and her soft, quiet voice. He took a last glance round the cabin. I shall probably never see it again, he pondered, but better to go this way than to fritter my life away in misery. He opened the door, ignoring the boarded-up radio room and its blackened bulkhead. "So long, Chao! I've put a good word in for you in my letter. You'll get a good billet after this!"

Chao's slanting eyes were wet. "I don't want good billet! I want to serve you!" He clenched his fists desperately.

Rolfe nodded thoughtfully. "I know what you mean. But," he shrugged, "you must remember your duty!" He closed the door, cursing himself. Duty—when have you cared about regulations? He sighed and walked loosely on to the bridge, already feeling a stranger amongst the orderly discipline of those on watch.

"We're runnin' in now, sir!" Fallow whispered ho
"First line of rocks are 'bout a mile on the port bow!"

The moon was now only a faint gleam, but
see the thin line of white breakers twi
distance.

Rolfe watched them and gripped

"Feel all

leaving a dancing trail of phosphorescence in her wake, and then she rolled uneasily silent on the swell.

Rolfe and Fallow climbed down to the deck where the sampan had been lowered to the waterline. At a soft command the boat was slipped from the falls and dropped quietly alongside.

Rolfe sensed that many faces were watching him from the darkened doorways and hatches, and several figures shuffled closer as he moved to the side. Herridge was already in the boat while the oarsmen sat stiffly on the thwarts, their arms folded. It only wants a guard of honour, he thought bleakly, and the scene'll be complete.

Ursula Laker stepped forward from the silent figures, her body wrapped in a bridge coat. "Good luck, Captain!" Her voice was low. "I know why you have to go!" She leaned forward and kissed him on the mouth. "Bring her back safely, we'll be looking for you!" Her tone was marred by the sob in her words.

Rolfe stared round blindly. He could just make out the blob of Louch's head peering over the engine-room hatch, while above, by his precious gun, Chase watched in silence.

He swallowed hard, aware of their loyalty and strange attitude of comradeship which was unique to the navy.

"I'm off then," he said sharply. "Have you got the weight, Number One?"

Fallow smiled, his face split by an automatic answer to the meaningless service jargon. "Aye, aye, sir! I've got it!"

The boat shoved off and Rolfe sat limply in the bows, his back to the fading shape of the *Wagtail*.

The oars creaked in the crutches, and the boat moved steadily the rocks. Rolfe studied the small compass which he had right wrist. No point in swimming round in but I shall have to watch out for those

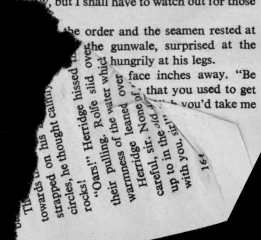

the order and the seamen rested at
the gunwale, surprised at the
hungrily at his legs.
face inches away. "Be
that you used to get
you'd take me

towards
strapped on his calm
circles, he thought calmly
rocks!
"Oars!" Herridge hissed
their pulling. Rolfe slid over
warmness of the water which
Herridge leaned over
careful, sir. None of
up to in the old
with you, sir

164

Rolfe steadied his breathing in readiness. "Keep an eye on things, Chief!" He wanted to say, try and help Fallow, but he lowered himself fully into the water, his palms resting on the smooth woodwork of the boat.

"I will, sir!" Then as a sudden afterthought. "He'll be all right!"

Rolfe thrust himself away and started to swim strongly, but slowly, between the black rocks. Behind him he heard the oars begin to creak, and when once he trod water and looked back, he found that the sea was empty.

The sea bottom was uneven and more treacherous than the warning shown on the chart. Sometimes his toes skimmed the sand, and then almost at once he was swimming in a deep gully, the powerful undertow dragging him down. Once he grazed his knee against a rock, and when, eventually, he began to think he had lost his direction, he saw the towering shape of the cliff right ahead, with its small apron of sand gleaming faintly at the bottom.

He stumbled ashore, alarmed by the apparent noise of the water sloshing from his shoes and the creak of sand under his feet.

Warily he stared round, his eyes falling on a broken rock pathway which started up the sheer face of the cliff, and then faded out in a series of jagged landfalls. It was the only way up, he decided, but its very appearance of desertion and decay made him feel confident of its being left alone by the Communists, or anyone else for that matter.

The silence, but for the gentle caress of the sea against the beach, made him feel completely alone and empty inside. It would be quite easy to panic now. I'd better get started, he thought grimly, and with slow caution, the beach grew smaller steep path. He tried not to look down, his fingers selecting his handholds. and more indistinct, and edged his way downwards. He gritted A piece of stone against the rock, his heart pounded, waiting for a shout from his teeth as he swore angrily, and a sleeping gull in his teeth his chin tucked into his chest, as loose stones

165

and sand pattered across his face, and his fingers sore and stiff from exertion. A hump of rock jutted temptingly as a final hold, which as far as he could tell, would take him to the top of the cliff. He reached out to the full extent of his arm, feeling the sand slipping under his toes. He breathed fiercely and flung himself sideways, his hand snapping at the rock like a limpet. For a moment, something held him pinioned, his waist was tugged obstinately backwards. He gasped—the revolver, it had caught. As he wriggled to free himself, he felt his belt slacken and then, below his straddled legs, the gun clattered and bounced into the darkness. He scrambled upright on the edge of the cliff. He had made it! He tensed, his nerves tight. He thought he heard a movement somewhere on the cliffs, but as he listened, his breathing slowly returned to normal. All the same, he thought, I'll have to be careful. It's quite likely that some people will be about.

From his new position the plateau opened up at his feet, and from behind the distant hills he heard the sporadic rattle of rifle shots and the occasional yammer of a heavy machine-gun. So it was still in the balance! The Communists were not finding it such an easy victory.

He consulted the compass. According to the chart, which he had memorized with grim determination, the island was only about four miles wide at this point. Once he got across the hills he would be overlooking the fishing village, and he would be able to by-pass the town and the fort.

He followed the cliff edge until he could see a break through the tangled mass of scrub and broken boulders, and then he struck purposefully inland, his rubber shoes slipping and stubbing against the rough surfaces. He found that he was on the extreme end of Laker's he could see the wide and even by the uncertain moonlight he black gashes of irrigation sweeping across the plateau and the of tangled, unclaimed land. The estate halted at the barrier forces for a fresh assault on its. Laker had been gathering his

Occasionally, on a hesitant to enlarge his property. burnt timber and a few sparks still out the smell of extent of Laker's fire.

Fool, he thought, as he stepped careful to mark the

nk,

"I'm afraid it has to be, Chao. There's no other way!"

Chao was silent for a while, but Rolfe could sense him watching his movements in the darkness. He closed the shutter again and switched on the small reading lamp. The boy stood blinking at him, his face wrinkled with worry.

Rolfe sat on the desk, impatiently glancing at his watch. His eye fell on the small leather case by his side. He opened it slowly and stared at the medal with its faded ribbon.

"Captain-sir? You take me with you?"

He ruffled the boy's spiky hair affectionately. "No, I'm getting into enough trouble as it is!" He snapped the box shut, and laid it on the desk.

I'm coming for you. The words repeated again and again. He tried to picture her face, but he could only remember her huge eyes and her soft, quiet voice. He took a last glance round the cabin. I shall probably never see it again, he pondered, but better to go this way than to fritter my life away in misery. He opened the door, ignoring the boarded-up radio room and its blackened bulkhead. "So long, Chao! I've put a good word in for you in my letter. You'll get a good billet after this!"

Chao's slanting eyes were wet. "I don't want good billet! I want to serve you!" He clenched his fists desperately.

Rolfe nodded thoughtfully. "I know what you mean. But," he shrugged, "you must remember your duty!" He closed the door, cursing himself. Duty—when have you cared about regulations? He sighed and walked loosely on to the bridge, already feeling a stranger amongst the orderly discipline of those on watch.

"We're runnin' in now, sir!" Fallow whispered hoarsely. "First line of rocks are 'bout a mile on the port bow!"

The moon was now only a faint gleam, but they could clearly see the thin line of white breakers twisting and writhing in the distance.

Rolfe watched them and gripped Fallow's arm in the darkness. "Feel all right, Number One? Not worried, are you?"

"I can manage the ship, sir. It's you I'm worried about!"

Herridge's head rose above the side of the bridge. "Boat's lowered, sir! Ready to slip!"

The telegraphs clanged and the throb of engines died away. For a while the darkened gunboat slid through the black water, leaving a dancing trail of phosphorescence in her wake, and then she rolled uneasily silent on the swell.

Rolfe and Fallow climbed down to the deck where the sampan had been lowered to the waterline. At a soft command the boat was slipped from the falls and dropped quietly alongside.

Rolfe sensed that many faces were watching him from the darkened doorways and hatches, and several figures shuffled closer as he moved to the side. Herridge was already in the boat while the oarsmen sat stiffly on the thwarts, their arms folded. It only wants a guard of honour, he thought bleakly, and the scene'll be complete.

Ursula Laker stepped forward from the silent figures, her body wrapped in a bridge coat. "Good luck, Captain!" Her voice was low. "I know why you have to go!" She leaned forward and kissed him on the mouth. "Bring her back safely, we'll be looking for you!" Her tone was marred by the sob in her words.

Rolfe stared round blindly. He could just make out the blob of Louch's head peering over the engine-room hatch, while above, by his precious gun, Chase watched in silence.

He swallowed hard, aware of their loyalty and strange attitude of comradeship which was unique to the navy.

"I'm off then," he said sharply. "Have you got the weight, Number One?"

Fallow smiled, his face split by an automatic answer to the meaningless service jargon. "Aye, aye, sir! I've got it!"

The boat shoved off and Rolfe sat limply in the bows, his back to the fading shape of the *Wagtail*.

The oars creaked in the crutches, and the boat moved steadily towards the rocks. Rolfe studied the small compass which he had strapped on his right wrist. No point in swimming round in circles, he thought calmly, but I shall have to watch out for those rocks!

"Oars!" Herridge hissed the order and the seamen rested at their pulling. Rolfe slid over the gunwale, surprised at the warmness of the water which pulled hungrily at his legs.

Herridge leaned over the side, his face inches away. "Be careful, sir. None of those madcap doings that you used to get up to in the old days!" His teeth gleamed. "Wish you'd take me with you, sir!"

Rolfe steadied his breathing in readiness. "Keep an eye on things, Chief!" He wanted to say, try and help Fallow, but he lowered himself fully into the water, his palms resting on the smooth woodwork of the boat.

"I will, sir!" Then as a sudden afterthought. "He'll be all right!"

Rolfe thrust himself away and started to swim strongly, but slowly, between the black rocks. Behind him he heard the oars begin to creak, and when once he trod water and looked back, he found that the sea was empty.

The sea bottom was uneven and more treacherous than the warning shown on the chart. Sometimes his toes skimmed the sand, and then almost at once he was swimming in a deep gully, the powerful undertow dragging him down. Once he grazed his knee against a rock, and when, eventually, he began to think he had lost his direction, he saw the towering shape of the cliff right ahead, with its small apron of sand gleaming faintly at the bottom.

He stumbled ashore, alarmed by the apparent noise of the water sloshing from his shoes and the creak of sand under his feet.

Warily he stared round, his eyes falling on a broken rock pathway which started up the sheer face of the cliff, and then faded out in a series of jagged landfalls. It was the only way up, he decided, but its very appearance of desertion and decay made him feel confident of its being left alone by the Communists, or anyone else for that matter.

The silence, but for the gentle caress of the sea against the beach, made him feel completely alone and empty inside. It would be quite easy to panic now. I'd better get started, he thought grimly, and with slow caution he groped his way up the steep path. He tried not to look down as the beach grew smaller and more indistinct, and concentrated on selecting his handholds. A piece of stone crumbled from under his fingers and he gritted his teeth as it rattled and banged its way downwards. He waited, his tense body crucified against the rock, waiting for a shout from above, or a shot. Only his heart pounded, and a sleeping gull in a nearby cleft mewed angrily.

Up and up, his chin tucked into his chest, as loose stones

165

and sand pattered across his face, and his fingers sore and stiff from exertion. A hump of rock jutted temptingly as a final hold, which as far as he could tell, would take him to the top of the cliff. He reached out to the full extent of his arm, feeling the sand slipping under his toes. He breathed fiercely and flung himself sideways, his hand snapping at the rock like a limpet. For a moment, something held him pinioned, his waist was tugged obstinately backwards. He gasped—the revolver, it had caught. As he wriggled to free himself, he felt his belt slacken and then, below his straddled legs, the gun clattered and bounced into the darkness. He scrambled upright on the edge of the cliff. He had made it! He tensed, his nerves tight. He thought he heard a movement somewhere on the cliffs, but as he listened, his breathing slowly returned to normal. All the same, he thought, I'll have to be careful. It's quite likely that some people will be about.

From his new position the plateau opened up at his feet, and from behind the distant hills he heard the sporadic rattle of rifle shots and the occasional yammer of a heavy machine-gun. So it was still in the balance! The Communists were not finding it such an easy victory.

He consulted the compass. According to the chart, which he had memorized with grim determination, the island was only about four miles wide at this point. Once he got across the hills he would be overlooking the fishing village, and he would be able to by-pass the town and the fort.

He followed the cliff edge until he could see a break through the tangled mass of scrub and broken boulders, and then he struck purposefully inland, his rubber shoes slipping and stubbing against the rough surfaces. He found that he was on the extreme end of Laker's estate, and even by the uncertain moonlight he could see the wide fields sweeping across the plateau and the black gashes of irrigation ditches. The estate halted at the barrier of tangled, unclaimed land, as if Laker had been gathering his forces for a fresh assault on the wilderness to enlarge his property.

Occasionally, on a hesitant breeze, he picked out the smell of burnt timber and a few sparks still drifted skywards to mark the extent of Laker's fire.

Fool, he thought, as he stepped carefully over a fallen trunk, what a nice piece of propaganda the Communists would make out of it. The retreating imperialists making a last effort to deprive the workers of their rights!

He squinted at the luminous dial of the compass, and as he halted, he felt his damp clothes cold against his skin. It was strange to feel cool again.

It was darker now, as the trees began to close in on him, and as his feet trod on fallen, rotting twigs and branches, the noise seemed incredibly loud. Each time he stopped to listen, the night was full of strange, unaccountable sounds. The muffled squeak of some disturbed creature or bird, and the distant ripple of a tiny stream from the hills. The trees and bushes were alive with rustlings and creaks which might have meant anything, and he began to regret, even more, the loss of the revolver.

The journey seemed endless, but as the ground began to slope beneath him, he found that the trees were thinning and that he had reached the sun-dried side of the first hill.

Another burst of machine-gun fire rang out quite close to his left, and instinctively he flung himself flat, his cheek against the rough stubble and earth. The firing sparked off another brief exchange of shots which echoed around the hills and then faded out into an uneasy silence. Rolfe raised himself to his knees and half-crouching, began to pick his way up the hill. He thanked God for the night's protection, knowing that under the glare of the sun this hill would have provided no cover at all.

A clump of trees, huddled protectively together in a dip on the shoulder of the hill, loomed unexpectedly in front of him and as he quickened his pace, he heard the scrape of metal, and then, as he dropped to the ground, his breath stilled in his throat, he heard a low cough. He waited, spreadeagled in the dirt, his ears straining into the darkness. There was something moving now and he caught the murmur of voices and the sounds of metal equipment. Then, as his heart pounded against the ground, he felt, rather than heard, the thud of boots approaching him.

He twisted his head towards the sounds, and as he watched, he saw the dim shapes of two figures strolling casually around the edge of the trees. They were chatting quietly in a flat, sing-song tone, and the moon touched the short barrels of their sub-machine-guns.

Nearer and nearer, and then they stopped, their feet twisting absently in the dust. Then they started to move towards his position. They were only a few yards away now and wouldn't fail to see him unless they were blind.

Rolfe gathered his strength, his eyes on the distant cover. They were sentries, he had been stupid to be so careless! He couldn't tell what uniform they were wearing, but it hardly mattered, as either side would shoot on sight, under the circumstances.

Almost without realizing it, he found he was on his feet, running like a madman up the slope. He heard the gasp of alarm and the snick of metal. As he twisted and turned around the first trees he saw their trunks suddenly glitter with reflected light, and the night was split in two by the rattle of shots behind him. With his breath choking and sobbing with effort, he flung himself on, regardless of the clawing branches, and conscious only of the whine and whistle about him, and the vicious slap of bullets against wood as they tore and thudded into the trees.

There was a shout from another direction, it seemed as if it was right ahead, and he swerved violently, his arm grazing against a broken stump. He must have shown himself, for the two guns opened up again with renewed hate. Rat-tat-tat-tat! The earth jumped in little spurts at his feet, and splinters rained down on his head. He halted, his back pressed against some thick branches, his chest heaving painfully. Immediately the firing stopped, too, and he heard the crash of boots stumbling through the undergrowth. There were several more of them now. He swore desperately, if only he could get over the brow of the hill, away from the moon. He might stand a chance then. He stiffened, the hair rising on his neck. He could hear the sound of breathing very close to him, and the very soft creak of leather. He waited, holding in his breath, until little lights danced before his eyes. An age passed, and then, very slowly, and with infinite care, the bushes by his elbow were parted, moved apart by a gleaming bayonet. Fascinated, he watched the rifle appear, and as the barrel wavered, a booted foot rose carefully over the scrub, and as it took the pressure of the ground, the man slid into view.

He was a thick-set, powerful man, his brown uniform criss-crossed by bandoliers of gleaming ammunition, and his movements controlled by all the instinct and training of a professional soldier.

Rolfe felt the dry leaves rustling his cheek, and he gripped the branch at his back, waiting for the exclamation, and the thrust of that cruel bayonet.

The soldier moved slowly forward, his head cocked for the least sound, a finger curled round the trigger. At that moment there was a savage burst of firing from another direction and more confused shouting. The soldier muttered irritably and dashed off in the direction of the new outbreak, his bayonet scabbard dragging coldly across Rolfe's thigh. He listened unbelievingly to the fading sounds, wondering what chance sound or error had drawn the pursuit in the opposite direction. He saw a ripple of flashes at the foot of the hill, and heard the whip of bullets singing across the clearing. Then there was silence, and with the sweat cold on his face, Rolfe scrambled up the last few yards to the summit and, as the sea glittered welcomingly before him, he ran recklessly down the slope, until a loose stone brought him crashing down, the wind knocked out of his lungs, and then he lay panting, and realizing for the first time just how lucky he had been.

They will come back eventually, he thought, as he began to recover from the shock, it's time to move and keep going!

The going was easier now, and with the black mound behind him he was able to watch his approaching objective, like a giant map.

He lost all sense of time as he twisted and turned through little gullies, and beneath towering humps of rock, and his brain became so tired with concentration that he had to force himself to stop and listen at each piece of open ground, and when he crossed the faint hill tracks, which seemed to run in every direction.

As he drew nearer to the sea he caught an occasional glimpse of the fort, its high, rugged outline picked out by the distant flash of automatic fire and the deep thud of grenades.

Rolfe wondered if all the General's men were in the fort now, or whether some of them were still fighting from the other prepared positions. There seemed little point for the Communist sentries, unless there were other forces abroad.

His heart began to beat faster as he saw the white ribbon of the coast road and heard the soft murmur of the sea.

Not far now to the hospital. And then—and then, what? He halted by the road, his face twisted into a frown. How would he get them to the other end of Santu? And then, how could they cross the water to the little island where they might be safe? He shook himself angrily, time enough to worry about that when you're on your way back here!

By keeping to the edge of the road he was able to study the fishing village for some time, but he was quite unable to see any sign of life, or, for that matter, any sign of damage or fighting. A tinge of hope moved in his breast. The attack would have by-passed the town, as he was now doing, and it was still likely that the Communists were too busy to deploy their forces away from the main objectives, at least until the daylight.

Taking a deep breath, he padded across the road to shelter in the deep shadow of the first hut.

He realized then just how unused and untrained he was for this type of behaviour. At sea, in any ship, he could carry out his duties practically without conscious thought, and the more difficult and improbable tasks he had met with equal calmness and confidence. Yet here, in the silent village, the small houses and huts slashed into strange black and white shapes by the moonlight, he felt uneasy and defenceless.

He waited until another burst of firing awakened the echoes, and then he stepped from his shelter and along the narrow lane between the squalid dwellings, his footsteps drowned by the barrage.

The walls seemed to move in on him and he had to duck repeatedly to avoid the dangling nets and the untidy coils of fish line which hung from every roof.

He blundered blindly past a deserted food stall, its cheap earthenware platters scattered in the dust and crackling beneath his feet. The moon was again masked by the buildings and he walked stiffly forward, his arms outstretched like a sleepwalker, and his face tensed for the expected collision from some fresh obstruction.

The firing stopped and, as he waited in the deep doorway of what appeared to be a storehouse, his eyes stretched in an effort to pierce the darkness, he heard the slow step of boots upon the road, accompanied by a soft humming. A pleasant sound, like someone taking a quiet evening stroll in the country before returning home to bed, but singularly out of place here.

But as he listened, Rolfe felt a surge of hope, the tune being hummed was familiar, and even the slow, slouching steps could not be a piece of his imagination.

He trembled with suppressed excitement. Major Ling, he breathed, it had to be! And that meant that here in the village at least, all was well.

Opposite to where he crouched in the doorway was a high white wall, and as the other man crossed in front of it, Rolfe saw the familiar stooped shoulders, the long legs and the strange, shambling gait. It was like a dim shadow, immediately swallowed up by the darkness as soon as it had passed the white wall. The shape moved carelessly and with a confidence born of familiarity with this very street.

Rolfe stepped out into the road. "Ling? Major Ling? Is that you?"

The humming stopped and he heard the scrape of feet as the man turned round with a sharp intake of breath.

For one terrible moment Rolfe thought he had made a mistake, and half-expected the crash of shots, and the searing shock of bullets hitting his body, but instead, a soft voice called out, "Captain! Well this is a surprise! Where did you come from?"

Rolfe groped his way towards him, impatient to be going to the hospital. "Just swam ashore," he answered, aware of the incredulous sound of his explanation. "I came back here at once!"

"But your ship, Captain! Where is it?" The teeth gleamed eerily.

"Gone! Out to sea!" He shook aside the questions and grabbed Ling's arm impatiently. "The hospital, are they all safe there? I'd like to go there right away, if I can!"

Ling laughed softly. "Certainly, Captain, they are quite safe, and I am on my way there myself. I shall now have the additional pleasure of your company!" He touched Rolfe's arm. "But do not talk. I must be sure to hear my sentries if they call out. I do not wish to be shot by my own men!"

They turned into an even darker alley, which was quite unknown to Rolfe, but as he was about to question Ling's judgement, a sharp challenge rapped out of the darkness. Ling called back some unintelligible words, and taking Rolfe's arm, he guided him between the upended shapes of two wagons, from behind which he could see several prone riflemen. He forgot them at once, as the corrugated iron roof of the hospital rose above him. No wonder he didn't recognize the route, this was the back entrance. Along the bottom edge of the ill-fitting door he saw the hard light of the pressure lamp, and at that moment it was the most welcome sight in the world.

Ling stood back to allow him to enter, and with something like shy excitement, Rolfe opened the door and stepped, half-blinded, into the little room.

His words of welcome died on his lips, and an ice-cold shock stabbed at his heart, until he reeled dazedly on his feet. Facing him across the table was a short, brutal Chinese soldier, his automatic rifle trained on Rolfe's stomach, and his tiny, slitted eyes unwavering in terrible concentration. As he spun round to face Ling, he knew then how miserable was his failure.

Like the little soldier, Major Ling was dressed in the plain brown uniform, with its red stars of Communist China.

Ling eyed him impassively, his shoulder resting against the door, in an attitude of bored detachment. There was nothing slack about the pistol in his fist, or the two soldiers at his back.

He smiled sympathetically. "So sorry you fell into the trap, Captain!"

Rolfe swallowed hard, fighting back the feeling of shame and defeat. "Trap?" he repeated wearily, "what trap?"

"The trap of the night! As you say in your country, 'All cats, look alike in the dark'." He glanced down at his uniform. "And I suggest that if you had seen my change of appearance you would not have hailed me with such a welcome in your voice!" He snapped a brief order, and then smiled apologetically. "A mere formality, Captain. My men are going to search you!"

Rolfe stood helplessly while the two soldiers ran over his clothing, their rough hands jerking at his pockets, as if he were already dead. I might just as well be, he cursed, as he watched the soldiers lay his compass down on the table. What a fool I've been! I've thrown my life away for nothing!

"A compass?" Ling smiled blandly. "A little unusual? But then, you say you swam ashore?" He waited for an explanation, his dark eyes watchful.

Rolfe's brain began to whirl. If he told them about the *Wagtail's* rendezvous, it was as good as signing a death warrant for the ship and everyone in her. "I was in action with two of *your* landing craft," he said slowly, his hatred for this man helping to overcome his feeling of defeat. "I was blown overboard by an explosion, and," he shrugged, "the ship carried on without me. She had no alternative under the circumstances!" It sounded a stupid story, but he stared defiantly at the impassive face, waiting for the challenge.

Ling nodded thoughtfully. "Then you swam ashore? Most interesting, Captain, and very unfortunate for you. However," he continued briskly, "it is a fortune of war, and at the moment, a most helpful solution to one of my problems!"

"You said that the Feltons were safe! What have you done to them?"

As if reading the menace in his eyes, the soldiers moved closer to him, and he became aware of their sickening stench and coarse, brutal features. They were not like the islanders or the Chinese he had seen in Hong Kong. They were the raw material from the mainland, swept up from the vast reserves of the peasant masses for service in the army. Their blank, unintelligent faces showed no interest or feeling, and their hard eyes merely mirrored an almost animal instinct.

"They cannot understand what you are saying, Captain." Ling followed his gaze. "But they make good soldiers. Cheap to run and easy to replace!" He laughed mockingly. "And as for your two friends, I was not lying. They are uncomfortable, perhaps, but quite safe!"

Rolfe clenched his fists. "If you've harmed that girl I'll see that you're paid back, if it's the last thing I ever do!"

Ling slipped his gun into the holster and patted it. "It would be! Now follow me. We have much to do!"

He pushed open the door of the surgery and with a gun at the base of his spine, Rolfe followed him.

Judith Felton and her brother were sitting on the bench at the far side. Their hands were behind them, and even as he stared, Rolfe saw the ends of the rope which pinned them against the supports to the roof. Felton leaned back against the wall, his eyes closed, the distorted side of his face clashing horribly with the other half, which remained still and pale.

Judith sat unmoving on the edge of the bench, her head low, and the mass of gleaming hair falling down across her shoulders. She was still wearing the patched dress, and Rolfe felt his throat tighten, as he saw the stains on the cloth and the bruise on her brown arm. She looked so small and alone that he felt a wave of fury sweeping over him. I'll get her out of this somehow, he swore.

"Visitor for you!" Ling snapped sharply, and Rolfe stepped forward, ignoring the soldiers and turning his back on Ling's amused stare.

Judith hadn't moved, and very gently he put his hand under her chin to tilt her face. "Judith," he whispered, "are you all right?"

For a second her lithe body twisted with a sudden violence to get away from his hand, and then as she looked up at him, her terror-filled eyes widened with amazement and hope, which like a brief flame died away, as she looked over his shoulder at the others. Her dry lips moved, "Justin, you've come back! You came back, just as you promised!" A tear passed down her cheek and she bit her lip cruelly. "Thank you for trying, Justin!"

Felton was watching them without expression or emotion. "So they got you too, eh?" He laughed harshly. "These are my friends! And Ling there has turned out to be one of the people I've been looking up to all these years!"

Ling sat on the edge of the operating table, his head glossy under the swinging lamp.

"That will do! I've a lot to do before the morning, and it will be much easier if you all co-operate!" He eyed each one of them separately. "I am sorry it has to be like this, but I am afraid that we are too busy to be concerned with small, individual problems!"

"What the hell are you talking about?" Rolfe's voice was trembling with fury. "Stop talking in riddles and come to the point!"

Felton strained forward, the rope pulling at his wrists. "He wants me to confess!" His good eye gleamed wildly. "Confess to being a spy for the Western powers!" He lowered his head, suddenly weary. "Me, a spy! After all I've done to help the spread of Communism amongst these people in Santu. Now I'm a spy for the imperialists!" Something like a sob broke from his lips. "The man I've loathed the sight of all these years, suddenly turns out to be the representative of the new China! What a ruddy laugh!" His head jerked back, as without apparently moving from the table Ling reached out and struck him across the mouth.

At that moment Rolfe lunged forward, his hand closing on Ling's wrist while he groped wildly for the pistol in his belt. As they toppled over on to the floor, Rolfe gasped aloud with pain, as a rifle butt struck him savagely in the back. As he twisted round to face his new attacker, the other soldier jumped across his shoulders, forcing him to the floor, with the others on top of him.

For a moment they rolled in a tangled mass of gasping bodies, but as he felt a man's throat between his fingers, another rifle butt crashed down into the pit of his unprotected stomach. A thousand lights exploded in his eyes, and he heard himself cry out in agony. He was still writhing, as they wrenched his hands behind him, and pulled a noose of thin wire over his wrists. Vaguely through the mist of pain he felt them drag him to the opposite wall and secure the wire to a rafter, so that he was forced to stand on tip-toe to prevent his arms from being wrenched from their sockets.

Ling watched him balefully. "Very stupid again, Captain!" Then he turned back to the others, his black eyes noting Judith's expression of horror and pity as she stared across at Rolfe's taut body.

"Now, we can go on." He sounded calm and unruffled again. "It was unfortunate that Mr. Laker and his friends were able to make good their escape. It would have been fitting evidence for the world to see, if we had caught them with their ill-gotten spoils! However, we have the next best thing!" He smiled coldly. "We find that we have the Western collaborator and spy who has made their escape possible right in our midst! Not only that, but the Captain of the imperialist gunboat is also found with him, without his uniform, and hiding in our territory!"

Rolfe ground his jaws together in an effort to still the pain. "No one will believe such tripe!" he gasped.

Ling spun round, his lips curled in a thin smile. "Everyone will believe it! Especially when we produce the written confessions and publish photographs! Oh, yes, Captain, we Chinese are not still in the Green Dragon era!"

"You can't make us sign anything!" Rolfe glared at him, his grey eyes glinting. "That idea failed in Korea, and it's useless to try it here!"

Ling stood up lazily, consulting his watch. "I must go to my office and prepare the statement for signature. That will be something to go on with!"

Felton struggled vainly with his bonds. "I won't sign! My whole life, all my hopes," his words were a meaningless garble, and Rolfe could see he was suffering from a form of shock. "I'll tell the whole world what a filthy impostor you are and what a lying, ruthless government you represent!"

Ling opened the door, smiling without humour. "When I come back you will sign. That, I promise you!" The door closed behind him.

Two of the soldiers followed him out, but the small man with the automatic rifle watched them unblinkingly from his seat in the corner.

"Sorry about this," began Rolfe softly, "I've made a complete muck-up of the whole business!"

The girl eyed him, her face resigned. "I knew that Major Ling was bad! When the soldiers burst in here today and started to attack the injured people in their beds, I knew then that all Brian's hopes were finished!" She shuddered, as the memories came flooding back to her. "It was terrible, I thought I was going mad!" Her voice shook, and Rolfe wanted to get to her, but the wire biting into his wrists reminded of his helplessness.

"Did they touch you?" He kept his gaze steady. "Was there an officer in charge of them?"

She nodded wearily. "They had their orders about us. Now we know why!" Her eyes filled with tears. "Poor little Chu, they took him away and shot him in the road! Right up to the

176

last he thought they were just playing with him. Like all the other villagers, he believed what Brian had told him about the Communists!"

Felton didn't respond to her bitterness, but slumped heavily against the wall, his eyes tightly closed again.

Rolfe could imagine the turmoil in the man's mind, but he avoided looking at him, he had eyes only for the girl. It made his heart ache to see her tired, frightened face, and the unsteady movement of her breathing.

"We will get away from here! We must remember that all the time!" He put all the firmness into his voice that he could find. "Don't forget I've promised to take care of you!"

She raised her face, her mouth quivering. "You did, didn't you? Don't worry, I'll try not to let you down!"

Major Ling entered the room, his face unsmiling and businesslike.

"You've been quick, Major," Rolfe remarked softly, "so it's only to be a short confession!"

Ling muttered under his breath, "It is enough."

Felton laughed. "Of course, you wouldn't by any chance have had them already made out in advance?" There was a sneer in his voice.

Ling was unmoved. "Yours, yes! The Captain's, no! But now they are done! So let us not waste any more time. Who will sign first?"

"What happens to us afterwards?" Rolfe watched the man's eyes for some small sign.

"Afterwards? Who knows? But it is not my concern! My Government will decide that!"

"Well, I'll not do a thing until you find out what's in store for us!" Rolfe began sharply, praying for time and searching for a plan.

"You will, Captain!" Ling snapped an order and the soldier laid down his rifle carefully and shambled obediently to Ling's side.

Here it comes, thought Rolfe coldly, the torture about which he had heard so much in Korea.

It was all like a nightmare, without beginning or end, and even the people about him seemed shadowy and unreal.

He chilled with horror as the soldier stepped jerkily forward, his yellow face intent and hard. He didn't even glance at Rolfe, but walked straight to the girl, and before he had time to realize what was about to happen, he jerked one of her feet off the ground, and as he crouched like a small, deformed animal on the floor he flung her sandal across the room and gripped the small bare foot in his two rough hands. Judith stared at the soldier, her eyes wide with terror, her body shrinking back away from him.

Ling smiled sadly. "You see, Captain, there is no chance for you! I understand that certain parts of the female body are quite tender and susceptible to pain!" As Rolfe strained madly at the wire he continued dreamily, as if repeating a lesson. "In a second or two, this soldier will cut open the sole of her foot!" He nodded sharply, and the crouching figure produced a short, wide-bladed trench knife and laid it against the soft brown skin.

She struggled wildly, but in that grip she was helpless. She turned her eyes desperately to Rolfe. "Don't sign anything! Don't give in!" Her voice was strangled.

Felton watched them, his face contorted with fury. "Don't touch her, you swine! She has had nothing to do with any of this! She's done more for these people than any of you!"

Ling eyed him thoughtfully. "Are you ready to carry out my orders?"

"Yes, yes! Only tell that beast to leave her alone!"

Ling spoke a brief order and the soldier dropped the foot reluctantly, his thick fingers stroking at her ankle. When he stood up, there was something else in his narrow eyes, and his mouth was slack with lust. He shuffled across to Felton and untied the rope, and watched blankly as Felton rubbed weakly at his bruised wrists. Shakily he moved to the table, his eyes unseeing, as Ling, his pistol again in his hand, indicated the long sheet of paper and the pen.

Felton snatched the pen and scrawled his signature across the bottom.

"Aren't you even going to read it?" Ling's voice was silky. "It explains how you have connived with the Captain to remove the bourgeois criminals from our hands, and how you have been a very active agent during your stay in Santu! The other paper which, unless I am very much mistaken, the Captain will willingly sign, explains his part in the conspiracy!" He waited until the soldier had re-tied Felton's hands and had released Rolfe. "I think that whatever happened out at sea, Captain, your ship will certainly not be far away. I suspect that it will be nosing around soon to look for you!" He watched Rolfe sign the paper and laughed shortly. "To think that you crack so easily! And all because of this woman!"

Rolfe writhed inwardly as the soldier slipped the wire over his numb hands. He had brought nothing but disaster and failure with him. Even the ship was in danger now! The ship—he had hardly given her a thought since he left her. It was strange how he had altered.

Ling glanced at the papers, apparently satisfied. "Good! I shall have to leave you for a little while, I'm afraid. I have to find our signals unit." He fixed his hard eyes on Rolfe. "I must inform my superiors that your ship is inside our new territorial waters, Captain! They will no doubt send a suitable vessel to deal with it! That should be fairly easy, as your incompetent government have nothing available, apparently, but that ancient ruin which you have the honour to command!" He crossed to the door, speaking softly to the soldier. "I shall be back! And maybe you will be allowed to watch the final assault on the fort and the destruction of the General's remaining forces!" He slammed the door behind him.

Judith trembled violently, "You shouldn't have done it," she sobbed. "You've thrown everything away for me!"

Rolfe was about to answer when he saw her eyes move to the soldier, her body straining with sudden, unrestrained violence.

The man was staring at her in that same dazed manner, his wide mouth hanging open, to reveal his thick, uneven teeth and lolling tongue. He leaned his rifle against the wall and walked slowly towards her.

"For God's sake!" Felton was struggling wildly. "Can't you stop him?" And he poured out a flood of Chinese at the advancing soldier. It was if he had said nothing, and with a sudden, hungry movement, he seized the girl's shoulders, his fingers digging into her as he pulled her body towards him. She was like a child in his hands, and as Rolfe struggled and cursed, he saw the blunt, dirty fingers itp open the top of her dress, the worn cloth tearing like paper in his powerful grip. Her writhing, sun-burned shoulders and naked arms were half hidden by the panting dwarf as he pulled excitedly at the remains of her dress, while from his throat rumbled a series of grunts punctuated by sounds of anger as he wrestled with the girl's struggling figure.

As her eyes rose above the man's broad shoulders she gasped to Rolfe, "Don't watch. Please don't look!" Her words were choked off short as he pushed her back against the rough wall.

The surgery door opened from the waiting-room, and Rolfe twisted round, his face contorted. "Stop him, for Christ's sake!" His mouth hung open, the frantic words stilled in his throat. It was more like a fearful nightmare than ever, but as he stared, he knew that the small, wet figure with the huge Service revolver gripped in front of him with both hands was his steward, Chao. He didn't know how that could be possible, yet when the room rocked with the savage blast of the gun, and the soldier was flung forward on to the girl's body, an ever-widening stain in the middle of his back, he knew that the impossible was happening.

Chao turned towards him, his face old and determined. A knife appeared in his hand, and with two strokes the wire was slack around Rolfe's wrists and he was running to the girl's side.

He gathered her shivering body in his arms, while Chao released Felton, muttering at the same time, "Quick, Captain-sir! Out through other room, no guards there!"

Then they were running and stumbling through the long waiting-room, while from behind them came the shouts of the two sentries, as they beat on the other door, which Rolfe guessed Major Ling must have locked, or else the dead soldier had done so to keep out his comrades. At the thought of what had nearly happened, Rolfe hugged the girl to his chest, but although she gripped him tightly around the neck, she could still only stare at him from shocked eyes.

They paused outside the hospital, and Rolfe's eyes fastened on the dull shape of a jeep, Ling's, no doubt.

"Quick, get in!" he barked, "I'll drive."

Felton clambered weakly into the back with Chao and the boy reached out to help Rolfe with his limp burden.

Rolfe grunted with satisfaction as he saw the automatic rifle which Felton carried awkwardly in his hands. "Well done, Brian!" he gasped as he slammed the car into gear, but Felton stared uncomprehendingly at the weapon, as if he didn't remember collecting it from the dead soldier. He sighed with relief as the jeep responded to his inexperienced handling and shot, swaying, down the coast road. There was a brief crackle of rifle fire and a bullet ricocheted from the metal bodywork, but the sounds were drowned by the mounting whine of the engine, and the sudden increase of explosions from the direction of the cliffs immediately below the fort.

"How did you get here, Chao?" Rolfe spoke between his clenched teeth as he swung the wheel in his hands.

"I jump overboard and swim after you!" the boy answered simply. "I think maybe you need me!"

Rolfe nodded his head in amazement. Of course, the sounds he had heard as he scaled the cliff. Chao must have just been pulling himself out of the sea. And to think that he had not only swum after him, but he had not had Rolfe's advantage of being carried half-way to the shore by boat!

"I shan't forget this, Chao! You don't know what you've done!"

"Bit of luck you drop your gun when you climb cliff, yes?" Chao grinned cheerfully. "Though it nearly knock off my head!"

The tyres screeched as the jeep rocked round the hairpin bend towards the harbour.

Two or three dark figures ran haphazardly from their path, but whether they were soldiers or fleeing townspeople, Rolfe didn't know.

"Where are we going?" Felton sounded vague.

"Harbour! Only chance! Must get a boat of some sort and get away to the other end of the island, now, before dawn!"

He was thinking of the *Wagtail's* motor-boat, which had been abandoned when the gunboat had been forced to withdraw in the face of the attack on the harbour. It was incredible to realize that the attack had only been about nine hours before. He shook his head furiously, nothing must stop them now!

He felt a movement from the floor of the jeep and from the corner of his eye he saw Judith trying to arrange the tattered dress to cover her nakedness. A warm flood of emotion surged through him. "You were wonderful, Judith," he said softly.

Her eyes swam in the pale oval of her face. "I thought—I thought," she faltered, "we were never going to get away!"

He knew what she really meant, and he reached out to squeeze her shoulder with understanding. As his hand touched the bare skin she quivered and almost pulled away, the torture of her recent experience making her reaction automatic and fearful. Then with a sound like a quiet sob, she leaned weakly against his leg, her hair spilling over his bent knee.

He cut the lights and allowed the jeep to idle quietly down the last slope towards the harbour entrance.

The whole area was repeatedly illuminated by the bright flashes of gunfire from the fort and the surrounding hills, and in the short, savage flashes, Rolfe saw that the market place and harbour approach were littered with dull, black shapes, some of which still moaned with the torment of their abandoned agony.

"Give me the rifle," he whispered, and as he pushed the others behind him, "follow me along the jetty and keep close!"

Chao, his huge revolver waving from side to side, brought up the rear, while Felton helped his sister to step over the dark twisted shapes and staring, distorted faces.

There was one extra loud bang, and a searing red flash from the cliffs made them look back. The front of the distant fort was completely ablaze, and a hoard of fantastic shadows flitted and ran from side to side in front of the glow as they waited for the signal to rush the main gates of the General's stronghold.

In the bright, flickering reflection of light in the still water of the harbour, Rolfe easily picked out the neat grey shape of the motor-boat as it drifted aimlessly amongst the abandoned hulks of the fishing boats. He seized Judith's hand and waved the rifle at the others. "Come on! We must get to the boat as soon as we can! They'll be after us any second now!"

They stumbled along the jetty, sliding across the congealing blood of the littered bodies and watching for any sign of a sentry. But, as Rolfe had guessed, the Communist soldiers were too busy and too confident to bother with ground already won in battle.

He helped the girl down on to the deck of the nearest fishing boat, ignoring the upturned white eyes of a mangled soldier and fuming with impatience as Felton hesitated on the top of the wall.

He was staring back at the town and watching his hopes burning in the flames.

"Come on, Brian," he called, as gently as he could. "It's too late now to do anything about it!"

The little motor-boat was unharmed, apart from a few bullet holes in the roof of the canopy, and Rolfe bent over the engine remembering what Fallow had told him about its irregular behaviour in the past.

With a series of coughing grunts it started, and as he sighed, it suddenly cut out again. He cursed and felt his way clumsily along the battery leads. "Damn! Don't you let me down now!"

"Soldiers coming, Captain-sir! 'Long the end of the jetty!"

As Rolfe glanced up to the warning, a bullet whined viciously overhead and hissed into the water beyond.

"Shove the boat away, Chao!" he barked, and the boy seized a boathook to thrust off from the fishing boat, so that they began to drift out into the harbour.

Judith ducked down with a gasp as another shot shattered the glass in the small cabin canopy, and the splinters tinkled into the bottom of the boat.

"Here, give me that rifle!" Felton sounded strange. As he took the gun, he stood up calmly in the rocking boat and aimed carefully along the wall. Rolfe paused in his fumbling with the engine to watch the twisted face pressed against the rifle stock. There was something terrible about it, something uncarthly.

The rifle cracked and they heard the bullet snicker along the stone jetty in a shower of sparks. Then as the running soldiers appeared on the top of the wall, Felton moved the rifle catch to the automatic position and fired a short burst into the weaving shadows. There were sounds of muffled cries and for a moment there was no more firing from their direction.

"That's for Chu!" shouted Felton wildly, his good eye peering watchfully along the sights. "Come on! What are you afraid of?"

"Please, Brian," Judith called out anxiously, "get down!"

But he shrugged angrily and moved the rifle to a more comfortable position.

Rolfe drew a deep breath and pressed the starter button again. The engine whined, picked up shakily, and then burst into an unexpected roar. Without waiting for further developments, Rolfe slammed the gear lever ahead and opened the throttle slowly, feeling the boat begin to gather way beneath him. With a quick grin at Judith, he opened the throttle wide, and as he kicked over the tiller with his foot, the boat swung throatily away from the other craft and steered for the harbour entrance.

Another burst of shots splashed into the water from a new direction and from a higher angle.

"The end of the jetty! They're up there now!" warned Rolfe, as the deck vibrated to the thud of bullets.

Damn them, he thought furiously, we shall have to pass right under them! We'll never make it!

Felton squinted up at the slimy wall as it coasted past. He rested the rifle on the cabin top and took careful aim. "Not too many shots left," he observed calmly, "but I think we can keep their heads down!"

Chao had also poked the revolver through the shattered window, and as the rifle began to snap, he squeezed the stiff trigger again and again, the heavy thud of the weapon sounding far more dangerous than its accuracy at that range.

They swept under the arm of the jetty, where Laker's car still perched forlornly, and then, as the boat turned towards the darkened sea, Felton gave a sharp cry and dropped the rifle on the deck.

Judith sprang from her shelter and helped him to lower himself across the lifejackets.

"In the back!" Felton spoke jerkily between his teeth. "Singularly appropriate—er, don't you think?" Then, as he twisted violently under her hands, "Christ, Christ!" his voice raised to a sudden scream, died away in a low moan.

"Chao, grab the tiller! Steer due south for a bit, till we're past the headland, and watch out for breakers!"

Rolfe slid down beside the girl. "Here, let me have a look," he said quietly, and gently they turned him on his side, bolstering up the twisting body with the padded lifejackets. By the light of the dim compass lamp, Rolfe tore open the back of Felton's soaking shirt. The bullet had struck him just above the waist, to the left of his spine. Rolfe fumbled for the boat's first-aid box, trying to estimate the extent of the wound. Fired from above and behind, the bullet must have burrowed deep into his pelvis, or perhaps still high enough for his stomach. He managed to extract a phial of morphia, and as he glanced at Felton's disfigured face he saw the blood coursing down his chin.

"God, must be a stomach wound!" he breathed.

Judith tore off a strip of her tattered skirt and dabbed the blood away. She shook her head quietly, her eyes sad but steady. "No, Justin, he's bitten through his lip!"

Rolfe dug the phial into Felton's arm, and after a while his movements became easier, but as his bloodied lips opened in a deep sigh, he whispered, "My legs have gone. No feeling." Then he fainted into a drugged sleep.

Their eyes met across his body. "We must try and make him comfortable," Judith said. "I'll look after him while you look after the boat!"

Rolfe nodded, knowing that she was more experienced than he at such work. He'll never live until morning, he thought bitterly, even if he wanted to.

Once clear of the rocks around the harbour reaches, and sheltered from the roadway by the dark cliffs, Rolfe swung the boat on to a new bearing and tried to memorize the island's coastline, and watched for the vague outlines of the rocky slopes along the shore, which were his only guide.

"D'you know the little island at the southern end of Santu, Judith?" He kept his voice low. "That's where I'm making for. I think we'll be able to hide there until the *Wagtail* arrives!"

He saw her head nod in the shadows. "Yes. It's just a pile of bare rock, really. The natives avoid it, and think it's an evil place!" She smoothed her brother's hair, "You must be careful, there is no beach, just a sort of rocky shelf around the bottom, by the water's edge."

"We'll manage," he smiled. He peered ahead, knowing that it would be hard enough to get alongside the rocks without smashing the boat, but with a badly injured man it would be doubly dangerous.

The engine coughed and faded, and then spluttered into renewed life. Rolfe ground his teeth. The petrol, it must be just about dry by now! The little boat dipped and curtsied over the sullen swell, the loose gear and broken glass making the only sounds, apart from the labouring engine.

Chao saw the island first, as he crouched in the dipping bows, still holding the empty pistol. It rose, stark and menacing out of the sea like a huge decayed tooth, its sheer rocky sides black against the oily waters which surged and creamed into an angry froth at its base.

Rolfe knew that it was only about two miles from the main island, and that it was merely a crude formation of rock thrust up defiantly from the sea bed, with neither vegetation nor shelter. But he also realized that the rock's flat surface, once they reached it, would provide a good vantage point for watching for the gunboat, and it was unlikely that any search party would come their way. The search would either move across Santu to the other side, or they might think that they had tried for freedom in the motor-boat itself.

He reached out and began stuffing a few useful pieces of the boat's gear into one of the cabin cushion covers. "Put on those lifebelts!" he called. "We may need them if we strike!"

Even as the boat moved uneasily towards the shining rock shelf at the foot of the sheer, cheerless wall, the engine gave a last cough and died. Rolfe snatched up a small emergency paddle and shouted to Chao, "Quick, boy! Try to keep her head round to the rock!"

Playfully the heavy swell lifted the boat and banged it against the half-submerged shelf, and the shock threw them off their feet. In a flash Chao was up again and leaping ashore, the boat's painter trailing behind him. Rolfe hurled his makeshift bag after him, and as Chao dug himself behind a slippery crag, the rope curled round his body, the boat struck once more with a splintering crash. Rolfe staggered to the girl's aid, the water already gushing through the timbers, and swilling around his ankles. Felton moaned faintly as Rolfe slung him hastily across his shoulder and swung his legs across the tilting gunwale.

"Hold on, Judith!" he gasped, as he strained his leg muscles to control the heaving boat. "Feel your way past me!"

She scrambled over the widening gap, her bare feet slipping on the smooth rocks and her breath panting painfully.

The boat shuddered, and Chao called out anxiously, "Can't hold it! Too big pull!"

Rolfe tumbled on to the shelf, pulling Felton after him. Before he had time to steady the man's body in a more comfortable position, the boat groaned against the rocks and rolled over on its side, the shattered planks gaping at the sky. Then she was gone, and the loose painter snaked over the edge of the shelf, following the boat to the bottom.

Another surge of water splashed over their legs, and Rolfe stared up at the high cliff. "Come on," he muttered. "Chao, get that heaving-line out of the bag!"

Judith watched silently, her brother's head pillowed in her lap and her long hair sleek with spray, as Rolfe knotted the end of the strong line round the boy's waist.

"Can you manage it?" he asked, as he untwisted the slender line.

Chao grinned. "You an' me old hands at this game, Captain-sir!" And with a quick leap he was creeping up the rock face like a monkey.

They waited in silence, Rolfe tensed to catch the boy's body. But Chao suddenly called out, "O.K.! Line fixed!"

Rolfe smiled. "You go up first, Judith. Then I'll make one journey with Brian."

He watched her anxiously as she laid Felton's head on her discarded lifejacket. She'll not make it, he realized, she's still shocked, and he gripped her arm tightly to prevent her from swaying over the edge. She started up the rock, gripping the rope desperately, and feeling for holds with her feet. With a quick glance at Felton, Rolfe followed her, praying that the line would hold both of them. Each time she faltered, he heaved his shoulder up the cliff to act as a prop beneath her body, and when he thought that his muscles would crack, he saw Chao's thin arms reaching out for the girl, and he knew that she was safe. He slithered down the rope, heedless of the burning pain in his palms, and with all the care he could muster, he began to drag Felton's limp form to the end of the rope. He tied a bowline under his arms and padded it away from his body with the lifejacket. That should do, he thought, and then, with a final deep breath, he hauled himself up the cliff.

With Chao and the girl behind him, he heaved cautiously on

the rope, listening to Felton's agonized groans getting nearer and nearer. He heard the lifejacket scrape the lip of rock and breathlessly they pulled him up over the edge.

As far as he could see in the darkness the rock island was about fifty yards long, and hollowed out in the centre by the constant wear of time and weather. Once in the rough crater, the sounds of the sea were muffled, and as the moon bathed their refuge in pale light, they made Felton comfortable on a flat piece of ground and gave him some more of the precious morphia.

Rolfe sat wearily on his haunches and looked across at the girl. Her clinging rags had fallen practically to her waist, and her skin gleamed in the light like pale gold.

Rolfe jerked off his shirt, feeling the cool air on his sweating body. "Here," he called softly, "slip this on. It's better than nothing!"

She took it hesitantly and moved away to the edge of the crater. Chao was already lying down, his eyes closed, and as Rolfe lay back gingerly on the hard surface, he caught a brief glimpse of the pale, shimmering figure, poised like a statue against the moon, before she pulled the shirt over her head.

She crossed shyly to his side, the remains of her dress in her hand. "This will do for bandages," she said. "Thank you for giving me the shirt," she added gravely.

They stared at each other in silence, and Rolfe was moved beyond words. He patted the rock beside him. "You'd better stay close." His voice was suddenly husky. "You must try and keep warm!"

She dropped to his side and curled into the crook of his arm. As the warmth of her supple body seeped into him, and she slowly began to relax, Rolfe forgot the danger and the threat of the dawn. He felt a new inner warmth of contentment and desire.

7

ROLFE awoke from his exhausted sleep, his eyes and his senses groping for an explanation to his surroundings. For some moments the painful stiffness in his limbs made him lie quietly, staring up at the clear blue morning sky, which rose above the rocks around him like a distant sea. He stared blankly at the ground beside him, the memories of Judith and the previous night flooding back, and he twisted his head in the direction of the voices, which he now realized had awakened him.

Chao and the girl squatted by Felton's side, readjusting the makeshift bandages and trying to soothe away the fierce, agonized mutterings which issued from his dry lips.

Rolfe stood up, feeling guilty that he should have slept while the others were occupied with this new problem. Judith glanced up at him and smiled brightly, her even teeth white against her brown face. As she rose from the ground, Rolfe saw that she had pulled the tails of his shirt down between her legs and knotted the ends together to form a shapeless khaki smock. He smiled tenderly, remembering the brief vision of her curved beauty which he had witnessed on the edge of their crater.

As he moved to join them, every muscle and bone in Rolfe's body protested in unison, and he grimaced as he glanced down at his bare skin. Apart from the red marks left by the rocks on which he had slept, there were the angry bruises where the rifle butts had beaten him to submission at the hospital.

"I didn't want to wake you," Judith talked quietly, her small hands resting on her hips. "We need you too much to have you collapsing on us!"

Rolfe grinned, feeling his parched lips crack with the effort. It was strange indeed that he had not thought of drink since that first visit to the hospital, when Felton had eyed him with pitying contempt. And now the doctor, shrunken and pale, lay helpless in the dust at his feet, and he was thinking of a drink of a different nature. He ran his tongue round his mouth and stared carefully about their hiding-place. The dust-dry rock bowl in the centre of the tiny island was devoid of shelter, and apart from a few loose pieces of stone, and age-old piles of seagull droppings, was completely bare. As he walked to the lip of the high cliff the sea glinted up mockingly, and a few of the hunting gulls rose screaming from the surface as his distorted shadow fell across them.

Santu shimmered sleepily in the distance, the reds and greens of its contrasting cliffs and trees giving a lush and tempting picture, which belied the slaughter and terror on the other side of the island.

He frowned and wished he had a watch. It was very early in the morning, and the warm breath which fanned across his naked back was only a gentle threat of the heat and discomfort which would soon be upon them.

He stared out across the flat, inviting sea, to the south, wondering where the *Wagtail* would be at this moment, and remembering the new danger threatened by the possible approach of a Chinese warship.

As if reading his thoughts, Judith moved closer to him, her shining hair barely reaching to his shoulder. "We must make some shelter for Brian," she said gravely. "He is asking for a drink already, and he will be in agony when the sun reaches him!" There was a great depth of sadness in her voice, but her tone was steady, and as Rolfe looked at her, she smiled up at him, her eyes clear and bright.

Rolfe nodded slowly, thinking how small and perfect she looked, and the torn, flapping shirt was unable to hide her proud figure. Apart from the shirt, she owned nothing, and as he forced himself to consider the problem of making a shelter, he realized that he, too, had nothing but his trousers, his battered shoes, and a few pieces of boat's gear to help them through their ordeal. He grinned ruefully, "We don't seem to be very well equipped, do we?"

She shrugged, the movement sending a fresh pang across Rolfe's heart. "We must do what we can!" she answered simply.

Rolfe and Chao began to gather the loose pieces of worn stone, and in the deepest corner of the crater they laboriously erected a wall. While they were grunting and panting across the crater with their finds, they all noticed that the rock floor was growing steadily warmer, like a giant hot-plate, and before they were half finished, Rolfe was running with sweat.

Judith carefully padded out the lifejackets into a bed, and when they had finished, Rolfe knelt down beside Felton, waiting until the pinched face was turned wearily towards him.

"We're going to move you, Brian. D'you think you can manage to put up with it?"

Felton smiled crookedly. "Why bother? I'm finished!"

190

"Once we can get you away from here——" began Rolfe, but a claw-like hand gripped his wrist with sudden force.

"Let's not kid ourselves! You seem to forget, *I'm* the doctor! I know what has happened!" His head fell back and he stared unblinkingly at the brightening sky. "Finished!" he groaned again.

They lifted him tenderly, expecting him to cry out, as his loose, seemingly disconnected legs jerked with their combined efforts. But Rolfe's heart sank as they lowered Felton into the shelter, he had seen that air of resigned defeat before, that disregard of pain on the faces of other dying men. He strode desperately round the crater, leaving the others to make the man comfortable.

How had it all happened? He racked his brains, but only succeeded in obtaining a jumbled mass of pictures and events. When he had staggered aboard the gunboat to assume command, his will and energy sapped with self-pity, he could never have dreamed such a transformation possible.

The evacuation had nearly ended in slaughter and he had deserted his ship. He knew that if he turned his head he would see the reason for his actions, as she knelt watchfully over her brother, but try as he might, he could not see how the future would permit his dreams to mature to a reality.

He suddenly noticed, for the first time, a faint pall of black smoke hanging thinly across the hills of the distant island. He wondered if the battle still raged, and if the General had been beaten. The scene was so beautiful that these cruel facts hardly seemed possible.

Chao leaned across the rocks, his body clad only in a small loin cloth. "Think I go down and try a bit of fishing!" he said thoughtfully, and Rolfe cursed himself for thinking of his own worries.

"What'll you use?"

Chao laid out his crude line and hook. A piece of gut from the First-Aid box, used normally for stitching wounds, and a bent safety pin.

"Good Lord!" Rolfe breathed admiringly. "But be careful how you go. Keep to the other side of the rock, away from Santu, and if I shout to you, keep down out of sight!"

The boy grinned, his dark eyes slanting against the sun. Then, with one of his quick leaps, he lowered himself nimbly down the rope, which Rolfe pulled up, and settled down to keep watch, conscious of the growing pain of his thirst.

A warm hand slid under his arm. "Don't look so worried, Justin! What are you thinking about?"

He grinned, startled. "You mostly! I keep thinking what a mess I've made of things!"

Her eyes widened. "Nonsense! If it wasn't for you, things would have been very different. Mr. Laker would have bamboozled you into delaying the evacuation, and then they'd all have been caught!" She lowered her gaze. "And anyway, we might not have been alone together, ever!"

He gingerly slid his arm about her slim shoulders and together they stared out to sea.

"A lot of things are clearer to me now," he said suddenly. "I couldn't understand at the time why Major Ling allowed your brother to stay in Santu, when everyone knew his views about the General, and other things. But, of course, Ling realized that Brian was doing his own work for him by spreading discontent against the General's rule, and he could carry on with his deception in safety until he thought fit. Until yesterday, in fact." He squeezed her gently as she stiffened. "But it's over now or at least that part of it!"

"What are our chances Justin?"

"We *have* to make it!" He spoke harshly, to convince himself. "I must get to my ship before anything else happens!"

She snuggled against him and his skin tingled as her hair floated across his shoulder. "You will be a captain again! And I will just be in the way!" But at that moment they both knew there was something strong and exciting growing between them, something which the outside world could not offer, or destroy.

"I might let you cook for me," he grinned. "I might even let ——" He jumped up without finishing, his head cocked on one side. "Listen!"

They stared at each other, their eyes mirroring their doubts, and then as the low-pitched buzzing mounted to a throb, Rolfe shouted, "Chao! Keep out of sight! There's a plane of some sort!"

192

He saw the boy lower himself into the water, his head against the rock shelf, and then gripping Judith's hand, he ran to the shelter, pulling the first-aid box against the uneven wall.

"Keep here with Brian," he breathed, listening to the throb which vibrated noisily around the crater. "I'm just going to have a look!"

He slid cautiously up to the edge of the cliff, blinking in the growing glare. At first he could only see the sea and the green of Santu, but as he watched, he saw a black, ungainly shape hovering and darting, dipping and turning, just above the land, like a giant dragonfly. A helicopter, he thought, the implication twisting in his mind. They were still searching for them with that same cold determination which seemed to motivate all their actions.

The sun glinted on the Perspex front of the aircraft, as it gained height, its long blades blurred with power. For a while it remained motionless, as if the pilot was undecided, then with a sudden haste it swooped lazily towards the lonely pinnacle of rocks.

Rolfe ducked back to the shelter, his face grim. Carefully he checked the rifle. Only three shots left. He bit his lip, as he lowered himself on to his elbows, and cradled the weapon against his cheek. He watched the lip of the crater, black against the sky, and listened to the growing roar of the engine.

How low will it be? What can they see from up there?

He jerked as she touched his back. "If they come here, Justin," her voice trembled, "don't let them take me! Promise me you'll kill me first!"

The words struck a chill through him, and he met her gaze steadily. "No one will take you from me now!"

The roaring grew to a deafening intensity, and without warning the bulbous front of the helicopter rose slowly over the edge of the crater like the hideous head of some forgotten monster. Overhead the blades slashed at the air, churning up the dust around them in a thick yellow cloud, until Rolfe was forced to close his eyes and pull the girl's face against his side for protection. The sun vanished, as a great black shadow hovered over them, and when Rolfe squinted up through the flying grit and sand, he saw the two helmeted figures crouching behind their Perspex screen, barely twenty feet away. A fresh cloud was stirred up by the blades, and Rolfe's throat was filled with dust, until he began to cough, helpless, and gasping for air.

It was the dust which saved them, for as they lay together against Felton's covered body, they heard the engine's note rise with sudden power, and with a graceless leap, the helicopter left the crater and glided back towards Santu, leapfrogging with its shadow across the ruffled water.

Rolfe pulled Judith closer and with his grubby handkerchief, began to wipe the dust from her face. Then her slender arms were pressing the back of his neck and he felt her warm mouth against his, in a breathless, sobbing kiss. They clung together without speaking, until Chao called shrilly from below, "I have fish! You ready up there?"

They smiled secretly at each other, and Rolfe went for the rope.

* * * * *

As the sun rose higher above the Eastern sea, and the deep water shed its cloak of mysterious blue, and glittered and shimmered in a sheet of pale green glass, the last cool breath left by the night was crushed and vanquished, until even the fish swam deep to avoid the scorching rays.

A few gulls, hardier and more greedy than the others, still glided hopefully after the gunboat *Wagtail*, and whenever anything appeared in the creamy wake, which stretched across the sea in a white line, they dived, screaming, to investigate its possibilities.

Apart from the lookouts and a few of the duty hands, the decks were deserted, for without the protection of the awnings the bare, unsheltered spaces were made heat-traps under the dazzling glare. The engines throbbed placidly, and the bows of the ship hardly tilted over the gentle swell which bubbled against the stem.

Lieutenant Fallow studied the chart carefully, and with the pencil gripped in his ungainly fingers, he marked the estimated position of the ship on the straight line of their course. He half listened to the toneless chant of two Chinese seamen as they daubed grey paint along the scarred plating of the abandoned wireless room, and was thankful that he, at least, was in the comparative shade of the chart room.

He tried again to visualize what would happen when night eventually came, and he would have the task of searching for the Captain. It still seemed strange to be left in charge of the ship, yet stranger still, it had become almost a relief. By attending to his new duties he had been able to keep away from the questions and arguments of his passengers, and Vincent, apart from his spells of duty on the bridge, had become almost a stranger.

He had seen him occasionally, pacing around the main deck, as if he was also avoiding contact with the others, although from his strained face it appeared that his were different reasons. Fallow groped for his handkerchief, already sodden and limp. It was amazing that such things could happen, and he wondered gloomily what the Admiral would think when he read the reports.

The injured man, Edgar Lane, was comfortable enough, physically, but nothing Fallow, or anyone else could do, would make him talk, or take an interest in his condition. His companion in the sick bay, the Chinese seaman wounded in the brief encounter with the Communists, was all smiles, and lay back proudly in his comfortable bunk, relishing in the visits of his comrades. Fallow shook his head, putting the most gnawing worry to the back of his mind.

He kept thinking about Rolfe and torturing himself by gauging his chances of survival. Pretty slim, he decided. Then there was the steward, Chao, who had disappeared overboard without a trace. There was more to that than met the eye! He peered round the door to ensure that the helmsman was attending to his duties. Tempting fate, that's what it is, he thought vaguely.

A shadow fell across the deck, and Fallow looked up irritably. Vincent stood uncertainly in the doorway, his eyes hot and tired.

"Well?" Fallow forced himself to consider the reasons for Vincent's visit.

"It's about tonight." Vincent seemed to be groping for his words, in a manner quite foreign to him. "Are we really going back to that damned place?"

"You know we are!" So that's what was biting him. He's more windy than I guessed! And so am I, he thought bitterly.

"Well, I don't think it's right!" Vincent's eyes blazed with sudden anger. "He'll be dead by now, and in any case, it's his own fault! I—I mean, it'd be hazarding the ship to go back there!" The words poured out in a wild torrent. "He's left the ship to you, and it's your duty to get us, I mean these people, back to Hong Kong!"

Fallow listened uneasily, he had already considered that possibility, and although Rolfe was, in effect, still engaged in an evacuation of sorts, he had ordered Fallow to consider the ship first, in his absence. He clamped his jaws together vehemently. "What the 'ell are you sayin', man? D'you want me to leave the skipper to bloody well rot?" He thrust his purple nose towards Vincent's face. "You're windy! That's what's up with you!"

Vincent clenched his fists, a flush on his cheeks. "It's not that! I just don't think the risk is justified!"

"Well, who's bloody well askin' you what you think?" The heat and the additional nagging worry of Vincent's remarks were beginning to wear down Fallow's reserve of outward calm. "I'm bloody fed up with you an' your sort! Always showin' off, and playin' the big man, with yer lardy-da ways! An' when it comes to the showdown, what 'appens?" He poked the man's jacket with a fat finger. "I'll tell you what 'appens! You blow yer top! No guts! So if that's all you've got to offer, you'd better 'op it!" He glared belligerently, all the pent-up rage clear on his red face.

Vincent turned away, his slim body shaking with either rage or fear, Fallow didn't care which. He had said it at last, he had told one of 'them' off, and he felt immensely better.

He caught the helmsman's eye. "'Ere, watch yer course!" he growled. "You Chinks need a white walkin' stick instead of a compass!"

He walked to the wing of the bridge, and stood breathing heavily, and tried to think of Mary.

In the wardroom Vincent groaned with anguish as he stared at the occupied seats, and breathed the foul air of tobacco smoke and gin. Blast them, they were making the place into a combination of a club and a public meeting place.

Laker glanced up. "What's the news, eh? Are we still bent on self-destruction? I'm goin' to have a word with that Lieutenant Fallow in a moment and tell him what I think about it!"

Vincent jerked his hand at the steward, trying to shut out the angry voice which beat mercilessly into his brain. "Large whisky, steward!" Peng glanced at him impassively, as if to question the sense of Vincent's order. All the stewards knew that Vincent was normally meticulous and careful about his drinking habits when the ship was at sea.

He swallowed the drink, his eyes far away and desperate. What's got into me? To let that fat oaf speak to me like a damned rating! He twisted in his chair, his disordered thoughts making him re-live all the miseries and insults which he had suffered. Wait until I get back. He tried to fan up the old familiar gloating feeling, but he could feel only emptiness. He tried to think methodically about the future, but there was nothing. Nothing! He stood up, startled, that was it! He was going to be killed! He glared round wildly, as if looking for a way of escape. What could he do? Now that the last pretence had fallen, he could only think of the dangers ahead. That was the future, there could be nothing else.

He stumbled from that hateful place and hurried along the deck to his cabin. With a trembling hand he unlocked the cupboard and drew out a bottle of whisky. Fool, fool! he told himself, but with an almost frantic eagerness he felt for a glass.

The door opened, and Ursula leaned quietly against it. Her eyes were anonymous behind the sun-glasses, but her full lips twitched in passing alarm as she studied him.

"Going to hang one on, David?" Her voice was soft and cool.

He gazed at her uncertainly. "Come in and shut the door, if you want to."

"This isn't quite the pleasure cruise that I'd hoped. I thought I might have seen a little more of you," she shrugged. "But everybody seems to be in such a panic!"

He coloured, but before he could answer, she had sauntered lazily past him to stare at the framed photographs which were arrayed neatly about the cabin.

She paused at each one. The self-conscious uniformed group taken at Dartmouth College. Another of Vincent smiling whitely beneath a rowing trophy, and the rest a photographic record of his career.

"This looks like the way I've always imagined the navy," she said, her voice still casual. "It's so vast, so impartial, some-how!" She turned to face him, pulling away her glasses. "You can't let all this go, David!" Her eyes blazed with green fire.

197

He shifted his feet, suddenly conscious of the weight of the bottle in his hand. What was she talking about? Why was she tormenting him?

She crossed to him, gently removing the whisky from his nerveless grip. The warm, animal smell of her full body stirred him, in spite of himself.

"Don't you see, David? Your Captain's doing what he thinks is right! He messed up his career, nearly lost everything," she waved away the numbed protest. "Yes, I know all about it! But even though this was his last chance, he didn't hesitate in what he knew was his real duty!" She ran her hands along his shoulders. "He's a man! A real man, and you should be man enough yourself to realize it! Follow his example and show a little trust!" She pouted, "Hark at me! I didn't think I had it in me!"

Vincent gaped at her in amazement. "You're a queer girl, Ursula, and no mistake! I'm just a bit weak, I suppose."

She twisted the buttons of his tunic between her fingers, her lashes lowered. "I know differently!"

Vincent pulled her against him, but there was no passion in his heart, only the desire to hide and be protected.

She led him to the narrow bunk and together they laid in a tight embrace. Vincent's forehead was screwed into a tight frown, and as the girl eased his head against her breast, he shivered violently. Ursula stared up at the whirring fan, a distant smile on her mouth.

• • • • •

The deck canted slowly as the gunboat swung away on to her new track, and Louch watched his engine dials morosely. I hope they know what they're doing, he thought. There's not enough fuel to spend all our lives steaming round and round in ruddy circles. He accepted the mug of tea from his leading stoker. "Ta!" he remarked distantly, and when he sipped the strong beverage, he spat with sudden anger. "For God's sake, let's get away from this blasted island!" But only the tired engines heard him.

Chief Petty Officer Herridge stepped on to the bridge and saluted. "You wanted me, sir?"

198

"Er—yes! About tonight, Chief. I'm not too 'appy about you goin' after the Captain in a pullin' boat!" Fallow eyed him sombrely, waiting for the tough Cornishman to pass judgement.

"No option, is there?"

They studied the chart and noted the seemingly endless tangle of reefs and shoals around their objective.

"Think he'll be there when we find the place, sir?" Herridge asked quietly. "He was taking on a hell of a lot, if you ask me!" Normally he would never have thought of discussing the matter with an officer, but he knew that Fallow wanted to talk to him about it, and he had not forgotten his own unspoken promise to Rolfe.

Fallow rubbed his chins worriedly. "Lord knows! But whatever 'appens, we're not out of the wood yet!" He glanced quickly around the bridge, some of his old nervousness showing in his eyes. "Why did we 'ave to lose the radio? If only we could tell somebody what 'as 'appened!"

Herridge watched him calmly. Easy there! he thought, watch it now! Aloud he said, "I reckon he'll get those people away all right. If he can't, nobody can!"

"Er—Chief," began Fallow awkwardly, "there's something I'd like your opinion on." He paused, swallowing hard. "Some of the passengers think I should leave the Captain behind and clear off! That's what Laker 'as just been to see me about!" He looked straight at the other man, his brown eyes desperate. "I know I shouldn't be talkin' to you like this, an' it's not fair of me to ask you. But I shall be out of the Andrew soon, and anyway, I'd like to know what you think about it!" he ended defiantly.

Herridge watched the ensign flapping dejectedly from the gaff, his face cautious. "Well, sir, what exactly did you say to Mr. Laker?"

Fallow's face was comical. "I told him to bugger off!"

Herridge's eyes widened. "Then I reckon that was the correct answer, and very diplomatically put!"

They grinned at each other, and then lapsed into a companionable silence.

The *Wagtail* ploughed on, her fate decided.

Rolfe watched in silence as the girl cut open the small striped fish with Chao's knife. She laid it on the tin first-aid box, and began to remove the bones.

He was fascinated by even her casual movements, and as she tossed the hair back from her eyes and glanced across at her brother, he saw the serious pressure of her lips. She beckoned quietly, and held up the fish for his inspection. Already it was curling under the relentless heat.

"I think we had better try to get him to eat. It might help to moisten his mouth."

Brian Felton moaned as Rolfe gently removed Chao's white jacket from his pain-racked face. His eyes seemed to have fallen back into his head, and the scarred side of his twisted features no longer appeared so stark when compared to his grey, lifeless skin.

"Here, Brian, have a go at some of your sister's cooking!" Rolfe forced a grin. He was horrified by the appearance of Felton's legs through the rents in his tattered trousers. The skin around the groin gleamed an angry yellow as if lit by an inner fire.

Felton stared up at him, his eye at first blank and wavering. Then the thin mouth twisted, and he moved his hands weakly. "Try anything once! Hope it's not poison!"

Rolfe put a small piece between the man's lips and watched him move his jaws in slow, jerky bites.

"Chao says it's good stuff," Rolfe added. "If you just chew it, it might keep away the dryness a bit!"

"Well said, Doctor!" the voice was just a mumble. "But I wish you'd take the rest for yourselves! It's wasted on me."

Rolfe heard the girl draw in her breath and he looked up quickly as she rubbed her eyes with the back of her hand.

Chao crouched beside them, a cheerful smile on his face. "I feed him, Captain-sir! Me more experienced!" He slid his hand under Felton's head and prattled away cheerily, while he fed the fish into Felton's parched mouth.

Rolfe stood up, his bare shoulders feeling stiff and dry with the growing pain of sunburn. It was as if all the air had been sucked out of the crater, and indeed from the whole islet, to leave a glowing bowl of heat and pain. He no longer sweated and his mouth burned continuously, making his tongue feel twice its size.

He moved slowly around the crater, forcing himself to strain his eyes across the inviting green sea, and watch for any possible danger. He swayed slightly, and leaned his hands on the rock, unable to move, yet aware of the heat coursing up from the dry surface.

He turned as Judith's shadow crossed the ground. She had untied the shirt-tails from between her legs, and as she crouched down by the edge of the cliff, she drew her brown legs up inside the shirt, making a small tent for her body. Her hair, dusty and loose, draped protectively around her shoulders, but her lips were dry, and his heart ached as he saw the pink tip of her tongue trying vainly to ease their discomfort.

"Your shoulders are getting very burned," she said gravely, "I think you had better take the shirt for a bit!"

Rolfe tried to laugh, but it was a cracked sound which he heard. "Much as I'd like that, Judith, I think we'll carry on as we are!"

She dropped her eyes and rubbed the sand with her bare foot. "I don't know how you can say such things! I wish I could be as calm as you are."

He slipped down beside her, his breath pounding with the effort of movement.

"I'm not a bit calm, as it happens," he said soberly. "I keep thinking of what might happen if the *Wagtail* doesn't come for us, or if we find we can't get to her. I'm worried about moving Brian. He's pretty bad, as you know, and any shock might finish his chance of survival!"

She rested her chin on her knees and pulled the shirt collar up across her neck. Rolfe trembled as he saw the warm curve of her breast through the sagging front of the shirt. He clenched his fists helplessly. She looked so small and perfect that he had to tear his mind away from the prospect of being left either to die of thirst on this god-forsaken place or to submit to recapture. The thought of what could happen to her as a prisoner in Santu made him feel sick and weak.

Her hand found his wrist and her wide, hazel eyes studied him with concern. "We shall be safe soon, Justin, I feel it!"

She said it with such calm assurance that he had to turn his face away lest she should see the anguish in his eyes.

"Tell me about Hong Kong," she said suddenly. "I want to know about so much. I'm afraid I'm rather inexperienced, as you've probably gathered."

He moved closer to her, letting his sore skin rest against her small body. "I don't know it really well, but if we get there we'll tour the place together!" He twisted round suddenly. "Judith, there are so many things I want to tell you!" He watched her worriedly, but she smiled across at him, her face encouraging. "I've made a mess of everything here for you, and I've not done much better with my own life! I wanted to tell you before about ———" he groped for the right words—"about my marriage, and all that happened!"

"You don't have to say anything about it," she answered softly. "I may be pretty innocent in some ways, but your trouble showed on your face the first day you arrived!" Her grip tightened. "It's all over now, isn't it?" He nodded dumbly. "Well, that's that, then!" She laughed quietly, "I'm mean and grasping, I don't care about her, whoever she was! She couldn't have been any good, or she would have appreciated you, as I do!"

"Judith," he felt his eyes smarting, "while we've got the chance, let me tell you now. I love you! I want you!"

She leaned against him. "What, looking like this?" But her words trembled with pleasure.

"Just like this, just as you are! You've known it all the time, haven't you?"

She nodded dreamily. "All the time!"

He knew that she was forcing herself to be brave, and trying to shut out the misery which surrounded them like a wall, but they both drew comfort and fresh strength from each other.

The day dragged on, and their bodies became weaker and more parched, while from above the sun searched out their last reserves of strength and drove them from their scanty cover.

Talking became impossible, and the journeys back and forth to tend to Felton's needs had the makings of a new nightmare.

Rolfe pulled himself alongside the man's twitching form and examined his bandages. His stomach protested against the vile smell of the wound, but he could only stare wretchedly at the sunken face, knowing that he could do nothing to help him.

It was late in the afternoon when he saw the ship. At first he could only stare dully at the long grey hull, his mind vacant and uncomprehending. Then as the shape hardened in his brain, he croaked over his blistered shoulder. "A destroyer. Making for the harbour!"

He felt rather than saw that the others had joined him, and he watched the strange ship curve slowly away from the shore, to skirt the long line of creaming reefs. A faint trail of smoke whispered from the squat funnel, and as she moved, her fittings and equipment flashed brightly in the glare. Above her powerful bridge the radar aerials turned slowly, while from her gaff a red flag fluttered half-heartedly in the humid air.

"One of theirs?" Judith's voice asked hoarsely.

He nodded, feeling his hopes fading in the wake of the ship. "I know the type. Ex-Russian, 'Gordy' class destroyer." His trained mind ticked off the grim facts. "She's mounting four big guns, five-inchers, and a hell of a lot of other stuff!"

They waited, watching the ship and still half-hoping that it might turn away again, for the mainland.

Judith sighed, as the raked stem slewed round the last reef and past the distant headland. The destroyer was making for the anchorage outside the harbour.

"So Major Ling has kept his word," Rolfe muttered, as he stared at the sea, which was again empty.

Judith's mouth quivered slightly. "Does that mean that your ship won't come?"

"Fallow'd be a fool to risk it now!" he answered flatly. Then, as the new thought penetrated his swimming brain. "We must signal them to keep away!" He swallowed hard, not looking at them. "*Wagtail* has no radar, nothing! And the radio is finished! By the time we got Brian down to the water the destroyer would be on us, and the *Wagtail* would be sunk!"

Chao padded quietly away, his features dull and fatigued.

"What do you want us to do?" Judith asked at length.

He gripped her shoulders, searching her upturned face. "You mean, you agree with what I just said?"

"It was the only decision, Justin!" She tried to smile, but her eyes were misty and her mouth trembled uncontrollably. "We must find another way!"

They laid down, their precious reserves spent.

"I want to be with you, Justin. Nothing else matters any more."

He laid his forearm across his aching eyes. The rock seemed to be searing right through to his spine. "It's as if someone never intended us to be happy together!" He felt her tears running hotly across his arm, and they lay, clinging to each other in silence, closing their eyes against the mocking sun.

When she eventually spoke again, her lips were practically against his ear, and her voice sounded dry and weak.

"How far will the *Wagtail* be from here when it comes?"

He glanced at her, worriedly; wrenching his sodden brain back into consciousness, but she shook her head gently. "It's all right, Justin, I'm not going to break down again! I—I just wanted to know if we shall see the ship from here."

He lay back again, seeing the picture of the quaint little gun-boat in his mind. "I told Fallow to approach from the south-east and lie off outside the reef barrier. Santu harbour is in the north-west corner of the island, and I thought it advisable to keep the mass of the land between the ship and the main bulk of Communist forces!" The effort of speech made him more tired, but he felt the girl suddenly wriggle up on to her elbow. When he squinted painfully towards her, he saw that she was frowning and her eyes were thoughtful.

"Suppose, Justin, just suppose that the destroyer has been looking for your ship?" She seemed to be trying to stop herself from appearing excited. "It might be possible that they've given up the hunt and that's why they've gone to the harbour?"

He wrestled with the idea as she hurried on before he could interrupt.

"After all, they still don't know we're here, and they probably believe we got away somehow in the motor-boat." Her eyes were so full of sudden hope that he hated himself for having to spoil her eagerness.

"Well, just supposing you're right in your idea, Judith," he began slowly, "and it's quite a possibility. We would still have the task of lowering your brother down the cliff and getting him

204

to the boat." He shook his head heavily, suddenly weary of the whole business. "It would kill him."

"It was just an idea," she said in a small voice.

"That reef barrier is about two miles from here, and the *Wagtail* will haul off about a mile beyond that. I did think that the boat would be able to come right through to this islet for us, but," he shrugged his sore shoulders, "it would take a long time and it would be risking the lives of every man and woman aboard, each minute that we were making the attempt." He wanted to tell her that he was prepared to sacrifice the ship and everyone in it if it meant saving her life, but he knew that he couldn't bring himself to do it.

As if reading his thoughts, she said quietly, "It would be too great a risk!"

He stirred himself as he heard Felton moaning from his shelter. "I'll go," he called, as Chao rolled over in the dust, his thin arms pushing at the rock.

Felton regarded him fixedly, while Rolfe wiped the dust from his mouth. "That ship, Justin," he croaked, and Rolfe groaned inwardly. Not again! I shall crack in a second!

"It's ruined everything, hasn't it?" Felton persisted. "You're going to tell the gunboat to clear off, aren't you?" It was like an accusation.

Rolfe ran his fingers through his matted hair, his brows throbbing. "Try not to excite yourself, Brian. There's not much we can do at the moment!"

Felton struggled angrily in his stained covering. "You can! That reef barrier, Justin, the one which the General thought would save his precious skin!" Rolfe tried to soothe him, but the broken body was gifted with a burst of strength. "You could swim there, from here!"

Rolfe had thought of that while Judith had been outlining her ideas. Once on the reef they would be within reach of rescue, although the very thought of making such a swim in their condition made him sicken with frustration. "Forget it! We'll make out somehow!"

"It's me, isn't it? You won't chance it because of me?" The eye gleamed redly. "Go on, answer me, damn you!"

Rolfe readjusted the bandages, trying to ignore the distorted face. "I shall try and steal a boat from Santu tomorrow," he was almost startled by his own calm voice, and the lie. "I'll think of something!"

A hand fastened on his wrist. "Just admit that my idea is a good one! It is, isn't it, Justin?" He was pleading now.

Rolfe stood up, his shadow across Felton's dead legs. "Very good, Brian!"

An expression of triumph and peace crossed the man's face, and he let his body go limp again. "Thank you, Justin." Then, as Rolfe stared at him dully, "You love her, don't you? You'll take care of her?"

He's delirious, he thought, and he smiled quickly, not wishing Felton to become excited again and lose the last of his failing strength. "I love her! And I've told her so."

Felton smiled, and some of his old self seemed to flicker momentarily across his face. "You think I've been a fool! Well, perhaps I have about some things, Justin." He gritted his teeth savagely to control another spasm of agony. "But I have been right about a lot of things, and about these people. I belong with them." His eyes closed, and as Rolfe stepped quietly away, he called, "You're a friend, Justin!"

Judith was still huddled beneath the shirt, and for a terrible moment he thought she was unconscious. Her head was sunk across her knees, and one hand lay upturned on the dust.

She stirred, her breath coming in short, hot gasps. "How much longer, Justin?" He stared at her anxiously and she lifted her tired eyes to his. "When will the night come?"

"Soon!" He gathered her body in his arms, feeling her skin moist and hot through the cloth. "How do you feel?"

She lolled her head from side to side, her lips tortured and dry. "Fine."

Chao was over by Felton's side, although Rolfe's mind was now so unreliable that he had not seen him move. Their distant voices floated unevenly across the shimmering expanse of heat.

Chao crawled past, his face peering over the edge of the crater, as if to reassure himself.

"What did the Doctor want, Chao?" He cursed himself for wasting his breath in speech. Each word was like shedding some of his blood.

Chao slumped across the rock, staring vacantly down at the water. "He say he bored, Captain-sir."

Rolfe squinted at Chao's black silhouette. "Bored?"

"Yes. He say he want to clean his rifle. The one he take from dead soldier."

Rolfe grunted and fell back. Judith started to lean against him, her damp body becoming more and more unsteady. She jerked away as Rolfe scrambled to his knees, his cracked lips mouthing incoherently. His mind fumbled with the warning which suddenly screamed through him. "The gun!" he gasped. "Quick, the gun!"

But even while he was swaying to his feet, the ground reeling beneath him, his head split open to the echoing crash which seemed to erupt from the very rock itself.

As the sound of the shot died away, and only the gulls screaming disturbed the air, Rolfe stood looking down at all that remained of Brian Felton. The one good eye still gleamed defiantly, as if watching the growing pool of bright blood soaking across his chest. The smoking rifle, its butt jammed against the rock shelter, was pointing at his heart.

"Hold her, Chao!" Rolfe barked, as Judith ran whimpering across the crater. He bent and covered the body with Chao's old jacket, and then stood quietly, his head bowed.

Then, shaking his head to clear away the sick dizziness, he stepped between Chao and the writhing girl. She collapsed sobbing in his grip, and he stroked her hair, unable to find the right words.

Chao's face was torn with anguish. "I not know, Captain-sir! I deserve to die!"

Rolfe shook his head across the girl's body. "No, Chao," he was speaking as much to her as to the horrified boy, "he knew he was going to do it! If it hadn't been the rifle, he would have thought of something else!"

He paused, feeling Judith's nails biting into his chest. "He did it to give us a chance!" Gently he lifted her chin, holding it until her streaming eyes opened and her sobs quietened. "Will we take that chance?"

She stood back from him and he reached out to replace the shirt as it began to slide off her shoulder.

"Poor Brian," she murmured, and then very slowly she walked

across to the still form on the ground. Rolfe and the boy watched her helplessly.

She knelt down and very gently pulled the jacket from her brother's face.

Chao groaned softly as she said, "Good-bye, Brian. I understood, and so did Justin!" She lowered her lips to the still face and the ends of her hair strayed across the glistening blood.

Then she stood up, her slim body straight, but somehow pathetic. "We will bury him now," she said, her voice firm. "He will be happy here!"

Rolfe made her sit by the lifejackets while he and Chao covered the body with the pieces of stone from the crude shelter. It took a long time, and cost them all a great deal, but when they had finished, they stood looking down at the rough mound.

Judith looked across at him, her eyes pleading. "Will you say something for him, Justin? He didn't believe in anything like that," she faltered and bit her lip cruelly, "but it would be nice."

Rolfe spoke the same words that he had read across the body of the dead telegraphist, and as if ashamed of its presence, the sun began to move towards the horizon and threw their three shadows starkly across the grave.

Their eyes met and Rolfe knew that he must do something to break this terrible silence. "Are you ready, Judith?" he asked quietly. "We must get ready to leave."

She began to knot the shirt between her legs, her small face determined. "What must we do?"

He crossed to her side, worried by her tight composure. "Why don't you just lie down for a bit? Chao and I can get the gear ready."

She stepped quickly away from him, shaking her head wearily. "Just let me be quiet for a bit, Justin. I don't think I can take any more kindness!" She stared up at him, her eyes trying to explain. "I must try not to think about what has been happening! Perhaps later," she finished softly.

Rolfe jerked his head to Chao. "O.K., Chao, get the lifejackets over here. I want to be sure they're in good condition!"

He bent his head at his task, dimly aware that the sun had changed its coat to a deep orange ball, and its rays were no longer flaying his skin. He examined the small, red battery-lamps which were fitted to each lifejacket, to make sure that they were still working. He thought of how he had intended to use one of them to signal a warning to the gunboat. To tell her to keep away, and leave them to die. Brian Felton had changed all that, and had given them their only chance. The ground swayed beneath him, and he cursed anxiously. A two-mile swim, even with lifejackets, would be a pretty hazardous effort, especially when the moment came to climb out of the water on to the knife-edged reef.

"We'll tie ourselves together with the heaving-line," he murmured, and saw Chao's sad eyes glimmer with understanding. "That way we'll stand a better chance. There's a big undertow around this coast, and we might easily get swept apart!"

"When we start, Captain-sir?"

Rolfe eyed the softening sky, with its long golden shadows reaching across the hazy horizon.

"Sunset is about four hours before midnight," he answered thoughtfully, "so I think we'll start in about one hour. Without knowing the exact time, it's better not to take any chances." He tried to clear his throat, but the hard, prickling dryness clogged his aching mouth like hot sand.

He looked across for the girl, and saw her standing at the foot of the grave. She was quite still, and her head was bowed.

He wanted to run to her. To pull her against his chest, and let her cry out the misery which was stored in her heart. She was holding it back, he knew that, and he could imagine what it was costing her.

He stretched his shoulders and winced as the tight, sun-blistered skin made him stiffen with pain. He tried not to think about his thirst, and the great pounding in his ears, but each time that his guard dropped and his ear picked out the slap of water against the foot of the rock, he imagined that he was hearing the sounds of cool, fresh water running from a barrel.

He concentrated on the distant reef, feeling a note of alarm at the sight of the deep feathers of spray which rose and fell unevenly about the grinning rocks. Once out of control, and their bodies would be torn to shreds.

He kept his sagging body occupied, and his screaming mind busy, doing every little thing he could think of, not daring to lie down, in case he collapsed completely.

He noticed that the lip of the crater had cast a deep shadow across the silent figure by the grave, and a momentary panic gripped him and made him wonder whether he had misjudged the time.

Judith shivered slightly as his hands gently cupped her shoulders from behind.

"I think it's time now!" he whispered against her soft hair.

She turned slowly, as if reluctant to leave, and he was at once made more anxious by her frail appearance. But she smiled wanly, "I'm ready!"

They struggled into the lifejackets, Rolfe gritting his teeth as the rough covering ground across his back.

Judith went first, lowered carefully by Rolfe, until her feet were resting on the smooth rock shelf by the warm water.

Rolfe took a last look round, and with a savage heave, sent the rifle whirling out to sea. He dropped the tin box, and all their spare pieces of tattered clothing over the side of the cliff, and stared grimly at the darkening shape of the grave. So long, my friend, he breathed, you have had your wish. You are with the people you tried to help. Then he swung himself over the edge and down the rope.

Chao, slower but still sure-footed, followed him, without using the line, which he had first thrown down to Rolfe.

Now that they had left the shelter of the crater, their weakness and pain made them feel unprotected and naked, and it was almost with relief that they lowered themselves into the tugging water and pushed away from the rock.

The orange and blue lifejackets bobbed brightly on the heaving water, and Rolfe swam cautiously ahead, the line around his waist jerking slightly as Judith twisted into a more comfortable position. Like a brown shadow, Chao swung out on the end of the line, panting with the exertion of movement, after the blazing inactivity on the rock.

Rolfe was finding it even more difficult than he had imagined, for now that he had lost the advantage of height, he could rarely see the reef, except when a freak wave lifted him momentarily above the others, and he caught a brief glimpse of the white foam of breakers.

Each time he saw them he felt like crying with frustration. They still looked the same distance away, and the rock still loomed over his shoulder.

He twisted round, treading water. "How are you managing?" he gasped.

Judith's hair floated around her like chestnut sea-weed, glossy and sleek, but when she tried to answer him, a small wave slapped her across the mouth, and she retched painfully as the salt tortured her raw throat.

They swam grimly on, Rolfe feeling the weight growing on his rope. But for the lifejackets, he realized numbly that it would all have been over now, and the sea would have finished what the sun had started.

He was getting so weary that repeatedly he misjudged his own movements, and his head ducked beneath the jostling water. He rose, choking and spluttering, and trying to find the reef.

He looked back again. Chao was still swimming with savage determination, his eyes almost closed with strain. But the girl had practically given up, and her arms were moving only disjointedly, while her legs hung limply down beneath her.

For God's sake, he gasped, how much farther? It was much darker now, and everything was becoming more distorted and unreal. Perhaps I'm going under, he thought coldly, maybe I'm already unconscious.

A ghost rose in the water ahead, and fell with the hiss of spray. As he beat the water frenziedly with his aching hands, he saw it again and heard the dull boom of the breakers trying to force their way in over the reef.

He back paddled, and for a moment the three of them floated together in a confused tangle. He had to shake Chao's arm to stop the fierce, jerky strokes, and even then the boy didn't seem to realize that they had reached their objective.

"Slip your rope!" He had to shout, suddenly aware that the noise of the surf had grown much louder. His legs felt as if leaden weights were pulling them down. The cross-current, he thought desperately, and kicked out with the last of his strength. "I'm going to tackle it first! You follow on! Have you got that?"

Chao nodded, gulping noisily at the air.

Rolfe fumbled with the girl's lifejacket, aware that she was watching him, and conscious, too, that they were both moving rapidly through the turbulent water. He put his lips against her face, feeling the smooth skin rubbing against the stubble of his chin.

"Going to swim for the rocks! Can you hold on to my back?"

He turned over and felt her hands slipping and snatching at his neck. Then she was holding him, and her knees straddled across his back. They plunged forward and Rolfe kicked and thrust madly, as each creaming roller threatened to tear the girl from his body, and carry them helplessly on to the waiting jagged teeth.

Suddenly he saw the reef, and all at once it was below him, and he was flying through the swirling water over the first line of submerged rocks. Ahead lay the main barrier, and for one terrible second he thought they were going to be dashed against it and broken like the surf. The water dropped into a trough, and he started to fall towards the glistening crag which rose to meet him. He cried out as the thick pad of kapok on his chest ripped into the rocks and all the breath was driven from him.

Then, while he wallowed and struggled like a landed fish, his legs were dragged mercilessly over and down, and he stared in disbelief as the water was tinged with red.

He was staggering to his feet when the next wave rolled, thundering over the reef, and he hurled himself against the rock, dragging Judith against his body.

The sharp edges tore at his knees and hands as he pulled her to safety, and together they stood shaking on the top of the rock barrier, while the foam plumed and roared beneath them. They could neither hear nor think, but he squeezed her limp figure tight against him, careless of the blood which poured from his lacerated legs, and which was washed away by the high-flung spray.

He watched Chao swimming strongly along the line of gleaming teeth, and when his body was picked up by the waves, Rolfe plunged to the edge to catch him. It was a turmoil of noise and lung-bursting frenzy, but as they stood clustered together on the slippery crag, they knew that whatever else lay ahead, they had done the impossible.

Rolfe braced his body and mind against the playful fury of the sea, until time and suffering became meaningless. It was dark, but the night was torn apart by a continuous and terrifying ballet of leaping white waves, and when the pin-point of red light jabbed across the heaving black water beyond the reef, it was some time before he could bring his reeling brain to function, as with slippery, numbed hands he groped for the life-light, and flashed it dazedly towards the distant signal.

Perhaps it was all his imagination, and the red light had just been one more part of the nightmare.

He hugged the two limp bodies against him, squinting into the spray.

An age passed and just when he felt his reason and hope beginning to fade, he heard the steady creak of oars, and as he swayed awkwardly on his precarious foothold, the pale shape of the boat skimmed towards them.

"Here! We're over here!" The sea flung the words back into his mouth.

The boat faltered, and then its shape shortened as it turned towards the reef.

Blindly Rolfe clutched Judith's shoulders. "Jump!" he yelled, and together they were engulfed by the waves once more.

He clung to her body with grim desperation, and only when he felt the eager hands pulling at his body, and the smooth wooden sides of the boat, did he allow himself to falter.

They lay panting in the bottom of the boat as the oarsmen pulled strongly away from the beckoning reef, and as the keel cut into the calmer water, Rolfe saw Herridge kneeling at his side.

"Thanks, Chief," he gasped. "Couldn't have held on much longer!"

Herridge eased the girl's limp body against his knees, brushing the tendrils of hair from her face.

"Seems it was all worth while, sir!" He smiled as the girl opened her eyes and gazed at him in disbelief.

The next minute he saw the gunboat's swaying bridge above him, and summoning up his strength, he helped the girl on to the low deck. They swayed dazedly on the sturdy planking, still unable to believe they were alive, and as the boat was being hoisted briskly to the davits, and Fallow rushed forward to meet them, Judith fell limply against him in a dead faint.

"Thanks, Number One! You can get under way now!"

He carried her carefully to his darkened cabin and laid her across the bunk. Ripping off the remains of the shirt, he began to dab tenderly at her body with a towel, listening to the sound of her steady breathing.

Beneath him a bell clanged and the engines began to throb once more.

8

FALLOW watched silently from a corner of the dimly lighted wheelhouse, his shadowed face filled with unveiled curiosity and awe. He was an unimaginative man, but as he followed his Captain's movements he pondered over the story which Herridge had told him, of how Rolfe had been found 'standing in the sea'. The very fact that Herridge was so obviously impressed by all that had happened was in itself enough to make him wonder.

Rolfe, naked but for a new pair of duck trousers, was noisily draining the last of a punctured can of beer. He laid it down gratefully beside two similar cans and breathed deeply. As his broad shoulders twisted under the small pilot-light, Fallow saw the angry red blisters and the bruises, and he wondered if Rolfe would eventually explain what had been happening on Santu.

Rolfe dragged the chart roughly across the flag locker, and tapped it with his scarred hand.

"We'll stay on this course, Number One, and if the Chief gives us all the revs. he can manage, we should be able to get sixty miles between us and the island by daylight!" He rubbed his lips gingerly with the back of his wrist. "In the morning we'll alter course towards the coast and steer right along the edge of the international limit, so to speak, just in case we're attacked!"

"Er—this destroyer you mentioned, sir," began Fallow cautiously, "d'you think she'll be after us?"

Rolfe eyed him distantly. "Could be. Once we're clear of

the coast she may pick us up on her radar, although I don't think they're all that well equipped in that direction. Still, we shall have to be ready to take avoiding action." He indicated the chart. "If we are attacked, our best chance will be to close the Chinese coast, and try to shake off the chase amongst these islands and reefs. With our draft we could do it. A destroyer would find it very difficult!" He smiled bleakly. "It's a good chance, anyway!"

Fallow fidgeted awkwardly. "Suppose we meet them in the open sea, sir? I mean, we're safe 'ere, surely?"

"If I'm forced, I shall fight! They'll soon realize we're not using our radio, and they'll put two and two together."

"I see," Fallow nodded his big head, but inwardly he felt a strange sensation of calm, as if all his forebodings were coming to a head, and the realization gave him a distorted satisfaction.

Rolfe fingered his unshaven chin and shook his head to clear away the feeling of exhaustion. "They're out for revenge, and there's no saying what they might do."

The door from his quarters slid open and Ursula Laker peered across the wheelhouse. She watched Rolfe in silence, until he looked up, and then smiled gently.

"I've made sure that your little nymph is comfortable," she said quietly, "and I'll sit by her in case she needs anything."

Rolfe stared at her thoughtfully, as if seeing her for the first time. "Thank you. I'd appreciate that very much."

Ursula glanced around at the quiet, businesslike scene, and began to withdraw. "She's very lovely, Captain! I'm glad you were able to find her!"

Rolfe sighed as the door clicked behind her and Fallow stepped forward anxiously.

"You sure you're feeling strong enough, sir? I mean ter say, you look about all in."

"I shall have a shave," answered Rolfe vaguely. "That might do the trick."

"Er, pity about 'er brother, sir. That Major Ling seems to 'ave fixed things very well fer 'imself?"

Rolfe's face hardened. "I'm not so sure, Number One, I think I'm just beginning to understand these people, and I don't believe Ling's superiors are going to be too pleased with him!

He's allowed all the scapegoats to get away, and all he's got to show for his years of plotting and spying are two worthless confessions, which he might easily have written himself. No, I don't fancy his chances at all!"

"The bastard!" muttered Fallow hotly. "That poor girl must 'ave gone through 'ell until you got there, sir!'

Rolfe walked stiffly to the compass. "She went through hell afterwards, too. And she'll still be suffering now, I think!"

The bridge door banged open and Chief Petty Officer Chase marched in. "All guns crews at the ready, sir! Ready-use ammunition lockers checked, an' ship at first degree of readiness!" He glared round belligerently.

"Very good." Rolfe eyed him grimly. "If we are engaged, Chief, it'll be very much a hit-and-miss affair. You must make every shot tell, as we're no match for five-inch guns!"

Rolfe had already explained the situation to his heads of departments, and it still seemed unreal to be discussing a possible naval engagement when every inch of his throbbing body told him he was still lying on that sun-scorched rock.

"Oh, I dunno about that, sir!" Chase sounded hurt. "These Chink gunners ain't so 'ot!"

"Don't forget you'll be using Chinese gunners, too, Chief!" Rolfe smiled at Chase's puzzled expression.

"That's different, sir," Chase smiled placatingly. "Y'see, sir, they ain't 'ad the trainin'."

"Whale Island?"

Chase flushed awkwardly. "Well, that's about it, sir!"

"Carry on, then. And remember what I said!"

Fallow sighed deeply. "'E means well, sir."

Rolfe listened to Chase's distant voice shouting instructions. "Right now, he's about the most important chap aboard!" He patted Fallow's fat forearm. "Except you, of course!"

"That's all right, sir. I'm used ter 'avin' me leg pulled."

Rolfe eyed him seriously. "If it hadn't been for you, that girl in there would be dead, and so would Chao, and I! You're a good chap, Number One." He paused, remembering Felton's last words. "A friend!"

Fallow twisted with embarrassment. "Vincent an' me knew what we was gettin' into. We knew what 'ad to be done!"

Rolfe lifted his eyebrows. "Vincent? Was *he* keen to come back?"

Fallow stared out of the bridge window, fumbling for words. "'E's young, sir. 'E'll learn in time! To tell you the truth, I'm fair worried about 'im! 'E's not been the same since this lot started to blow up!"

"I don't think any of us has! We've all changed round."

"Pardon, sir?"

Rolfe shrugged tiredly. "Nothing. But it's quite a thought."

"I was wonderin', sir. 'Ow did you get to that rock place? Did you pinch a boat?"

The gunboat quivered as her blunt bows thrust urgently into the flat sea.

"The boat was provided by *Wagtail*! It was lucky we left the harbour in such a hurry that the motor-boat was left behind!"

Fallow grinned admiringly. "Lucky? It was Providence!"

In his cabin beneath the bridge Vincent lay staring at the deckhead, his eyes wide and unblinking. Could it be that his fears had been stupid and groundless? Had he given himself away so completely and without cause? He bit his lip with torment as he tried to assess his own capabilities.

Ursula must surely be laughing at him now. And where was she, now that he needed her? Probably with that other girl, the one that the Captain had brought aboard. He suddenly closed his eyes tightly and tried to shut out the ship and everyone in it.

It would be different at Government House. His thoughts began again, testing the strength of his reasoning, but it was still useless. The picture of safety and well-being simply would not form.

God! When would it all stop? Every beat of the engines seemed to be throwing a challenge to this Chinese destroyer, instead of reminding him they were on their way home.

He heard the door slide back and he lay completely still, hoping that whoever it was would go away.

"Ah, Vincent!" Laker's thick voice bored down at him. "I wondered if I might find you here."

Vincent grunted, but kept his eyes shut.

"We've been having a discussion in the mess and we've decided that we shall leave this ship at the first opportunity."

Vincent sat up slowly, blinking at the other man in amazement. "Leave? How d'you mean?"

Laker smiled blandly. "Well, I think we shall be meeting other ships soon. I understand that your Admiral intended to send ships to escort us home, once the evacuation was completed, and if we can get aboard some faster craft, we can be back in Hong Kong before your Captain!" He waited to allow the words to sink in. "We'll have a nice warm welcome waiting for him, by the time he gets to Hong Kong!" He leaned back, puffing at his cigar.

"What can you do?" Vincent asked eventually, staring at Laker with startled interest.

"Do? I told you I'm not exactly unknown in the right places! I intend to make it known how he has behaved; how he has endangered all our lives; how——" he broke off as Vincent's tight face collapsed into an uncontrollable fit of laughter. When he could speak again, his voice was high and cracked.

"Laker, *Mr*. Laker! Or whatever you call yourself! You're the one who is in for a shock! Do you spend all your time thinking up these ideas of yours? Because if you do, I'm not surprised that the Chinks hated your guts!" He lay back weakly, the tears running unchecked down his chin. "You know we've no wireless, yet you seem to think we can make a rendezvous right in the middle of thousands of miles of ruddy ocean! You live in the past, man! Don't you realize that people at home have never even heard of your damned island? I know that I, for one, wish I'd never seen the blasted place!"

Laker jumped to his feet, his face contused with rage. "Don't you dare to speak to me like that! I was going to help you, but I can see you're as worthless as the rest! And for your information, I happen to know that we may be meeting a destroyer tomorrow!" He glared down in triumph.

Vincent blinked incredulously. "You heard that?"

"I did!"

He rolled over on to his pillow, his words muffled with a sudden paroxysm of sobs. "Didn't you know it was a Chinese destroyer? God, leave me alone! Go back to your friends and tell them about your fresh bit of news!"

As Vincent buried his face in the pillow, Laker walked unsteadily to the door. His face was grey, and he looked a very old man.

.   .   .   .   .

The clear morning sunlight rippled its dancing reflections across the white paint of the wardroom and threw little golden daubs across the tablecloth. Through the open windows the sea rose and fell, calm and majestic, on either side of the ship, and gurgled cheerfully along the steel hull.

The stewards pattered to and fro between the pantry and the table, serving breakfast and watching the people with impassive faces. Fallow paused automatically at the door, to find his personal napkin, a habit he had found hard to cultivate, and now with the mounting tension in the ship, he found it even more difficult to break.

He had just been relieved from the morning watch by Vincent, who had stared dully at the chart and the log, without his usual list of biting questions and lofty remarks. Instead he had fixed his eyes on the endless wavering line along the horizon, the dull undulating mass of China, and Fallow had seen him shudder.

Fallow had avoided unnecessary conversation, and had been discomforted by the growing change in the other man. He had left him staring over the starboard wing of the bridge, his jaw tight and strained.

He lowered his bulk into the chair at the head of the table, and busied himself with the napkin, using the opportunity to dart a quick glance at the others, who sat moodily waiting for the food to arrive.

Laker stared straight in front of him, his face the picture of mixed emotions, and his eyes trying to remain in focus.

Grant and his wife were experimenting with some of the ship's biscuits, which had been brought out to replace the stock of fresh bread, long since consumed.

Anthea Masters peered across the table at the sparkling sea. "It rather reminds me of that trip we made to the Channel Islands," she began shyly, and her husband smiled uneasily. Laker frowned, as if her words had shattered his train of thought.

Fallow watched her thoughtfully. Scared to death, he concluded. It didn't seem possible that anything bad could happen in such a pleasant setting, but he was past guessing now.

Mrs. Laker eased her fragile figure forward in her chair, as the steward placed a plate of ham and eggs in front of her. She toyed with it and fumbled with her fork.

Fallow looked at his own plate and rubbed his hands with a rasping sound. "Ah! Just the job!" He glanced round the table. "This'd cost you five bob in Lyons, y'know! So you'd better eat up!"

Mrs. Laker smiled at him gratefully and began to eat.

Laker scowled at Fallow, his eyes smouldering with his pent-up dislike. Fallow munched noisily, fully aware of the hostile stare, and waiting calmly for some fresh outburst. He smiled inwardly when Laker merely asked petulantly, "Where's Ursula? She's late for breakfast!" Not risking another row, he decided gleefully.

He jerked his head as one of the stewards dropped a plate in the pantry. That was very unusual. The Chinese stewards were normally very careful. He sighed heavily, but then nothing could be normal any more.

The steward in question, Chu-pei, slouched miserably across to Fallow with the teapot. As he reached across the First Lieutenant's shoulder, Fallow saw that the thin brown hands were unsteady, and without making his movements too obvious, he craned round to stare into the man's black eyes. Chu-pei, normally a dreamy, cheerful character, dropped his glance to avoid Fallow's scrutiny.

As he moved away, Fallow nodded slowly as if to confirm his thoughts. The Chinks aboard the ship are more than just scared, he pondered, they know what'd happen to them in particular if we happened to run ashore around here.

He stirred his tea gloomily. What a mess it all was. Chinks in every direction. The General's lot, ours, and the Communists. All wanting different things, and us stuck right in the middle. He resisted the temptation to belch and tried to concentrate on what Grant was saying.

"How long d'you reckon it'll be before we're out of the woods?"

Fallow played with his spoon, wondering how he should answer. "Well, of course, we might run into a friendly ship at any time. Then we could pass a message for them to radio to Hong Kong."

"Yes, but supposing we don't meet a friendly ship, what then?"

"We'll jus' 'ave to potter along on our own. We'll be off Formosa in another thirty hours, an' we'll be all right then for sure!"

Laker tapped impatiently with his knife, listening intently to the cautious exchange of ideas.

"We seem a bit close to the mainland," persisted Grant, his face tired and uneasy. "Isn't that asking for trouble a bit? I mean, couldn't your Captain push out to sea a bit more?"

"'E knows what 'e's doin', Mr. Grant. If we are attacked, it'll call for some fancy manoeuvrin', and the closer we are to shallow water, the better."

Laker could contain himself no longer. "But they wouldn't dare to fire on a British ship! Why, it's piracy!"

Fallow munched persistently at a hard biscuit. "I bin out 'ere a good few years now," he spoke to the table at large, but he saw Laker lean forward to listen, "an' all that time I've seen British ships fired on, under every possible condition. In Formosa now, Chiang Kai-shek's boys are always shootin' up British merchant ships which are tryin' to do business with the Communists!"

"So they should!" barked Laker angrily, glaring at Fallow. "Doing deals with those scum!"

"Reckon they feel 'bout the same where you're concerned! Doin' deals with the bloody Nationalists, eh?" He guffawed loudly. It was surprising how easy it was to irritate Laker.

Laker swallowed fiercely. "This is different! This is a ship of war! And although it's not much of a ship, it is representing the British Navy!"

"Ah, you know that, but do they? You see, Mr. Laker, we've 'urt their dignity, runnin' off like this, an' I reckon it spoilt their plans!"

"Running off is right! No guts!" muttered Laker, his mouth quivering.

Fallow leaned back comfortably, his hands behind his head. "Maybe you'll get all the fightin' you want, pretty soon!"

"For heaven's sake!" Mrs. Laker's voice was shrill in its impact. "Can't you men stop baiting each other for a bit? Why don't you remember the rest of us?"

Laker snorted, but Fallow flushed humbly. "Sorry, ma'am," he murmured. "I gets a bit carried away somehow!"

Grant breathed out in sudden surprise and Fallow turned to stare at the door, following the other man's amazed glance.

Ursula Laker, in her cool frock and carrying her sun-glasses, stepped aside to allow the other girl to enter. The silence was complete, and even the stewards paused to watch.

A shaft of sunlight caught and caressed the chestnut hair and gave a warm glow to Judith's brown legs and smooth arms. She was wearing a pair of neat white shorts, with a simple blouse to match. As she walked quietly to the table, Fallow saw the glint of the medal about her neck. She looked fresh and incredibly young, but when she smiled openly at him, Fallow could see the deep sadness in her eyes.

Ursula slumped into a chair and smiled secretly at the others. "Well?" she raised her arched eyebrows. "Don't you think she's a peach?"

No one answered, and Judith's small chin jutted defiantly. "How is the Captain this morning?" Her soft voice was directed at Fallow, and by her calm assurance she seemed to exclude everyone else.

"Pretty tired, miss," he beamed at her admiringly. "'E'll be right pleased to see you about so soon agin! Are you feelin' a bit better?"

She smiled dreamily. "Much. Ursula has been looking after me, and she's fitted me out with some clothes." She dropped her eyes. "I didn't have much in the way of a wardrobe when I arrived aboard!"

Ursula chuckled. "Had to root about in your hold, or whatever you call it, to find those! Masses of bags and boxes everywhere!" She paused, frowning slightly. "By the way, who's that magnificent man, I think his name is Herridge? He helped me to search."

"Oh, 'e's the Chief Bosun's Mate, miss. A very fine chap!"

Got her eyes on old Herridge, has she? Well, well. Do him good, he thought.

Ursula winked at Judith. "Well, why isn't he here? Has he had his breakfast already?"

Laker banged his fist on the table. "Oh, for God's sake, girl! He's an N.C.O., he doesn't eat with us! He's only a——"

"Ranker?" Fallow's face was deceptively amiable.

Laker ignored his interruption. "And anyway, why the devil have you been messin' around in the store?"

"But I just told you," Ursula answered slowly, her eyes watching her father like a cat.

"I heard! It makes me sick to see a daughter of mine mixing with that little, little——" he spluttered helplessly, trying to find a suitable insult.

Judith turned her wide eyes in his direction for the first time. "Why do you hate me so much? What have I done to you?"

Laker ran his eyes over her slim body, his face bitter. "You and your kind have ruined everything my country stands for!"

Mrs. Laker fluttered at his arm. "Really, dear! What has she to do with what's happened? I'm sure she's quite a nice girl really."

Judith bowed her head, her mouth half-smiling. "Thank you very much! I am very grateful for your kind remarks!"

Fallow, who had been preparing to throw something at the other man, relaxed slightly. This girl was, as Ursula had described her, a little nymph. But she could take care of herself all right!

Mrs. Laker coloured, making her sallow cheeks appear more waxen. "You must understand that it's been a terrible shock to my husband, after all he's done! It's not his fault that you avoided us in Santu!"

Laker shook her hand from his arm, and Mrs. Laker sank back, exhausted by her own outburst.

"You and your brother were too busy with the Reds for that, eh?"

One of her small hands darted to the medal at her throat, and when she looked up, her hazel eyes flashed with anger.

"He tried to help those people you were exploiting! The Communists killed him, or didn't you know?"

Ursula jumped up angrily. "For God's sake, shut up, Father!

Judith's suffered more in the last twenty-four hours than you have in a lifetime! You make me sick!"

Fallow decided it was time to intervene. "Er, I think you'd better keep quiet, Laker! Miss Judith is still on the sick list, as far as I'm concerned, an' I'm not 'avin' 'er disturbed!"

"I'm all right!" Judith's eyes were moist. "I'm not afraid any more!"

Fallow patted her hand gently. "I know. But our old friend 'ere seems to delight in upsettin' people!" He glared threateningly at Laker. "An' I'm not 'avin' it, see?"

A dark shadow fell across the wardroom, and Rolfe stood black against the clear sky. He watched Judith quietly, and she smiled up at him, her face suddenly alight and clear.

Without taking his eyes from her, he announced slowly, "An aircraft was just sighted, circling astern." His words fell heavily into the stillness. "It may have reported our position, I'm not sure. But I am going to close up the ship at action stations and I shall want all the passengers to be ready to go below to the storeroom again!"

Fallow was already on his feet, his face impassive, but his eyes dull.

"Does it mean that we shall be attacked?" Ursula spoke calmly, watching her mother.

"It might." Rolfe's voice was unemotional and cold. "If we are, we shall try to keep our distance from any hostile ship until darkness comes. That will be our best chance."

Laker leaned on the table, his small eyes blinking "What can you do in a ship like this? We won't stand a chance!"

Reluctantly Rolfe dragged his gaze from the girl. "There is always a chance," he answered calmly. "The evacuation is completed, with the exception of Mrs. Lane and Doctor Felton, and we must face up to future events, whatever they may be. When we return to Hong Kong you can see the Governor and find out what proceedings can be opened with the Communist Government with regard to compensation, that is, if you're not too busy making accusations about my conduct." He smiled coldly, his grey eyes tired and red-rimmed with fatigue. "So you see, there's plenty for all of us to do!" He cocked his head, as the alarm bells began to jangle throughout the ship. "Right

I must leave you now. One of my Chief Petty Officers will be here in a second to assist you."

"Herridge?" Ursula's voice was casual

"Yes, Miss Laker, Herridge." He watched her, his mouth relaxed.

"Would you come to the bridge for a moment, Judith? I'd like to have a few words with you."

She smiled at the formality of his words, and he grinned awkwardly, aware of the curious and bitter glances around them.

Fallow noticed how stiffly Rolfe carried his shoulders beneath the white jacket. No doubt the blisters were playing hell with him. He sucked at his denture admiringly. He was a cool customer, right enough. In spite of his inner coldness, he smiled, drawing some confidence from the Captain's tall figure as he piloted the girl out on to the deck.

They climbed up the swaying ladders to the upper bridge, where the gun's crew sat inertly on their small seats, while the waiting shells gleamed brassily in the racks.

"Well, Judith?" He guided her to the far corner of the open platform, and together they looked down at the deserted decks. "Are we dreaming? Or are we still together, and away from that place?"

She moved closer to him, and he felt the gentle pressure of her thigh against his leg.

"We are together. Now and always!" she answered simply, but he could detect the warmth and emotion in her words.

He reached for her hand. "In a few moments I'm going to be pretty busy." He felt her body tense. "But I want you to know that whatever happens, I shall be thinking of you!"

"Lieutenant Fallow has said I'm still an invalid," she said gravely, and for a moment he thought she had not heard him, "so I can't be expected to go down below with the others, can I?" She gripped his arm tightly, her eyes pleading. "Don't make me go, Justin! I want to be close to you all the time, just in case——" She left the sentence unfinished.

He turned his face away, a burning in his eyes. "You can stay in my quarters, Judith. I'll have someone keep an eye on you."

She pressed her head against his arm and he gently stroked her hair, ignoring the intense stares of the gunners. What difference will it make? he thought. If we are hit by those big guns, no hiding place will be safer than any other.

It was sometime before she spoke again. "Last night, Justin," she faltered, "I thought I was dreaming, but was it you touching my body and looking after me?"

"Yes, Judith. I hope you understand." He watched her anxiously. "I didn't want anyone else to be near you at that moment!"

Her lips curved into a slow smile. "That's what I thought. And that's how I wanted it to be."

"Deck there!" The ringing voice of the masthead look-out shattered the peace of that perfect moment. "Ship, hull-up on the horizon! Bearing Red One-three-five!"

Rolfe grabbed for his glasses and focused them on the shouted bearing. At first he could distinguish nothing, but as the gunboat hung momentarily on the top of a lazy swell, he caught a brief glimpse of the tiny black smudge on the very rim of the sea.

He lowered his glasses. "Time to go, Judith. But don't forget what I told you."

She lowered herself over the side of the bridge and hung motionless on the metal rungs of the ladder.

"I won't forget. And I shall be thinking of the times when we will not be separated, ever again!"

The sun kissed her loose hair before she vanished from his view. For some moments he stared blankly at the empty ladder, realizing how he had changed, and how he suddenly wanted to live again.

The other ship was still visible on the horizon, but her outline was shrouded with haze, and carried no defined shape. He glanced at the silent gunners, and Chase, who was checking the shell racks. It was an air of resigned calm which hung over the gunboat. Rolfe had felt such tension many times in the past, but never had the odds seemed so grim, or the prospects so cruel.

He nodded curtly to Chase, and then lowered himself to the wheelhouse, where Vincent and Fallow were waiting for him.

"Ship closed up, sir," announced Fallow tonelessly. "I've told the engine-room to stand by for another emergency speed order."

"Very good."

226

Vincent rubbed his palms against his tunic, and stared round at the steel shutters. He seemed to have difficulty in breathing.

Rolfe eyed him keenly and caught Fallow's meaning look. "It's a bit stuffy in here," he remarked. "It'll be worse when the sun's high!"

Vincent looked at him blankly and licked his lips. "How long have we got, sir?" His voice was unsteady.

"All the time in the world," snapped Rolfe. "Now let's take a look at the chart again."

He felt their bodies closing in behind him as he switched on the chart light in the darkened space behind the bridge. He traced the ragged outline of the coast with his finger, picturing it in reality, as it lay off the ship's starboard beam.

"Shoal waters and three groups of small islands," he murmured softly, "all within the next sixty miles. The Taichau group are already abeam, and there are these smaller ones next. Not much in the way of habitation on this part of the coast, apart from the odd fishing village." He heard Fallow's heavy breathing and sensed them both watching his hand on the chart. "We'll have to chance there being any coastal batteries and drive in amongst these islands if it comes to a running battle!"

Vincent groaned. "Then there's no chance of, of getting away without fighting?"

Rolfe pivoted round sharply, his eyes cold. "Very little, I should imagine!" He dropped his voice, enclosing just the three of them in his words. "I think this is going to be a pretty tight situation and when it breaks, there'll not be much time for fresh thoughts. I shall do what I can, and I am relying on you to see that we make the best of ourselves! This is an old ship and a forgotten ship at that. But for this work, she'd be under the breaker's hammer right now! But she's a British ship, and part of the Service to which we belong! We were chosen for one job, which we've now completed, but there's something else quite different happening now, which the planners didn't bargain for. No doubt it'll be argued about and fought over in the United Nations, if the worst happens, and protests will be exchanged by all the governments concerned; but that's not our worry! What we must realize is that we are quite alone, and this is still a naval ship!" His mouth twisted into a grim smile, which made

227

his taut face look cruel. "We will act accordingly. Any questions?"

He watched each of them in turn, Vincent, pale-faced and hollow-eyed, and Fallow grimly set into a mould of determination.

"We ain't exactly cut out for this sort of caper, are we, sir?" Fallow forced a grin.

Rolfe smiled. "The impartiality of Admiralty often carries remarkable effects in its wake!"

Vincent made some effort to gather himself together. "It's all so unfair!" He sounded like a small boy. "So damned unfair!"

Fallow coughed nervously. "'Ere, come off it, Vince! Let's 'ave some of the old flannel you used to give me! I'd feel better if you bucked up a bit!"

Vincent shook his head dazedly and for a moment Rolfe thought he was going to break into tears. "I'm all right," he muttered, "I don't have to be told what to do!"

Fallow breathed deeply. "Good! 'Cause if you don't start showin' me 'ow a proper officer should behave, Vince, I'll never forgive you!" He shrugged helplessly at Rolfe, and began to tighten the strap of his binoculars about his neck.

"Very good, Number One. Carry on with the gunnery control, and good luck!"

Fallow tore his eyes from Vincent. "Aye, aye, sir. This'll be somethin' to tell the wife about, anyway!" He shambled away, his fat shoulders hunched under the load of his worry.

Rolfe stepped on to the wing of the bridge and felt the probing rays of the sun piercing his tunic, as if eager to irritate his raw back. The ship was nearer now and he could detect the faint trail of smoke hanging motionless across the clear sky.

It would be soon now, he thought. It was so brutal and final, and yet so slow, that he wondered if Nelson's officers had felt as he did, when the fleets of tall ships drifted closer and closer, across waters as flat and calm as these. He ran his eye wearily over the deserted decks. There was an air of expectancy which seemed to chill him, despite the heat, and even the engines sounded subdued.

From each mast and from the stern the huge White Ensigns flapped gently, and across the boards at his feet he saw the black shadow of the gun, like a pointing finger, as it silently followed the other ship.

I wonder what Laker thinks now? And the others, stuck down there in the storeroom? And what of Edgar Lane in the Sick Bay? Was he still mourning the loss of his trees, or had the impact of his wife's death reached his tortured mind?

Judith. Her name hung in his mind as he tried to picture her behind the steel shutters. What would she be thinking?

He banged his hands on the rail with sudden anguish. It was bad enough, without having to risk her life again!

The muffled voice of the range-finder drifted down to him. "Target altering course! Target's course One-nine-oh! Range Oh-eight-double-oh!" He watched the destroyer's low shape lengthening. She's trying to head us off. That shouldn't be too difficult with her speed, he thought bitterly. What'll her first move be, I wonder?"

Vincent spoke flatly from the wheelhouse. "We are closing first island, sir. We are inside Chinese waters now!"

Rolfe watched the destroyer narrowly through the glasses. "Hold your course!"

The Chinese captain was anticipating that, he thought. Just waiting for us to pull away, and then. And then, what?

The islands, yellow and green in the sunlight, were so many and so closely bunched that it was impossible to determine the channels between them. From the gunboat they looked like part of the coast itself. He caught his breath as a small orange flash darted from the destroyer's grey shape, and seconds later the dull boom of the gun echoed across the glittering water.

Rolfe counted automatically, and as he watched, a tall water-spout rose high in the sea, about a hundred yards ahead.

"First shot. Half a cable, at Red-one-five!" The range-finder's expressionless voice might have been noting the score at a darts match.

The two ships moved on, their courses practically parallel, while Rolfe watched the islands, and waited. The seconds passed, and then the minutes. He felt the sweat gathering at his waist and running freely down his arms.

Fallow's voice from above was hushed. "They're holdin' their fire, sir. What are they playin' at?"

"Listening!" Rolfe's voice was flat and uncompromising. "They're waiting for us to start wirelessing for assistance." He paused. "And when we don't, they'll know it's safe to go ahead!"

Fallow's head disappeared, and Rolfe frowned. He had wanted to reassure Fallow, but the false words had eluded him.

"How are the islands, Vincent? Are we still closing?"

It seemed an age before he replied, and his voice shook. "First one on the starboard quarter now, sir. There are the next little group opening up on the bow." He faltered. "Those shoals marked on the chart are visible, too!"

He could see the destroyer clearly now. The range was about three miles. Something told him it was time to act.

"Tell engine-room, full emergency!" His voice was a metallic rasp in the still air.

He felt the bridge trembling and the wake frothed and mounted under the low stern.

There it was! A ripple of four flashes along the grey hull and the louder crash of heavy guns following quickly behind.

"Hard a-starboard!"

"Hard a-starboard, sir," repeated the helmsman, "thirty-five of starboard wheel on!"

As the triple rudders bit into the surging water, the flat-bottomed gunboat tacked round like an experienced boxer. Even as she turned, the calm sea was torn apart by the tangled, leaping walls of spray. The four shells landed as one and amidst the din and the roar of cascading water, Rolfe heard Vincent cry out involuntarily.

"Midships! Steer Two-seven-oh!" He watched the swinging compass repeater and then stepped into the wheelhouse, slamming the steel door behind him. He cursed the inadequacy of the observation vents and rested his glasses on the warm metal, conscious of the sour taste in his throat.

Again the roar of distant gunfire pommelled his eardrums, and once more the salvo clawed towards the twisting gunboat.

Vincent turned his agonized face from the front of the bridge. "God! We're almost on those rocks!"

"Signalman, read back the reports from the echo-sounder, directly they're passed to you!"

Randal, the signalman, his face screwed up with concentration, held his ear against the voice pipe.

"Six fathoms!" he reported almost at once.

Rolfe pushed past Vincent and watched the unbroken line of reefs ahead of him. The gleaming necklace of rocks seemed to clash with the placid island beyond, and the mottled sheen on the shallow water.

He forgot the chart and tried to memorize the details of the islands.

"Four fathoms, sir!"

Rolfe forced himself to concentrate on the rocks, and with his eye he tried to estimate the distance between each wave-washed tooth.

"Port twenty!" The bows seemed to take a year to respond. He waited until they were practically masking the narrow strip of water between two of the reefs, then, "Midships! Steer straight for that gap!"

Leading Seaman Davidson leaned heavily on the polished spokes of the wheel, his narrowed eyes peering ahead. What gap? he thought desperately. We'll never make it!

"Three fathoms, sir!" The voice trembled.

The sea erupted into a blinding flash as a shell struck one of the rocks. Rolfe gritted his teeth and darted a glance at the helmsman, as something clanged against the shutters.

The hull of the gunboat quivered as if dealt a body blow.

The helmsman hissed between his teeth. He had practically lost sight of the tiny gap in the rocks, it had been blotted out by the overhanging bow. So great was his sweating concentration that Rolfe noticed that he didn't even quiver as the shell splinter screamed away across the bridge.

"Two fathoms, sir!" It was like a death chant.

"Christ! Turn back! You'll kill us all!" Rolfe turned to face the screaming face. "We can't get through there! You'll smash the ship to pieces!" Vincent's face had collapsed completely.

"'Ere we go!" Leading Seaman Davidson's voice was a mere rasp.

Rolfe ignored Vincent and sprang to the side of the bridge, to stare at the line of rocks skimming along the side of the ship. He ran to the other side, almost knocking Vincent down, and saw that they were passing between the gap, with barely feet to spare.

"One fathom, sir!" the signalman reported stubbornly, his voice weak.

Rolfe caught the helmsman's eye. "We're through, sir!"

Rolfe nodded, watching the distorted shapes of sunken rocks passing along and under the ship. They were less than four feet under the keel.

"Hard a-starboard!" he snapped, and the *Wagtail* strained valiantly round on her invisible pivot. The deserted beach of the nearest island was rushing to meet them.

He straightened the ship's creaming wake and called up Fallow on the voice pipe. Vincent was watching him with the eyes of a madman.

"Where's the target?"

"She's 'auled off, sir!" Fallow's voice was shaking. "I thought we was goin' on that load of rock, sir! I thought you'd been 'it, or somethin'."

Rolfe smiled in spite of himself. "Not quite, Number One! Now watch for the gap between the next island and get ready to fire just as soon as you get the chance. Concentrate on her bridge, if you can!"

The gulls and cormorants rose screaming and flapping from the beaches in a white cloud, as the strange craft thrashed recklessly along the narrow channel, and once, Rolfe saw a group of running figures darting between the trees. This will be something for them to remember, he thought. It was like a rabbit twisting and turning through the labyrinth of its burrow, with the ferret sniffing and scratching at every opening and exit.

The small island towered above them, and he tried to estimate the destroyer's approximate position on the seaward side. They would be coming to the end of the island soon, and there was another wide gap of open, shallow water to cross before the gunboat could find cover and temporary safety amongst the next scattered group.

He snapped his fingers impatiently without lowering his eyes from the green and blue patchwork of the channel. "Depth, man, depth!"

"Two fathoms, sir!"

He was sweating freely now, and felt strangely light-headed.

The depth of water was only a narrow margin of safety. At any second an unmarked and hidden reef might tear out the bottom of the charging gunboat, like a knife cutting through cheese.

"Oh, God! Why doesn't it stop?" Vincent's strangled voice was close to Rolfe's ear and he started with surprise. In the excitement and danger he had all but forgotten him.

"Hold your course!" he snapped to the helmsman, and moving swiftly, he jerked Vincent by the arm and led him roughly into the chart room.

For a moment he stood glaring at this wreck of a man, half of him wanting to deal reasonably and patiently, and the other half screaming out at himself to get back to the bridge, begrudging every second of wasted pity.

"Vincent! You've got to get hold of yourself!" He spoke harshly, his eyes holding the other man's frightened gaze. "It's your only chance! Do you understand?"

Vincent swallowed nervously and with cold deliberation, Rolfe struck him hard across the cheek with the back of his hand. Vincent fell back against the chart table, his hand fluttering against his reddening face. His eyes were still filled with fear, but the fear was fresh, and Rolfe knew it was because of him. He lifted his fist again, and Vincent cowered back, his mouth quivering.

"Well? Are you ready?" The grey eyes flashed with rage. "Or do I have to kill you first?"

Vincent nodded violently. "I'll try, sir! I'll try!"

Rolfe turned his back and ran back to his position, with Vincent following dazedly behind.

When Rolfe issued his next orders, his voice was calm and detached, as if he had never moved.

"Inform the guns to stand by to fire immediately we clear the land and sight the target!" He waited, his mind stilled, as Vincent's unsteady voice passed the instructions.

He spoke to the bridge at large. "We should be in the open again for about ten minutes. That'll give us time to have a shot or two at them." He could feel Vincent's eyes watching him as if mesmerized. "The destroyer still can't get at us in these shallow waters, but she'll have a good try to finish us off the moment we show ourselves!"

The yellow beach started to curl away, and the sheltered water began to widen. The open sea and the distant horizon sparkled with quiet malice, and every eye was watching the widening gap, every heart pounding faster with each beat of the racing propellers.

Above his head Rolfe heard the clank of metal, and in his mind he could see the gunners crouched around their puny weapon.

The edge of the island fell clear, and in the sunlight the green slope seemed to harden, but as they watched, they recognized the sharp stem of the waiting ship.

The world exploded as the six-pounder barked its challenge, and close behind it came the staccato rattle of the Oerlikon. The bridge rocked and echoed with the trapped noise, and the stench of cordite made their eyes smart and their throats contract.

Again and again the guns crashed out and the hoarse commands and range orders mingled with the clang of empty shell cases on the steel platform and the sharp clicks of the breech block.

The destroyer's hull was masked by the flame and smoke of her own guns, and Rolfe jammed his smarting eyes into the eyepieces of his glasses, taking in the long, threatening shape, the squat funnel, and the long guns, which seemed to be pointing directly at him.

The weaving gunboat was shrouded and straddled by the tall columns of water, and the hull bounced and shuddered as the heavy shells hissed and screamed into the water around her.

The destroyer turned slightly as if to intercept them, and then swung away. Her echo-sounder must have warned her of the danger just in time. In that brief moment of manœuvring, her guns fell silent, and Rolfe heard a scattered cheer as a bright flash lit up the rear of her bridge.

One hit to us! One tiny pinprick. But it will give them something to think about.

All the air and light was sucked from the bridge with the ease of a pump drawing water. One moment Rolfe was listening to the cheers and watching the next group of islands, and the next he was staring at a line of rivets in the grey-painted plating. He tried to concentrate, and as his shattered mind cleared, he realized that he was lying full length on the deck, his face against the steel bulkhead.

He pressed his hands on the deck and tried to lever himself to his knees. He could feel the pain in his ribs where he had fallen, but he could hear nothing.

Vacantly he stared round the smoke-filled wheelhouse, his eyes and mind registering a slow jumbled mass of terrible detail.

The wheel clinked gently from side to side, unattended and loose, and Rolfe seized the shoulder of the helmsman, who was twisted into an untidy heap beneath the compass.

The sudden urgency of what had happened made Rolfe stagger wildly to the front of the bridge, where he clung breathless to the shutter, and stared at the deck beneath him. The flat fo'c'sle deck had gone completely. There was only a wide, blackened hole reaching from one side of the ship to the other, leaving the bows and anchors marooned in a tiny island. The guardrails and plating of the hull were bent and twisted, like plants wilted by the heat. He stared at the great gaping gash left by the shell, and through the black smoke and evil-smelling vapour he saw the glint of water.

We're done for! He choked back the flood of fury and despair which rose unrestrainedly in his aching throat. As he tried to pull his wits together, his hearing began to creep back, and with it came a torrent of disjointed and terrifying sounds from all around him. Voice pipes rattled and shouted, and somewhere he heard a high-pitched scream, which rose and fell with a terrible persistence.

The helmsman staggered to his feet, his face white and shocked. Without looking at Rolfe, he grabbed the spokes of the wheel and spun them cautiously in his hands.

"Course, sir?" He could hardly get the words out.

Rolfe jerked his head towards the peaceful islands, realizing for the first time that the engines were still throbbing, although with a different beat. "Keep straight for the next island!"

He staggered to the demanding, screaming voice pipes, noting as he went that Vincent was slowly rising to his feet. Their eyes met, and Vincent smiled, his teeth gleaming strangely through the dust on his face.

Rolfe called up the gun's crew. "Report damage!"

He was surprised to hear Chase's voice from the other end of the brass pipe.

"Gun still in action, sir! Lieutenant Fallow's been 'it! An' there's a good bit of damage forrard!"

"Very good! Carry on firing!"

He fumbled with the engine-room speaker. "You all right Chief? Is that bulkhead holding?"

Louch sounded tired and far away. "Aye, sir! But one engine has packed up for the moment. I've got my men working on it, an' I think some of the fuel pipes have been sheared off by a splinter."

Rolfe sat silent, watching the Signalman crouched at his station. Poor Fallow, he thought suddenly. I wonder how bad it is?

The ship rocked wildly as another shell sliced along the upper deck and exploded harmlessly in the sea beyond. It looked as if a giant branding-iron had been scored right across the decks and had left one wide, blackened trail of damage in its wake.

One engine only, he thought desperately, watching the helmsman struggle with the wheel, as the gunboat staggered in a twisting, crablike motion, its rudders fighting for mastery over the uneven thrust of the remaining engine.

"Damage Control Party just gone forrard!" reported the signalman, and he saw Herridge and a handful of seamen ducking and slipping over the shattered deck, their faces turned away as each salvo screamed over their heads.

Rolfe watched them helplessly, as Herridge and his men began to lower themselves into the gaping crater. He could now hear the deep, pulsating thud of the main pumps, as they fought against the inrushing water. There ought to be an officer with them, he thought. Herridge would have his work cut out just keeping the men at their posts.

"Vincent! Get forrard! See what you can do, and report damage!"

Vincent did not reply, and Rolfe waited for some fresh outburst, but instead, the door clanged shut, and a few seconds later he saw Vincent walking slowly along the rim of the shell crater, his hands behind him, as if he was inspecting his division on a Sunday morning.

Another shell whined across the bridge, and with amazed eyes, Rolfe saw the forward mast plunge over the side, dragging a mass of rigging and halyards after it. The useless wireless aerials clattered and squeaked against the bridge, before they, too, were sucked into the sea.

Herridge ran to the foot of the bridge, his grimy hands cupped. "Bulkhead's holding, sir! But quite a large fracture abreast the keel! The pumps are just about holding their own!"

"Lower the boat, Chief!" Rolfe saw the man's jaw drop. "Lower it to the waterline, and put all the ship's awnings in it!" Herridge still hesitated. "Jump, man! I want that boat ready to drop as we come up to the next island!"

Herridge ran aft to the davits, calling out a string of names. The *Wagtail's* canvas awnings were dragged from their racks and laid in the boat by the small, frightened seamen.

"Engine-room!" Rolfe had to yell above the head-splitting roar of gunfire. "Three drums of oil on deck, at the double! And get it to the boat!"

A freak shell exploded in the water, and Rolfe gritted his teeth as one of the Chinese seamen running to the boat faltered in his stride and slid to the deck. For some moments he thrashed about wildly, as his white jumper burst open to reveal what looked like a mass of scarlet rubber hose. Before their eyes, the man had been disembowelled by one savage splinter.

Herridge, tight-lipped, punched a staring seaman in the shoulder. "Don't stand there like a tart in a trance! Man the falls!"

The terrified seaman wrenched his eyes from the glistening thing on the deck and ran to the boat.

The islands opened up their green banks to welcome the *Wagtail*, as with smoke streaming from her wounds, loose planking and twisted plates dangling from her sides, she wallowed forward to safety.

Rolfe watched the oil being poured into the boat and soaking into the piled awnings. The boat was lowered until its keel almost skimmed the moving water.

Come on, old girl! Just hold on! He gripped the rail, as if sharing her pain, as another shell burst under the sagging bow with a blinding flash. When the spray had fallen, he saw with amazement that Vincent still paced stiffly across the unprotected deck.

The destroyer was gone, hidden again by the little lumps of land. She would be getting ready to finish the job at the next gap.

"Right? Light the awnings and slip the boat adrift!"

Herridge moved briskly to the buckled rail. "Stand by! Lower away!"

The boat yawed sluggishly against the side, and while the axes were still hacking away at the falls, Herridge hurled a lighted rag into the oily mound across the thwarts.

The next minute the boat had bobbed astern, and when Rolfe craned over the rail to watch, he saw it rocking forlornly in their wash, almost hidden by the great black pall of dense smoke which floated straight up into the bright sky.

They'll see that and think it's us, he mused. It'll give us a bit of a respite, anyway, if it works!

The wheelhouse door clanged back as three seamen staggered in and laid their burden across the flag locker.

Fallow lay back on the coloured bunting, his brown eyes tightly screwed into little islands of pain.

His face seemed shrunken, and when he tried to speak, Rolfe realized that he must have lost his dentures.

"Too—bad—sir!" His breath was fast and wheezing. From the rough dressing on his shoulder, Rolfe saw the widening scarlet stain seeping across the outflung arm. "Sorry to leave you like this!" Fallow was still apologizing, and Rolfe dropped to his knee, gripping the man's hand. It was ice cold.

"Hold on, Number One! Don't forget you're due for a discharge!" He tried to grin, but the expression of misery in Fallow's eyes made him turn away. "Just lie quiet, Number One."

Vincent walked shakily into the wheelhouse, wiping his mouth with a filthy handkerchief.

"Take over, Vincent!" Rolfe eyed him sharply. "Watch your course! I'm going up top to look at the damage!"

The upper bridge seemed even more unsheltered now that the mast had gone, and he found Chase leaning tiredly against the breech of the gun, his red face heavy with strain.

One gunner lay at his feet, the inside of his head splashed across Chase's trousers.

"Good shooting, Chief!" Rolfe felt his stomach heaving "What happened to Lieutenant Fallow?"

Chase was staring vacantly at the human wreckage on the deck. "When we was 'it, sir, a splinter got Mr. Fallow in the shoulder. 'E was up with the range-finder. This is 'im down 'ere!" He cleared the phlegm from his throat. "Gun's still all right though!" He patted the breech with a beefy hand. "Bloody Chinks!" he added flatly.

Rolfe noticed that one of the gun-loaders was crying openly, the tears pouring unchecked down his yellow cheeks. Chase looked across at the man. "Stow it! Or I'll croak you an' all!" He scowled and the seaman moved miserably away. "Bloody Chinks!" Chase said once more.

Rolfe slid down the ladder, his eyes checking the pathetic wreckage and damage, which seemed to be confined to the forward part of the ship.

He waited, as the stewards carried Fallow into his cabin and laid him on the bunk. He didn't see Judith come from the other cabin, but he found her in his arms, her slim body pressed against him.

"Is it over? Are we safe?" She stared searchingly at his worn face.

"Not quite! But we've left a decoy in the water for them! I am hoping that the destroyer will try to see what's back there making all the smoke, and that will give us time to pass the next bit of open sea!"

"They can't get at us while we're amongst these islands, can they?" Her mouth quivered slightly.

"We shall have to move out eventually, Judith," he answered slowly. "I'm just fighting for time."

She watched Fallow's heavy breathing, the morphia beginning to take effect. "Is he, is he going to be all right?"

Rolfe smiled gently. "I am hoping so." He held her tightly, trying to find words to reassure her.

"I'll stay with him, Justin. He looks so ill!" she said simply.

"Yes." He turned wearily, as Herridge poked his head round the door.

He looked at Fallow and then stared at Rolfe. "All the passengers are fit an' well, sir. Bit shaken up, of course!"

"I can imagine," Rolfe answered grimly. "Still, it's lucky they weren't at the other end of the ship!"

"Is the Lieutenant badly hurt, sir?"

"I can't tell yet, Chief. But he's lost a lot of blood!"

Herridge eased his stiff shoulders. "Lieutenant Vincent told me to tell you we're passing between the main group of islands now, sir."

"Good."

There was no more firing. The gunboat was momentarily safe amidst the maze of green humps. The destroyer must soon discover the ruse Rolfe had left behind, and would be thrashing after them. But at the moment they were secure.

He gripped her shoulders. "Lie down on the deck if it starts to get noisy again!"

As he returned to the bridge, he saw her kneeling by Fallow's side, wiping his damp face with her hand.

Lieutenant Vincent found he could not stay still, and every bone in his body felt loose and unsteady. He continually shook his head and licked his dry lips, and tried to remember what had happened on the forward deck.

He had left the bridge at Rolfe's orders, and as he had gone to look for Herridge, he had felt as if he was giving up his life and throwing away his last chance of survival.

With crazy deliberation he had paced the rocking deck, shutting his ears to the screaming shells and the turmoil of water. He had held his body erect, waiting for the sudden impact.

A seaman had been cut to ribbons by the lowered boat, but he had felt nothing, not even shock.

He stared around the wheelhouse, unable to realize he was still alive. I must be going mad, he thought. Nothing seems real any more. I can't feel anything!

When he thought of Fallow, he was strangely affected, but he saw Fallow as himself, and felt pity rather than sadness.

He looked up, startled, as the Captain strode to the open shutters. Rolfe looked gaunt and completely exhausted. His dirty tunic hung open, and his bare chest was pockmarked by the tiny wooden splinters which had whistled up from the torn decks.

Vincent found himself grinning again. "They built this ship pretty well, didn't they, sir?"

Rolfe regarded him calmly. "Just as well!"

In the dim cabin Fallow stared up at the deckhead, his eyes dark with inner misery. He could feel no pain any more, merely a pricking sensation in his shoulder, like pins-and-needles. He felt as if his body was suspended in space, lighter than air.

He saw the girl's brown face close to his and noticed that her huge eyes were brimming with tears.

That worried Fallow, and he tried to tell her not to cry. But he found that no words came, and that he could not even raise his hand to her hair, which hung close to his cheek.

He felt himself sinking again into another bank of cloud, the cabin swayed and receded before his eyes. Mary, he thought desperately, what will she do without me? What about the garden, and the rockery I was going to make? Judith's face had faded to an oval blob, but her presence gave him comfort.

Poor little *Wagtail*. I've looked after you all this time and now they are trying to destroy you, as they've destroyed me! All the light had gone now, but it didn't matter any more. It was easier to see Mary and the distant liners making for Southampton.

.   .   .   .   .

The *Wagtail*'s engine-room was an inferno of noise and steam. Above the straining beat of the remaining engine, Louch listened gloomily to the screech of a hacksaw and the thud of hammers, and tried to read some sound of success.

He stared at the silent mass of steel and brass, which a short time ago had been a living symbol of his power. Now, deprived of its precious fuel and drive, it lay inert and useless. A Chinese stoker was rubbing the shining shaft with a piece of oiled rag, as if in some mysterious way he was going to set it in motion again.

Louch thrust his bird-like body away from the warm bulkhead, the very movement sending a fresh stream of sweat down his angry face. He had to do something, anything, to take his mind away from what was happening overhead and around him. He listened to the water sloshing against the hull, and wondered why the firing had stopped. When the five-inch shell had ploughed into the fo'c'sle, and exploded below the waterline, he had thought that the moment dreaded by all ships' engineers everywhere had arrived. His heart seemed to stick in his throat, as he waited, crouched like a trapped animal, for the bulkhead to burst open and a wall of water to surge in on him. Once that happened, and the savage water reached the boilers, there was no escape. It was said to be a quick death. He shuddered again and spat. Who knew what it was like to be fried alive?

Herridge was thinking along a similar line of reasoning as he watched the pumps squirting a steady stream of sea-water over the side. It was amazing to think such a small ship could stand so heavy a blow and survive.

He smiled sardonically. Survive for what? he wondered. Far behind he could still see the oily spindle of smoke rising from the abandoned sampan. Trust the skipper to think of something like that, but perhaps it was only prolonging their agony just a little longer.

He scratched his chin, watching the small islands skimming past, and feeling the gunboat roll and sway, as she twisted between the threatening sand bars. Sixty miles of islands the skipper had said. But even if they survived that, the open sea still lay between them and safety.

Rolfe's head appeared over the top of the scarred bridge. "Check the passengers, Chief!" he called. "Make sure they're comfortable, and get Mr. Lane out of the Sick Bay and put him with the others. I want 'em all together."

Herridge made his way quickly to the storeroom, glad to have something to do. He grimaced as he stepped around the cruelly rejected pile of rags and flesh on the main deck, and lifted the heavy hatch over the twin storerooms.

In the dim light of a swinging inspection lamp he saw their eyes gleaming whitely, as they turned towards him. They think I've come to tell them we are sinking, he thought, and grinned cheerfully.

"S'all right, everybody, everything's under control!" He glanced about the wide compartment and had to stoop to avoid crashing his head on the low supports. He saw the white jackets of the stewards as they moved between the stooped forms, adjusting lifejackets and passing around cups of fresh water.

Laker's face shone distortedly in the swinging light. "How far have we got? Has the other ship gone away?"

Herridge shook his head, his eye straying to the pale shape of Ursula Laker. Her long legs were directly beneath the lamp and shone with a disembodied brightness, which fascinated him. She was a fine girl, he mused, well built, and she knew it, too. His thoughts were interrupted by Laker's demanding voice, and he wearily gave the man his attention.

"We'll have a bit more firing in a minute, I expect, sir." Charles Masters gripped his wife even closer in the darkness, and Herridge softened his tone. "But the Captain knows what he's about!"

"Those damned Chinks!" Laker rocked back on his seat with sudden rage. "I'd like to get my hands on some of them!"

Herridge glanced quickly at the two stewards, but their blank faces told him nothing. "Well, try to remember, sir, that two of them have just been killed up top. Fighting for you," he added mildly.

There was a pregnant silence, and Herridge began to mount the ladder. "By the way," he spoke across their heads, "if you get the order to come on deck. Do it at the rush! And keep together!" He pushed back the hatch and felt the sun hard on his head.

"There's no need to throw your weight about!" Laker seemed to be trying to regain his prestige in front of the others.

Herridge glanced at him stonily. "You'll do yourself a bit of good to obey orders, sir." He spoke with flat politeness. "You're next to the magazine!"

He felt childishly pleased with his lie as he climbed out on to the deck. He stood aside as two seamen carried Lane down into the darkness on a stretcher. Stuck-up bugger, he thought. I hope his daughter hasn't got any of his ways.

Rolfe's eyes were beginning to dance and burn in their sockets, as he stared from the bridge to the islands, and from the rocks to a small feather of spray, which might be hiding a reef.

He almost jumped as a voice spoke quietly at his elbow.

"Nice mug of iced beer, Captain-sir?" Chao stood respectfully at his side, his dark eyes tired and fearful. He nevertheless smiled as Rolfe lifted the huge mug to his parched lips, and drank deeply. "Sorry about mug. All wardroom crockery smashed!"

243

Rolfe watched the boy affectionately, wondering if he and Judith had really been marooned on a distant rock with this brown elf. "That's too bad, Chao. But the beer tastes all the better!"

Chao still waited.

"Well? What's on your mind?" Rolfe kept his eye on the nearest strip of beach.

"Miss Judith. I think we better get her down to deck, Captain-sir! It not safe up here any more!" He glanced around the shambles and fallen wreckage.

"It's as safe as the rest of the ship," he said slowly, "but I am relying on you to keep an eye on her for me!"

Something of the old smile flashed across the round face. "Very good! I stay up here too then!"

"That's what you really wanted, isn't it?"

Chao placed the mug carefully on the tray, his features masked in tired gravity. "That is so, Captain-sir."

"Two fathoms, sir!" The voice was getting weary and cracked. but Rolfe nodded briefly and raised his glasses to study a small fishing boat which had appeared round one of the beaches. It was being sculled by a thin, bearded man in a wide straw hat. He neither looked up nor slackened his stroke with the long sweep-oar, as the gunboat bore down and passed him.

Overhead, a white line of gulls circled watchfully above the tiny boat waiting for the fish to appear. It was so peaceful and so strangely beautiful that he felt a lump in his throat. How could anyone begin to understand China?

Vincent stirred on the other side of the bridge and cleared his throat. "Alter course, sir? I estimate our position to be just to the north-west of the last group. That means we've got two more hours of cover to go." He seemed to be speaking half to himself, and Rolfe watched him thoughtfully.

Vincent seemed to be making an almost superhuman effort to appear calm and natural, and he felt relieved that the man was trying to help him. "Yes, alter course," he answered distantly.

"Port fifteen!" Vincent peered at the compass. "Midships! Steady!"

The gunboat tugged rebelliously at the rudders, but slowly swung on to the new course.

"Steady, sir! Course One-eight-five!" The helmsman looked as if he was riveted to the wheel. As if he had been there for ever.

"Steer One-eight-six!" Vincent chuckled strangely, amused by his own preciseness.

Rolfe caught his eye and smiled grimly. It did seem rather stupid to imagine that any careful effort of navigation could be of any assistance to them.

"Two more fishing boats!" the look-out reported. The small wooden craft floated motionless on the glassy sea, their sails folded like the tattered wings of sleeping birds.

The machine-guns on the bridge swung menacingly towards them, but the harmless vessels drifted past, and bobbed gaily in the gunboat's wake.

Food and drink was passed round the ship, the stewards creeping furtively between each group of waiting seamen. Nobody spoke, and few noticed what they had eaten. Their throats became dry almost as soon as they had finished the water, and they knew that, for once, the sun was not solely to blame.

Rolfe examined the pencilled line across the chart. Their escape line from Santu. It was as if a magnet had drawn them closer and closer to the waiting mainland. He cursed aloud, defying his weakness and imagination. The islands were fading away, and he remembered when he had waited for the fog to lift, so long ago, in the North Sea. He had been searching for a crippled U-Boat, which was hiding in the fog, hanging on to the thread of life.

The fog had gone, and they had gone in to the kill.

He stared at the printed shapes of the islands on the chart and realized just how that U-Boat commander must have felt when his cover and protection faded away.

There was one island, quite apart from the remainder, which would be their last barrier against the destroyer. After that, the sea-bottom shelved down and dropped away to a bottomless cavern. The field would be open then.

"Tell the guns to prepare to shoot when we clear this group," he called wearily. "We shall cross to the last island, and although the water is still shallow, it's a bit deeper than here, and the target will close in a bit more, I think."

He heard Vincent passing the instructions and he straightened up, feeling the stiffness in his limbs.

He listened to the empty shell cases rolling across the gun platform as the ship swung heavily into a sullen roller, and dipped her waterlogged bows with tired resignation. Poor old girl, he thought, it's unfair to you, as much as the rest of us.

The islands began to fall away, and they moved into the open stretch of sea with what appeared to be terrible slowness. Unlike the first time, there were no sharp commands, and few sounds of any kind, but for the muffled hammering in the engine-room. Their uneven shadow twisted across the water, and Rolfe could feel every eye on the distant sea and its threatening emptiness.

"Three fathoms, sir!"

He pulled the creased chart urgently against the rail and studied the tiny figures denoting the various depths and the positions of the nearest rock formations.

The sea ahead of the *Wagtail* was empty and flat, yet the chart showed the continuation of the reef barrier, which seemed to surround most of the islands in grim detail and closely packed profusion.

He cursed himself for not taking it into consideration earlier. The echo sounder would give little warning of a sudden shelf or rocky crag just beneath the surface. The muscle in his jaw began to twitch, and he dashed the sweat from his eyes with the back of his hand.

Vincent sucked in his breath in a loud gasp. "There she is, sir! Dead astern!"

Rolfe plunged to his side, his glasses already to his eyes. He found that he did not need them. The destroyer, frustrated and angered by his decoy, was charging recklessly along the islands, her guns trained inland, covering every inlet and creek. Her high, raked stem was covered by her powerful bow-wave as it cu savagely through the sea. Less than a mile away she seemed to fill the horizon with her plunging shape, and blot out their chance of even reaching the last island.

The bells rang once more, and the *Wagtail's* gun barked viciously overhead. It was pointing practically dead astern, and a hot shock-wave forced its way into the bridge and made Rolfe stagger with its intensity.

He saw the four guns swing round towards him, and in no time at all, the sea about the *Wagtail* was a raging torment of boiling water and screaming shells.

The little gunboat halted in her uneven track as a shell struck her dead on the superstructure.

It penetrated the seamen's messdeck and exploded with a deafening roar inside the small steel compartment. For a few moments the ship vibrated and cracked, as a hail of white-hot splinters whined and banged in every direction, and pieces of heavy equipment were hurled high into the air, with the ease of a boy throwing stones.

Something rolled noisily across the Battery deck and clattered over the side. Rolfe saw that it was the barrel of the Oerlikon gun. It had been directly above the explosion, so it was pointless to look for the gunner.

Chase could still be heard shouting and cursing above the noise of burning woodwork and exploding ammunition, while his men tried vainly to spot the destroyer through the billowing pall of smoke, which was rising above the decks in an impenetrable cloud.

Rolfe heard Herridge, too, as he led a party of seamen with fire extinguishers and axes towards the blaze, and watched their puny figures swallowed up in the smoke.

The helmsman was retching helplessly, but grimly holding to the wheel, his eyes smarting and pouring in the fumes which were rapidly filling the wheelhouse.

"Open all the bridge shutters! Vincent, check with the engine-room and report damage to hull!" He noticed that the destroyer had stopped using her main armament, probably because of the smoke which was masking her target, but his heart felt numb as he heard the rattle of machine-guns and the lashing of steel hail along the gunboat's hull.

"Hull not making any more water!" Vincent's eyes rolled as a burst of bullets hammered at the bridge. "But Chief says that the port fuel tank is damaged and we're leaking fuel behind us all the time!"

Rolfe looked for the last island, but it was as far away as before, jeering at him beneath the sun.

"Very good. Get the passengers on deck. Midships, starboard

side. That'll give them a bit of cover from the machine-gun fire."

Vincent faltered at the voice pipe. "Does that mean we're baling out, sir?"

"It means, do as you're told!" barked Rolfe, his body tensed as another burst of firing echoed and clanged around them.

Even if we shook her off now, he thought, we'd never make it. They'd just follow our trail. A nice clear track of oil, with the prize at the end of it!

"Herridge has gone to get the people on deck, sir." Vincent's voice was a mere whisper.

Rolfe nodded, his slitted eyes watching their remaining mast drag alongside, held only by the trailing mess of stays and halyards. He raised his voice harshly above the din.

"Chao! Get Mr. Fallow in here! See if you can get a lifejacket on him!"

It didn't really matter if he had a lifejacket or not, he thought, not any more. But Judith would be kept busy until the end. Perhaps too busy to see what had happened.

Herridge fought his way over the twisted plates, feeling their heat through his shoes and marvelling that the ship was still beneath him.

He wrenched back the hatch, ducking, as a bullet whined hotly over his shoulder, like an enraged hornet.

"On deck there! Clear the storeroom at the double!"

He seized their groping hands and steadied their shoulders, as they scrambled over the coaming, and followed the beckoning seamen to the safety of the other deck.

Herridge gripped Ursula's hand as she stumbled against the torn planks and thrust his face close to hers.

"Keep calm! No need to start falling all over the blessed place!"

She seemed to take hold of her reeling senses and paused to stare at his brown, grinning face.

"I'm trying," she gasped. "I thought that last bang was the end!"

"We've not even started yet!" He squeezed her hand warmly, and pulled her after the others.

Laker slumped against the guardrail, his face ashen. He fumbled blindly with his bright lifejacket, his mouth hanging

248

loose and wet, and his body jerking to each crash of the gun, and with every nerve-jarring explosion.

"Done for!" His voice was thick and almost inaudible. "Trapped like rats!"

Herridge half listened to him, and kept his eyes on his men, as they hacked at the broken mast with their axes. It fell away and was immediately lost astern in the smoke.

"All right, drop those axes and get below to check the bulkheads! Any new cracks report to me at once!"

The stocky Chinese seamen ran aft, jumping across Lane's stretcher like nimble rabbits.

Laker closed his eyes and gripped the rail more tightly. "Will it never stop? What will happen to us now?"

Herridge jerked round as the silent figure on the stretcher suddenly bounded to its feet. Edgar Lane, in his pyjamas, and with a sheet still flapping loosely round his thin body, looked like a newly arisen corpse.

He cleared the space between himself and the cringing man at the rails in one bound, and thrust his bandaged head close to Laker's face, before anyone realized what was happening.

"You cowardly swine!" His voice was like a thin scream. "You're to blame for all this! You bloody murderer!"

He swung up his arm, and Herridge saw the axe which Lane must have taken from the deck.

Laker bellowed in terror and forced his huge body backwards over the rail.

Herridge's fist fastened around the man's wrist like a steel band and, as he forced his knee up into Lane's back, he saw the blade of the axe falter and fall away harmlessly to his side.

The guardrail, scarred and weakened like the rest of the ship, creaked beneath Laker's sudden weight and then, with a soft crack, the wire parted and Herridge caught a brief glimpse of Laker's kicking legs and wide, soundless mouth, before he disappeared into the thrashing foam at the ship's side.

Rolfe, at the wing of the bridge, heard the sudden commotion and saw the pointing arms and frantic gestures. He felt dead inside, as Herridge dived cleanly over the broken rail and started to swim after Laker's bobbing lifejacket. We were never meant to escape. I doomed them to this, before I even left Hong Kong.

"Stop engine!"

He stared calmly at Vincent's twisted face, shutting out the torrent of words from his tired brain.

"You can't stop for him! You can't go back for that useless swine!" Vincent jerked his hands helplessly. "Why are you doing it?" He broke down into a spasm of sobs.

Rolfe listened to the fading engine. There was no time to explain anything to Vincent. No time even to think. He watched the girl standing in the doorway. He blinked away the film which threatened to cover his eyes and saw Fallow's arm across her slim shoulders. Chao was supporting Fallow's body from the other side and between them he glared wildly from side to side, like a vanquished prize-fighter.

"We've stopped?" Her mouth framed the question. "Justin, is this the end?"

Fallow tore himself free and staggered drunkenly across the broken glass and splintered woodwork.

"End? End? Course it ain't! By God, I'll kill the first man wot steps aboard!" He stared blankly from Rolfe to the girl, as if unable to understand how he had got there. "Tell 'em, sir! Show 'em what we can do! The old *Wagtail* can 'andle any bloody Chink!" He fell against the helmsman, muttering vaguely.

Rolfe walked past him and on to the open wing of the bridge. He saw Laker's head, wet and shining, close to the quarterdeck, and watched Herridge treading water, getting ready to assist him aboard. He lifted his eyes dimly to the destroyer. He had often watched sharks circling their prey, and it was no surprise to see the long grey shape of the destroyer curving sharply inwards, closing the range to finish the unequal battle once and for all.

He glanced around at the remains of his last command. There seemed very little of the ship which had neither been destroyed completely nor badly mauled.

One ensign, smoke-blackened and torn, still flapped defiantly, and the gun still remained pointing straight at the enemy.

He watched the warship growing larger and larger. She was heading directly for the hidden reef barrier now. In a few seconds she would turn and deliver the final broadside, with every gun she possessed.

Unless—he felt himself twitching uncontrollably—unless she went straight on the rocks! He ran breathlessly up the ladder, ignoring Chase and his dull-faced gunners. It might be just possible, he thought wildly. The Chinese captain would not be seeing the *Wagtail* as any menace now. She was outwardly a wreck, stopped and helpless, and with lifejacketed people already thronging the rails.

"Chase!" His voice was hard and cold. "Can you still fire?"

"Yessir. But, but what for, sir? It'll only make 'em kill us all off!" He sounded tired and deflated.

"One shell, Chief. When I tell you. And I want it right in the middle of her wheelhouse! Aiming mark, just below the upper bridge!" He glared at Chase's red face. "Can you do it?"

Chase rubbed his fat palms on his rumpled trousers, his piggy eyes already gleaming. "Move over, Clinton!" he growled. "I'll show you a bit of fancy shootin'!" He slid into the gunlayer's seat and rested his eye against the telescopic sight.

Rolfe clenched his hands until the nails bit into his flesh. His nerves screamed, and although he had lost his cap and the sun was strong across his neck, he felt as cold as death.

Vincent burst into view beneath him. "Herridge is back, sir! He saved that——" He stopped, feeling the acute tension around him. Slowly he turned to face the other ship.

On the battered rim of the engine-room hatch Louch perched tense and watchful, his eyes following their enemy. Around him, and throughout the ship, everyone was waiting and watching. Not knowing why, or for what, but aware that something else, something even more terrible, was about to happen.

Laker, sodden and limp, lay across his wife's lap, moaning miserably. He, at least, was missing the final act.

Herridge gripped Ursula's arm and pulled her unresisting body closer. He stared bleakly up at the bridge, watching the lonely figure silhouetted against the clear sky. Poor bastard, he thought.

The destroyer moved nearer, slackening speed. Rolfe could visualize, without effort, the calm scene on her bridge, the telltale squeak of the echo-sounder and the Asdic. The captain getting ready to alter course.

The glass screen along the top of her bridge flashed in the sun like a signal. She's starting to turn, he breathed.

"Fire!"

He was deafened by the whiplash bang of the gun and the spot on the front of the distant bridge, the place which he had mentally marked, erupted flame and smoke.

The ship faltered and then plunged forward. Seconds later, she began to turn again, a new helmsman at his post. But it was too late. With a metallic groan she struck, and for a brief moment hung against her hidden adversary, the powerful screws still beating the water into a frenzy. Then her decks canted, and she slid off into deeper water, heavy and lifeless.

Rolfe found that his limbs were trembling uncontrollably. He clenched his teeth.

"Full ahead!"

The *Wagtail* swung slowly away, making for the island. A few sporadic shots whistled overhead, but even those died away, as the destroyer turned to the first task, of self-survival.

Soon she was lost from sight, blotted out by the calm green of the island.

Rolfe had been standing motionless by the rail, his eyes unseeing. Chase saw the hard features soften slightly, as a messenger reported, "Both engines working, sir! Full ahead together!"

Beyond the island the open sea lay ready to welcome them.

EPILOGUE

As the shiny staff car, with his miniature flag fluttering from the bonnet, lurched and bumped over the dockyard's cobbled road, the Admiral had to restrain himself from leaning over the driver's shoulder and control the rising excitement which had mounted steadily from the moment he had watched the battered *Wagtail* steaming slowly past his flagship.

The two destroyers, which he had despatched, without much hope, to look for her, followed at a respectful distance, their clean grey hulls contrasting starkly with the listing, shell-scarred gunboat, which was half-hidden by the black smoke from her riddled funnel, and so low in the water, that it was difficult to imagine what was keeping her afloat.

A great, hushed silence had fallen over the anchorage, and the silent crews of the fleet had lined their rails to watch and wonder. Absent were the jeers and cynical comments which had followed her from this harbour such a short time before, and as her battered shadow had crept past the first line of moored ships, the silence broke with the force and suddenness of a typhoon.

The Admiral had felt a sting in his pale eyes, as he followed the little ship's progress, and listened to the wave of cheering which rippled wildly along the ships.

His ships, and his men. Cruiser, or outmoded gunboat, what difference?

Yelling for his Chief of Staff, he had sped for the shore, conscious of the Commander's worried stare, but more excited than he had cared to admit for a long time.

The car nosed between a line of marine police, which wavered and swayed against a cheerful and curious mob of dockyard workers, coolies, and anyone else who could get near enough.

The car halted near the dry-dock. The same one from which *Wagtail* had left on her strange mission to Santu.

The Admiral stood blinking in the sun and staring at the growing pile of suitcases and crates on the dock wall, and at the ambulances and waiting repair gangs.

He brushed past the gaping workers and saluting seamen, and stood on the edge of the dock.

He thought afterwards that it was like standing by on the side of a grave to say good-bye to an old friend.

As the water seethed and roared from the dock, the gunboat seemed to sag, and then, as her worn keel rested on the blocks, she slowly settled down, the last life draining from her, as the receding water laid bare her cruel wounds.

"What a mess, sir!" Commander Pearce muttered.

The Admiral shook his head slowly, watching the procession of gaunt men and women being guided up the sloping brow to the reception party. "But not a waste," he murmured. "People at home don't realize that such things as this can happen in peacetime. But this is war in reality of a different kind! I think the *Wagtail* would have liked to end her life in this way, rather than go submissively to the scrapyard!" He smiled softly, as he saw a Chinese seaman painstakingly adjusting the tattered ensign. "She has made her gesture, small though it may be, and it will give faith to others!"

He straightened his trim figure as the tall Lieutenant Commander strode towards him and saluted.

He studied the tired, calm face, and noticed the difference. "Welcome back, Rolfe! You've worked wonders!"

Rolfe smiled briefly and handed a sheaf of papers to the Operations Officer. "It's all there, sir. From beginning to end!"

"I have read and re-read your signal, which the destroyers sent to me, a dozen times, and I'm more than satisfied." The Admiral gave one of his rare laughs. "You'll be disappointed to learn that the world press are not giving you much prominence! The Communists are saying that they fired on a British 'invader' of their waters, and our people are saying much the same about them!" He rubbed his hands, "But dealing with a destroyer the way you did, well! I think a new command is indicated for you right away, eh?"

Rolfe's smile faded, as from the corner of his eye he saw Laker, in company with some officials from Government House, approaching them along the wall.

He stepped back as Laker was introduced, and waited while they conversed in low tones.

He watched as Laker stepped into a waiting car and drove away. He did not once look back.

Rolfe tightened his lips, some of the old bitterness welling up in his tired mind.

"Is the offer of a new command still open, sir?" The words were out before he could stop them. "I expect Mr. Laker has had a few words to say about me?"

The Admiral cocked his neat head on one side. "He told me some things I didn't know, yes. That you risked the ship to save his life, for instance! And that I should be proud of you!" He waited, an amused smile on his lips. "You've changed him, Rolfe."

Rolfe stood looking at the silent gunboat, his face expressionless. "We've all changed, sir." His voice was soft, as if he was speaking to himself, or to the *Wagtail.* "Mostly for the better, I should think." So Laker's nerve had finally failed him, he thought.

He watched Vincent walking unseeingly through the excited groups, his eyes on some invisible objective. "And some are still changing!"

Then his frown vanished, and he beckoned boyishly to the slim figure who stood apart from the others.

"I should like to introduce someone to you, sir!"

The Admiral looked into Judith's wide, candid eyes and grave smile, and wondered.

"I think you'd better accept a shore appointment for a bit, Rolfe." He saw him grip the girl's hand, unconscious of their stares. "In case you want to make any other arrangements, eh?"

They walked slowly away from the wall, the Admiral already planning his retirement and letting routine reassemble his life.

Rolfe and Judith paused at the top of the ramp and looked back to the shadowed dock.

"She did well," he said slowly.

"We all did," Judith answered, and together they walked contentedly away from the harbour.

.   .   .   .   .   .

The high sides of the luxury liner, homeward bound for

England, were thronged with passengers and tourists taking their last glimpse at Hong Kong.

As the great ship glided steadily towards the wide approach, several people were pointing to the thin funnel and splintered upperworks which showed above the distant dry-dock.

One of them turned, as Fallow, his bandaged shoulder stiff and cumbersome beneath his uniform, leaned heavily on the rail beside him.

"Say, what sort of a ship is that, then?" He watched as Fallow stared emptily across the widening gap.

"That's the old *Wagtail*." He smiled sadly. "I used to be First Lieutenant in 'er!"